Cole Stallings

Deep Texas

Deep Texas is a work of fiction. Any resemblance to persons living or dead, places or events is coincidental. Names and characters are used fictitiously.

ISBN:1463749872
ISBN-13: 9781463749873
LCCN: 2011913175
CreateSpace, North Charleston, SC

Dedicated to mothers everywhere:

The thanks we offer are, sadly, posthumous. Dorothy Cole Butler and Lela Stallings Kinghorn believed in us from the moment of our first breath, to the moment of their last. Our mothers left each of us the priceless gifts of eyes that could cry, and hearts that could be broken. Not a day goes by that we don't offer our thanks to them.

Cole Stallings

Prologue

Long-haul truck driver Raleigh Poole had been pushing his power-ful, twin-screw Kenworth diesel through the early morning Texas darkness for nearly ten hours, and in spite of the wide Velcro brace he was wearing, his back ached like an impacted tooth. Raleigh had kept the "hammer" down on his beloved, metallic red diesel for forty-two straight days, carrying everything from bathtubs to blankets to bad-minton sets. He and his "K Whopper" had literally been hauling ass and teakettles over 35,000 miles through fifteen states and had roam-ing charges of over $800 to show for it.

Raleigh winced and groaned as he stretched his left leg, pushing hard with the toes of his boot against the floorboard in an attempt to ease his aching hamstring. He glanced into the outside mirrors to check on the double set of trailers that hummed and bounced along behind him over the smooth tarmac of Texas State Highway 12. He had picked up the doubles in Austin and was "deadheading" them back to the Interstate terminal in Wichita, Kansas, his home base.

Raleigh let the big rig drift a little, thinking about anything that might take his mind off his full bladder. His goal was just a couple of more miles down the road. Pocatello Pablo's Truck Stop was at the top of the Grace hill, and that was where he planned on sinking his teeth into what Pablo's road signs claimed was the "Biggest chicken-fried steak in the world!" He wouldn't say no to a fresh-fried scone, either. As he spotted the *"SHILOH ROAD - REST AREA - NEXT RIGHT"* sign, he knew he couldn't make Pocatello Pablo's. He immediately flipped on his turn signal and downshifted while simultaneously hitting the "jake brake," slowed the big Kenworth with a trumpeting of released engine compression, and pulled the 80,000-pound rig into a parking lot that was bathed in an unnatural yellow glow from lights mounted on top of high metal poles. He parked his rig alongside a half-dozen other idling big rigs and gathered a handful of trash from the cab, stuffing it into an empty Taco Bell sack before climbing down and out, immediately stretching his legs in relief. He tried to bend down a little to stretch his distressed hamstrings, but his back threatened him, and he wisely gave up that notion. As Raleigh walked stiffly toward the rest rooms, he spotted a dumpster set against a nearby fence. When he approached it, a night critter of some sort scurried out through the half-open lid and tore off into the bushes. In his haste to flee, the critter had brushed against the metal arm that released the lid on the dumpster, causing it to fall with a loud, tinny crash that startled Raleigh. "Probably a possum," he said to himself. Lifting the lid, he tossed the Taco Bell sack inside, lowered the lid, and started to walk away before he froze in his tracks. The truck driver's twenty-twenty eyesight had picked up something that his road-weary brain had taken a second to register and interpret. This *something* was not only out of place, but it was unsettling as well.

Lifting the lid again, Raleigh saw almost immediately what it was. A *human hand* was protruding through a rip in the side of a black garbage bag, its delicate female fingers extending upwards as if it had just dug itself up from the bottom and then had frozen in mid grasp.

Raleigh released the lid with a loud *bang* and hurried to find a telephone.

1.

The puppies were getting on Pinky's nerves. Deprived of their mother's warmth and nourishing milk for the first time in the six short weeks of their lives, they constantly squirmed over, under, and around each other in the large cardboard box. There were seven of them, each a mix of yellow lab and golden retriever that produced a light coat of fluffy fur. They were soft and helpless, almost irresistible, but not to Pinky.

"Can't you do something for those squirming little shits?" he barked over his shoulder as he left Interstate 35 and headed toward the center of Waco.

Kitty had been riding in the back of the van since they had picked up the puppies in Bancroft, taking turns snuggling different ones against her neck. "They miss their momma," she replied, replacing one puppy and picking up the small male runt that cowered in the corner of the box.

"Hell, I miss my momma, too, but you don't see me crying and whining about it." He glanced into the mirror and saw Kitty stroking the puppy. "If you're so hot to hold something, come up front here. I got a one eyed puppy you can play with. Careful, though, or he'll spit at 'cha!" Pinky laughed at his tired joke just as hard the hundredth time as he had the first time he had told it to Kitty. Her response was also the same.

"Don't be crude."

"Hell, where I come from, crude is in. You ain't *crude*, you being *rude*."

Kitty eyed the puppy for a moment. It whimpered softly. "I don't think this little guy is going to make it."

"Life's a bitch, ain't it? You want to try the Safeway?" Pinky asked.

Kitty was silent as she considered their options. She would have preferred driving to Houston or Dallas again or even an all-night trek to Oklahoma City. Waco was a little over two hundred miles from home, but it still felt too close. Pinky didn't plan things out like she did. Like her other helpers, Pinky was careless, counting on audacity and brute strength to get him out of situations that a minimum of planning could have avoided altogether. He was still in training although he would have laughed at the thought. She was going to have to get him under control, but right now she wasn't quite sure how to do it. He was smart, but arrogant and far too wrapped up in *his* needs to understand *hers*. At this point in their relationship, Pinky still thought he was using her –believed he was the one making the decisions–and it suited her purposes to let him keep that illusion, at least temporarily.

If they were going hunting, she wanted to be far from home. She didn't want to risk a chance encounter with a customer she knew or someone from church.

"Let's try that little mall again," Kitty finally answered.

"I roger that," Pinky said, taking a left on Newton Road to enter the mall from the rear entrance. He parked away from the half-dozen buildings that housed a bowling alley, a used bookstore, a Cash and Carry Market, a Taekwondo Martial Arts center, a video store, and a Laundromat. They had been unsuccessful at this spot two months previously.

As Pinky turned the engine off, thirty-five year old Kitty removed a wig from a paper sack and pulled it on. She had bought it at a Salvation Army thrift shop for two dollars. The hairpiece fit snuggly against her scalp, and the tight blond curls dramatically changed her appearance, somehow softening her finely chiseled features. She checked herself in the rearview mirror, adjusting the wig slightly, and then slid open the side door and stepped out into the warm night air.

"Do it baby!" Pinky urged her on.

Kitty pulled the Ft. Howard Paper Company box toward her and picked up the squirming puppies. "We don't take any chances; if it's not going to work, we bail, got it?"

"I hear you, darling'," Pinky said, sliding out from behind the wheel and moving on his knees to the sliding side door. He liked to tell people, especially the geezers at church, how he'd found God, that he didn't want to spend anymore time behind bars. In fact, he'd told Kitty several times that he'd kill himself before he went back. It wasn't true, but it sounded good. "Hell," Pinky thought, "prison wasn't that bad. Not that bad at all."

As Kitty carried the box of puppies away from the van, Pinky pulled the door shut, sat back on the carpeted floor, and watched his chunky wife walk across the lot and then set up in front of the Laundromat. As he waited, he opened a storage box and took out a roll of duct tape, tearing off several four inch strips and sticking them on the window so they hung down, ready for use. He tore off a half-dozen foot-long strips and stuck each of them to the window casing. While handcuffs would have been more efficient, they would also be harder to explain to a cop if they happened to be stopped and searched for any reason.

Pinky looked out the window. A man and two young boys were looking at the puppies. "Move along, assholes," he muttered softly as he sat back and waited.

Pinky was one person who didn't mind waiting. In fact, he preferred waiting. He had spent more than half of his adult years locked away from the real world in small cells where waiting was a way of life. Pinky was so good at waiting that he could just shut down all systems and let the clock and the world go on, for hours, days, weeks, even months without him. He had refined those skills the old fashioned way; he worked at it.

Pinky chuckled as the man and boys walked away from Kitty carrying one of the puppies, got into a pickup truck and drove away. "One less mouth to feed. Hell, we're doing a good deed finding homes for unwanted puppies. What a fucking joke." He sat back and waited, pulling the quartz crystal necklace from his pocket, letting it dangle from the light gold chain. The crystal revolved in a slow, lazy circle, sending muted colors that danced over the wolf's head tattoo on the back of his hand, making the red eyes of the beast appear to sparkle. He had taken the necklace off one of the girls as a reminder. He would have liked to have kept that one alive longer, but Kitty wouldn't allow it, nearly going crazy when she discovered the bruise on the girl's cheek where he had back-handed her. He had awoken that night with Kitty standing over him, a razor-sharp boning knife at his throat. She made it clear that the girls they hunted were not to be battered. "Better to humor her for a while," Pinky thought.

Five minutes passed before he saw the girl exit the video store and pause next to Kitty. This was his fantasy, played out on a nightly basis over a period of eight long years; 2,922 nights that he had spent in a ten-foot by twelve-foot cell at Huntsville Prison. This was what he lived to do. He was on the hunt again.

Sandy haired Sonya Koontz, twelve, with bright, sparkling eyes and a wide, attractive smile, kneeled next to the box. "Can I hold one?"

"Be my guest," Kitty replied.

Sonya leaned over the box and picked up the sleepy runt, cuddling it gently under her chin. "This is the most beautiful puppy I have ever seen."

"You two go together." Kitty played her part well, interested, but not too eager.

"He's so precious," Sonya said, entranced by the soft, fragile dog.

"That's a little male. Why don't you take him home with you? He'd be a great playmate."

"I'd love to, but I'd have to ask my momma first," Sonya replied.

"Yeah, you should do that." Kitty leaned down and picked up the awkward box. "Tell you what. I'm not having too much luck here. I think I'll call it a night. Would you carry the puppy out to my van for me?"

"Sure," Sonya replied, glancing over her shoulder at the Laundromat and then falling in step with Kitty as she walked toward the white van parked off in the corner. Sonya thought it odd that the woman would park so far away, especially when she had to carry such a heavy load.

Kitty read Sonya's look and quickly moved to put her at ease. "What grade are you in, 9th?"

"I wish," Sonya said, pleased to be mistaken for a freshman. "I'm just a seventh grader."

"Could have fooled me. So, do you like school?" Kitty asked as they approached the rear of the van.

"It's okay."

"What's your favorite class?" Kitty reached for the side door that somehow magically opened as they approached.

"Oh, I don't know. I like my Language Arts teacher okay, Mr. Michaels."

Kitty leaned into the van and set the box on the carpeted floor, pushing it as far into the van as possible. "Just put the puppy in the box, will you?"

The unsuspecting Sonya kissed the puppy on the nose one last time. "Bye, little guy," she said, and as she reached into the van, her mother's loud, clear voice stopped her short.

"Sonya, come over here. I need your help!"

The fortunate Sonya turned and sheepishly handed the runt to the startled Kitty. "Sorry," the girl said over her shoulder as she hurried to where her mother was loading two baskets of freshly laundered clothes into the rear of their well-used Ford Explorer.

"Mom, can I have a puppy?"

After spending ten hours behind a cash register at Payless Drug, Kay Koontz was less than receptive. "Good Lord, Sonya, as if I didn't have enough to worry about. No dogs!"

Sonya didn't care so much about the puppy, but somehow it was an issue she wasn't going to drop easily. She became petulant. "You never let me have anything I want. You are the meanest person in the world."

"I know, Sonya, absolutely the meanest, nastiest mother around. Any other mother would have welcomed the whole darn litter. And since we're talking mean, nasty mothers, you know better than to talk to strangers. What were you thinking?"

"Geez, Mom, she had puppies, for crying out loud. What do you think she was going to do? You are way too suspicious."

Kay Koontz shut the back gate of the Explorer and climbed into the driver's seat as Sonya opened the passenger door, slid in, and slammed the door in protest.

When Kitty crawled in behind the wheel, her hands were shaking, and she was close to hyperventilating. As she fought to regain her breath, she glanced up and saw Pinky staring at her from the back like a cat watching an injured bird.

"Quit getting so bent over everything. Hell, woman, you'll drive yourself nuts that way. "

Kitty struggled for a deep breath as she retrieved the inhaler from the console and quickly pumped two shots of soothing mist into her lungs. It took nearly a minute before she was calm enough to breathe normally.

"We almost had her; another five seconds and..."

"Almost don't cut it in the real world, woman. Out here it's results that count," Pinky said, rubbing his erection through his pants. Every time they were out he became aroused by the possibilities of what he could do once the prey was snared. "Let's set up somewhere else."

Kitty shook her head firmly. "No, not tonight. She saw me real good, and her mom might remember the van. We'll try again tomorrow."

Kitty took the key out of her purse and was putting it in the ignition when she heard him.

"Come back and help me out." His tone was suddenly flat, devoid of emotion, but Kitty knew exactly what he wanted.

"You don't mean here? Now?"

He sprang forward and, forgetting for a moment that the tight blond curls weren't hers, he jerked Kitty's head back, only to have the wig come off in his hand. "Ohh, I like that. It's like I scalped you!" he laughed.

Kitty resisted. "Please, Wesley, not now. At least wait until we..."

Pinky grabbed her by the neck and yanked her into the rear of the van. He was so incredibly strong; it was useless for her to resist and she didn't.

As he moved on top of her, she gritted her teeth and winced from the pain. Kitty forced herself to submit, thinking of the girl, Sonja, with resentment. She could have saved her from this humiliation. Kitty knew that Pinky's lust was only partially satisfied, and he would be at her again tonight, using her as a surrogate for the pretty teenage girl. She would force herself to submit because it was a bargain she had knowingly made; only this time the prize had escaped from both of them.

Later that night, lying beneath him on her soft bed, as Pinky's movements intensified, Kitty heard the sounds coming from her throat and marveled at her own detachment. It was as if she were listening to an old, familiar phonograph record played over and over so many times that she knew the exact inflection of the sigh or groan that would come from her mouth next. As usual, Pinky finished quickly and rolled off her. As she lay in the darkness she tracked his silhouette as he moved into the bathroom.

After a moment, Kitty heard the toilet flush and her eyes followed his shadowy figure as he emerged and left the room, leaving behind only the cold stickiness on the sheet beneath her. She heard his bare feet moving across the hardwood of the living room and then the familiar creak of the storage room door opening.

Pinky's prison years had made it impossible for him to share a bed with anyone, and the day after he arrived, he had built himself a narrow platform in the windowless, small storage room, thrown a mattress on top of it, and had slept there every night since.

At one point he had attempted to explain his problem to Kitty and was relieved and surprised when she simply smiled and said she understood. In point of fact, she despised everything about him and preferred to sleep as far from him as possible. Now, she lay in the darkness and listened to the old building as a thousand of its rusting metal joints contracted, and it creaked and groaned like a tired old man. The sounds were part of the phonograph record also and stirred within her the familiar longing to be with them again. The yearning rose from deep within her stomach and into her chest, choking off her breath. Her hand quickly located her inhaler on the small side table. Two quick shots into her mouth eased the tightness in her chest, and she lay back against the pillow and waited patiently for Pinky to fall asleep. When she heard the sounds of his snoring, she got up and, dressing quickly, moved noiselessly through the familiar darkness to the long staircase that led up into the building. Her heart raced in anticipation as she silently climbed the twenty-two steps that ended at the metal door. She removed a heavy coat hanging from a brass hook on the wall and, putting it on; pulled the door open and entered.

2.

~

The morning commute was sluggish and getting worse. Jessi Cole had set her clock radio for five A.M. in hopes that clearing the apartment by five-thirty would put her well ahead of the morning rush on Interstate 45. The only trouble was that a half million other Houston commuters had the same heat-beating, brilliant idea, and now, twelve hours later, they were all right back where they left off on the slow ride home the night before—hot radiators and tempers, side by side, coming to a boil, ready to explode.

Jessi tensed as she jerked her heavily-oxidized, 1949 GMC pickup to a squealing stop as a bald man in a blue Toyota Celica cut her off and somehow managed to squeeze his car into a half car-length space in the lane in front of her.

"Jerk!" she muttered under her breath as she mentally ticked off his violations, which included an unsafe lane change and failure to signal. She hit the radio scan button, letting it run through the electronic forest of conservative talk, liberal talk, jock talk, news talk, hip hop, elevator classics, modern country, classic country, salsa and mariachi before settling on Houston's golden oldie station, KDMK, where Maggie and the Silva Brothers were singing David Kinghorn's hit "Boat that Floats."

You can fly planes that soar way up into the stratosphere,
take a train through Spain way down here in the atmosphere,
but the best way I know when you don't mind going slow...

> *Gimme a little boat that floats on any kind of water, a boat
> that floats on any size of sea, gimme a boat that floats, and a
> grandson to sail with.*

The song brought a smile to her lips as she remembered her dad's off-key, gravelly voice warbling the words as he guided the faded green "Jimmy" down this same highway. They had spent dozens of similar hot days in the fourteen-foot-long metal fishing boat Deke had christened *The Bloodworm*, casting bright-colored lures into the gray-green waters of San Jacinto Bay as he chain-smoked Camel cigarettes and drank his way easily through a twelve-pack of Budweiser.

> *And everything is right with me.*

She was surprised by the tears running down her cheeks. She hadn't consciously thought about her parents since her last visit to their gravesite the month before. Her mind drifted as the predawn traffic slowed to an idle, and she was momentarily startled when she caught a glimpse of her mother staring back at her from the pickup's rearview mirror. She saw her mom's short, dark hair framing ivory skin, a sprinkling of rust-colored freckles on her slightly crooked nose, and her mother's large gray eyes. She was pleased, in a way, to look like her mother, having always considered her beautiful. Jessi squinted at the reflection, and the sameness dissolved to a resemblance. At twenty-eight, she preferred the resemblance.

"You're too young to become Mom," she said aloud.

> *And it will all make sense to you.*

The song finished as Jessi parked the Jimmy in the fenced-in lot reserved for officers' private vehicles and headed to the small gymnasium located in the basement of the Hall of Justice. Dressed in well-worn sweat pants and an Astros t-shirt, she spent twenty minutes on various weight machines, ending with three miles on the stationary bike, followed by a quick shower. She was soon dressed in the dark trousers and distinctive light green shirt and tie that accented her five-foot-seven frame and identified her as a Houston police officer. She pulled the heavy leather Sam Browne from her locker, strapped it around her narrow waist, removed her 9MM Sig Sauer pistol from her purse and slid it into the holster on her belt. Grabbing her clipboard, Jessi headed back upstairs, ducking into a cramped kitchenette where an ancient coffee pot sat, steaming as it slowly but relentlessly turned a quarter pound of Hills Brother's Columbian Supreme and three gallons of water into a deep brown battery acid. Balancing her Styrofoam coffee cup on her clipboard, she entered the spacious roll call room, where she settled behind one of the twenty-five well-used oak tables at the rear of the room. Glancing around she saw that three of her academy classmates had beat her in. Martinez, Lindsey, and Odom were already engrossed in completing leftover paperwork or studying the four-inch Texas statute book that Houston police officers referred to as "The Bible."

"Morning,"

Only muffled "Mmms" emanated from the distracted trio.

"Hey, Officer Odom. I think you can do better than that," Jessi said as she removed two credit card slips from her clipboard and studied them.

Tom Odom's low-key manner of dealing with the ebb and flow of the job's ever-fluctuating stress level made him an ideal partner, and as a happily married father of two small children, the muscular African

American was as grounded in the common sense approach to law enforcement as Jessi was.

"Good morning, partner, how goes it?" Odom asked, his husky drawl pinpointing his upbringing to one of two southern Texas counties.

Jessi winced as she tasted the coffee for the first time. "Ohmygawd, did you make this?"

Odom shook his head and nodded toward the young, short Chicano officer sitting at the next table.

"I did," Joe Martinez volunteered without looking up from his Bible. "And it isn't my fault. I cleaned the pot and everything."

"It tastes like you tossed a whole damn can in there," Odom offered.

"I put in five big scoops, just like it says on the note," Martinez responded testily.

"Joe, that note went with the old five gallon pot. So tomorrow try *three* scoops and notice the difference," Jessi said with a grin.

"If you got a problem with it, Cole, make it yourself," Martinez replied.

"Don't be so sensitive, Joe. You make shitty coffee. That doesn't make you a shitty person," Jessi said.

"Yes it does," Odom countered.

Jessi continued reading the new credit card slips. The watch commander had stuck them in her mail slot with a terse message on a Sticky Note: "More Braxton?"

Jessi's patrol area had seen a rash of unauthorized credit card charges perpetrated by two small-time thieves named Vonzell and Tyrell Braxton. She removed the credit card slips from the reports and checked the signatures, easily identifying them as belonging to the brothers, who had been leading a team of detectives from the CAP (Crimes Against Property) desk on a game of hide-and-seek that had lasted for well over four months. The Braxton brothers were small-time career criminals who had fallen shamelessly in love with other people's credit cards and had turned that love affair into an enormous moneymaker. Over a fairly short period of time the brothers had run up charges on such wide ranging purchases as $5,000 leather coats to groceries at Safeway. The brothers were successful at their scam in large part due to their boldness, but also because they took care not to max the stolen cards out and call undue attention to themselves. In fact, they would normally use a stolen card to make only one or two purchases within a very short window of time. The rightful owners of the card would usually be unaware of the theft until their monthly bill arrived. The Braxtons' M.O. was simple: Steal a card, use it for two, three hours max, and then toss it somewhere it was sure to be found and used by another thief. Nogoodnick number two comes along, finds the card and uses it until he's caught, thus taking the fall for the Braxtons' charges, as well as their own. So far the scam had netted the Braxton brothers over $750,000 in goods and services.

The first slip was for $900 worth of metal cooking utensils from Yankee Trader, a high-end department store and the other was for a $3200 gold bracelet "purchased" at a small jewelry store named Davy J.'s. Both businesses were located a stone's throw from each other within the high-rent downtown Galleria Shopping Mall.

As Jessi read the attached report, she saw that the reporting party was a Mr. Henry B. Pursell but there was nothing in the report about where Mr. Pursell had lost his credit card or had it stolen. Jessi glanced at the clock on the wall. She still had ten minutes to go until roll call began. On a hunch, she removed her cell phone and dialed Mr. Purcell's number. Pursell answered on the first ring.

"Mr. Pursell, this is Officer Cole from the Houston Police Department. I'm sorry to call so early, but I'm doing a follow-up investigation on the theft of your credit card. "

"Yeah," Pursell responded, "I called the credit card people the minute I saw the bill. Scared the hell out of me. I'm not going to have to pay for it, am I?"

"No, sir, you're not. The card company will absorb the loss," she responded, foregoing her usual, somewhat tired-sounding pitch that eventually we all ended up paying for it in higher credit card interest rates.

"That's good, 'cause I never had a gold bracelet in my whole goddamn life. The only gold I have is in my teeth, and I'll bet the ambulance driver pries that out before I get to the goddamn mortuary."

"Do you have any idea how these people might have gotten hold of your card?" Jessi asked, choosing a well-used pencil from a dirty glass tumbler on the desk and grabbing a new, yellow legal tablet from the desk next to her's.

"The only place I can figure is Chez Peyo," Pursell answered, "the fancy French restaurant downtown. I took my wife, Claire, there for lunch for our 45th anniversary. I know I had it then because I used it to pay the bill. After that I went into the rest room, and when I came out my wallet was gone. I figured I might have dropped it in the can, but when I went back in, it wasn't there. Somebody must have picked it up. Seven hundred bucks and all my plastic. Claire had to pay for the parking, for chrissakes. Some celebration. I called the credit card people the same day, but as it turned out, the bastards had already used it! The nerve! Houston is full of thieves now. We're thinking of moving away. Maybe Miami."

Jessi reached into her briefcase, retrieved a file folder from under a stack of papers, and opened it to reveal the grainy mug shots of Tyrell and Vonsell Braxton. "Mr. Pursell, while you were in the rest room at that restaurant, do you recall seeing two well-dressed men? One of them would have been..."

"A big black guy?" Pursell interrupted. "And the other was thin and kind of greasy looking. Also black. Lots of jewelry. The big guy bumped into me... Oh, no, you don't think...? Sonofabitch! They lifted my wallet!"

"Sounds like it, "Jessi offered. "If I hear anything I'll get back to you."

As Jessi hung up, she noticed the roll call room was quickly filling with noisy officers. Sergeant Leroy Tobin entered the room from the hallway and took his customary place at the wooden podium. "Sarge" was sixty-one and closing in on retirement and at 280 pounds was a walking, talking advertisement for an impending coronary. The likable supervisor's well-worn uniform appeared to be glued to his barrel chest and bulging stomach. The material in the rear of his pants had been polished to a high sheen from ten-hour days buffing the chair behind the duty desk. Tobin was one of the last of the old breed, the hard-charging, hard-drinking, head-knocking "dinosaurs" that roamed somewhat uncomfortably through the well-lighted, modern infrastructure of the "new" police department. He watched in puzzlement as the contemporary breed of sharply tailored, well-educated officers headed for health clubs at the end of shift rather than smoke-filled cowboy bars.

The room quieted quickly as Tobin cleared his throat and spoke in a surprisingly high pitched voice.

"Good morning, ladies, you too, gentlemen. Today is July 15 and the first day in the rest of your law enforcement career. Let's all make the most of it by going home safe and sound, shall we?"

"It's going to be another scorcher out there today, at least 105, maybe 110. Be aware that dehydration is a concern for you, as well as the general population. Keep a bottle of water close by, and be prepared to answer some heat related 911 calls. Keep in mind that rug rats and geezers are extremely subject to heat related problems. I know this to be true, people, 'cause I'm a geezer, O.K.?"

A training officer sitting at the front table yelled out "You're the head geezer, Sarge!"

"Yeah, and fuck you, too, Officer Hadley. Memo from…" Tobin rolled his eyes and pointed upward to indicate the powers that be that loomed above them, as he read from a typed letter. "Officers arriving late for shift change have been parking their private vehicles in the covered parking structure."

A collective groan swept through the room. At least half of the officers present were guilty as charged. The city had provided only enough parking spaces for half of the day shift's private autos. This insured that the other half would try to sneak into the covered garage rather than park on the street where a relentless squad of Cushman-driving meter maids delighted in ignoring the improvised signs the cops would place on their dashboards. They enjoyed placing the tickets over such messages as "Do not ticket- Police Officer Risking Life And Limb For You."

Tobin continued.

"A reminder to all concerned. The covered parking structure is reserved for official police vehicles."

"Yeah, like the Watch Commander's Lexus!" an officer shouted from the rear of the room.

"Settle!" Tobin warned. As the murmur died, he continued. "Starting July 16, that's tomorrow, folks, all private vehicles left in the covered structure will be cited and towed."

A loud chorus of "boos" stirred Tobin to shake his head in mock sadness. As he did, his double and triple chin swayed, reminding Jessi of the brandy keg the fabled St. Bernards carried through the snowy Alps.

"Your 'boos' are like arrows to this faithful heart. I am simply the messenger. Use the information I offer, or ignore it and pay the fine. The choice is yours, and quite frankly, I'm almost out the door, and I don't give a shit!"

"Memo from Lt. Baker in Records: 'To all patrol personnel. The unauthorized use of Department computers and data bases to do background checks for any purpose other than those established by statute, are expressly forbidden. Those officers found to be in violation of this order will be terminated and punished to the full extent of the law.' "

Tobin glanced around the room, noticing the exchanged looks and raised eyebrows.

"This is no joke, folks. From now on when Uncle Roy wants you to run the name of the scroad with prison tattoos who's hanging around his sixteen-year-old daughter, tell him you can't do it. The paper boys upstairs and the State Attorney General are very serious about this. I don't want to see any of your asses in a sling."

A former Marine M.P. named Phil Brownell unconsciously stroked his buzz cut as he addressed Tobin. " So, Sarge, let's say this scroad is thirty-eight and he's not only bangin' my pimply little niece who's fourteen going on thirty, but he's providing her with crystal meth. Is this *not* a legitimate law enforcement issue?"

A wave of agreement and nodding heads swept through the sea of blue shirts.

"Settle!...Officer Brownell, if Uncle Roy comes to you directly, and you in turn, call in Detective Banks from the Sexual Battery Unit, *then* it's a law enforcement issue. But if <u>you</u> run the scroad through the computer and give that information to Uncle Roy directly and he kicks the scroad's ass like he should, *your* ass will be the one in the sling. Got it?"

"Incidents of note: A homicide occurred at Cheap Charlie's on Second Avenue at 3:46 this A.M. The perp made off with an undetermined amount of cash. We've got him on video tape, but he had a scarf around his face. We can surmise he's a male hispanic, 18 to 30, 5'10', 150 to 175 pounds. Let's hope the murder squad can give us a little more by the end of shift."

Jessi and Odom exchanged a quick look. Cheap Charlie's was in their patrol sector. They knew the store well. It was a run-down, graffiti-stained gas-and-go hangout for drug dealers and gang bangers and a nightmare to nearby residents. There had been numerous assaults and at least two homicides in and around the litter-strewn parking lot. An Arab family named "Shalonn" had recently purchased the business and were trying gamely to clean it up, a nearly impossible task for that particular neighborhood. A knot formed in her stomach as she tried to recall what brother or nephew worked the graveyard shift.

"All Central units, make it a point to be highly visible in and around Cheap Charlie's today. Even if you just do a drive-by. I think the neighbors could use the reinforcement. And Edward Forty–Two, see me after roll call, please."

Jessi nodded, slightly uncomfortable with the special attention.

"Make sure you pick up the new 'hot sheet' and warrant lists from my desk, and like I said earlier, let's all go home on two feet at end of shift. Okay, folks, our training session for today will be conducted by Officer Joe Martinez who will explain to us the intricacies of when and if a citizen can lawfully refuse to give a police officer identification. Officer Martinez."

Tobin quickly removed his papers from the podium and exited the room as Joe Martinez stood and made his way nervously to the front. As he started to speak, he made eye contact with Jessi and got a thumbs up in return.

As Jessi listened, she realized her session on gang graffiti was scheduled in two weeks, and she had barely begun her research. She made a mental note to contact Chris Chavez in the Gang Task Force Office and then turned her attention back to Martinez.

Leaving roll call Jessi saw Sergeant Tobin exiting the copy room with a stack of "hot sheets" and warrant lists. "You wanted to see me, Sarge?"

The distracted Tobin looked momentarily puzzled.

"I did? Oh, yeah. The credit card slips. Make sure you do the follow up on them and call it in. The watch commander is getting all kinds of pressure from upstairs. Apparently one of the city hall muck-a-muck's mother had her card stolen and used by our friends, the Braxtons. "

"Yeah, Sarge, I'll do it first thing," Jessi said as she peeled a "hot sheet" and warrant list from the stack in the sergeant's beefy hands. The "hot sheet" was a listing of recently stolen cars, and the warrant list was a printout of outstanding felony warrants.

Tobin started to walk away, but he paused and looked at her. "God you look like your mother. That's a huge compliment, you know?"

Jessi nodded. "And a welcome one. Thanks, Sarge."

They stood in silence for a moment before Tobin spoke again. "You still got your dad's Old Mr. 44?"

Jessi smiled. "Of course I've still got it. I keep it right next to his badge."

"How about Boom-Boom?"

"It's on my belt," Jessi said, patting the worn, wooden night stick on her waist.

"I'll be damned. Jesus, Jessi, how long's Deke been gone now?"

Jessi shook her head. Nine years had passed since that terrible night when her father had suffered a massive, fatal coronary while chasing a burglary suspect through a downtown Houston alleyway. Deke's long-time partner, a tall, skinny man named Wally Tripp, had come to the house with a faceless watch commander and the department chaplain and had woken her up at two-thirty in the morning, explaining to the pretty nineteen-year-old that her fishing buddy was dead. Jessi barely remembered the chaplain's, or the watch commander's face and only snatches of meaningless words as he gave her his prepared statement by rote: "On behalf of the City of Houston... regret to inform you your father passed away while serving the citizens of... You should be proud..."

After the chaplain and watch commander had departed, Wally had sat down beside her on the couch and laid it on the line. "We was chasing a little hair bag through an alleyway off Leland. Deke hopped out, and I stayed with the car. One minute he's running flat out, and then boom, he was down. He didn't feel shit, Sweetheart. He was dead before his head hit the pavement. EOW, Sweetheart, end of watch." He then handed her a sack that contained her dad's wallet, "Old Mr. 44," and his badge. "I want you to know that the last thing he talked about was how great you were doing in college," Wally had said, adding, "You were everything to him."

Within a half an hour a group of veteran cops Deke had dubbed "The Dirty Dozen" had filled the small living room, and they spent the rest of the night drinking, swapping Deke Cole war stories, and taking turns letting Jessi cry on their broad shoulders. Leroy Tobin had been one of those men, and when Jessi had graduated fifth in her class from the police academy, the Dirty Dozen had shown up in force; and when Wally Tripp had pinned Deke's badge on the beaming Jessi, the entire group had stood in mass and given her a loud, raucous cheer.

Sergeant Tobin nodded. "Nine years. Doesn't seem that long ago. Some days I expect to see Deke coming through the door bringing in some shit rat he'd chased down, giving me a detailed visual on the action. I miss those days. Nobody else takes the time to even talk to a dinosaur, 'cept you of course."

Jessi's silence made Leroy uncomfortable. "Your old man liked it out on the street, Jessi."

"I know. I'm not angry with him for leaving me anymore. Tackling a shit rat and dying from a heart attack with your arms wrapped around his legs is a scene that Dad would have thoroughly enjoyed."

"He got that shit rat," Tobin smiled.

"Yeah, Sarge, he got him," Jessi repeated as she watched the huge man lumber to his desk.

Jessi joined Odom at the armory cage, where they each signed out their short-barreled Ithaca shotguns and portable radios and headed for their cars. After leaving the garage, their first stop was inevitably at a portable coffee wagon in the parking lot of the nearby Albertson's supermarket. The coffee cart was owned by a middle-aged Hispanic man named Rueben, who sported a well worn Oaxca baseball cap and who greeted them daily with a smiling "Buenos dias," and a piping hot "mule" for each of them—"mule" being Rueben's rendition of a triple espresso mixed with his personal blend of 'open your eyes in a hurry' beans. Coffee safely in hand, Jessi and Odom were headed for the freeway when they got their first call.

"Edward 42. An ADW just occurred at 1-0-0-5-6 Old Highway Six. The reporting party is an unidentified female. She asked for you by name and said that the subject was still there. Your call is Priority three."

An ADW was an assault battery, but since the response was priority three meaning get there quickly, but don't use your lights and siren, Jessi assumed the situation was not a "hot" call. She keyed the mic on her collar. "42 roger."

The dispatcher's voice came back. "Edward Forty, back up 4-2 on the Highway Six ADW."

Jessi heard her partner's voice. "40 rogers. In route."

As she punched the accelerator and felt the car surge forward, Jessi glanced in her rear view mirror and saw Odom right on her bumper. They both knew the address. This was definitely *not* the way to start the day.

Jumping on Interstate 45, they crossed the bridge and immediately took the next exit circling until the ramp dumped them onto a littered frontage road that was once the main highway through the city. When Jessi was fresh out of the academy, she and her training officer had taken this road almost daily, and she could have found the encampment with her eyes closed. She followed the deteriorating asphalt frontage road, her car dipping and slipping and rattling like a stagecoach. In less than 100 yards, she made a sharp left onto a pock-marked dirt trail that didn't appear on any street map but was called "Rags Road" by the cops who patrolled it. It snaked under the Interstate 45 over crossing and into the makeshift homeless encampment above Buffalo Bayou known as "The Arches At 45." Its name coming from the curved span of the understructure of Interstate 45 that passed over the top. It offered the ever-changing population of homeless people who lived there a minimum of protection from the bleaching sun and pounding rain. The name was also a tongue-in-cheek knock-off of the million dollar gated community five miles further down the highway, known as "The Arches At Canyon Road."

A thin layer of heavy, acrid smoke drifting over Rags Road was pushed aside as the patrol cars breezed past the rusted or burnt shells of a dozen gutted cars and trucks and pulled to a stop alongside one of the huge, cement support columns. Shopping carts, stuffed with filthy clothes, ragged blankets and other street treasures, were lined up like junky vehicles in a low rent housing tract.

As the officers stepped out of their cars, and started up the hill, a dog barked a distant warning. Had they been watching they would have seen the ghost-like face of a woman appear in the back window of a weathered Chevrolet van parked beneath one of the arches.

Inside the twenty-five- year-old van, the woman watched the officers with interest as she fingered a quartz necklace that hung around her thin neck. She smiled as she recognized the female officer.

"God I hate this place," Odom said as he stepped gingerly around an imposing pile of fresh dog excrement.

With the drone of the heavy morning traffic passing over their heads, Odom followed Jessi into the shadows and onto a concealed path that wound its way up and around the metal underpinnings of the freeway crossing. As they cleared another support column, the putrid odor of unwashed bodies, unwashed clothing, untreated sewage, and other trash blindsided them.

"I should have brought the Vicks," Odom said, covering his nose and mouth and fighting his gag reflex.

"It's not too bad yet. Wait until this afternoon," Jessi offered.

"No thanks," Odom answered.

The path continued uphill for another twenty yards to where a ragged piece of canvas had been strung between arches like the shredded sail of a broken-down ship that had run aground long ago. The canvas served as a windbreak of sorts for a listless, ragged crew of men and a sprinkling of women who were circling a fire. Their attention on a simmering blackened canning kettle that was giving off the wonderfully incongruent rich smell of bubbling coffee.

For a few moments, the inhabitants watched their approach suspiciously. Then, without seeming to move, they evaporated into the surroundings. A hyper black dog, part Lab, part Shepard, darted out of the shadows and yapped nervously as it caught the unusual scent of washed bodies and leaned cautiously to sniff at their clean clothes in hopes of finding the source of this interesting odor. Jessi reached down and scratched the dog's ears before pulling a Milk Bone dog biscuit from her pocket and tossing it to the excited mutt.

Odom gave her a curious look as the dog snagged the biscuit in mid air and quickly disappeared into the shadows.

"My dad taught me to never leave home without one," she shouted over the drum beat of passing traffic directly over their heads. Jessi walked closer to the fire where a tall, skinny man wearing a worn Nike baseball hat and a dirty Guess t-shirt ladled out coffee to the others. The man's watery left eye seemed to float lazily in its socket, tracking just a split second slow, as if it were somehow working independently of its fraternal twin on the other side of the weathered face.

"Hey, Snooky, how goes the battle?" Jessi said in a friendly, familiar tone.

"Oh, comme ci comme ça," the man answered, smiling to reveal a bottom row of dark, rotting teeth. "How you doing, Officer Cole?"

"I'm staying in the car with the AC going as much as possible," Jessi answered.

"It's been hot, but I hear it might rain soon," Snooky replied, filling a Styrofoam cup with hot coffee and holding it out to Jessi. Odom politely waved off the same offer.

"Rain, huh? Sounds wonderful," Jessi said, taking the cup and tasting the familiar brew. It had the same dark, bitter taste that her father's coffee had. "You got plenty of egg shells in there?"

Snooky nodded. "Got to add those egg shells. Takes some of the bite off."

Odom watched his partner a moment longer. He was determined to let Jessi run the call at her pace, but he was getting impatient. Jessi worked people better than anyone he had ever seen, but he hated everything about this place, and it showed in the way he stood: his head on a swivel, his dark eyes darting, tracking each and every move.

"So, what's the problem? Somebody get hurt?" Jessi asked.

"Sort of," Snooky replied, turning away from the imposing figure of Odom and facing Jessi. "You remember 'Little Hondo? Had that big purple birth mark on his face?"

Jessi scratched her neck unconsciously as she mined her memory. "The little guy who used to climb up and sit on the edge of the freeway and spit on cars?" Jessi asked, pointing up at the freeway that formed a roof over their heads.

Snooky nodded.

"Last I heard he was committed to Ridgeway Psyche," Jessi said.

"And that's where the crazy, pardon my French, bastard should be, but he's out again. This morning he steals a TV dinner from Loopy Larry's cart. Larry gets pissed and tries to take it back, but Little Hondo grabs a baseball bat and breaks Larry's arm. Then after Hondo eats the TV dinner, he starts threatening the rest of us. We got enough problems out here without that kind of shit going on."

The invisible, ragged group suddenly reappeared around the fire and mumbled their agreement.

"Where's this Little Hondo now?" Odom asked.

Snooky turned and pointed off. "He's sleeping on the other side in a Kenmore box he took from Corky here."

A small, bearded man wearing a heavy, long coat in spite of the heat stepped forward, shaking with anger and pent up rage that he was incapable of resolving. "He did, by God, and I carried it all the way from Sears."

"He evicted you from your house, huh?" Jessi asked before turning back to Snooky. "How about Loopy Larry's broken arm? Is he O.K.? " Jessi asked.

"Lela drove him to the Emergency Room couple of hours ago," Snooky answered.

Jessi nodded. "O.K., I think my partner here and I can handle this. Does Hondo still have the bat?"

"No," Snooky answered. "He tossed it down, and I burned it in the fire."

"You ever see him with any other weapons, a knife maybe, or a gun?" Jessi asked.

"No, nothing like that. But he's mean and he'll bite," Snooky said, adding quickly, "Come on, I'll show you."

Jessi nodded and followed Snooky away from the fire and further up the hill. With Jessi and Odom one step behind, Snooky followed the path around a pillar and passed a stretch of dry dirt where mounds of human forms slept on the ground, sandwiched between dirty blankets and sheets of cardboard. On the far side of the clearing, Little Hondo's relatively new Kenmore Box stood in sharp contrast to his neighbors' substandard structures. Snooky pointed at the box and nodded. A pair of worn army boots attached to a set of demin-clad legs was visible protruding from the front entrance. As Jessi approached the box, she slid her father's nightstick from her belt.

"Hey Mrs. Hondo, can Little Hondo come out and play?" she asked as she unceremoniously gave the soles of the boots a sharp rap. "Let's go! Let's roll out of there!"

The boots kicked back at the club. "Get the fuck away from..."

Odom moved quickly, grabbing the boots and jerking the little man easily out of the box and onto the dirt. The officer then squatted on the man's back, letting his 250 pounds do their work as his big hands grabbed Hondo's thin, tattooed arms and pinned them behind his back. Jessi knelt and cuffed his wrists in a well rehearsed give-and-go that she and Odom had used dozens of times. As Jessi snapped the cuffs in place, she noticed the angry rash of red needle tracks on both of Hondo's forearms and regretted not having put latex gloves on.

"Before we search you, do you have any needles or anything sharp in your pockets?"

"I ain't got nothing in my pockets you fucking bitch, now let go of my..."

In one easy motion, Odom grabbed the denims by the cuffs and jerked them completely off Hondo's body, exposing the man's spindly white legs and his filthy Fruit Of The Loom briefs.

"Hey, you just can't..."

"I just did, idiot," Odom said, jerking the man to his feet and tossing the useless pair of pants into the Kenmore box before pushing Hondo toward the path.

"I love it when you do that," Jessi said admiringly.

Odom grinned, then quickly covered his nose. "He's a ripe one."

Hondo's stench was quickly becoming unbearable, and Jessi was forced to cover her nose and wipe her watery eyes as she took Hondo's upper arm and attempted to guide him down the path, when he suddenly spun nimbly and tried to bite her on the hand.

"You bite me and that will be the last time you use those teeth, got it?" she barked, grabbing the end of his thumb and bending it back with such force that Hondo squealed like a pig.

"O.K., O.K.," he said as they half led, half dragged him down the hill. Before placing him in a car, they flipped quarters, odd or even, to see who would drive him to the station for booking. Odom took even and lost two out of three.

"Shit," was his only response as he pushed Hondo into the back of the patrol car and slammed the door.

"Be sure to keep your windows down," Jessi teased, pushing her luck.

Odom shot her a dirty look. "Thanks a lot, partner," he said as he swung his large frame behind the wheel.

Jessi watched Odom drive away before moving back to her car. She was just opening the door when she had an odd feeling she was being watched. Glancing up, she caught just a blur of a woman's face in the rear window of the old van that was parked in the shadow of a highway arch. The face quickly disappeared, leaving Jessi looking at a faded, swaying green curtain. For some inexplicable reason, she felt a twinge of dread. She quickly shook it off and climbed back into her car.

The woman in the van was still clutching the quartz. It had grown warm in her hand, and she held it to her lips as she watched the police cars pull away. "So, Officer Cole, today is the day we finally meet," she half whispered.

She waited for a few seconds and then, starting the van, followed.

3.

❀

Jessi cleared the Arches ADW with dispatch and drove straight down Second Avenue to the scene of the early morning homicide. The normally crowded parking lot of Cheap Charlie's was empty except for a Chevy Suburban from the Crime Scene Unit, the Medical Examiner's white Econoline van, and an unmarked Crown Victoria that belonged to the Murder Squad detectives. The front of the run-down store was still cordoned off with yellow crime scene tape, and several neighborhood people had gathered in a tight, hushed knot on the sidewalk.

As Jessi exited her car and walked toward the entrance, an older black woman approached carrying a bouquet of brightly colored flowers. "Officer, would you please put these next to the door? I don't dare cross over that tape there."

Jessi took the flowers and smiled. "I'll be glad to, ma'am. Thanks for your concern," she said, ducking under the tape.

"That man that got shot was a good man. He never cheated us. Ever. Damn shame that these animals 'round here do this to him. He's got a wife and two kids. Dear God above, we're in deep trouble out here," the woman said, her voice a troubled plea.

Jessi nodded and, moving to the doorway, placed the flowers against the wall with several other floral offerings. As she entered the store she paused and looked around. Two crime scene techs were busy, one dusting the counter for prints, while the other took flash photos with a

35MM camera. The two detectives, a middle-aged balding man named Steve Tyley and his long time partner, a tall, gangly veteran with a full, bushy black hairpiece named Merle Eisom, stood in the rear by the beer coolers, watching as the woman from the M.E.'s office hovered over the body that lay in a three-foot-wide puddle of coagulated blood.

Jessi instantly regretted stopping and tried to back out of the store without being seen. She had had several encounters with the detectives, mostly bad, and was nearly out the door when Tyley turned and spotted her, a leer flashing instantly across his ruddy face.

"Well if it isn't Officer Cole!" he bellowed, stepping around the dead man and walking toward her. "How nice of you to join us," he added as his full-eyed gaze threatened to swallow her whole.

Tyley was one of those aging men who actually believed his wife of thirty-five years when she told him that he was not only handsome but seductive as well. He was blissfully unaware that he had been voted the "Most Repulsive Senior Officer" in an unofficial tally posted on the bulletin board in the women's locker room.

"I didn't mean to interrupt. Sarge told us to do some drive throughs."

"Interrupt? I'd take looking at a beautiful woman like you any day over looking at a dead body, he said, giving her another head-to-toe mental undressing that made her skin crawl.

"Who's the victim?" Jessi asked, hoping to divert his attention.

"There lies one Romeer Fei Shalonn, thirty-nine. Night clerk and brother of the owner."

"Not Romy!" Jessi felt sick. The dead man had waited on her many times. He was a tall, dark-eyed, nice-looking man, always smiling, always polite. He loved to show her pictures of his wife and babies.

"He got it three times in the neck and once in the head with a small caliber handgun. As near as we can figure, the perp got about one hundred and forty bucks and a bunch of cigarettes."

The stupidity of this type of crime always made Jessi angry. "Don't internalize it," she repeated the rookie mantra to herself for the hundredth time, but her heart still ached. "Any leads at all?"

Tyley shook his head. "You know how that goes. There was probably thirty little gang bangers and other assorted scumbag assholes in the parking lot, but nobody saw shit. These people out here deserve the life they make for themselves."

Jessi's non response irritated Tyley. "Oh, sorry, I keep forgetting that you're one of the 'new breed' of cop: Joey College, social worker, no, teacher, right? You'll learn."

"Well, got to run," Jessi said, turning and leaving the store.

"You're welcome at my crime scene anytime, Officer Cole!" Tyley said, watching her exit the store and move to her car. "Anytime," he repeated to himself.

Jessi climbed into her car and picked up her clipboard. With her partner off the radio, she could use the time to check out the latest credit card thefts. Studying the addresses on the slips, she instantly constructed the usual Braxton pattern. As was their MO, Jessi theorized, the brothers probably enjoyed a scrumptious meal at the highly rated French restaurant, Chez Peyo, which they always paid in cash. Their appetite satisfied, they walked down the block to Davy J's Jewelers, where they used the stolen card to purchase a man's $1500 gold bracelet. From the jeweler's, the thieves had moved a block east to The Yankee Trader Store, where they had charged a $900 set of pots and pans.

It took Jessi six minutes to drive to Chez Peyo. The restaurant was still closed. She made a mental note to return later in the day and then walked to the nearby Davy J's Jewelry Store, where the elderly owner described the man who purchased the bracelet as "A very large Negro man who laughed a lot. He was in the company of a white woman who wore lots of makeup and appeared to be inebriated."

Mr. Morgan then showed Jessi a bracelet similar to the one the man had purchased. Jessi studied the gaudy piece.

"Very nice," she said, handing it back. "Mr. Morgan, did you ask the man for a picture I.D.?"

The owner shook his head. "Sometimes I do, but with the blacks, if I ask for I.D. they sometimes accuse me of being racist, and I'm not, by God, but it's easier to just let it go."

"I know, but next time, ask. I have it on good authority that most African American people want you to."

"You think?"

Jessi nodded and left the store.

Jessi walked the half a block to The Yankee Trader store where she quickly located the female African American clerk who had handled the $900 pot and pan purchase. "He was a skinny little black dude, silk shirt, all kinds of gold necklaces, the works. And this ugly-ass white woman was falling all over his nasty self."

"Did you ask him for a picture I.D.?"

"His cologne was awful! I just wanted him out of my face," the clerk explained without apology.

Jessi left the store and returned to her patrol car where she used her cell phone to confirm to the CAP detectives who were investigating the case that the Braxton brothers had struck again. She then called Odom on her cell phone and learned that he had cleared the jail and was on his way to their sector. They agreed to meet at the local donut shop, but as Jessi started the car, the radio crackled to life.

"Edward 42, 911 disconnect." The call was one of the biggest time wasters for the average patrolman, but one that couldn't be ignored.

Jessi keyed her mic "Edward 42, go ahead."

"3-1-0-5 Temple, cross of Kearny. No history." The dispatcher's reference to "no history," told Jessi that no previous 911 calls had been made from that number or address.

"10- 4, in route."

Jessi made a u-turn, heading east toward and into an older neighborhood that had once been on the fringes of downtown Houston. The neighborhood had been through several transformations over the years. Originally it had started as nice, two-story houses with yards large enough to plant grass and flowers and to hold a swing set with neighbor-friendly fences designed not for privacy or security, but simply to keep the dog home.

As the oil rich city grew and sprouted suburbs, the neighborhood was slowly but steadily abandoned, leaving the entire section looking prematurely old and run-down. The once proud, spacious houses were cut up into unkempt, square apartments, and the busy streets were soon littered with blowing garbage and a small, drifting army of down-on-their-luck homeless that spent their welfare checks drinking cheap wine purchased from the few remaining mom and pop stores that were bought up and modernized by hard working, ambitious Arab immigrants.

The area was on its way to becoming an advertisement for urban blight when some insightful city planners and a smart developer decided to reclaim it under the banner of urban renewal. The garbage was removed, and the growing homeless population was encouraged to move along, which they did, grudgingly, but not too far, to a sprinkling of overcrowded shelters and National Guard Armories. The hardcore homeless resisted the idea of four walls and fled instead to out-of-sight places, swallowed up in concealed, festering holes like the nearby "Arches." The houses were gutted and upscale flats and lofts replaced the squalid apartments. A Starbucks was added so that the residents could conveniently buy their lattes and espressos, as well as an upscale grocery store, complete with subdued lighting to accent the produce department and gourmet olive bar. The bakery offered eight different kinds of bread and over a dozen different croissants and scones, but not one donut or chocolate bar could be purchased there.

Jessi pulled to a stop outside 3105 Temple Street, a restored two-story home with a new flagstone walkway leading up to freshly washed cement steps and a forest green front door.

Jessi stepped out of her car and looked around, assessing her surroundings. Everything appeared quiet, except for the traffic noises coming from the end of the block. People going about their daily business; no one shouting, no one concerned, no one standing outside bruised and battered waiting for the police to arrive.

As Jessi rang the doorbell, she noticed that the front door was unlatched, immediately setting off mental alarms and instantly increasing her adrenalin flow.

"Edward 40, meet Edward 4-2 at 3105 Temple for a backup."

"Roger that Edward 42. I'm three–four minutes out."

Jessi took a deep breath and started to nudge the door when it suddenly flew open, revealing a middle-aged, blond man dressed in a business suit and carrying a briefcase. He dropped his briefcase and jumped back, obviously startled to see a uniformed cop on his doorstep.

"What's the problem, Officer?"

Jessi's right hand was resting on the butt of her pistol, ready for any contingency. "I'm Officer Cole. We received a 911 call from this residence."

"911? I'm sure not. No reason for it. Everything is fine here. Now, if you'll excuse me, I'm late," he said, a hint of acid lacing his pronouncement as he turned to lock the front door.

"I'm sure everything is fine, too, sir, but the call did originate from this residence. Computers have virtually eliminated any room for error, Mr. ah…."

"Somers, Arnold Somers. I'm a practicing attorney and I'm due in court. I really don't have time for this."

"An attorney? I would have never guessed. Believe me, I understand completely, sir, that this is an inconvenience for you, but I would be derelict in my duty if I didn't see your ID and clear the residence," Jessi said, shaking her head in dismay at the inconvenience she was causing.

Somers sighed as he put down his briefcase and retrieved his wallet, thrusting it toward Jessi.

"Please take your license out of your wallet, sir," Jessi asked politely.

"Seems like you'd have something better to do than …"

Arnold's response was interrupted by the screeching siren of Odom's patrol car squealing around the corner, light bar flashing, and roaring down the block, where it skidded to a hot, smoky stop behind Jessi's car. Odom jumped out and was quickly alongside her.

"Situation under control, Officer Cole?"

"Situation under control, Officer Odom, but I thank you for your speedy response. Mr. Somers here was just about to take his I.D. out of his wallet and show it to me. Isn't that right, counselor?"

Somers gave Jessi a look as he dug into his wallet for his driver's license.

"Been through the house?" Odom asked.

"Just waiting for you."

"Is this really necessary?" Somers protested as he handed her his plastic driver's license.

"Just part of the service," Jessi positively beamed as she checked the license and turned to Odom. "Mr. Somers and I were just wondering how to avoid these pesky 911 disconnect calls. He's a busy man, and, of course, you and I are wasting the taxpayer's money."

"That's not quite what I meant," Somers reluctantly stepped away from the door, allowing Jessi and Odom to enter.

"What is it Arnold?" An attractive young woman, her hair uncombed and wearing flannel pajamas, stepped out.

"The police are here," Arnold snapped, stating the obvious.

"We're checking out a 911 disconnect call that came from this residence," Jessi explained. "And you are…?"

"Sally, Sally Somers. Excuse my attire," Sally giggled. "I work at home three days a week, been online to Taiwan since six this morning. Don't you just love it? Arnold's got to go downtown, fight the traffic, and punch a time clock…"

"I *don't* punch a time clock," Arnold countered.

"You know what I mean," Sally smiled. "My husband's a little jealous because I get to lounge in my pajamas and drink tea and eat crumpets at my leisure."

Arnold looked pained.

"Well, we'll just check the house and get out of your way," Jessi said as she and Odom did a quick walk through of the tastefully decorated premises, upstairs and down.

"Nice place. I wonder what they paid for it?" Jessi asked as she slid her fingers over the soft, golden top of a beautifully restored oak library table in the dining room.

"Half a mill, I'll bet," Odom responded as he followed Jessi back to where Arnold and Sally were waiting.

"You might want to have the phone company check your lines," Jessi suggested. "And make sure you keep your door locked."

"Have a great day, O.K.?" Sally said with a smile.

"You, too," Jessi said over her shoulder as she fell in step with Odom. The grumpy Arnold had already picked up his briefcase and hurried past them.

"You have a good day too, Counselor," Jessi called to Arnold's back. The red -faced attorney ignored her on his way to the three-story, corner parking garage to fetch his Jaguar.

"I hope you don't meet him in court next week," Odom said.

"That's a scary thought," Jessi replied.

Odom looked at his partner and smiled. "You know what I like about you, Cole? You got a little bit of a mean streak, and your sarcasm? First rate and highly polished. I'd give you a nine on the ten scale."

"Thank you, I appreciate you noticing. I guess I just wasted your gas, though. Sorry about that," Jessi apologized as they returned to their cars.

"Hey, don't ever make the mistake of thinking that a call like that doesn't warrant backup. You have an unlatched door, you aren't psychic, you have no idea what's waiting in there. I get a similar situation, I'll call you."

"Okay, okay, you're sounding like a training officer," Jessi said. "Tell me something, Tom; why is it that when you show up, all arguments just seem to suddenly dissipate, *poof,* gone?"

"Well, if I were to be objective, I'd suspect it's my charm," he said, his deep voice breaking into a rolling chuckle that Jessi loved.

"Nothing to do with you height, width, and brawn?" Jessi asked.

"Nah, besides, you almost had yourself talked around that pipsqueak."

"Yeah, but only *almost*. Sometime I'd love to go on a call and just strike fear into their cold hearts,"

"You mean," Odom's thick voice attempted to take on a shrill tone, 'Yes officer, no officer, anything you say officer, just don't hurt me officer.'"

Jessi laughed. "Yup, just like that."

"You want to strike fear, hell, put on 150 pounds and flatten your nose like mine, and then grow some big old biceps like these," he said flexing his arm. "That'll strike fear into anybody's heart!"

Jessi laughed again.

"Tell you what, Cole. I'll trade my brawn for your brain any day. I'd love to go on a call and have a perp spill their guts to me like they do with you. Remember Ronnie Walton?"

The Walton incident had occurred the first week of Jessi and Odom's partnership, when they had responded to an "unknown disturbance" call at a run down, six story, federal housing project on Sixth Avenue known as "The Brickyard." When they had arrived on scene, the nervous duo had had exactly two weeks of solo patrol experience between them. Enter Ronnie Walton. Fresh out of Huntsville prison and a rigorous weight training regimen, Walton was a buffed out, twenty-five-year-old crack head robber who beat his common-law wife nearly to death before putting a 44 Magnum pistol to his terrified, six-year-old daughter's head. He swore she was "infected" with wood ticks and had to be put out of her misery.

The thought of Walton and his sobbing daughter still gave Jessi chills. "Yeah, I remember him."

"Well, no amount of muscle was going to get that asshole's finger off the trigger. Lord knows we all tried. Hell, if that frigging idiot, Tyley, would have gotten his way, we would have busted the door down and that bastard would have killed his own kid."

"I didn't do anything, just got lucky."

"Hell you didn't. You kept him talking, you didn't get rattled, and you didn't rush it. You talked him into letting his little girl go. It was pretty much all you, girl."

"Thanks, John," Jessi said quietly.

"We're doing our job, Cole. I'm smart enough to know that there's more than one way to get it done."

"Oh, I get it; it's all about you, is it?"

Odom smiled. "You got that right. Now it's all about me needing a buttermilk bar and a cup of D & D coffee. You coming?"

"Right behind you, partner"

Jessi smiled as she got into her patrol car and pulled out.

She stopped for a red light, her mind still trying to figure out the 911 call and the unlatched door. Probably was a telephone glitch. Honking horns got her attention. Halfway down the block, a stalled vehicle was creating a traffic jam and flared tempers.

Jessi pulled into traffic, flipping her siren off and on to clear the line of cars, if only partially, and pulled in front of the crippled auto. Exiting her car, she noticed a growing crowd of street people waiting at a nearby city bus stop, watching the drama of a frightened old woman trying in vain to start a perfectly cherry, 1948 Pontiac sedan.

"What's the problem, ma'am, out of gas?

The elderly driver, fighting panic, stuck her head out, "No, dear, I just filled it up. It just quit on me. Nothing I could do, I swear. All this honking is giving me a headache, and if it doesn't stop, I might just start bawling like a baby," she said, her thin voice breaking.

"Hey, no tears, O.K.," Jessi soothed, patting the woman's shoulder. "Pop the hood latch and I'll take a look."

The woman was puzzled. "This is Ralph's car. He's been dead for two years. I've never opened the hood."

"My dad had a car like this when I was little. If I remember the latch is right down here..." Jessi reached in, "There," she said, as she pulled the lever and heard the latch snap open. "Let me check something."

Jessi's lifted the heavy hood and let her eyes sweep methodically over the spotlessly clean, bare engine compartment, noting with pleasure the lack of smog devises, fuel injection cells, turbo packs, and computer modules.

Everything looked normal.

Jessi frowned, ignoring the honking cars.

"There it is," she said aloud, a grin washing across her face. The lead wire from the distributor cap had come loose. Jessi quickly reinserted it and closed the hood. Returning to the driver's side door, Jessi leaned down. "Try it now. Let's see if it starts."

The old woman turned the key, and the old engine fired immediately.

"Thank you so much," the old woman smiled. "Do they teach you to fix engines at the police school?"

"Not exactly," Jessi replied, returning the smile as she headed back to her car. As she opened the door, she again felt someone's eyes on her. Pausing half in, half out of her door, she scanned the sea of faces at the bus stop. Again, the strange feeling in her stomach flooded over her. She caught a glimpse of a woman with long, gray hair watching her from the sidewalk. The face triggered some kind of recall. Was she the face in the van at The Arches? Probably not. She shook off the feeling and slid onto the hot upholstery of the patrol car. Checking her rearview mirror to make sure that the old Pontiac was moving, she hit the AC button and drove off.

Halfway down the next block, she pulled into an open space behind Tom Odom's patrol car. The feeling in her stomach returned. "Am I getting paranoid?" she asked herself as she checked the rearview mirror and caught just a flash of movement behind her car. Frowning, she adjusted the mirror. Nothing. She took a few moments to shuffle some papers and leaf through her notebook before getting out, locking her door, and walking toward D&D's Donut City which was around the corner and down two doors. She heard the footsteps behind her, and as she rounded the corner, she stopped abruptly and turned, hand on her pistol grip, waiting for the shadow she knew was not far behind.

Within a heartbeat she saw the approaching shadow and sprung, grabbing the woman and twisting her arm behind her back, shoving her, face first, against the brick wall. The pungent odor of musk oil filled Jessi's nostrils.

The frightened woman screamed, thrusting her head back in a vain attempt at a head butt, her long, gray-black hair getting tangled in Jessi's fingers.

When that didn't dislodge her attacker, the woman barred her teeth and growled, forcing Jessi to twist her arm even harder.

"Help! Police! Help!" the woman shrieked.

"Be quiet," Jessi said coolly. "I *am* the police and you are two seconds away from a trip to the county lock up! Now tell me why you've been following me." Jessi released a little of the tension in her tight restraint hold.

"What makes you think I'm following you?" the woman asked unconvincingly.

Jessi twisted her arm a little higher.

"Alright, alright, I wanted to talk to you. Is that against the fucking law?"

"So now we're communicating," Jessi stated, giving the woman a quick pat down before releasing her hold.

The woman turned defiantly to face her. "I could sue you for police brutality," she hissed, irritably rubbing her arm.

"Yeah, probably," Jessi agreed. "No doubt we're being recorded," Jessi said, looking off and faking a wave. "Hi, Mom!"

"No way. With my luck, this is an episode of *Cops* and I'll look like a wild-eyed hooker or something," the woman said with a glimmer of a smile.

The woman had high cheekbones and a narrow, strong chin that hinted at a soft beauty that had been coarsened by unequal parts of sun, alcohol, drugs, and heartache. She looked like a refugee time traveler from San Francisco's Haight-Ashbury, wearing thin, jeweled rings on each finger, a rumpled, loose-fitting, hippy-style dress, made of a flowered print that hung off her shoulders and was long enough to cover her filthy feet, which were protected by a well-worn pair of handmade leather thongs. Her long hair was a salt-and-pepper mix of black and gray, and she carried an oversize, multicolored cloth bag, made of brocade, that appeared to hold as much as a good-sized suitcase.

"Back to the point. Who are you, and why have you been following me?" Jessi demanded.

"My name is Lela Starr, and I haven't *exactly* been following you," Lela amended her previous statement to her fall-back position. "I mean, I do have a van, but traffic's terrible and *I* can't turn on my lights and siren like *you* can. So really, there's no way I could keep up to actually follow you."

"What are you talking about?"

"Well, since I couldn't keep up with you, I kind of like, ahh, how do I say this? I had to figure a way so you'd come to me, sort of. Know what I mean?"

"No, but I'll tell you this: if you don't get to the point in the next five seconds, I'll take you in for annoying the hell out of me!"

"You're a lot more patient with old ladies in stalled cars than you are with me," Lela complained.

"So it *was* you in the crowd?"

"Yeah," Lela admitted. "I know you patrol out here, I see you all the time, and I know they assign you all the grunt calls."

"Grunt calls?" Jessi was puzzled for a moment before a strange idea took root in her consciousness. "Just a minute. The 911 disconnect? You had something to do with that?"

"Yeah," Lela said, obviously pleased with herself. "People are incredibly foolish. It was a spur of the moment thing, really. I mean I was on the block; I used to live there, you know, had my own business in that very house. But when the yuppies *discovered* the old neighborhood, I and about 10,000 others were tossed out on our ass."

"Get to the point—911 disconnect."

"Mr. Moneybags ambulance chaser came out of *my* house, all in a rush, didn't even get down the steps when *Sally* dear called him back in. He left the door wide open. The rest was just inspiration and improvisation on my part."

"Inspiration? Sounds pretty stupid to me, because now you're looking at not only the improper use of 911, but a trespassing charge as well," Jessi stated, deadpan.

"Like I said, I wanted to talk to you, and you know both those charges are bullshit misdemeanors and both are going to take about an hour of your valuable time to write up. Am I right, or what?" Lela said, rubbing her upper arm where Jessi grabbed her.

"You could have just called dispatch," Jessi said as another 60-watt light bulb went off in her brain. "Ah ha, but you did. You were the reporting party on the ADW, the Little Hondo thing at The Arches, right?"

Lela nodded. "That man has the worst karma I have ever encountered. He should be horsewhipped."

"Why didn't you talk to me out there? You do live at The Arches, right?"

"If I had talked to you out there, you would have considered me a deranged bag lady, and besides, it's not that easy."

"I'm asking you again, there are five hundred police officers in Houston. Why me?"

Lela offered an exaggerated sigh as she rummaged through her bag. "I don't see why I've always got to explain everything to you people. It's like you close off...here it is." Lela pulled a wrinkled newspaper article from her bag, carefully unfolded it and passed it to Jessi. "I've seen you on the street and at the Arches. You're still open to people, and besides you were a teacher."

Jessi took the clipping. It was a feature article printed in the Houston Examiner that told the story of a junior high school social studies teacher who had followed her mother's footsteps into the classroom, but when that road became a dead end decided to detour and become a Houston police officer like her father. It was a feature on Jessi Cole with photos of her surrounded by a group of seventh graders.

"*Was* a teacher," Jessie corrected. "I'm a police officer now, remember?"

"But you still have a connection with young people. You know how vulnerable those girls are, how fragile."

Lela's words triggered a flood of emotions and memories, the giggles, passed notes, the tears. Jessi shook away the past. "Look, I don't have time for this. I've got work to do."

"I had to be sure you were the right one."

"And you're *sure* now?"

"Maybe, I don't know," Lela said, her voice laden with uncertainty.

"O.K., you wanted to talk, so talk," Jessi said. "You've obviously got my attention."

Lela took a deep breath and pursed her lips. "I need to report a kidnapping."

Jessi was interested despite herself. "When did this happen?"

"I don't know."

"Where did it occur?"

"I don't know."

"Who was kidnapped?'

"I don't know that either."

Jessi stared at Lela for a full five seconds before stepping back. "You know, I think it might be easier for you just to go to the station and talk to a detective. They can probably..."

"I have talked to every detective down there. They won't listen; they think I'm a crackpot, some kind of loony tune."

Jessi turned away and rolled her eyes before turning back to face Lela. "If you've gone through the detective bureau and they don't take you seriously, what makes you think that I won't agree with their conclusion? After your 911 call today, I'm already well on my way to the loony-tune theory," Jessi said, silently cursing the gods for putting some kind of mark on her that crackpots seemed to spot a mile away.

"I know," Lela said tiredly. "I guess the difference is, I *know* you'll listen. You'd worry if you didn't."

"Worry? Trust me, I won't worry. I don't internalize," Jessi said quickly, already feeling the familiar beginnings of the disquieting knot in her stomach. She took a deep breath. "Alright, I'll listen, but only for five minutes. Not one second longer. Agreed?"

"Agreed,"

"You want a cup of coffee?"

"I've been craving a custard-filled chocolate bar for about a month," Lela said, following Jessi down the sidewalk.

Odom was headed out just as Jessi and Lela entered D&D's Donut City.

"I thought I'd been stood up," Odom smiled at Jessi, his curious eyes instantly sweeping over Lela Starr.

"Ms. Starr here thinks that she has some information on a kidnapping, and she would like to share that information with us," Jessi said, her tone and body language giving her partner an unspoken warning that Lela was a possible nut case.

Odom quickly sized up Lela and decided to bail. "I'd love to stay, but I've got a domestic disturbance call pending."

"Pending, huh? I must have missed that call," Jessi said raising her eyebrows.

"You and Ms. Starr don't need me. Take notes; you can fill me in later." Odom quickly backed away and fled to the safety of his car.

"See, he thinks I'm a nut and he doesn't even know me," Lela said, nodding at the fast disappearing Odom.

D&D Donuts was not fancy, the only decorations being a few uninspired travel posters, but it was spotlessly clean, and the eight Formica-topped tables scattered around the high-ceilinged room allowed you to read the morning paper without being crowded or rushed. A half dozen regular patrons were doing just that when Lela followed Jessi into the familiar shop, where they were instantly enveloped by the sweet smell of fresh hot donuts.

"You just missed you're partner," the middle-aged woman behind the counter said. "I know, I saw him. He had to run," Jessi replied.

The woman's name was Danielle, and she owned the business along with her baker husband, Don. "What can I get you, honey?" she asked with a warm smile. She was short and heavy and wore a blue, baseball-style hat and a clean, white t-shirt, both silk-screened with "D&D" on the front.

"I'll have a double latte with chocolate, vanilla, and cinnamon sprinkles, along with a crumb donut. And my guest, here, will have...?" Jessi nodded toward Lela.

Lela's eyes swept over the glass counter hungrily "Let's see here, no need to rush. Mmmm. I want one of those pumpkin spice lattes with extra chocolate sprinkles and two chocolate bars, two French donuts, and a cinnamon twist."

"You want these to go?" Danielle asked.

"Yeah, put them in a bag," Lela replied.

If Danielle noticed Lela's street appearance, she gave no indication as she quickly filled the order, putting everything in a bag and placing it in front of Lela and doing the math in her head. "That'll be $8.75."

"She's paying for mine," Lela nodded toward Jessi.

"I guess I am," Jessi said, removing her wallet and handing Danielle a ten and three ones to cover her own purchase, which was sure to cause a discussion.

"We don't want you to pay, dear," Danielle smiled. In truth, she and her husband, who had been robbed over a dozen times, would have gladly paid Jessi or any of her fellow officers just to have a patrol car sitting outside for a few minutes twice a day.

"Hey, we got to keep you guys in business," Jessi responded as she grabbed the tray and moved to a table by the window. Several of the customers glanced up as they passed, aware of the odd couple appearance of the cop and the bag lady. As Lela sat down opposite Jessi, she dropped her multicolored bag on the floor and immediately removed a chocolate bar from the white paper sack and hungrily devoured the whole thing, only then taking the time to take a tentative sip of her steaming latte.

Jessi watched the woman opposite her closely, taking the opportunity to check her eyes for pupil dilation and her forearms for needle tracks or the tell-tell scars of a chronic drug user. There was something about this woman that flipped a toggle switch deep in the recesses of Jessi's long term memory bank. Had she met her somewhere?

"I'm not a junkie," Lela said, noticing Jessi appraising her.

Jessi shrugged, not convinced. "Okay, so you're Lela Starr, right? And I'm Officer Cole, and you went through a lot of effort to talk to me about a… kidnapping, right? So let's get to it. Four minutes and counting," Jessi prompted, checking her watch for effect.

"How'd you fix the old woman's car? I thought you were a cop, not a mechanic," Lela gave Jessi her own appraising look.

"It was just a loose distributor wire," Jessi explained. "My Uncle Gary owned a garage, worked on cars. I used to stay with him sometimes."

Lela raised her eyebrows. "Amazing."

"Yeah," Jessi agreed, "truly amazing, but not as amazing as someone reporting a kidnapping while she eats donuts and sips lattes. Three and a half minutes."

"Do you mind smoke?"

Jessi frowned, but slid a tinfoil ashtray across the table. Lela retrieved her cloth bag from the floor and, placing it next to her on the table, started rummaging, quickly coming up with a foot-long, deep brown incense stick that she lighted with a wooden match.

"Nice, huh? It's called Indian Summer. I find that incense stimulates the olfactory senses and enhances communication, don't you agree?" she asked as she swirled the smoldering stick above her head, sending a line of lazy, sweet-smelling smoke drifting around the table and into the nostrils of those sitting nearby.

As Danielle waited on a line of customers, she watched the smoke rise and frowned. If the bag lady had been alone, she'd have called Don from the back and had her tossed out.

Jessi sneezed and, after wiping her nose, tried to refocus Lela. "Let's try it again from the top. Who was kidnapped?"

The question seemed to hang in the air with the swirling smoke as Lela brought a small, wax candle from the bag and lighted it, placing it in another ashtray.

"The burning flame offers my life continuity. I find in my present circumstances that continuity is something I really need," Lela said, replacing the box of matches in her bag and turning her tired eyes once again to Jessi.

Jessi sneezed again and fanned the air in a vain attempt to clear the pungent smoke before picking up the smoldering incense and dousing it in Lela's latte. She then leaned over the table and blew out the candle. "You seem to be a little distracted," Jessi said to explain her actions as she took out a small tablet and pencil to indicate she was prepared to take notes. "You are going to tell me about a kidnapping, or I'm out of here in exactly two minutes and forty seconds."

"I already told you I don't know, exactly. I mean, I'm not sure."

Jessi's pencil froze in mid air. "You don't know? O.K., let's deal with what you do know, alright? Now, is the victim a member of your family, a friend, an acquaintance, what?"

Lela paused, pursing her lips in a worried-looking curl as she carefully considered her response. "No, I mean I don't actually *know* her. We've never met, if that's what you're asking. I *do* know that she's a young girl, a teenager. I heard her sobs, but they were far away."

"You heard her sobs," Jessi shook her head in frustration. "You happen to get a name?"

"Mickey."

"Now were progressing. Mickey what?"

"I don't know, but she frightens me. She looks like this," Lela was suddenly excited as she yanked her spiral-bound sketchpad from her bag and thrust it at Jessi, unconsciously locating the quartz crystal dangling from her neck and stroking it with her thumb and forefinger, sending a band of rainbow colors dancing over Jessi's face.

As Jessi looked down at the pad, she felt a cold chill pass through her spine and into her heels. It was a professional, detailed, black-and-white pencil sketch of the terror-filled face of a young girl. After studying the drawing for a moment, Jessi pushed the pad back to Lela, and the women exchanged a long, measured look.

Again the colors from Lela's necklace flashed in Jessi's eyes, sparking a memory that surged into her consciousness. "I knew I'd seen you before! You used to go the University of Houston and set up your stuff on The Quad. You drew caricatures and sold crystal necklaces. You read Tarot cards and palms."

"I can read eyes and tea leaves, too," Lela bristled, her defensive sarcasm coming to the fore. "I still go out to the University sometimes, but the kids nowadays are such material buttheads I can't stand them. Absolutely zero social consciousness. No depth whatsoever."

Jessi nodded and unconsciously closed her small notebook, relaxing with the self confirmation that she was dealing with a nut case. She picked up her crumb donut and took a bite. "This kidnapping? Would it possibly be what you might call a..." Jessi raised her fingers in the international sign for quote marks "'materialization,' or something like that?"

Lela's expression froze in an angry glare. "Look, goddamnit, I don't..." She spit the words out, her volume increasing slightly as she raised her hands, giving her own rendition of quote marks using her middle fingers, "*materialize*, I *visualize*, and I don't have the time to waste on your juvenile skepticism. Mickey's dead, and you're wasting my fucking time!"

Jessi's volume also increased. "Oh, she's dead now? I thought you said she was kidnapped. Which is it? How do you know?"

"I don't know how I know. I just know," Lela shot back, thumbing quickly through her sketchpad and sliding it back to her increasingly skeptical questioner. Jessi turned the pad and studied the second sketch. It was a well-drawn recreation of a female hand, frozen in place, reaching out and up from a black background. In the left-hand corner of the sketch, the numbers *1305* were printed about two inches high in stencil-style block letters. "Mickey is dead. I told the detective about her before, but he thinks I'm a head case."

Again, Jessi felt a strange chill sweep down the small of her back. "What are the numbers about? The 1305? Are they part of the Mickey visualization or are they like a, a totally separate thing?" Jessi asked, trying with only minimal success to filter the increasing skepticism from her tone.

"I don't know. The numbers just came and I wrote them down. They're on the same page, so you can assume they're related, okay? They sure as hell mean something, or I wouldn't have written them down now, would I?"

The two women stared at each other in silence for a few moments before Jessi set Lela's sketchpad aside and finished her donut and luke-warm latte. "Look, if you want me to help you, I need names, dates, addresses..."

"You're just lazy," Lela blurted, reaching across the table and snatching the sketchpad back. She shoved the pad into her carryall and stood, rattling the table and slamming her chair back with a loud screech.

"Lazy?" Jessi's anger levitated her slowly upright and reddened her cheeks as she faced off with the equally angry Lela Starr. "I will make probably twenty runs today and write a dozen reports before I can go home. And if I'm really lucky, I'll make it home by seven tonight. That's not a visualization, nor is it a materialization; no, it's just plain, hard ass work that the taxpayers of Houston pay me to do. Now if you don't mind, I'll get at it!"

Jessi glanced around the donut shop noticing that they were providing a great deal of entertainment to owners and customers alike. "See you later, folks," Jessi said to Don and Danielle as she headed out the door. She was nearly to the corner before she heard Lela's dogged steps behind her.

"I'm telling you about a dead little girl, and you're whining about working late!"

Jessi froze, turning slowly to face the source of her uncharacteristic anger. "You are telling me nothing. You give me some rambling story about a kidnapping, or maybe now it's a murder, and some bizarre drawings, and you expect *me* to figure it out. You," Jessi said, poking her finger in Lela's chest, "are not going to make me a part of your hellish imagination. End of story. Your five minutes are up." Jessi moved away, then turned back quickly. "Oh, and have a nice day," she said, pinching off a very small piece of smile as she turned and walked away.

"Wow, how totally original! Maybe you should quit being a cop and go to work for Hallmark!" Lela jeered, following close behind.

Jessi ignored her, turning the corner toward her patrol car.

Lela hurried to the corner. "When you're ready to do your job, look me up!" she shouted at Jessi's back. Slowly, and with deliberation, Lela started singing.

It took Jessi a full second to realize what she was hearing.

> *Gimme a boat that floats and a grandson to sail with and it will all make sense to you. Yes, it will all make sense to yooooouuu!*

Jessi hesitated but didn't stop, and for the first time in her short career as a police officer, she fled *from* a call.

4.

Lela shook her head in frustration as she watched Jessi's patrol car disappear into traffic. She vented her anger on an unfortunate, elderly man who happened to be standing nearby, tethered to his aging cocker spaniel that was peeing on a sun burnt shrub. "If it wouldn't be too much trouble, could somebody please tell me how to report a fucking murder?" she screeched, sending the old man and his dog retreating over the hot cement.

Lela felt the unrelenting Texas heat envelop her as she made her way down the sidewalk, laboring under the weight of the cloth bag. She had parked her van in the next block, and now she wondered if she could make it that far. Her thoughts returned to the female cop. How could she have been so stupid? She had been so sure that Jessi was the right one that she was somehow different from the others and would certainly understand. Lela sagged, suddenly feeling very old and very tired. She stopped momentarily and, spotting a sliver of shade, leaned against a boarded- up store front, closing her eyes and turning inward to gather strength for the homestretch to her van.

"Dammit! She's got to understand. I need help! My girls need help!" She fought for air, short, raspy, shallow pants that failed to quiet her growing panic. As she stood there catching her breath, a dark shadow fluttered behind Lela's lids, terrified eyes imploring her. "I'm trying, little ones, I'm trying," she mumbled aloud.

"You got a problem, lady? Can I help you?"

Lela blinked her eyes open to see a bearded young man with spiked pink hair wearing a dirty, tie-dyed t-shirt staring at her. Both of his nostrils and one eyelid were pierced with gold studs. Lela pushed herself away from the wall and extended her ringed hand toward him.

"Your life force is very strong and your aura radiates blue!"

The words and her sudden movement startled the young man, and he started backing away.

"Wait! Don't leave. I have something for you," Lela quickly withdrew her notebook from her bag and did a caricature of him in under a minute. "This is for stopping," she said, tearing it out and thrusting it toward him.

The young man smiled in surprise as he admired the sketch. "This is nothin' but cool."

Lela grabbed her bag and hurried down the block, glancing up and down the busy street, seeking her precious van which she had left in a twenty-minute yellow zone. When she finally spotted it, there was a white parking ticket under the windshield wiper. The meter maid was still visible halfway down the block, writing another citation, oblivious to the fact that she had just thrown gasoline on Lela's already burning anger. "I try to report a murder, and they fine me forty-five fucking dollars! Well you know something?" Her mumble graduated instantly to a full-blown scream. "I am not fucking going to pay it!" The volume of her voice caused several nearby street people to veer away and speed up to avoid Lela's field of vision.

Out of habit she checked the garbage can on the corner, spotting a McDonald's Value Breakfast Meal sack that contained a half-eaten potato patty. She quickly added the greasy patty to her donut bag and continued to her van.

Jessi returned to the stationhouse and made her way through the busy squad room and down a hallway that led to another large room buried in the far southeast corner of the building where a dozen cubicles were set aside for patrol officers to use for report writing. Most of the cubicles were in use by other day shift officers and Jessi was forced to use the "rookie cube," which was next to the men's restroom and guaranteed constant foot traffic and little privacy. The meager area housed two, coffee stained oak desks butted up against one another so that when she and Odom were both there, they looked directly at one another. A well used computer monitor and keyboard sat on each desk. The monitor was up and running twenty-four and seven, attesting to the in house line "We never close."

Jessi sat down at the desk and used the computer mouse to bring the internal data base up. She typed in the name of Lela Starr, hit "Enter," and waited.

Nothing.

No internal report forms, called "1017s," had been entered on any interviews Lela Starr claimed to have had with any detectives, homicide or otherwise. The bag lady was not only a total nut case, she appeared to be a liar as well. Jessi shook her head, she wasn't surprised. She should just forget it, she had enough to occupy her time, but she couldn't, not quite yet.

Jessi pushed herself away from the desk and made her way back to the spacious squad room where dozens of over worked detectives processed the grisly incidents that a population of two million people could generate on a daily basis. Jessi slowed and then froze as she approached the front-line desks where the homicide detectives known as the *Murder Squad* resided.

Detectives Tyley and Eisom were manning their desks. Tyley was talking on the telephone so she pointed herself at Merle Eisom.

She momentarily considered the option of fleeing, but she forced her reluctant legs to propel her toward Eisom's desk, admonishing her inner demons not to stare at the tall man's goofy looking, jet black hair piece.

Eisom looked up at her and grinned. "Twice in one day? We're blessed again. What's up, beautiful?"

"I know this is a long shot, but do you know anything about a woman named Lela Starr?"

Eisom sat back in his chair and pursed his lips. "Lela Starr you say?" He contemplated the name for a few more seconds before shaking his head. "Nope. Don't ring a bell. Where am I supposed to know her from?"

"Bag lady type. Claims to have visions about a kidnapped girl. She's some kind of psychic."

Eisom's puzzled expression slowly dissolved into a sneer. "*Psycho* you mean?"

"Whatever. When did you talk to her last?" Jessi asked.

Eisom turned toward his partner and hooted. "Hey Tyley, you got to hear this."

Jessi sighed, instantly cognizant that she was about to become the butt of a bad joke. At this point, she was hoping to minimize her exposure and escape. "Look, Detective Eisom, I know you're busy and I don't want to take up too much of your time. All I need to know is if you've talked to her or not?"

"Oh, we communicated with her, sort of," Eisom chuckled.

"Who took the report, you or your partner? I can't find any 1017s," Jessi said.

"That's because there is no 1017," Tyley replied loudly from the next desk as he hung up the phone and stood.

"Why not? Who took her statement?"

"I took her statement, if you want to call it that," Tyley answered, moving uncomfortably close to Jessi. "But I only fill out 1017 reports on interviews conducted on human beings, not on every conversation that every friggin' lunatic who stumbles in off the street waving incense and ranting about abductions. She's a fucking head case."

"So you guys *do* know her?"

"The spook? Hell yes, everybody knows the spook," Eisom declared as he made an exaggerated show of closing his eyes and rubbing his temples with his fingers. "Through my magic rocks I see a body of water with a railroad track close by. That's where you'll find the corpse, officer."

"Cole, please don't tell me you're gullible enough to write a report on anything that dirt bag says?" Tyley shook his head in disbelief.

"Yeah, I'm that gullible," Jessi said, surprising herself. "I interviewed her so I'm going to write a report. Isn't that the procedure we're supposed to follow? At least that's what they taught us at the academy."

"Well, let me put it this way, teach, if you're going to play liberal social worker, have at it, but you'll have to excuse me, I've got a homicide to work," Tyley declared, summarily dismissing her as he moved back to his cluttered desk where he slumped heavily into the chair.

Jessi could feel her face redden as she watched the arrogant detective busy himself in a mound of files. One thought flashed through her mind: "You're blowing it!" But she couldn't stop herself from approaching him again.

"Detective Tyley, I would really appreciate your help. When was the last time Lela Starr was in here? It's important."

"Oh, Christ, you're really going to push this aren't you?" he asked, clenching his teeth. "O.K. I surrender. Your case is obviously more important than my homicide. I saw the spook, I don't know, hell, maybe a couple a weeks ago. What's the big deal?"

"What did she talk about? Remember?"

Tyley looked up from a file and, puffing out his cheeks, blew hard enough to make his lips flutter. If looks could kill, Jessi would have been DOA. "Hell, Cole, I don't know. What do those friggin' spooks usually talk about? She blew smoke up my ass and rambled about 'sensitives' and evil spirits and "ying" and "yang" and psychic energy, and it was all one hundred percent certified horseshit, O.K.? Now can I please go back to work?"

"Did she mention anything to you about young girls getting murdered? Did she mention any names?"

"Names? What names? Christ almighty, the woman's a friggin' fruitcake. I don't know any names."

"Try to remember, please."

Tyley scratched his head as if that simple act would somehow rekindle his memory. It worked. "I think she mentioned a missing girl, but that's nothing new. She's been doing that for months. Mandy, Mindy?"

"How about Mickey?"

"Could have been. Then she fired up her incense, and I kicked her butt out. Now, Inspector Closeau, may I please be excused to get back to some real police business here?"

Jessi made it three steps before she turned back around. "You know, if you had filled out a 1017 like every one of your fellow detectives find the time and energy to do, you would have saved us all this hassle, and I might have a little bit of usable information."

As the two detectives watched Jessi walk away, they exchanged lustful looks. Tyley unconsciously rubbed his bald head. "Excuse me, Detective Eisom, but does Officer Cole have the tightest little ass in

Houston, or am I going as blind as the one-eyed Cyclops that lurks in my shorts?"

Tyley's tone was loud enough to carry to Jessi's ears. She stiffened, but didn't bother turning around.

"Better watch it," Eisom said wagging his finger at Tyley. "You're being what they called in the workshop, *sexually insensitive.*"

This time Jessi did turn around.

"Don't worry about it, Detective. Rumor is that the Cyclops *Detective Tyley* keeps talking about is more fiction than reality. Besides, I'll reserve my sexual harassment charge for someone who's a real threat. Not someone who's just a pain in the...excuse me, a pain in my *tight little ass.*"

Jessi turned quickly and walked away, leaving Tyley and Eisom to avoid each other's eyes as they returned to their desks.

Jessi was still fuming from her encounter with the detectives as she hurried past the watch commander's open door, hoping that he wouldn't notice her and force an explanation of why she wasn't in her patrol car. She didn't make it.

"Hey, Cole, come in here a minute."

Lieutenant Mike Sakelaris sat behind the cluttered desk in his cubbyhole of an office reviewing crime reports from the graveyard shift. He was a tall, gruff, no nonsense third generation Greek American with a wide, bushy mustache who, like every Sakelaris male for untold generations, had pursued law enforcement as a career. He was now fifty-five and a confirmed workaholic who was both liked and respected by his subordinates. As Jessi entered, he leaned back in his chair, yawned, and stretched his arms above his head. "How's it going on the credit card thing?"

"I checked out the newest slips. It was the Braxton brothers alright. I've got two positive I.D.s. It looks like they lifted the credit card from a guy at Chez Peyo restaurant. I'm going to check that out this afternoon."

"Did you let the detectives know?"

"Yeah, that's why I came in," Jessi fibbed.

"Good. These creeps are taking up too much of our time and they're robbing our citizens blind. Anything else?" he said.

"That's it, Lieu," Jessi said as she started out.

His deep voice caused her to pause. "I'm getting good reports from you and about you. Keep it up."

"Yes, sir. Thanks."

"I got a call a few minutes ago from a little old lady who said you fixed her car. Do you rotate tires too?"

"Nope, don't do tires," Jessi smiled as she turned and walked to the stairwell that would take her back to the parking garage. As she took the steps three at a time, she passed the door to the Records Division slowed and then stopped. "You really are asking for trouble," she said to herself as she turned around and opened the door.

The spacious Records Division housed long rows of light green file cabinets interspaced with work stations. This was where over a dozen overworked civilian employees, all but two of them female, entered an unending stream of crime reports onto permanent records. Other employees initiated wants and warrant searches, or processed routine information requests from various police agencies within the state or around the country.

One of the two males in the room was a thirty-five-year-old dedicated computer nerd named Murray Crook. He had gone out of his way to assist Jessi on several occasions over the last few months, and the two of them had developed a comfortable friendship. Murray was openly gay and celebrated it daily by wearing an assortment of Hawaiian shirts he had purchased on line from Hilo Hattie's in Hawaii. Jessi's easy and honest acceptance of his lifestyle made Murray's life on the job just a touch more pleasant, and he smiled as he looked up from his monitor to see her enter and approach his desk.

"Officer Cole. How is my favorite peace officer doing this fine day?"

"Morning, Murray, you busy?"

"You tell me," he answered, gesturing toward a foot high stack of files sitting next to his computer monitor. "I'm backed up about six hours worth."

"No problem. I'll see if somebody else can do it," Jessi said, but as she started off, Murray grabbed her wrist.

"Like hell you will. I said I was busy, but I'm also open to bribery, and I think you're aware of that one, tiny little flaw in my otherwise rock-solid character."

"Bribery is a criminal offense. However, I suppose a simple lunch or dinner couldn't be classified as bribery," Jessi answered.

"I guess it depends on just how simple a lunch or dinner we're talking about."

"Simple enough that you can put mustard and relish on it?" Jessi responded.

"God, cops are so cheap. I'll be damned if I'll put mustard on it. I deserve much better. No deal."

The two of them faced off, exchanging their best rendition of "I draw the line here" look, before Jessi pursed her full lips and threw in the towel. "O.K., O.K., a sit-down dinner."

"I'm bought and paid for. What's the favor?"

"Can you run a name through N.C.I.C. for me?" Jessi asked.

Murray glanced nervously around the room. "Ahh, Jessi, I'm assuming you're read the latest directive regarding accessing records? I mean, this *is* an official police matter, is it not? I mean, otherwise, I have to log your name and what you are investigating and oh shit, so much paperwork." His look pleaded for a positive response.

"Yes, it's police business."

"Good. Let me bring it up." Murray cleared his monitor and typed in a four-number code. With the click of a button the format screen for National Crime Information Center popped up. "Here we go, name?"

Jessi glanced at her legal tablet. "Mickey."

Jessi didn't miss Murray's skeptical look, which she deflected with a shrug.

"Let's assume female. That's the best I can do, sorry," she said.

"Missing since?"

"Who knows? Maybe never. Let's say within the last couple of months."

"Why don't you make it easy on yourself and try to find the proverbial needle in a haystack or a BB in the ocean? Or a...?"

"I know, I know, but it's all I got. Add 'at risk.'"

By giving the inquiry the seemingly simple "at risk" designation, the N.C.I.C. would give the search for information priority over less urgent requests.

Murray shrugged and typed "Mickey," and hit the enter key.

A message appeared on the monitor: "PROCESSING DATA - STAND BY."

"The system will go nationwide first, then regional, then state, and then county. It will also access the National Missing Children's Registry".

Murray hit enter and waited. "Did you know that over 2,000 kids were abducted or otherwise reported missing last year?

It took a full 20 seconds before the "NO DATA AVAILABLE" message appeared on the monitor.

"No hits. "Murray said, glancing over his shoulder at the disappointed Jessi. "You know, I got a cousin everybody calls Mickey. But her actual name is Michelle."

"So try it and make your search open ended," Jessi responded.

Murray entered the name Michelle. Again the "NO DATA AVAILABLE" message appeared on the screen.

"Sorry, Jessi."

Jessi shrugged and headed for the door. "I actually didn't expect any, but thanks anyway. I'll see you later."

"Remember our date!" Murray smiled as he opened the top file folder on his stack and prepared to go to work. As he looked back at his monitor he came instantly alert. "Hey, Jessi, hold a minute!"

She was halfway out the door when she heard Murray call her back. His eyes were locked on the monitor as Jessi returned and looked over his shoulder. "You got something?"

"Yeah, but it's not a *missing* girl. This one was found, *dead.* Michelle 'Mickey' Sandoval, 13. Reported missing June 15th last year by her parents in Dallas. Her body was found at a highway rest stop in Grace County, Texas on June 19th."

"Print it for me, please."

"Where's Grace County?" Murray asked, clicking the print button with his mouse.

"I haven't the vaguest idea," Jessi said as Murray removed the report from the printer tray and handed it to her.

"She said Mickey was dead," Jessi said as she quickly scanned the printout and headed for the door.

"*Who* said she was dead?" Murray called after her.

Jessi was so intent on reading that she didn't hear his question. "Thanks again. And Murray, don't make plans. We're going to dinner tonight after work. I'll meet you out front of Chez Peyo at six-thirty?"

"Where's Chez Peyo?" Murray shouted at Jessi's back as she hurried out of the office. Not getting a response, he shrugged. "I'll use my nav."

Jessi bounded back up the stairs, two at a time. As she exited the stairwell, she nearly collided with a hurried and somewhat impatient Lt. Sakelaris. The watch commander was on his way to the weekly meeting of division heads and was in no mood to visit. He quickly scanned the N.C.I.C. printout as Jessi gave him a shorthand account of her unsettling encounter with Lela Starr.

"Come on, Cole, you know better than to take this woman seriously. She's a nut, a chain rattler. These people will tell you anything you want to hear just to get some attention. If you go along with her on this, she'll run you ragged. Forget it."

"But the report?"

"This?" Sakelaris held up the N.C.I.C. printout. "This is nothing. No, this is less than nothing. Look, Officer, I've got a meeting to get to where I have to justify every goddamn paper clip and piece of paper we use down here!" Sakelaris flared as he pushed the printout back into her hands and disappeared through the swinging doors of the squad room.

Jessi stood mute, her mind racing over whether or not this particular issue was worth rocking the boat over. She decided it was and, hurrying out the door, fell in step with Sakelaris as he headed for the elevator. "Lieutenant, you're not asking me to ignore this, are you?" she asked, holding the printout up for emphasis.

Sakelaris stopped abruptly and pushed the elevator call button, his tone impatient as he unconsciously stroked his baldhead. "No, I'm not asking you to ignore it. I'm telling you to ignore it!" The elevator door opened noisily, and he stepped on, pushing against the rubber cushion on the inside frame to stop it from closing. "Memo to probationary Officer Cole, would you please put all your psychic thoughts and energy into completing more positive pursuits, like finding the Braxton brothers ASAP! O.K.? Thanks for your anticipated courtesy in this matter. Sincerely yours, The Boss!"

Jessi nodded meekly as the door slid shut. She waited for the familiar *whirr* of the rising elevator, but the door slid open instead, and Sakelaris looked out at her somewhat sheepishly. "Listen, if you can get one of the Murder Squad interested, have at it. But if you can't, drop it. End of conversation," he said as he allowed the elevator doors to slide shut.

As the elevator *whirred* its way upstairs, Jessi returned to the squad room, but as she approached the Murder Squad desks, she veered off. Being berated and laughed at again seemed very unappealing. Leaning against the wall, she reread the printout before a voice startled her.

"You look troubled, kiddo, what's wrong?"

Jessi looked up to see Sergeant Tobin standing next to her.

If you've got a couple of days I'll tell you about it," Jessi replied.

"Follow me," the big man said walking deliberately through the hallway to the patrol desk. "I ain't got a couple days, but I can give you a couple minutes," Leroy said, sitting down and interlocking his beefy fingers and tucking his thumbs under his third chin as he listened patiently to Jessi recount her interview with Lela Starr including the N.C.I.C. report.

After hearing her out, Leroy sighed. "Jessi, you're about the most levelheaded person in this stationhouse. You're also one of the smartest, so when I say to you that, in my opinion, you will look like a total idiot to your fellow officers if you involve yourself with this nut, you'll understand it's nothing personal, right?"

Jessi shook her head and exhaled in frustration. "You're always hearing this crap about going with your instincts, you know, but every time I want to follow a hunch somebody says, 'Hey, you don't have enough experience to play hunches. Do your job, and go home. Hell, if I had wanted to just do my job and go home, I'd get a job in a bank."

"That's certainly one option. I'll tell you this, though," Leroy continued, "If your old man was here, you know damn well what *he* would say." Leroy's voice dropped two octaves. "'If you got a hunch, play it. Screw these paperweight suits!'"

"So what do *you* say, Sarge?"

"I say do what you're going to do and after you've done it, get your butt back in your patrol car and hit the street. I'm short cars as it is."

Jessi smiled as Leroy pulled his bulk out of the chair. "Believe me, honey, if something you do pans out, these assholes upstairs will be falling all over themselves trying to take credit for it."

"Thanks, Sarge."

Leroy tossed her a wave over his shoulder as he disappeared into the nearby rest room. Jessi stood in silence for a few moments before picking up the sergeant's telephone and asking the operator for the phone number of the Grace County Sheriff's Office.

5.

☙❧

The sun-bleached wooden sign marked the trailer at 1032 Kearney Street as:

Grace County Municipal District- Sheriff.
Street, Water, and Sewage Departments
"Pay water and garbage bills inside."

From her desk in the center of the double-wide trailer, Janie Cortez could see outside where the lone star flag of Texas hung limply beneath the equally exhausted Stars and Stripes. Janie, a full-blooded Comanche Indian, stood and moved to the large, upright fan that "whirred" loudly nearby and tilted it a little more to the left. In that way, she could at least feel its cooling breeze without having it blow everybody's paperwork all over the small office. "Nice time for the air conditioner to go down," she thought, right in the middle of the fifteenth-straight day of 100-plus-degree temperatures. Janie marked each day's temperature on the calendar which hung above her communications console. There was something satisfying about having one more day to add to the record: 105 yesterday, 107 today, and tomorrow looked like it'd be another scorcher.

The water department phone jangled and Janie answered it on the first ring. "Grace County Water Department. This is Janie. May I help you?... Oh, hi, Thirl, how's Joan doing?... So what's going on?... You're kidding, right?...Thanks, hon., Frank will be right there."

Janie stood, unplugged her portable headset from her console and, with it dangling around her neck, moved to the other side of the trailer where her husband, Frank Cortez, was using the Water Department desk as a makeshift workbench, mounting a pulley on the shaft of the new electrical motor for the broken air conditioner. She moved quietly, suddenly leaning down to give the stocky, dark-complexioned man a peck on the cheek.

"You're going to give me a heart attack, woman," Frank responded, failing once again to sound truly grouchy as his phony frown dissolved into his usual warm, easy smile that she loved so much. "Don't be kissing on the head of the Water, Street and Sewage Departments without an appointment."

"That was Thirl Butler on the phone. Lloyd Herring just hit the fire hydrant at Hughes and Van Keppel with his tractor. I guess it looks like Old Faithful over there."

"What the hell's that old fool doing driving his Johnny Putt-Putt on the sidewalk?" Frank grimaced, setting the motor aside and pulling on his dirty Dallas Cowboys hat over his wavy, dark hair, and headed for the door. "Tell the Sheriff I'll have the new motor in the air conditioner as soon as I can get back. Hang in there, honey," Frank said as he hurried out to the yellow Grace County Water Department pickup.

Janie could hear the pickup pull away as she continued through the office, passing by a vacant-eyed, uniformed deputy sitting numbly in front of a brand new computer, its cursor blinking an unwanted invitation. The deputy was a fifty-six-year-old former Marine named Vernon 'Red' Cordell, a muscular six-footer with a severe flattop gouged into a thick head of bright red hair. The computer sitting in front of him was

74

a complete and total enigma to him. He knew how to hunt-and-peck on a typewriter well enough to get by, he knew how to arrest people, he knew how to shoot any gun that was ever made, he could duke it out with the meanest bad guy around, and he knew how to fight bulls, but the blue screen with all the colored boxes had brought him meekly to his knees.

"You're fighting it again, Red. Relax. Experiment with it. If Ray Tucker over at the miniature golf place can figure out a computer, I suspect you can. You know Ray's never going to make the finals on "Jeopardy," either."

"Well, someone should set a trap for this mouse and string the damn thing up!" Red bellowed as he pushed himself up from the chair. "I'm going to go outside and have a smoke; it can't be any hotter out there than it is in here. Maybe I'll find some inspiration or get sunstroke. Probably the same thing."

Janie laughed as Red went out the door of the trailer and headed for his favorite smoke spot, a lone, live oak tree that cast a small puddle of shade around a well-used picnic table next to the trailer. Janie watched through the window as Red lit up his usual Pall Mall and took a deep drag. The heavy, hot air refused to allow the smoke to dissipate, causing it to float in a lazy circle over his head. A trace of the tobacco smoke snaked through the open window and touched her nostrils, stirring Janie's dormant craving. She had quit her two-pack-a-day Viceroy habit cold turkey eight years ago but she still loved the smell of burning tobacco.

The ringing telephone jerked her back to the present. The pitch of the ring told her it was a police-related call, and she plugged her head set into the nearest jack. "Grace County Police Services. This is Janie. Can I help you?" she asked, automatically picking up a pencil and a tablet from the nearest desk. As she listened to the caller, she noticed Red move back to the window and glance in at her under the assumption that any call on the police line was worth taking note of. Janie held up one finger, signaling to Red that the call was not an emergency, and Red went back to his cigarette. "You did say the Sandoval case?" As Janie listened to the caller's positive response she felt her stomach muscles tense. "Could you hold for a moment? I'll get the Sheriff."

Putting the caller on hold, Janie unplugged from the jack and hurried to the back of the trailer where she opened the door that lead to an outside garage. A tall man in a greasy pair of overalls was working under the hood of perfectly restored 1957 Chevy Bel Air convertible. "John, a police officer from Houston's on the phone. Wants to talk to you."

Sheriff John Cutler, sweating heavily in the still air of the overheated garage, looked up from the engine of the turquoise Chevy. The tall, gangly, thirty-five-year-old's handsome face was weathered a deep brown and his blue eyes sparkled when he talked.

"On the way," he said as he put aside a wrench and picked up a clean cloth which he used to wipe his greasy hands. As he entered the trailer and moved to his desk, he absentmindedly leaned down to pet a scroungy looking, overheated Lasso Apso that was lying stretched out, belly down, in an attempt to maximize the coolness of the linoleum floor. "How you doing there, Henry boy? Pretty hot, huh?" The gray-haired Henry immediately rolled on his back in hopes of receiving a full-fledged belly rub and was disappointed when Cutler reached for the phone instead. Before pushing the blinking hold button, he turned to Janie. "Who'd you say it was?"

"Officer Cole from Houston."

"What's he want?"

"Something about the Sandoval case, and it's a *she*, not a he," Janie replied.

Hearing the name *Sandoval,* Cutler's smile faded and, as he set his jaw, he punched the flashing button. "This is Cutler. What can I do for you?"

"Hello, Sheriff. This is Officer Jessi Cole from Houston. Would you mind giving me a brief rundown on the Michelle Sandoval homicide?"

"Don't mind at all. Michelle Sandoval was grabbed off the street on her way home from a Dallas middle school. Four days later and about three hundred miles southwest of Dallas, her body was discovered by a long-haul truck driver in a trash dumpster at a rest stop off State Highway 12, about three miles from my office. That's it. We got nothing. So what's your interest in Michelle Sandoval?"

Jessi cleared her throat, suddenly feeling very foolish. "Sheriff, I know this sounds a little bizarre, but I took a report this morning from a person who claims that they, ahh, somehow *sensed* the death of a girl named Mickey. I got the name Michelle Sandoval off N.C.I.C."

Jessi heard Cutler exhale tiredly. "What exactly does 'sensed' mean? I don't understand," he replied, the disappointment in his voice quite obvious.

Jessi winced inwardly at his tone, thinking that she must sound like a total idiot. "I'm not really sure, Sheriff. The woman claims to be a psychic."

Jessi wouldn't have been surprised if the man had hung up on her.

"Is this person a reliable source? Someone you've dealt with before?" he asked.

"Personally dealt with, no. I don't know anything about her. She does, ahh, have a history with the department, though. She's come in numerous times volunteering information," Jessi explained.

"So far we've had about twenty calls from psychics claiming knowl-edge of the Sandoval murder. The girl's face was all over the papers, and her family put flyers up all over the South."

The sketch of the girl the psychic had shown her popped into Jessi's mind. Lela could very easily have taken the likeness off one of the fliers, she reasoned.

"Your fortune teller probably read about the case in the paper or saw it on TV like the rest of them," Cutler continued, his tone taking on a slightly impatient edge.

Jessi picked up on the sheriff's impatience and, for some inexplica-ble reason, it irritated her. The man was, after all, only voicing her own skepticism. "I'm sure you're right, but I thought I'd better follow up on it no matter how far fetched. I felt I should at least give you a call."

"I appreciate it. Anything else I can do for you?" Cutler asked.

"Yes. You can tell me where Grace County is?"

"We're up by Brownwood." Cutler replied.

"Never heard of it."

Cutler laughed an easy, deep laugh that made Jessi smile through the phone. "Let's see, Grace is about 300 miles southwest of Dallas. Does that help?"

"I'm not very good at geography. When I travel it's usually from city to city, and most of the time I fly, so I haven't seen much of what's in between."

"O.K., go to Waco, then take Highway 84 westbound until you're in the hills, and just when you think you're hopelessly lost, that's Grace County. We like to say we're out here in *Deep* Texas," Cutler said.

"I'm still lost, sorry," she said, suddenly realizing that she was flirt-ing with a complete stranger over a telephone line. "I guess I'll have to look it up on a map. Thanks for your time, Sheriff."

"Anytime."

"Oh, one more thing. My psychic connection gave me a number - 1305. I realize it probably doesn't mean anything, but...?"

"One three zero five?" Cutler asked as he picked up a pen and wrote the number on a yellow sticky note.

"That's it. Again, sorry I bothered you," Jessi said.

"No bother; thanks for the call."

Cutler hung up the phone and sat in silence for a moment. Mickey Sandoval's body had been found a little over a year ago, but the case was never far from his thoughts. He had seen his share of shocking crime scenes, but he wouldn't allow the carnage to touch him. Sandoval was different. The image of her pale-white hand rising from the trash in the dumpster was indelibly burned into his mind and would pop into his consciousness at unexpected moments. He held the sticky note up and looked at the number *1305* again. It made him inexplicably uneasy. Why? He hated wasting his time, but there was something about it. Something...

Cutler stood and approached Red Cordell just as the stocky deputy returned from his smoke break. "Do you still have the Sandoval book?"

"Janie's got it," Red answered, immediately curious. "Why? You got something?"

"I doubt it."

By the time Cutler walked the few steps to Janie's dispatch console, she had already fished the heavy red binder out of her basket and handed it to him. "Everything should be in there. Something going on you want to share?"

"Not yet," Cutler responded as he took the binder from the curious Janie and moved purposely to his desk.

Janie sat at the dispatch console and watched the sheriff with affection. She had worked for John Cutler for five years. She liked everything about her job and her boss especially his easygoing manner and even temper. The crazier things got around them, the calmer he seemed to become.

Cutler was soon totally absorbed in crime scene photos, newspaper clippings, autopsy photos, and witness interviews. He cross-checked reports and clippings, studying them closely, looking for...*what?* Hell, he thought, he didn't even know what he was looking for! How would he know it if he saw it? As he re-examined the crime scene photos for the thousandth time, the gnawing urgency to find the monster that could abuse this girl and then so callously discard her body sent a familiar angry heat over his face and neck. He looked at a photo of the dumpster, and the number *"13"* stenciled on the side jumped out at him. Another photo from a different angle gave him the completed number *"1305."* His heart was racing as he got to his feet and moved quickly to Red's desk.

"Red, check with Sel Turner at the Tribune. Ask him which photos of the Sandoval crime scene went out on the wire service. Then call the Dallas and Waco papers and ask them the same thing."

Cutler hurried away, knowing that Red was already making the necessary calls, and returning to his desk, removed a videotape from his bottom drawer. Moving to a television set that was sitting on top of a metal file cabinet, Cutler fed the tape into an outdated VCR and watched various news reports that had aired when Mickey Sandoval's body had been discovered.

Janie joined him, her interest tweaked by Cutler's sudden intensity. "Are we looking for anything in particular?" Janie asked.

"Yeah, if you see the number 1305 anywhere, yell at me," Cutler replied, his fingers locked onto the fast forward button of the gray plastic remote.

One by one, the two of them studied the footage as the on-scene television reporters from the network affiliates did their live remote segments from the parking lot. None of the reports made any mention of the number "1305," and it was not visible in any of the background shots. "But why would it be?" he asked himself. It was simply the shop number of a dumpster, of which there had to be tens of thousands.

Red approached just as Cutler finished rewinding the news tape. "Sel said the only photos that were used are on the news clippings right there in the binder."

"Red, you're a betting man. Tell me, what're the odds of someone in Houston just accidentally coming up with the shop number of the dumpster Michelle Sandoval's body was in?"

Red rubbed his chin in mock thoughtfulness. "Ahhh, how about slim and none?"

Cutler nodded in agreement as he returned to his desk and re-examined the entire book again. It was too important not to. The sheriff had interviewed enough witnesses to know that there was more than one way to come into possession of crime scene information, but he was certain it wasn't through any damn *psychic revelation!* This woman, whoever the hell she was, had knowledge that only someone close to the crime could possibly have, and Cutler had every intention of finding where and how she got it.

He closed the book and turned to Red. "I'm going to Houston. Call Kiko and get him out of bed. You two are 'it' until I get back." He leaned down to ruffle the fur on Henry's neck. "Janie, can you take Henry home with you?"

"Sweet Jesus, I not only get to listen to Frank snore, now I'll get the whole chorus. I'll take the mutt, but you let us know what's going on, comprende?"

"Roger that. I'll give you a call later," Cutler said, sticking his straw Stetson on his head. As he turned to leave he paused and picked up a framed photo, half buried by a stack of files, off his desk. It was a colored photograph of a beautiful young woman standing alongside a turquoise-colored 1957 Chevrolet convertible. The same car that just moments ago he had been working on. He held the picture for a moment, touched the image gently, and then replaced it, unaware that Red and Janie were watching him.

"Call Kenny and tell him to get the Cessna ready," Cutler barked as he headed for the door. "And Janie, tell your husband that if that air conditioner isn't working by five o'clock, Red will arrest him!"

"And I will too!" Red chimed.

The sheriff covered the ten miles to the Grace County airfield in less than six minutes, keeping the mud-splattered white Chevy Blazer's speedometer buried. Turning off the paved county road, the 4x4 threw up an enormous cloud of dust for the last mile and a half before skidding to a dusty stop in front of a large metal hanger.

Grabbing his shaving kit off the front seat and retrieving a freshly laundered shirt from the hook behind the driver's seat, Cutler locked the Blazer and entered the hanger. A faded, peeling sign above the door marked the building as:

"Kenny's Flying Service- Grace County, Texas - Elevation 1,346
Unicom: 122.8"

If you knew how to fly and you lived in Grace County, chances were excellent that gravelly voiced Kenny Braren had taught you how. The short, wiry seventy-five-year-old former Army aviator scrambled around on his collection of eight airplanes with the agility of a thirty-year-old.

"Hey, Johnny, catch any bad guys lately?" he asked, glancing up from under the Cessna 152 trainer he was changing the nose wheel on.

"Not yet, but the day's still young. How's three one zero looking?" Cutler asked, knowing that the plane would be ready and waiting.

"Fueled, tooled, and ready for school. Where you headed?"

"Houston."

"Go into Hobby field, it's easier," Kenny called, continuing his tire changing.

"Thanks, Kenny, I'll see you later." Cutler replied, continuing out of the building and quickly walking fifty yards to where the shiny blue and white Cessna 172 was tied down on the sticky-hot tarmac.

Cessna 82310 had come into the possession of the Grace County Sheriff's office in August of 1996 when Cutler, acting on a tip from a hay farmer, found it abandoned on a dry lake bed nearly fifty miles due west of downtown Grace. The plane had been wiped clean, with all identifying numbers carefully removed. Three of its four seats had been taken out in what Cutler assumed was an effort by drug runners to cram as much cocaine into the plane as possible. The smugglers had most likely loaded the plane in rural Mexico, flown to the dry lake bed, off-loaded their cargo into a four-wheel drive vehicle, and then simply abandoned the aircraft and drove away. In the drug trade the profit margin was so high that a $50,000 aircraft became more of a liability than an asset.

Cutler opened the front door of the small plane and felt a rush of hot, stale air hit him in the face as he set the keys on the dashboard and removed the glass fuel tube from the pocket in the rear of the seat. Cutler trusted Kenny's preflight check of the aircraft, but the fuel check he always performed himself, draining a small amount of light blue aviation fuel into the glass tube from each of the four release valves located under the nose and belly of the aircraft and checking for the presence of water.

Cutler was soon strapping himself into the left seat and mentally flipping through the pre-flight checklist as he put on his headset and turned on the radio and transponder before starting the aircraft and guiding it effortlessly onto the 60-foot-wide runway to begin his take-off roll.

6.

◠◠

Murray Crook watched from the sidewalk as Jessi parked the old pickup and climbed out. She was wearing beige slacks, a simple white blouse and a khaki jacket. The contrast with her uniform was striking.

Murray smiled. "For some reason I expected you to arrive in a little Beamer convertible or something."

Jessi laughed. "Me, in a Beamer. You're kidding."

"Well, I even find your choice of vehicles charming. That is a cool truck." Murray said.

"It was my dad's. Sorry I'm late, we had a domestic call that got really ugly," Jessi explained.

"No problem. I was a little late myself. You look great by the way. You went home and changed. I'm flattered." Murray smiled, giving her a peck on the cheek.

"Actually, these are my court clothes. I keep them in my locker. Let's eat, I'm starved," she said, turning and approaching the stairway that led to Chez Peyo Restaurant. The business was located on the second floor landing of a spacious, trendy shopping mall that soothed evening shoppers with surround sound elevator music.

As they climbed the brick steps, Murray took Jessi 's arm and his voice took on a strong, brotherly tone. "And another thing, young lady,

I looked this place up on the internet. This is four-star establishment. You can't afford this. We'll go Dutch."

"Absolutely not, I promised you dinner; I'll buy your dinner. But while we're here I'm going to talk to the manager about a credit card case I'm working on, which means it's a business expense, which means it's —"

"Deductible!" Murray said with a flourish. "My favorite word," he finished as they approached the classy, double glass doorway of Chez Peyo, which was flanked by two huge potted ferns. Murray moved ahead and held the door open for her. "Do you think they'll mind my Levis?"

"Why would they? You look great," Jessi said as they stepped into the tastefully decorated lobby.

"You know something? If I wasn't so flaming gay, I'd steal your heart," Murray said, and they both laughed as the maitre d', a slightly built man with a built-in French accent, named Pierre, guided them to their table. The elegantly furnished dining room was crowded with an assortment of successful looking young businessmen and women who had filtered in from the surrounding financial district for an early dinner. Pierre melted away as their waitress quickly and efficiently recited the dinner specials, and they were soon savoring thin slices of warm wheat bread as they studied the menu. Loud laughter erupted from one of the corner tables, but it soon dissipated.

Murray smiled weakly as he perused the menu. "Oh, oh, the cheapest entree is $35.00. We *will* go Dutch."

"Not another word about money. I told you I was buying, and I meant it," Jessi said, leaving no room for argument.

"I know, but I feel guilty having a... having someone else pay for me. Something from one of my many past lives, maybe, and don't give me that crap about *deductible*. The Houston Police Department wouldn't reimburse you for a hotdog."

Jessi's response was drowned out by raucous laughter emanating from the corner booth behind Murray.

Murray watched Jessi as she perused the menu . "You're one of the best cops in the department, and I mean that. How many of those Neanderthals in Central can show you a Teaching Credential or a Master's Degree?" Murray paused a full two seconds for effect. "One, and he's a captain on the night shift. Only one patrolman on your shift even has a B.A., and that's in Management and he got it on-line."

"How do you know that?" Jessi asked.

Murray raised his index finger to his lips. "I read their 488s."

"Reading personnel records are against the law, you know?"

"Not if you work in Records it's not. *Daaaa!* It's your job. "

Jessi resumed studying the menu and had just settled on the *Gravenstein Chicken* for $35.50 when the loud, annoying laughter erupted again from the table in the corner, irritating Murray. "If those creeps over there are annoying you half as much as they are me, I'll ask them to be quiet."

"Don't worry about it, they're just having a… " Jessi froze in place and her mouth dropped open as she glanced over Murray's shoulder at the rowdy group in the corner.

Murray noticed her stunned expression. "What's the matter? You look like you just saw a ghost."

Jessi blinked and looked again. She had a strange sensation that she was participating in a dream, for there, at the corner table, sat all two hundred and eighty pounds of *Tyrell Braxton*!

The enormous man was dressed in a twenty-five hundred dollar grey suit, dark glasses, and an assortment of gold necklaces that hung loosely from his open collared satin shirt. Jessi's mind worked like a calculator for a few seconds, matching stolen credit card reports with every item of his apparel. Sitting next to Tyrell, and the source of much of the obnoxious laughter, was an attractive African-American female who was hanging breathlessly on Tyrell's every word. She had large, sleepy brown eyes, and was dressed in knee high black leather boots, a very short leather skirt, and a leather vest that covered as little of her midriff and upper chest as was legally possible.

Directly across the table from Tyrell, his younger brother, Vonsell, was busy snuggling the neck of a thin-boned, white woman. The underside of her surgically-altered thin nose was flame red from a daily exposure to countless lines of cocaine. She was wearing a low-cut white blouse that highlighted the dark circles under her watery eyes and displayed her ample bosom to maximum advantage.

Jessi wondered briefly whose credit card had paid for the woman's large and no doubt expensive breasts.

Tyrell, however, was the center of attention and was obviously enjoying himself as he leaned back and, raising a champagne glass, offered a toast to his fellow diners. The gesture set the inebriated foursome howling with laughter.

"I can't believe this!" Jessi's tone betrayed surprise, excitement, and pleasure, simultaneously.

"That did it. I'll complain to the waiter," Murray responded as he shot the occupants of the corner table a cold look.

"No, no, Murray, don't say anything. Don't even look, not now."

"Why not? What's the matter?"

"Those guys chug-a-lugging Dom Perrion are the creeps I've been chasing for the last five months."

"The Braxton brothers? No shit?" Murray asked in a loud whisper.

Jessi nodded and then came alert as she noticed Tyrell flag down a waitress and ask for his check. The waitress nodded and disappeared through the swinging doors that lead into the kitchen. "Ah, man, they're going to take off... Murray, listen, I need you to do something."

"Sure. What?"

Jessi's voice was at once calm and firm. "I want you to get up like you were going to the rest room. Don't even look in their direction. Go out to the lobby and use the pay phone. Call 911, and tell them that an officer needs help at this address."

Murray looked ready to panic. "You're not going to get hurt, are you?"

"I'll be fine. Now remember, don't look at them. They might get nervous," Jessi said as she gave Murray's hand a reassuring squeeze.

"Now?" Murray asked in an unsure whisper.

She nodded, and Murray grimaced, stood, and moved quickly through the dining room and disappeared into the lobby. Jessi opened her purse under the table and felt for the comforting weight of her pistol. Her fingers also felt for and located a set of handcuffs that she had fortunately forgot to leave in the pickup. Jessi rose and, carrying her purse, walked through the swinging doors into the busy kitchen where she found the waitress leaning on a stainless steel counter preparing a check while other waiters rushed past laden with steaming stacks of balanced dinner plates . The woman saw her coming and forced a tired smile. "The rest rooms are back through the lobby."

"Actually, I'm not looking for a rest room." Jessi removed her I.D. case from her purse and opened it to reveal her badge. "Is that the bill for the party of four in the corner?"

"The party of four from hell? Yes."

"Could I borrow your apron for a minute?"

Tyrell Braxton emptied the last drops of the Dom Perrion into his little brother's goblet. "Your turn to make a toast, Vonsell. And at 225 a pop, it better be a good one, hear?"

The skinny, pock-faced Vonsell had gone to sleep loaded at 0' dark thirty and had been drinking Jack Daniels straight from the bottle since waking up at 10:30 that morning. "Toast? I don't know no fuckin' toast, dude."

The women howled with laughter, which tickled Vonsell to no end but made Tyrell scowl. His dark eyes flashed as he turned suddenly on Jolene and hissed, "Shut up, bitch!" The big man once again turned his attention to Vonsell. "I said I wanted you to offer a toast. I didn't say I wanted you dissin' me in front of everybody."

"I wasn't dissin' you, man. What the fuck you talkin' about? You want a toast, I'll give you a fucking toast. What to? Ahhh..." Vonsell massaged his tender temples trying in vain to force his cocaine-and-alcohol stewed brain back on duty. Tyrell had an awful temper and Vonsell didn't want to bear the brunt of it in front of Jolene and Sherry. "O.K., I got it," he said, raising the crystal glass in the air. "Here ya go, my brother. To life, liberty, and the pursuit of pussy!"

Tyrell slammed the table with his fist and howled. "I'll drink to that!"

All four of them were roaring when Jessi approached the table and placed the tray holding the $458 check in front of Tyrell. As with most criminals who depend on their wit for their daily bread, the appearance of a stranger at the table set off a silent alarm somewhere in the back of his paranoid brain, and his laughter faded quickly.

"So what happened to the other one? We wear her out or something?" Tyrell asked Jessi, checking her out from head to toe.

"She went on break. Union thing. I hope your lunch was enjoyable. How was the Gravenstein chicken?"

"It was big time great, sweetheart. So was the service," Tyrell said as he glanced at the check and peeled five one hundred-dollar bills from his large roll. "I put a nice tip in there to show my appreciation."

As Jessi reached for the tray, her hand went instead to Tyrone's left hand, touching the gold bracelet that hung from his thick wrist. "What an incredible bracelet."

Tyrell held up his wrist for Jessi's inspection. "Solid gold, baby, seventeen diamonds."

"How gorgeous. How much would something like that cost, $1,000, $1,500?"

The big man beamed. "Fifteen hundred hell; you're looking at $3,200 dead George's." Tyrell chuckled as Jolene snuggled closer to him. She was not enjoying the way this white interloper was scoping her squeeze, and her dark eyes flashed Jessi a warning.

"I'm impressed," Jessi said, "and since you were kind enough to show me yours, I'll show you mine." She had the handcuff snapped onto his left wrist before Tyrell realized what was taking place.

Tyrell got only two and a half angry words out, "What the fu...?" before Jessi snapped the other cuff over the brass railing that ran close to the table and flashed her shield in his face.

"It is my pleasure to announce that you, and *you*," she nodded at the stunned Vonsell, "are under arrest."

"Say what? Who do you think you got, woman? This is a big mistake!" Tyrell shouted.

"Big mistake!" Vonsell echoed.

Jessi reached into Tyrell's inside suit pocket and pulled out his wallet. She took out a plastic credit card holder that accordioned out nearly to the floor, displaying more than two-dozen credit cards.

"I know exactly who you are," Jessi said, quickly reading off the names on the cards. "You're John Pittman? How about Mike Butler? Not him either, huh? Mr. John Necker, maybe? Pat Cochran? Bruce Robb? Neil Van Natta? Mike Naylor? No? None of the above? Hmmm, then my only other guess would have to be Tyrell and Vonsell Braxton! Correct?"

Vonsell exploded out of his chair, pushing the table aside and sending glasses, plates, and champagne bottles flying in all directions. Sherry and Jolene quickly covered their heads, and screamed as the edge of the heavy table caught Jessi flush in the stomach and bounced her onto her back. By the time she sat up and pulled her 9mm, Vonsell was disappearing through the swinging kitchen doors, and Tyrell was trying in vain to remove his handcuffs.

Murray was still in the lobby waiting for the backup officers when he heard the commotion in the dining room. He found Jessi pulling herself off the floor. "A patrol car is on the way! Are you alright?"

"Watch this one!" she said, as she turned and dashed toward the kitchen, nearly bowling over an unsuspecting waiter, who was exiting the double doors carrying two flaming shish kebabs.

Murray was left to stand guard over the hulking and angry Tyrell Braxton. The big man had given up on the handcuffs and was now using his ample strength in an attempt to pull the brass railing from the wall while the startled diners watched. Murray hurried to the waiter, grabbed one of his flaming shish kebabs and pointed it at Tyrell's throat.

"This kebab is loaded, and I'm not afraid to use it!" Murray yelled.

As the huge Tyrell settled onto his chair, and Jolene and Sherry whimpered, the other diners rose to their feet in unison, whistling and applauding their support. Murray blushed but held his ground.

Vonsell Braxton had a good block lead, and given the totally inappropriate shoes Jessi was wearing, there was no way she could keep pace. Removing her shoes on the run improved her speed momentarily, but a stretch of rough, hot sidewalk forced her to stop in the alcove of a book store where she quickly pulled the shoes back on. Jessi was considering returning to the restaurant when the Number 17 cross-town bus squealed to a stop at the curb. She didn't hesitate, but jumped aboard through the double rear doors, pushing her way around and through a dozen lethargic passengers and pulling out her badge as she approached the slender, African-American female driver. "I'm a police officer. Follow that man!"

"Do what?" The driver asked, staring in disbelief at the out of breath Jessi Cole.

Jessi leaned down and pointed up the street to where Vonsell Braxton was just disappearing around a corner. "See that guy running? Follow him!"

Shauna King had driven a bus through the streets of Houston for most of her adult life and had dreamed of just such a moment. She flipped the toggle switch, closing the doors with a hiss and pulling the bus out into traffic, grabbed the microphone.

"Hold on back there folks 'cause we are in hot pursuit!" She laughed as she expertly steered eight tons of metal and glass through the heavy, downtown Houston traffic.

As the bus approached the red light at Main and Prairie Streets, Jessi kneeled on the floor next to the token box and called out traffic. "Clear on the right!"

"And I'm clear on the left!" Shauna steered in between cars like an elephant tip-toeing through a room of ballerinas.

Vonsell had sprinted out of Jessi's vision at the corner of Main and Texas Street. The adrenalin coursing through his skinny, 138-pound frame propelled him for another block before he suddenly realized his lungs where only taking in half of the oxygen his body required to keep functioning. Marathon runners call it "hitting the wall," and it usually occurs somewhere between mile twelve and mile seventeen of the twenty-six mile, three hundred eighty-five yard run. Vonsell Braxton hit the wall at approximately nine-tenths of mile one with sweat literally pouring off his face and his lungs burning like they were on fire. To compound his problems, his legs started trembling as they usually did during the third day of detox, and he finally pulled up, coming to rest against the hot brick wall of a drugstore where he continued to sweat and pant.

When the city bus squealed to a stop at the nearby corner, Vonsell decided to count his blessings and get on. Were he not so physically spent, he might have noticed two important facts: the first, that there was no bus stop at that particular corner; and the second, that there was no city bus service whatsoever on this section of Texas Street.

Too late.

Vonsell pushed himself away from the wall and lurched like a drunk toward the bus, and as the doors hissed open, he staggered up the steps and shoved a twenty-dollar bill into Shauna's hand.

"Keep the change, sister!"

"Why thank you very much, *brother!*" Shauna answered, the sarcasm in her voice so thick that even the exhausted Vonsell noticed it and paused briefly. Vonsell shrugged as he turned away from Shauna and took two steps before he tripped over someone's outstretched foot, falling heavily, face down in the dirty aisle. What oxygen remained in his lungs was suddenly jettisoned when the 130-pound Jessi launched herself onto his back and jerked his limp arms behind him, applying enough pressure on both of his thumbs to solicit a painful yelp!

"You are under arrest, and if you blink, I'll dislocate both your thumbs. Got it?"

Vonsell struggled briefly as Jessi repeated the warning and emphasized it with harder thumb pressure. The man screamed before accepting the inevitable. Jessi glanced over her shoulder at Shauna and got a smile and a thumbs up. "Hall of Justice, please."

"My pleasure, honey. I'd drive you to Dallas if you wanted me to," Shauna said, releasing the air brakes with a loud "hiss" and sending the bus into motion.

As the bus gained speed, the spent Vonsell finally managed to inhale enough oxygen into his lungs to form a protest. "You can't do this to me. I got rights!"

"Not on my bus you don't!" Shauna retorted. The other passengers laughed as the blue and white number 17 bus made a left turn back onto Main and headed nonstop for the Hall of Justice.

7.

It was a little after seven in the evening when the broken screen door of the old house exploded outward and the two girls hurried out into the blast furnace that was Grace County, Texas. Their mother's shrill voice nipped at their backsides, "And I want your butts back here in one hour, by God! You hear me, Samantha?"

The older of the two girls, fourteen-year-old Samantha "Sammy" Deavers, didn't bother looking back but continued walking toward Hughes Road, forcing her heavyset mother, Glenda, to open the creaky screen door and repeat the warning. "I said be back here in one hour, or you'll get a whippin'! Do you hear me, young lady?"

"If you'd get me my own cell phone you could keep better track of me," Sammy mumbled.

"One hour, girl!"

"Yes, ma'am." Sammy's over-the-shoulder response was laced with the typical fourteen-year-old smart-mouth tone that Mrs. Deavers hated but was too tired, hot, and ineffectual to argue about. She had lost control of five other children at precisely this age, so it seemed only natural that Samantha would backtalk her from the time she arose in the morning to the time she retired at night. It was only a matter of time, Glenda knew, before Sammy would end up in trouble like each of her big sisters had. Glenda's seventh child, nine-year-old Nicole, still listened, and for that she thanked the Lord daily.

"Nicole, you make sure your big sister comes back with you!" Glenda shouted.

The younger Nicole turned without stopping and shouted back, "I will, Momma! Don't worry about us."

Watching the girls wind their way through the junky front yard and exit through the broken front gate, Glenda Deavers was thinking only about her aching back and the terrible heaviness of the heat. She had absolutely no inkling that this would be the last time she would see Samantha alive.

The girls walked quickly through the hot dust of Hughes Road and headed toward the central Texas town of Slocum, population 8,561, that lay half a mile due west of their house. The Deaver's three mongrel dogs, Rusty, Dusty, and George, watched from their lounging area under the broken down porch, their long tongues hanging limply from the sides of their mouths. The dogs didn't want to go for this walk, but their instincts made them rise and trot loyally after the girls.

Sammy and Nicole were both wearing shorts and halter-tops. Nicole looked like the skinny, knobby-kneed nine-year-old she was, but her older sister was a young woman with shapely, tanned legs and well-developed breasts that turned the heads of males of all ages. Sammy liked being attractive, and she enjoyed the feeling of power it gave her over not only boys, but men as well. She loved teasing Mr. Jensen, her ninth-grade math teacher, who would stand over her daily and pretend to help while he looked down her blouse.

The girls cut off the road and moved through the borrow pit to the fence, where Sammy turned and yelled at the dogs to go home. Normally the animals would stubbornly refuse to obey, and the girls would be forced to pick up rocks and chase them back. Today, however, the three dogs turned and trotted back toward the cool dirt that awaited them in the shade under the house.

Sammy started to climb through the fence when her quartz necklace caught on a strand of barbwire. "Damnit! Nicky, help me. I can't get it loose," Sammy swore, trying in vain to free the delicate gold chain that bound the crystal to her neck.

"Hold still," Nicole responded as she dropped to her knees. She hardly ever got the opportunity to help her older sister, and she relished the few seconds it took to free the necklace from the barb.

The sisters continued, taking their usual shortcut through the abandoned Starlight Drive-In Theater that marked the Slocum city limits. The drive-in theater had been closed for three years now, but it had been a part of their life for as long as both girls could remember. Over the years Sammy had watched countless movies here with her brothers and sisters. They would sneak under the fence with blankets and pillows and lay on the hard ground next to a speaker box until a car would pull in and force them to move elsewhere, or until the owner, old Mr. Tillis, would spot them and they would have to run and hide. Watching movies at the Starlight and running from Mr. Tillis were some of Sammy's happiest childhood memories.

Nicole, on the other hand, had never seen a movie at the Starlight, but she and her friends rode their bikes here almost daily. They'd zig and zag over the sloped ramps, and around the poles that once held aluminum speakers that were long since destroyed or stolen, only to turn up periodically at various Grace County flea markets. The poles now seemed to stand at mute attention before the large screen that was as worn and tattered as an old battle flag. On the back side of the screen, a faded marquee that once announced the current Starlight feature now displayed only the letter "W" that the residents of Slocum had developed into a game of "Do you remember where you were when *Dances With Wolves* played for the last time at the Starlight?"

Climbing through the fence on the west side of the Starlight, the girls had to hurry across the four lanes of State Highway 12 to get to Slocum's only shopping center. There the IGA Supermarket shared billing with a Thrifty Drug, a U.S. Post Office, a Burger King, Erin's Video, Dave's Rifle and Ammo Shop, The Recovery Room Bar, and a new four theater movie complex called, appropriately enough, The New Starlight Cinemas, which was owned by old Mr. Tillis' two sons, Brent and Lance.

He had argued with Kitty for hours, trying to sooth her fear of working so close to home. He pointed out how her disguise made it virtually impossible for anyone to recognize her. He couldn't stand the idea of another twelve hour ride through this god forsaken Texas scenery. To his relief, Kitty had finally relented and agreed to another run.

Pinky tensed as he saw the girls hurry across the highway, and as they moved through the parking lot toward him, he felt the familiar rush of excitement that he had grown to savor. He tapped his horn three times to alert Kitty. The tattooed wolf's head on the back of hand seemed to quiver as he tapped his fingers lightly on the wheel.

Sammy and Nicole passed the rear of the white van, totally unaware that a predator was watching them through the van's outside rearview mirror. The girls were nearly at the IGA Supermarket when they heard the boys.

"Hey, Sammy! Looking good!"

"Hey, sweetheart, come on over here!"

The shouts came from a pair of tan faced cowboys sitting in a cherry red 1955 Chevy pickup that was parked close to the nearby video store.

Sitting behind the wheel of the souped up pickup was twenty-year-old Lenny Price and his carousing buddy, eighteen-year-old Ray Larson. Lenny turned down his blaring CD player and stuck his head out the window, openly leering at Sammy Deavers. "Hey, Sammy. Gey your cute little butt over here!"

Sammy turned to Nicole. "Go in and get started. I'll catch up."

Nicole frowned. She was too old to be sent away like a child, and she resented her sister treating her like a baby. "I'll stay."

Sammy pushed her off. "I said go! I'll be right there," she commanded.

Nicole gave her older sister a dirty look and reluctantly headed for the grocery store as Sammy approached the driver's side window of the Chevy. " Hi, Lenny, Ray. This truck is so buff. What you guys up to?"

Lenny smiled in response. "Nothing much. Just hangin'. What you doing with yourself these days, beside looking good I mean?" Lenny and Ray shared a leering laugh.

"Going to the store for Mom," Sammy answered, standing on tip-toes and leaning over the edge of the window so that both Lenny and Ray could catch a glimpse down the front of her halter top. Her necklace dangled enticingly.

Lenny took the bait and left no pretense as to what he was looking at. "You are one foxy little lady, you know that?"

Ray laughed and rolled his eyes. "Hey Sammy, this beer's so cold it'll make your brain go numb. Come on, let's go out to the river and have some fun," Ray patted a twelve-pack of Coors that was sitting on the floor at his feet.

"Yeah, hop in. Let's party!" Lenny added.

Sammy wasn't buying. Just as Lenny's hand reached out for the necklace, Sammy moved back. "How about your wife and baby, Lenny, you going to bring them along too?" she retorted as she turned and walked away from the pickup.

Lenny leaned out the window and shouted after her, "Lisa and I are separated, didn't you hear?"

"Damn liar! I know Lisa's sister, Amanda, and she didn't say nothing about it! She did say Lisa was three months along though!" Sammy yelled back as she continued toward the IGA Supermarket. She heard Lenny and Ray laugh before the 327 cubic-inch V8 roared to life, and Lenny laid a ten-yard stretch of rubber as the pickup squealed out of the parking lot.

The smell of the burning rubber lingered in the hot air as Sammy approached the automatic door of the supermarket, and it whirred open, releasing a gush of coolness that greeted her face and invited her in. A woman's voice caused her to pause.

"You wouldn't be looking for a puppy to take home, would you?"

A female customer brushed past and entered the store as Sammy turned and moved to where a large woman with long dark hair was kneeling over a cardboard box where half a dozen six-week-old puppies napped on a bed of shredded newspapers. Sammy's eyes lit up as she kneeled alongside the Fort Howard Paper Company box. "Ohmygawd, how cute. Can I hold one?" she asked the woman.

"Be my guest," the woman replied. She smiled warmly as Sammy reached into the box and came up with a squirming bundle of soft, yellow hair, which she pressed to her cheek, breathing in the distinctive sweet smell that only new puppies carry and children of all ages find irresistible. "That's my favorite, too, a male," the woman added, stroking the puppy's small back.

"You're so cute, aren't 'cha, little fella?" Sammy crooned as she snuggled the compliant puppy to her neck and giggled as it licked and then chewed softly on her ear.

Kitty studied the girl. She wore way too much makeup and obviously enjoyed flaunting her well-developed body. Her ears were pierced numerous times, her fingernails were painted a gaudy orange, and she guessed correctly that Sammy was sexually active. She could just picture the girl standing in front of a mirror, spending countless hours making herself look like a doe-eyed, punk rock princess. Yes, this one would do just fine.

"That little guy was meant for you, like maybe you two are star-crossed or something," Kitty said.

"I'd love to take him, but we already have three dogs. My dad would kill me if I brought home another one," Sammy answered.

So far so good, Kitty thought.

"Well, I'm not doing any good here. Time to try another location," Kitty announced suddenly as she bent down and picked up the box, then started carrying it toward the parking lot, leaving Sammy standing alone with the puppy.

"Hey, lady, take your puppy!" Sammy yelled as she hurried to catch up and fall in step with the much larger Kitty. Sammy tried to replace the little dog in the box, but Kitty swung the box away from her. "At least carry him out to the van for me, will you? This box is heavy."

"Okay," Sammy replied, and as she followed a few steps behind Kitty, she snuggled the puppy one more time and let it lick her cheek. Ahead of her, Kitty approached the side door of a nondescript white Ford Econoline van that was parked at the edge of the lot, away from the other cars. Sammy probably didn't notice that the van door slid open a split second before Kitty got there, allowing the heavyset woman to place the box down inside the van and step aside, gesturing for the girl to put the puppy in the box. As Sammy complied, Pinky's powerful right forearm exploded from the darkness, clamped tightly around her neck and jerked her into the van. In a blur of well-rehearsed motion, Kitty slid the door closed and walked quickly to the driver's side, crawled in behind the wheel, started the motor, and backed the van out.

In the rear of the van, Pinky's locked grip was so powerful around Sammy's neck that she couldn't move or even gasp. She was aware of a lack of oxygen, the stifling heat, and the heavy smell of stale body odor. Sammy's terror was so complete she couldn't stop herself from urinating.

8.

⊙⊙

Leaving the police station that morning Lela had driven her beat up 1984 Chevy van to the University, intending to set up a blanket on the quad next to the student union where she regularly peddled her assortment of quartz crystals, tie dye, and incense and occasionally sketched a caricature for whatever she could get. She never made much, ten or twenty dollars here and there, but it bought gas and oil for the van and an occasional meal at Denny's.

Arriving on campus it took her a few minutes to find a red zone to park in. She unloaded the blanket and her bag and trudged four blocks over the blistering-hot cement to find that the sweltering heat had swept the students off the open grass of the quad and sent them toward shade or anywhere blessed by air-conditioning. Lela debated whether to try to set up inside the student union again, but she'd been kicked out a half-dozen times and another major hassle with the campus cops was something she didn't need.

Lela slumped against the wall in the shade of the student bookstore alcove for a few minutes before using a nearby rest room to wash up. The cool water from the tap felt refreshing on her face and arms, and she lingered there for several minutes until a female janitor entered and chased her out with disdain in her eyes. Lela returned to the van just in time to see a meter maid pulling away on her blue Cushman after leaving a twenty-five dollar ticket under her windshield wiper. Lela removed the ticket and tossed it in a nearby garbage can before getting back in the van. She would have preferred to drive away from the heat of the city, but in reality she couldn't afford the luxury of wasting what little fuel she had in the gas tank. Besides, her old van was blowing blue smoke, and she didn't want to get stranded in the heat, so she drove directly back to "The Arches."

Emerging from the van she had immediately closed herself off from her neighbors under a castoff beach umbrella supported by a broken cinderblock that she had retrieved from a nearby flood channel after a recent downpour. Now the umbrella was decorated with dangling crystals that caught the hot sunrays and danced off Lela's sweaty face as she sat in a lotus position with her eyes closed. It amused her that even among this ragged, smelly crew who answered to such names as Goofy George, Sad Sam, One-Armed Mike, Spider Bob, Crazy Patty, Stretch, and Chef Snooky, *she* was a misfit. For the most part the other inhabitants avoided her. In ordinary circumstances, her crystals would be targets for theft, to be bartered for a cheap bottle of Thunderbird wine. But they were afraid of Lela, afraid of the fearful moaning and screaming that came from her van late at night as they tried to sleep.

As she sat under the umbrella, the ever present drumming of the cars passing above slowly faded, and she was left in peace to consider her next move. The interview with the female cop still rankled. She was accustomed to being laughed at, to being dismissed as nothing more than a foolish crank, a "full mooner," by the cops. She desperately needed someone to listen to her, to believe what she had seen. But who?

Lela spent the rest of the day under the umbrella, alternately dozing and reading, coaxed out after dark by the warm smell of simmering stew from the main fire. She returned to the van and rummaged in the back for the pink Melmac bowl and her last can of Campbell's Chicken

Noodle Soup. Returning to the overhang, she wordlessly added the soup to the simmering, blackened pot watched over by a half-dozen ragged men. Snooky used a glass coffee mug to fill her well worn bowl with the steaming liquid. Returning to the blessed privacy of her van, she removed another of the precious donuts the cop had bought her earlier that day and the hardened potato patty she had retrieved from the downtown garbage can. The potato patty thickened the stew and the hot liquid brought the drying donut back to life. In a few minutes the exhausted Lela was feeling surprisingly satiated as she wiped her bowl and spoon clean. After putting her utensils away she hung a well-used Garfield The Cat beach towel over the front window, hooking the faded blue material over the visors to insure herself at least a modicum of privacy. She then crawled into the back, climbing over a half-dozen plastic garbage bags stuffed with her dirty laundry, piles of books, and a large stack of sketch pads. She cleared a space on the dirty mattress and quickly undressed in the familiarly tight confines. Pulling on a frayed nightgown she fell into a fitful sleep that lasted until two-thirty in the morning. The inside of the van was still hot, and Lela had long since stripped off her nightgown and was lying naked in that place between sleep and consciousness that she had long ago accepted as her version of rest. She opened her eyes hoping to find daylight but found only the shadows of early morning. The van amplified the hollow sounds of the never-ending stream of cars and trucks that rumbled above her into a strangely primitive drum solo. She sat up, parted the frayed curtains, and glanced out the rear window of the van. Two cooking fires were still clinging to life, sending thin lines of acrid smoke and random sparks up into the understructure of the bridge. In the darkness she could make out several nests and the outline of the sleeping humps of ragged, smelly humanity. She lay back on the mattress and reached out to touch one of the dozen quartz crystals that dangled from the roof by foot-long lengths of fishing line. The feel of the crystals usually offered her comfort, but not this morning. As her fingers brushed the smoothness of a stone, she saw a tangle of tan puppies with cream-colored bellies. Their breath smelled of warm milk; their tongues were wet as they snuggled close together. Lela loved animals, and the vision should have brought her a feeling of well-being, but for some inexplicable reason, these fragile, innocent puppies filled her with dread. She shut her eyes and forced them away. She dozed for a few peaceful moments before the familiar metallic taste in her mouth signaled the oncoming electrical charge that surged through her body, leaving her helpless but totally receptive for the message she knew was coming. And it came like it always did, overwhelming her with voices screaming in terror, pleading for help!

"Momma, please help me. Sammy needs help. Please come and get me, please come and take me home!"

Lela willed her eyes to open, forced herself upright, grabbed her well-worn carryall bag from under her folded clothes, and hurried to pull out her spiral-bound sketchpad. She opened the pad to a clean page and felt around the bottom of the bag until her shaking hands located a pencil. She managed to draw two lines before the intensity of her grip snapped the graphite and she had to search for another pencil.

She started drawing the face.

The girl was young and pretty with sparkling dark eyes and a face bordered by long dark hair. Her mouth was open in horror and pain, and the words spurted out, "No, please don't hurt me anymore. No, I..."

As the sweat rolled off Lela's forehead and mixed with her tears, she let go of the sketchpad and, curling into a ball, cried for this beautiful child.

Jessi had spent the entire evening filling out in triplicate a mound of Braxton brothers' paperwork consisting of her probable cause statement, arrest reports, personal property inventories on the suspects that included a total of thirty-seven credit cards and nearly $2100 in cash, and property damage reports detailing the brass railing being bent and jerked out of the drywall, leaving a gaping hole. She also noted the exact number of coffee cups, saucers, and champagne glasses that had been broken during the melee at Chez Peyo. She had even included in the listing $29.95 for the flaming shish kebab that Murray had used so effectively against Tyrell Braxton. At a quarter after eleven, she was the only day-shift officer left on the floor, as she put the finishing touches on her "chase sheet." All vehicle pursuits involving Houston police officers required a detailed "Pursuit Report" in which the participating officers gave a minute by minute, block by block reenactment of the route they took while pursuing their suspect. This was done to establish, and put limits on, any liability actions against the city in case a police car sideswiped a parked car or plowed through someone's picket fence. Jessi had written dozens of such "chase sheets," but this was the first one in anyone's memory in which the pursuit vehicle was listed as a city bus. By the end of shift tomorrow, Jessi anticipated being called on the carpet by her superiors who would meticulously point out to her why a police officer should never put citizens at risk. In fact, Jessi agreed completely. She realized that when she commandeered the bus, she had put herself firmly in the clutches of the Tactical Interpretation Team, referred to simply as "TITS" by street cops. The "Team" would hold a catered luncheon meeting where they would dissect, analyze, and diagram every move she had made, and second guess every word she had spoken, from the restaurant to the apprehension of the suspect. Within a week "TITS" would issue a memo to be read at the roll call of every substation in the city, where patrol officers would "boo" and "hiss" the stilted language. After the reading, hats would be passed at every station house, and a well-used manila envelope containing nearly 1,000 one-dollar bills would eventually make its way to Jessi's purse.

She hadn't arrived home until well after midnight, and after taking a quick shower, she had spent the night tossing and turning, purging herself slowly of the adrenalin from the chase, reliving over and over the keyed-up exhilaration of the Braxton brothers' collar while trying to push the unsettling encounter with Lela Starr from her consciousness. One moment she was running flat-out after Vonzell, and the next minute the vivid sketches of the young girl Lela called "Mickey" floated through her dreams. If those weren't enough, her cat, Gussie, with half a queen sized bed to sleep on, chose instead to doze while perched heavily on her legs, giving her a nagging case of subconscious claustrophobia.

She had woken late, which surprised her because she could have sworn she'd never gone to sleep, and driven to work like a zombie. Her partner was waiting for her to arrive and pounced on her for details of the Braxton arrest. Jessi had just finished detailing her and Murray's adventure to an amazed Odom when Sergeant Tobin stuck his head in the roll call room.

"Hey, Officer Cole, the Head of Patrol wants you in his office, as in *now.*"

"Good luck, partner," Odom offered. "My prayers are with you."

"Well don't stop praying now," Jessi said as she stood and hurried out of the room. Sergeant Tobin winked as she passed. "I told you. Do something positive and they'll try to take credit for it. But fuck up, and they'll run you up the flagpole."

"Am I going up the pole?" Jessi asked, her voice betraying her real concern.

"I don't know yet," Tobin replied with a heavy shrug. "You're definitely my hero, but the Chief hasn't read all your reports yet. Depending on his mood, could go either way."

Jessi hurried to the second floor where she spent the next hour detailing every second of the Braxton scenario as the head of the Patrol Division, the watch commander, the chief of detectives, and the lieutenant in charge of the Public Relations unit sat around a long, polished table and took in every word she uttered. The men intermittently listened to her explanation and ruthlessly grilled her.

"And it never occurred to you that you were endangering the public when you commandeered the bus?" the head of patrol asked.

"Well, yes it did, sir, but I, I needed wheels and there they were. I assure you, the bus driver was fully capable of handling her vehicle in a safe manner." Jessi's response sounded weak even to her own ears. "This is not going well," she thought.

"One officer, female, two bad guys, one of which weighs close to 300 pounds. For all you knew, Officer Cole, they could have been armed. If there was ever a case for waiting for a back-up, this is it," the head of the Patrol Division said, his tone carrying equal hints of disgust and disbelief."

"Yes, sir, it was a poor judgement call and if I had to do it over again, I'd do it a lot differently," Jessi offered.

"You got shit house lucky out there," the chief of detectives volunteered.

"Better to be lucky than good," Sakelaris offered in weak defense of his fast wilting subordinate. "Hey, let's look on the bright side," Sakelaris added, doing his best to inject a little levity into the heavy air of the small room. "She got a couple of very bad actors off the street and she did it without anyone being injured or any liability issues arising."

"No liability? What do you call the twelve hundred dollars worth of damages to the restaurant?" the chief of detectives protested.

"Negotiable," Lt. Sakelaris volunteered. "I talked to him a few minutes ago. He's not only willing to eat the damage, but he's sending Officer Cole a $500 gift certificate to boot. Which, I might add," Sakelaris looked right at her. "She *cannot* accept."

The head of the Public Affairs unit cleared his throat. "Hey guys, reality check. The press is delighted. They interviewed the bus driver on the morning news and we've got all three networks asking for interviews with Officer Cole and this 'Shish kabob' Murray guy from Records. This is looking very much like a win-win for the department."

Jessi cleared her throat, relieved that the tension in the room had dissipated so quickly. "I really don't want to do any interviews."

"Yes you do, dear, yes you do," the deputy chief cooed. "And not to worry, the Chief will be right there with you."

The men laughed knowingly.

And the Chief of Police *had* been right there, standing directly behind Jessi and Murray Crook as they stood nervously in the press briefing room and suffered through interviews for all four Houston's major television stations. As the interviews progressed, the questions became increasingly predictable and after nearly thirty-five minutes, Jessi's answers were sounding forced and hollow in her own ears.

"No, I don't consider myself a hero. I do this for a living… Yes, being a cop is a lot like being a teacher. Both jobs are dangerous and unpredictable. Being a teacher is probably harder because you're not armed. Just kidding… Yes, my mother and father would be proud of me… Yes, next time I will certainly use a police car and not a city bus."

Murray, wearing a tight black t-shirt with "Longhorn Gay Alliance," silk screened on the front, kept his answers short and concise. "I just did what Officer Cole told me."

The chief of police ended the interviews by reading the following statement:

"Officer Cole and Mr. Crook represent the very best aspects of the Houston Police Department. This department strives to represent all segments of our society in such a way as to instill a sense of community, a sense of pride and a sense of purpose in our ranks. We will continue our daily struggle to bring the citizens of our wonderful city the kind of protection they need and deserve."

Jessi left the Public Relations office and headed for the closest rest room where she set her clipboard on a towel dispenser and glanced in the mirror. Her eyes were bloodshot from lack of sleep, her hair was a mess and her cheeks were bright red, a by product of the nerve racking interviews. She shook her head at her spent appearance and leaning over the sink, splashed cold water on her reddened cheeks.

"Well, if it isn't the local television star."

The voice startled her and, when she glanced up, she saw the reflection of Lela Starr standing behind her in the open doorway of a stall.

"What? What are you doing in here?"

Lela moved to the sink on Jessi's right and, ignoring the question, pumped a handful of liquid soap from the dispenser and washed her hands. Jessi shook her head and then winced as Lela removed a purple toothbrush and a small tube of Crest from her bag and proceeded to brush her teeth.

"I said, 'what are you doing in here?' This is not a public restroom. How'd you clear the metal detector downstairs with all this stuff? You're-"

"Excuse me, but I have to take advantage of the running water," Lela said, her voice muffled by the foam of her dental chores. She quickly took a mouthful of water, rinsed, spit, gargled more water, and spit again. Only after her toothbrush was thoroughly rinsed, returned to its plastic baggy, and pushed back in her cloth bag, did she even bother to look at Jessi.

"I don't believe I'm seeing this."

"There's another girl missing. I just visualized it last night. Does that make sense?"

"Oh, perfect sense. It couldn't be clearer. You just picked up a spiritual bulletin over the psychic airwaves, and you broke into a closed, guarded facility to inform me about it, right? And when you couldn't find me you decided you might as well brush your teeth. Can I get you anything else? Mouthwash maybe? Shampoo?"

Lela shook her head. "For somebody so young, you're awfully closed minded. I'm trying to tell you about a visualization."

"Tell me, in your latest close encounter," Jessi asked, "did you also visualize being arrested for trespassing?"

"There are young girls out there getting snatched off the street by a psycho, and you want to arrest me for trespassing? Wow, you *are* a true cop! Those testosterone apes that you work with would be very proud of you," Lela shouted angrily as she picked up her bag and headed toward the door.

Jessi shook her head in frustration. "For someone who says they've just witnessed a kidnapping, you seem pretty unconcerned. I mean you're the one in here doing dental hygiene."

"It isn't that simple. I know what I saw, what I *feel,* but I can't just go out there and...I need help." Lela lapsed into silence.

"You need help alright," Jessi said, folding her arms. "O.K., give me something I can work with. Let's start with the last name of the first victim, 'Michelle' was it? 'Michelle' what?"

A look of puzzlement washed over Lela's drawn features. "Michelle? I never said anything about 'Michelle.' I said her name was 'Mickey.'"

Jessi was silent, hoping that Lela would trip herself up.

"You found out something, didn't you? You know damn well I didn't make any of this up, don't you?" Lela asked, moving closer to Jessi.

"Yeah, I found out you can read about murders in newspapers or watch accounts of them on television news shows. That's what I found out."

Lela bristled. "I'm trying to tell you that there are monsters out there preying on little girls. You have to stop them!"

"O.K. Let's start with your latest victim. This happened last night?" Lela nodded.

"Good. That's a start. Now give me a name."

"Sammy. That's all I have."

"Sammy?" Jessi willed herself to be patient. "I'm going to need a hell of a lot more than that," Jessi said.

Lela's eyes flashed a warning, but she remained mute.

"O.K., give me a location?

Lela shook her head sadly before responding. "Officer Cole, your mind is so full of self indulgence and all that other yuppie crap, you can't even envision other energy fields, let alone experience them. You have more concern for your goddamn cat!"

A hint of a smile played over Jessi's lips. "Oh, that's right, I almost forgot, besides being psychic you're also a mind reader."

Lela bristled. "No wonder you're such a shitty cop, you won't get off your cute little affirmative-action ass and do anything!" Lela's voice echoed loudly through the small room.

Jessi felt the sudden urge to grab the woman's wrist and shove her sneering face into the tile wall and twist her up, but she caught herself just in time.

"You want to hurt me, don't you?" Lela asked.

"You say one more word to me and I'll arrest you. Now leave."

"All I want from you is-"

"I said *get out!* "

Lela was nearly out the door when she stopped and turned back.

"Now!" Jessi barked.

Lela swallowed her protest, turned, and left, leaving Jessi's face flushed with anger.

She turned and looked at herself in the mirror. "Hell, anybody could guess you had a cat. You've got Gussie's hair all over your shirt," she mumbled as she absently brushed the shoulders of her uniform and left the restroom, pushing into her subconscious the fact that her uniform had come from the dry cleaners and she hadn't worn it home last night.

9.

☙❧

She moved through the dark like a cat, sensing every corner, every sharp edge, every inch of the smooth, waxed concrete. The only sound came from her own labored breathing and the girl's soft whimpering which guided Kitty to the correct corner. The whimpering grew louder and then ceased as Kitty drew near and raised the camera. The flash of the Polaroid flared in the darkness, freezing everything in a numbing white that slowly retreated back into blackness.

"Don't be frightened. I'm here to be your friend, but you have to trust me," Kitty half whispered.

"Please let me go," the girl begged, her voice weakened by hours of futile, soft sobbing. "I promise I won't tell anyone. Just let me go and I'll keep my mouth shut. Please don't let him hurt me anymore."

Kitty ignored Samantha's pleas as she left the dark storage room, locked the stainless steel door, pocketed the key, and returned to her bedroom where she set the Polaroid on her bed and watched the image slowly develop. The process never failed to stir her - a picture from nothing. She studied the girl's face carefully. There were no bruises or cuts to mar her lovely skin. She would make a nice addition to her collection if she could keep Pinky from damaging her. She was glad she had the new lock installed on the storage room. The fiasco with Ralph Porter had been a good lesson. She had foolishly left him alone to watch over the Sandoval girl while she went out, and when she returned she found that the parolee had beaten the girl to death and disposed of the body in the dumpster. Even now it made her angry to think about it. That mistake could have cost her everything.

She hurried to the closet and, dropping to her knees, quickly cleared a half-dozen pairs of shoes from a spot against the wall. Lifting a loose board, she reached into the hole and brought out her scrapbook and carried it carefully back to the bed where she opened it and thumbed slowly through the pages of newspaper clippings, fliers, and photographs. Turning to the last page, she carefully placed the new Polaroid of Samantha Deavers in a plastic cover, being sure to leave room for the newspaper articles that would soon be written about the missing girl. She loved reading the stories, being the *only* one with true knowledge of the girl's whereabouts instilled in her a sense of power that she found both exhilarating and intoxicating. She looked once more at the photo of Samantha before turning back to the beginning of the scrapbook.

As always the familiar photo of Molly brought tears to her eyes: Kitty's eyes glistened, and she smiled as she stoked the photo, her fingers tracing the made-up lips and heavily rouged cheeks. She liked the effect of the lavender ribbons in the girl's dark hair.

Kitty's eyes suddenly hardened as she remembered. For thirteen years she had mothered that ungrateful, rebellious child. Their mother had died giving Molly life, and Kitty had willingly taken on the responsibility of raising her baby sister even though she had been a child herself. She had loved bathing and dressing Molly in sweet, frilly dresses that her father had let her choose. But Molly was always ungrateful and uncooperative, screaming when Kitty combed her hair, pulling out the ribbons, and bursting into tears when the darling little dresses got caught under her baby knees when she learned to crawl. Their father had laughed at Kitty's efforts, taking off the dresses and letting Molly crawl around in diapers. Over the years he had spoiled Molly, taking her fishing, teaching her to play softball, and allowing her to wear oversized t-shirts and shorts that left her knees perpetually scabby. He had attempted to include his big, awkward older daughter in the outdoor activities, but the sullen Kitty had hated it, all of it, especially the fishing. Her father soon stopped trying, turning his attention almost exclusively to the eager, bright Molly. Kitty had looked on, seething with resentment.

Then everything changed. When Molly was twelve and Kitty nineteen their father had died suddenly of a heart attack. Molly was brokenhearted, while Kitty had rejoiced in her liberation. Now everything would be different. She was sure Molly would turn to her, but she was wrong. Molly became even more unmanageable, refusing Kitty's attempts to guide and mother her. She would hide at their uncle's trailer until she thought Kitty was asleep and then sneak into the house. Kitty would hear her crying softly in the night, and the sound of Molly's muffled sobs filled her with rage. After Molly cried herself to sleep, Kitty would come into her room and watch the sleeping child, her face in repose, and imagine brushing her long brown hair. She could hear Molly thanking her in soft tones, but in the morning the sleeping girl would awaken, destroying the dainty image with her sloppy clothes and smart-ass mouth.

Kitty had planned carefully for Molly's thirteenth birthday. It had been six months since their father's death. Six months for Molly to mourn. It was long enough. Kitty was willing to give the girl another chance. She shopped carefully, choosing the perfect gifts: the chiffon lavender dress, Mary Jane shoes, and ribbons to match. She ordered the cake: a ballerina dressed in a lavender tutu. Kitty had been so excited, but Molly had ruined it all by bursting into tears and throwing the dress back at her.

Kitty remembered the white heat that had flashed over her, the roaring in her head, and Molly's face contorted in terror as Kitty's powerful fingers tightened around the girl's thin neck. It was a perfect solution and so simple that Kitty wondered what had taken her so long to think of it. Afterwards, she had lovingly dressed Molly in her new birthday finery, lighted the candles, and after blowing them out, cut each of them a piece of cake.

"Happy birthday, Molly," Kitty smiled. "You look perfect, just perfect."

After a moment she turned the pages and let her eyes caress the other photos. The heavy makeup disguised the young faces and blended them into a gaudy sameness. The different colors of the frilly dresses and ribbons were the only things that set them apart.

What Kitty didn't see, but the camera did, was the terror that filled their eyes.

She felt the familiar rush of warmth and anticipation that the pictures always gave her, but it wasn't enough. She felt a physical need to visit them again.

The buzzer from the shop sliced through her consciousness, abruptly canceling her moment with her *friends*. She quickly closed her scrapbook, returned it to its hiding place, and scurried downstairs.

It was nearly noon before Jessi cleared the squad room and walked quickly toward the parking garage. She could feel herself relaxing as she mentally went through her start of watch checklist, finding comfort in the familiar. It would be a total relief to be back in Edward 42, in a world where she understood the rules, and had at least some control of her actions. Jessi had been so distracted all morning she hadn't noticed that the blistering sun had quickly disappeared behind a thick layer of black clouds and the temperature had suddenly dropped twenty degrees. The sudden "BOOM" of a thunderclap startled her momentarily. Pausing, she moved to the edge of the stairway and looked down as heavy sheets of cool, welcome rain washed over the small island of blue and white patrol cars.

She was less than three blocks from the station, her shredded windshield wipers smearing her window, when her radio crackled. "Edward Forty-Two."

"Forty-Two, go."

"Return to station and report to Frank Seven," the dispatcher stated flatly.

Jessi's heart skipped a beat. Frank Seven was Lt. Sakelaris' call sign and he had *never* called her to the station. "Shit," she mumbled weakly.

As she made a quick u turn and headed back to the station, her cell phone rang. It was her partner.

"What the hell does Frank Seven want you for? What'd you do now?" Odom asked.

"I don't know. It's not good though. I'm hoping it's only a three day suspension," Jessi said as a heavy lump settled in the pit of her stomach.

"Call me the minute you know, partner."

"Will do," Jessi said as turned into the parking garage.

Jessi heard voices coming from behind the watch commander's closed door. She took a deep breath and knocked.

"Come in."

Jessi opened the door and entered. Lt. Sakelaris was sitting behind his desk while Detective Merle Eisom, the chief of detectives, and a man in civilian clothes sat opposite him. The stranger stood when Jessi entered, forcing the other men to their feet as well. Jessi was surprised at the man's height. He seemed to unravel from behind the desk as her curious eyes quickly took in his Tony Lama boots, pressed jeans, starched khaki shirt, well-worn, straw Stetson, and deeply tanned face.

"Officer Jessi Cole, I want you to meet Sheriff John Cutler."

Cutler's smile was open and genuine as he removed his hat and extended his hand. "Ma'am."

Jessi took his strong hand, noticing immediately the grease under his fingernails and the matted line his hat left in his thick, wavy hair. "Pleased to meet you, Sheriff."

"Actually, we met earlier."

Jessi's puzzlement was obvious. "I'm sorry, but I don't remember."

"We met over the phone. You called yesterday about the Sandoval case?"

Sakelaris shot Jessi an unmistakable dirty look, but she avoided his eyes. She had hoped her impulsive call to Grace County would have gone undiscovered.

"Oh, Grace County, out there in Deep Texas. Of course."

They realized simultaneously that they had been holding hands well past the deadline for first introductions and self-consciously released their grip. "I was hoping you could put me in touch with this psychic of yours," Cutler said.

Detective Eisom chuckled as he unconsciously adjusted his hairpiece. "You must be awfully hard up for leads if you came all the way down here to talk to the spook."

"I am hard up. In fact," Cutler said as he removed an 8x10, black-and-white photo from a manila envelope and handed to Jessi. "Officer Cole's phone call was the first break I've caught since the body was discovered."

The photo was a blowup of the murder scene dumpster. Sakelaris moved in and looked over Jessi's shoulder as she studied the glossy black-and-white print. "I assume this is where the body was found?" she asked.

Cutler nodded. "See anything else of interest?"

Jessi scanned the photo, looking for anything unusual that might catch her eye. She finally shrugged. "No. What am I missing?"

"Remember the number you gave me over the phone?"

Jessi's eyes darted to the numbers. "There!" she said, tapping the stenciled numbers on the side of the dumpster. "1305! That's the number Lela Starr gave me."

"I hope you didn't come all the way down here based on that. She probably saw the number in the newspaper," Sakelaris offered.

"That was my first reaction, too, but the pictures that ran in the newspapers didn't show the numbers. Neither did any of the TV news footage," Cutler added.

Eisom shook his head. "So what are you saying, Sheriff? That the old hippie actually..." he rubbed his temples and closed his eyes for effect. "...had a vision?"

Cutler's eyes locked onto Eisom's. "Maybe she was just passing by when all the commotion was happening? Maybe the 'somebody' who put the body in the dumpster told her about it? Maybe she was there and saw it firsthand as a participant. The maybe of it doesn't interest me," Cutler stated flatly. "The fact is, she knew about it, and I want to know why she knew it because this little girl's body was found in there."

The Sheriff brought out two more photos and set one of them down in front of Jessi. It was a colorized shot of a bright-eyed, smiling thirteen-year-old Michelle "Mickey" Sandoval that had been taken for the Sam Houston Middle School yearbook. It was the type of photo that came in a package of one 8x10 for Mom and Dad, four 4x5s for brothers, grandmas and grandpas, uncles and aunts, and two sheets of wallet-sized prints that the kids would carefully cut out and trade with only their best friends, whether they liked them or not. The resemblance to the girl in Lela's sketchbook was so close it caused the hair on the back of Jessi's neck to tickle.

"She had a drawing in a sketchbook that looked very similar to this," Jessi offered as she continued studying the picture.

"That was the photo that ran in the media and on the fliers," Cutler volunteered.

Sakelaris moved behind Jessi in order to look at the picture. "She probably reproduced it from the newspaper," he said.

Cutler hesitated slightly before passing Jessi a blowup that showed in vivid detail the sickly blue-white, bruised, puffy face of Mickey Sandoval exactly as it looked the morning it was removed from the Grace County dumpster. The girl's once sparkling eyes peeked out dully from swollen sockets and stared off into a clouded nothingness.

"Since it was a kidnapping, I'm assuming the FBI was all over it," Sakelaris said.

"Yeah, I had three agents living with me for about a week. They ruled out the family and the neighbors pretty quickly; even checked into the backgrounds of her teachers, but nothing developed. Early on they thought it might be linked to the disappearance of a local girl that occurred over fifteen years ago but that was a dead end. Then they tried to tie it to a series of kidnappings and disappearances that they'd been tracking all over the South. They felt Michelle Sandoval fit their general victim profile, which is a girl in junior high and pretty. It was a vague description at best. The one thing that didn't fit with the others, however, was that Michelle's body was actually found. That's a critical difference, because in the seven other cases they were looking at, no body was ever recovered. The girls just simply vanished."

"So how was it left?" Jessi asked.

Cutler shrugged. "We pretty much came to a consensus that it wasn't related to the others. Most likely it was a random-type thing. The killer spots the girl, snatches her off the streets in Dallas, does his thing, pulls off at an empty rest stop, dumps the body, and then continues on to grandma's house for dinner."

"What was the cause of death?" Jessi asked.

Cutler removed the autopsy report from the envelope and pushed it across the desk. "What they called blunt-force trauma to the head and body."

Jessi scanned the report, picking up on fragments of sentences "… ruptured pancreas…seven broken ribs… broken nose…numerous skull fractures."

"Poor kid," Jessi said, shaking her head.

"Yeah, she was obviously used as a punching bag and beaten to death by someone very strong and very…"

Cutler didn't finish the statement, Sakelaris did. "Sick sonofabitch…. Says here she was sexually abused?" The lieutenant made it a question as he tapped the autopsy report.

"Numerous times over an extended period. We figure he kept her alive for at least three days. After he killed her, he put her in a garbage bag, and dropped her remains in dumpster 1305."

The four officers were silent for a moment, each of them dealing with their individual ghosts of murders past. Cutler broke the silence. "I want to catch the person who did this in the very worst way. If I have to play games with a psychic, I'll do it."

Sakelaris rubbed his bald dome as he normally did when he was nervous or uncomfortable.

"Sheriff, could you give us a minute?" Lt. Sakelaris asked.

"Certainly," he said, quickly gathering his pictures and autopsy report and closing the door as he exited the room.

Sakelaris turned to Eisom and the chief. "So how do we handle this? You want to give it to the murder squad? Let them chase it down with him?"

The chief looked at Eisom, who simply shrugged his narrow shoulders.

"Chief, if the man had any kind of a legitimate lead, my partner and I wouldn't hesitate to jump in. But a fucking number on a garbage dumpster from a foul smelling spook seems a little thin, don't you think?"

Jessi willed her mouth to stay closed and almost succeeded. "Chief, I really don't think we can dismiss Lela Starr that easily. She seems to-"

Eisom's disgust boiled over. "Oh for chrissakes. Is this the voice of experience I'm hearing? Give me a break, Cole. Lela Starr should be in a mental facility."

The chief considered his options for a moment before setting his chin and nodding. "Go back to work, Merle."

Eisom departed, his cold assessment of Lela Starr lingering in the room. The chief cleared his throat as he turned to Sakelaris. "My detectives are overwhelmed as it is. If I throw this in somebody's lap they would make my life miserable and that sheriff's life miserable. Handle it some other way. Be creative," he said as he stood and opened the door. He was half way out when he paused and looked back at Jessi. "You know, for a probationary officer you certainly have developed a very high profile."

"Thank you, sir," Jessi answered.

"That wasn't a compliment," the chief said as he turned and left, leaving Jessi and Sakelaris staring at each other.

"You know, Officer Cole, I swear I gave you a direct order yesterday to leave this case alone."

"'Let it go,' I think you said." Jessi explained, weakly.

"So just what the hell does 'Let it go,' mean to you?"

"I'm sorry. I really am. I just got caught up in the moment. It won't happen again."

"Oh, that's a nice apology. But in the mean time, what do we do with the big cowboy out there? You brought him here."

Jessi shrugged. "I'll apologize and explain it was my poor judgment."

Sakelaris gave her a long look. "Like it's that simple, huh? Come on," he said, opening the door and walking out. Jessi followed as they approached the sheriff, who was standing at a window, looking out at the rain.

"Sheriff, Officer Cole here will be assigned to you as long as you need her. She has been instructed to give you any and all assistance that you may require for your investigation."

Jessi's puzzled look went unnoticed as the men shook hands.

"Thanks lieutenant, I appreciate it," Cutler said.

"Good luck to you," Sakelaris offered as his eyes locked on Jessi's. "Both of you," he added as he returned to his office and closed the door, leaving Jessi and Cutler to share an awkward silence.

Cutler's deep chuckle broke the ice. "You got the short straw, huh?"

Jessi smiled. "I hope you're not too disappointed."

"Are you kidding? I was afraid they were going to stick me with the guy with the hairpiece."

Jessi smiled. "Tell you what, I've got to get my briefcase out of my car. Meet me in the roll call room in about five minutes. Roll call is right through the door and to your left."

"Five minutes," Cutler repeated and watched as Jessi entered the stairwell and disappeared.

Three minutes later he was seated at a table in the roll call room when Jessi entered and, opening her briefcase, handed him the 1017 interview report she had prepared after her first interview with Lela Starr. Cutler quickly scanned the page.

"There's really not too much there; she couldn't offer any details whatsoever," Jessi said.

Cutler studied the page intently. "It's a whole lot better than the nothing I've been looking at the past year. Anything else you can add to this?"

Jessi shrugged. "This morning, Lela Starr somehow got around the security desk and snuck into a rest room on the second floor where, after scaring the hell out of me, she announced that a girl named 'Sammy' had also been kidnapped and was in danger. She even showed me another drawing, presumed to be this 'Sammy.'"

"First Mickey, now Sammy, hell, maybe we ought to call this the Mouseketeer Case."

"There was no Samantha included on the seven names the FBI had either," Cutler said as he studied the 1017 for another few moments. "I'd sure like to talk to this Starr woman, but I don't see an address on here."

"She's lives in her van on the street. Sometimes she parks out at The Arches. That's a homeless encampment under a freeway not too far from here. We can check it out if you want?"

"I thought you'd never ask," Cutler replied, standing and pulling his well-worn Stetson low over his eyes. "Do you mind if I drop my rental car off at my hotel? That way I won't need to come all the way back in?"

"I don't mind at all. Where are you staying?"

"The Howard Johnson on Fifth."

The left front brakeshoe on Edward 42 grabbed on the wet streets, and the worn windshield wipers scraped like a fork on a plate as they ineffectively slapped the rain from one part of the windshield to another. As she followed Cutler to the hotel, she used the radio to check DMV for the type of van Lela Starr might be driving. Less than a minute later the dispatcher came back. "I show no records of any kind on subject Lela Starr. I ran Star with one 'r' and two. No hits."

Cutler parked his rental car in the Howard Johnson lot and, using a folded newspaper to deflect most of the rain, hurried to climb in the patrol car.

"I ran Lela's name but they don't have anything on her or her van. She's probably got an alias."

"Or two, or three," Cutler added.

As they moved through the early afternoon traffic, the dispatch desk broadcast a steady stream of radio calls as the City was flooded with a crush of minor traffic accidents, mostly rear-enders. They rode in silence as Jessi concentrated on the sluggish traffic, moving slowly over the oily, wet pavement, slick and black in the afternoon gloom. Cutler wiped the fog off his window and looked out at Houston's impressive skyline, blurred in the downpour,

Jessi finally broke the silence. "I thought it would never cool off. I love the rain."

"Yeah, it's been hot up home, too. Plus our office air conditioning went out a couple of days ago." Cutler studied her profile. Her face was beautifully put together, he thought: high cheekbones, full lips. He tried to see if she was wearing a wedding band, but her left hand was turned away from him. "Sorry about cutting into your day. I loved my patrol hours and I hated sharing it with ride-alongs."

"I'm still on probation so I've never had a ride-along. You're my first, " Jessi replied, turning to see if his eyes matched the sound of his deep voice. When she turned she found Cutler staring at her, causing her face to redden. They both turned away.

"So, your boss tells me you had quite an experience last night? I mean chasing down a bad guy with a city bus is pretty exciting stuff to a country boy from way up in..."

"*Deep* Texas?" They both laughed, and then Jessi gave him a blow-by-blow account of the Braxton brothers' caper. As she recounted the events, Jessi noticed that a good deal of the last 24 hours worth of tension was starting to ease from her sore body. She winced slightly as she felt along the top of her belt line. She had a large, deep bruise where the table had hit her during the scuffle at Chez Peyo, but she hadn't realized until now that it was extremely tender to the touch.

Riding along she felt a sudden rush of warmth and realized that it was Cutler's presence in the car that produced it. It was a good feeling, being next to him, and it reminded her that it had been awhile since she'd been serious about anyone.

As she turned the car onto the freeway, an image of Brian Kinsey's face floated before her. They had met at the University of Houston in her sophomore year and had dated steadily for the next three years. She was convinced that Brian was the man she was going to marry, the love of her life. She had no doubt that he cared about her, probably even loved her, but she had slowly and painfully discovered that the passion they shared revolved around him and his goals. He couldn't love her as much as he loved himself. It was a stunning blow. She broke off the relationship, but it had hurt her deeply. A college roommate, Collette McMasters, told her that she'd get over him, that he wasn't worth crying over. Jessi had been resentful of Collette's cliches because she was positive they didn't apply to her. "Well," she realized, "Collette had been right."

She glanced at the sheriff and again found him looking at her.

We're almost there," she said.

10.

⊙⊙

The steady rain had transformed the thick dust and gaping potholes of Rags Road into slick brown mud and deep puddles that
rattled and shook the patrol car's undercarriage. As she steered the car
up a short, steep hill, the tires lost traction and the car bounced, rattled,
and shimmied as they hit a washboard of bumps that caused the car to
fishtail briefly before Jessi corrected the wheel and continued over the
top and into the parking area.

"To tell you the truth, I don't have a clue what we're looking for,"
Jessi said, rolling down her window and peering out into the wet gloom
at a hodgepodge of beat-up vehicles. The only van she could see was
missing all four tires and was up on blocks, every one of its' windows
shattered by vandals.

She parked as close to the under crossing as she could and turned off
the key. "When I was out here yesterday, there was an old van parked
right there. Whether it was her's or not I don't know." she said, pointing at a dry spot under the freeway arch where over a dozen refrigerator boxes had been hastily erected into uneven rows of corporate cardboard houses, sporting names like Kenmore, Hotpoint, Frigidaire and
Maytag.

"This place is infested with lice and all other manner of vermin.
You can stay in the car if you want," she explained.

"I guess I've seen some pretty unpleasant things over the years. Don't worry about me. Lead the way," he replied, opening the door and stepping out into the heavy rain, they hurried under the protection of the freeway arches.

Cutler winced as the stench hit him flush in the face. "Ohmygawd," he muttered, unconsciously covering his nose.

"Sorry, I forgot to warn you about that. Home sweet home," Jessi said, immediately remembering her shock the first time she had smelled it.

As they walked through the cardboard city, they passed boxes covered with a patchwork of plastic, cloth, and paper. These treasures had been gleaned from trash receptacles and dumpsters and packed carefully back to the encampment to be used as primitive insulation from the rain and cold. It was recycling at its most elemental, and every time Jessi saw the appliance boxes she thought of her dad. When she was small, Deke would bring boxes like this home to her. They would drag them onto the porch, and together they would cut out windows and a doorway for her and her friends to crawl through and play house.

As they followed the winding path up and around the pillar, the same dog she had encountered the day before signaled their arrival with a nonstop barrage of high pitched yelps. As they crested the hill and approached the fire, the hyper black mutt darted out at them and was again rewarded with a Milk Bone treat from Jessi's shirt pocket.

A sea of dirty faces turned and followed their progress, parting to allow them to approach the fire where Snooky stood watch over the blackened pot of bubbling hot stew. Snooky had a hand-rolled Bugler cigarette plastered to his badly chapped lips. "Well, if it ain't the best lookin' cop in Houston. Two visits in two days. I swear I didn't high jack no shopping cart, Officer Cole, I promise," Snooky held his arms up in mock surrender.

"Hey, Snooky, how you doing?" Jessi said, her eyes darting over the shadowy faces in hopes of spotting Lela Starr.

"Oh, can't complain too much. You sure as hell didn't come out in the rain just to roust our sorry asses again, did you?" he asked, his bad left eye drifting up to the freeway as his good eye locked onto Sheriff Cutler. "Got yourself a new partner there, huh?"

"This is Sheriff Cutler from Grace County and no, we're not out here to roust anyone."

Snooky made a conscious effort to force both eyes to focus on the tall sheriff. "Grace County, huh? Nice place out there in *Deep* Texas."

Cutler extended his hand toward Snooky. "You been there, huh?"

"Hell yeah, I did thirty days in that old jail of yours way out there in Bancroft. That must have been, what, over twenty years ago?" he replied, returning Cutler's firm handshake.

"You'd a dealt with my old man back then," Cutler said. "We got us a new jail now, right there in Grace, so we can take better care of you if you drop in again," the sheriff said with a laugh.

Snooky's cautious expression dissolved into a toothless smile. "You two are welcome to grab a bowl if you're hungry."

"Don't mind if I do. I haven't eaten anything all day," Cutler said, taking an offered aluminum foil pie tin from the wrinkled hand of a bag lady. The woman was wearing a mound of dirty clothing and her mouth was perpetually pinched from the absence of teeth. "Thank you kindly, ma'am."

Snookie quickly ladled out a helping of the thick stew for Cutler and then looked at Jessi. "No thanks, I had a late lunch," she said, swallowing the sudden urge to gag.

Snookie held up a plastic bag full of dinner rolls. "The rolls are day old, but they ain't too bad. No butter though."

Cutler took a roll and soaked it in the stew before taking a large bite. "This is just what I needed, something on my ribs."

"Something tells me you didn't come for my mulligan stew."

The way Cutler was putting away the stew indicated he might have come precisely for that, Jessi thought as she turned back to Snookie. "We're looking for a woman named Lela Starr. She's a white woman, about fifty, has a lot of quartz crystals. She's not in trouble, we just want to talk to her." Jessi said.

"That's what all cops say," a woman's voice wafted out of the group and others quickly seconded her sentiments.

"She's a crazy bitch," a short man with a wild beard and a dirty, San Francisco Giants baseball cap volunteered.

"She thinks she's better than us," said the toothless bag lady. Several of the others mumbled their agreement, but Snooky's look quickly silenced them.

"Lela's a little weird, but she's alright."

"Then she does live here?" Cutler asked.

"Live here? It's not like you check in and out of the damn place. Hell, man, people don't *live* here; people *survive* here."

Jessi handed Snooky her business card wrapped in a ten-dollar bill. "Do me a favor. Next time you see her, give her my card. Tell her I need to talk to her. Tell her it's important."

The card and money quickly disappeared into the pocket of Snooky's well worn Pendelton jacket. "She's a psychic, you know. She probably already knows you're looking for her," he grinned, exposing his decayed front teeth as his bad eye drifted upwards.

Cutler finished his stew and handed the pie plate back to Snooky along with a twenty dollar bill. "Like the lady said, it's important."

Cutler walked a few steps before he stopped and turned back. "You ought to bottle that stew and sell it, partner. You'd make a million."

As they walked back down the slippery path, Jessi could feel Snooky's surprised smile following them.

"The hell you say?"

Jessi obtained a list of homeless shelters from the County Office of Social Services and they spent the next two hours driving from one facility to another in a futile search for Lela Starr and her van. The last shelter on the list was The Full Gospel Mission on lower Eighteenth Street that required the homeless to attend a church service before rewarding them with a meal and a cot. The retired Lutheran minister who ran the mission knew who Lela was but wasn't any help in locating her.

"She's not allowed here anymore."

"Why's that?" Jessi asked.

"Because we have enough problems here without her, that's why. Not only did she refuse to participate in our prayer meeting, but she called me a fascist and used foul language and tried to get the others to go along with her. She wanted them to picket our mission. She called our program 'unconstitutional.' Can you believe that?"

"Yes, I can," Jessi replied.

After checking out several of the older, downtown residential hotels and coming up empty, they stopped for dinner at a small, downtown restaurant-bar called "Shorty's." Shorty's was unpretentious and loud, specializing in thick steaks and large helpings of deep fried potato wedges. It was here, with Deke and the Dirty Dozen, that Jessi had developed her habit of eating pancakes and eggs for dinner.

Cutler ordered a steak, and they ate in silence for a few moments before he spoke. "I don't mean to just sit here and stuff my face, but

I was so excited when you called yesterday that I've neglected to eat anything but a donut, two candy bars and Snooky's stew since." He was relieved to see that she wasn't wearing a wedding ring.

"You're a braver man than I, Charlie Brown," Jessi said.

"Actually, it was pretty good stew." Cutler took another bite of his steak before he spoke again. "Your watch commander said you were a teacher before you were a cop?"

"Yeah, I was," Jessi nodded. "My last year I taught seventh grade social studies and eight grade algebra. My mom was a teacher so Dad and I thought that's what I should do too. Mom died of a stroke when I was nine."

"Sorry to hear that," Cutler said, surrendering momentarily to a heavy silence that was broken by loud laughter coming from the bar area. "My mother was a teacher too," he volunteered.

"Oh, yeah, what grade?"

"High school English."

"She was brave. I prefer working with the younger kids. They haven't discovered that they know everything yet," Jessi explained.

"So if I'm not being too personal, may I ask what made you choose law enforcement over education?"

"My dad was a Houston police officer. He died of a heart attack on the job."

"How long ago?" Cutler asked.

"Nine years ago," Jessi replied, her mind drifting off momentarily as she recalled the numerous times she had sat at this exact booth with Deke.

"Excuse me, I didn't mean to pry," Cutler said.

"No, no. That's fine. My dad was... He was my life. He wasn't one of those cops that took off the job with the uniform. He brought it *all* home: The crazy stories, the people, his partners. I loved it. It all must of sunk in because here I am."

Jessica found herself telling him more about her childhood than she realized she even remembered. She had been six years old when she took Deke to her first-grade class for "What Does Your Daddy Do Day." She could still picture it in her mind's eye as clearly as if it were yesterday: the six-foot-three, 235-pound Deke in full uniform, complete with "Old Mr. 44" and his worn and scarred night stick that he had nicked named "Boom Boom," walking down the hallway of Oak Grove School holding her tiny fingers so gently in his meaty, strong hand. Once in the classroom, Deke had stood in a circle of thirty six-year-olds and kept them, several fathers and their teacher, a kind, grey-haired matron named Gladys Messicks, mesmerized for over an hour and a half with harrowing stories of lost kids, lost dogs, lost dads, kittens up trees, kittens down manholes, and weird men who tried to get innocent little children into their cars. "*Never!*" Deke's deep voice had boomed out, "*Never* get in a stranger's car!"

And afterwards, with almost three dozen kids clamoring and crowding around for his attention, Deke had picked her up and held her next to him and gave her that smile that made her realize that she was a part of this exciting life of his: a part of the stories, a part of him.

"So, you now know more about me than you cared to know. Now it's your turn," Jessi said as the waitress cleared the table around them and refilled their coffee cups for the fifth time.

Cutler laughed. "Not much to tell, really. My dad was the Sheriff of Grace County way back when. He was a good man, but he was a lot different about the job than your dad was. He left it at work. We weren't allowed to discuss it unless he brought it up, which he never did. My mom was as good as they come. I'm a total momma's boy," Cutler stared silently into his coffee cup for a moment before continuing. "They were both killed when I was in junior high. They were driving to watch me play in a basketball game and their car was broad sided by a hay truck that ran a stop sign. I was raised by my Uncle Merlin and Aunt Stella."

They nodded at each other across the table, silently recognizing their unspoken bond of shared pain and loneliness.

As Jessi pulled the unmarked Ford under the alcove of the Howard Johnson's, Cutler opened the door and started to climb out. Thanks for all your help." He hesitated briefly before stepping out, not wanting to go into the empty hotel room, but not wanting to make a mistake by suggesting they extend their time together with a drink at the hotel bar.

"Sorry we didn't have any luck," Jessi said. "We'll try again in the morning."

Cutler nodded. "Goodnight," he said, closing the car door.

"Goodnight, sheriff." Jessi watched as Cutler entered the brightly lighted lobby and the door closed behind him. He hadn't looked back.

Cutler watched from the lobby window as Jessi's car pulled away before taking the elevator to his eighth floor room where he pulled his boots off and slumped down on the king size bed in the stuffy darkness. As he laid back against the headboard, he grabbed the TV remote off the nightstand and thumbed through forty-six channels three times before settling on ESPN where an Australian football game was underway. Muting the sound he found himself again thinking of Angie, but when he tried to picture her in his mind, he couldn't summon her familiar image. Jessi Cole's face was there instead and, try as he might, Angie wouldn't appear.

He felt a hint of panic that quickly turned to guilt. Sitting up on the edge of the bed and pulling his wallet from his rear pocket, Cutler removed the well-worn photo of her from the cloudy plastic covering and smiled as he remembered Angie's face the first time he had seen her. He had been finishing up his Bachelor of Science Degree at the University of Texas and after four long years of lecture halls and labs he had felt he was due for a change. When the Marine Corps offered him a commission as a second lieutenant and guaranteed him entry into flight school, his lifelong goal to fly jets was within his grasp, and he jumped at the chance. He had met Angie Daniels at the University library, falling instantly and deeply in love with the beautiful brunette from El Paso who was enrolled in the University's archeology program. Angie hadn't been the least bit dissuaded by John's six year Marine Corps commitment, and the couple had signed their marriage license the same day John had signed his enlistment papers.

The newlyweds had one wonderful month together before Angie drove him to the airport in the turquoise 1957 Chevy four-door hardtop that his Uncle Merlin and Aunt Stella had purchased for him in high school. Angie had dropped him off and had driven away, laughing, not wanting him to see the tears that were pouring down her cheeks.

John never saw Angie again. She was killed four weeks later, struck down in a crosswalk as she was walking to the post office carrying a package addressed to his Quantico, Virginia training battalion. The contents of the package were scattered in the street: homemade chocolate chip cookies, a book of poetry with passages underlined, and a pair of wool socks. The brown paper wrapping was covered with lipstick kisses.

The thirty-four-year-old driver of the car that hit her had an alcohol level of .21 and claimed he didn't see either the red light or the young woman in the crosswalk. He wept at the scene but whether for himself or for the death he caused, no one knew or cared. Angie had been twenty-two-years of age and pregnant.

John was given thirty days leave to arrange Angie's funeral and get his life in order.

Returning to Grace County, he typed out a letter of resignation from the Marine Corps and addressed the envelope to his commanding officer. Before mailing it, he had ridden his horse to the highest point on the ranch and was sitting under a tree bawling like a baby when his Uncle Merlin found him. The two of them sat there in silence for a few minutes before Merlin cleared his throat, and spoke. "Johnny, don't waste your life looking back at what might have been. That's out of your hands. You just pick yourself a spot somewhere," he said, pointing off at the clear Texas horizon, " and you work yourself toward it. If you'll do that, if you promise me that you'll keep your eyes and your heart open and facing dead ahead, I promise you that you'll find what you need to get through this life. If you won't do that, and you decide to live back there," he waved his thumb over his shoulder, "in the past, you'll make yourself one miserable, bitter, sorry sonofabitch. The choice is yours, son."

Merlin had climbed back on his horse and had ridden off, leaving his brokenhearted nephew to make his decision.

John returned to Quantico and finished Officer's Candidate School and six months of infantry basic training with little recollection of having done so. He went on to the Naval Air Station at Pensacola, Florida where he threw himself into flight training with reckless abandon. Early on in flight training one of Cutler's fellow airmen nicknamed him "Hermit" because of John's habit of going off by himself rather than joining his fellow airmen at the local bars. The nickname stuck and became Cutler's call sign. During his training, his instructors quickly noted not only his obvious flying talent but also his propensity for taking unnecessary risks. He was reprimanded several times by his instructors and, on one occasion, was nearly washed out of the program because of his reckless behavior. The Marines wanted their pilots as tough and courageous as possible, but they didn't want them foolish and dead. Cutler's commander, a hardened Viet Nam-era pilot named Jeff Green, knew that John was hurting inside and was prepared to give him some time. Colonel Green's patience was rewarded. John's pain was eventually covered by scar tissue, and he won his gold wings, graduating sixth in a class of 124 pilots and getting his chance in the sky.

John spent a total of six years in the Marine Corps, flying twin-tailed F18s out of bases all over the world and launching off aircraft carriers in four of the world's seven seas. The last year of his Marine Corp service saw Hermit fly 134 sorties in the short, but devastating, Operation Desert Shield in the Gulf War. When the war ended, so did John's enlistment. John Cutler was ready to return to Grace County.

In the six years he'd been away, he found that very little had changed in his hometown. The changes were within himself. It could be said that he'd grown up, but it was more than that. There was a demeanor about him, a controlled intensity in his look, that caused people to pause but not question.

After being home for only two weeks, John once again signed papers; this time he was entering the Law Enforcement Academy in Austin for a six-month training program.

After the six months, Merlin and Stella drove to Austin to attend John's graduation ceremony where John gave Merlin the honor of pinning on his star. It was a special moment for both of them.

John returned once again to Grace County, this time as a fulltime deputy under Sheriff Clayton Pruitt. John was a natural for the work and quickly discovered something about himself that he'd never previously given any thought. He liked people, and he especially liked the people of Grace County. His philosophy of justice was simple: you commit a crime you pay the consequences. He dealt out justice impartially. If someone asked John to look the other way, which had become a Grace County tradition under Pruitt, they asked only once. While Sheriff Pruitt and many of his deputies were surly and unpredictable, Cutler was firm but fair.

John quickly became a familiar and respected figure in Grace County, and if two neighbors had a problem they couldn't solve themselves, it was John they called to handle it. "He's just like his daddy was," was a phrase often heard after Cutler had settled a dispute.

Sheriff Pruitt was as politically ambitious as he was dishonest, but what doomed him with the citizens of Grace County was his humorless nature. His constituents felt they could outlast his dishonesty, but they found his sour disposition almost unbearable.

When election time came, John Cutler was handed a petition signed by over 4,000 Grace County residents asking him to run for sheriff. On the day John accepted the challenge and filed his papers with the county clerk, Clayton Pruitt wet his finger, stuck it in the wind, and promptly had his name removed from the ballot.

Over the ensuing years the people of Grace had grown used to John's fairness. They liked his easy laugh and low-keyed sense of humor; they especially appreciated that he had one. Unfortunately, since the Sandoval murder, John Cutler's sense of humor had been almost non-existent.

11.

❦

Jessi pulled away from the Howard Johnson's and quickly drove the mile and a half to the police garage to turn in Edward 42. She changed out of her uniform and within twenty-five minutes she pulled the old GMC into her apartment complex and got out. It was nearly midnight and the fatigue that had been chasing her all day was catching up as she parked the pickup and hurried through the rain to the shelter of the alcove that protected her front door. She needed a hot shower and sleep in the worst way. She stooped to retrieve Gussie's food dish and looked around for the cat. He was usually there to greet her with his tail raised, brushing against her leg as she unlocked the door.

"Gussie, I'm home. Come on kitty. Kitty, kitty, kitty!"

The fat, grey alley cat with the scarred ears had strutted into her living room the day she had moved in and never left. He was always there, but apparently not tonight. He was probably hiding from the rain somewhere safe and dry. She shrugged as she inserted the key and opened the door. She had closed and locked the door and was three steps into the darkened living room before the wet cat wrapped himself around her leg and gave her his usual, raspy meow of a greeting.

She stiffened as an alarm went off in her brain! "Somebody's in here!"

Pressing her back to the wall she removed her 9mm from her purse and strained to pick up any sound that seemed even remotely out of place.

There was only silence and the thumping of her heart. She waited a moment longer before moving cautiously to the phone and dialed 911.

"This is 911, what is the nature of your emergency?" the female dispatcher asked.

"This is Houston police officer, Jessi Cole, badge number 1145. I'm at 172 Ravine Drive, number 7. Send a patrol car here code three. There's someone in my house. I'll leave the line open." Not waiting for the dispatcher to respond, Jessi laid the phone down and moved quietly down the hall, her 9mm held at ready. Entering her darkened bedroom she heard running water and could see light radiating from under the closed bathroom door. She moved silently across the carpeted floor and took a deep breath as she reached down and turned the knob, gently nudging the bathroom door open. Steam rolled out as she took a small step into the humid room. The shower was running, and through the steam Jessi could see the outline of someone behind the frosted glass door of the shower. As she took aim with the 9mm, she kicked open the shower door and screamed, *"Freeze!"*

Lela Starr, naked and wet, jumped in alarm, pushing herself back against the wall of the shower and folding her arms over her chest for protection. "Are you crazy? What the hell are you doing? Don't point that fucking gun at me! "she screamed back at Jessi.

"What the hell am *I* doing? You're joking, right?" Jessi responded, lowering her pistol and angrily flinging a towel through the shower doorway before retreating to the bedroom where she picked up the telephone extension. "This is Officer Cole. Cancel my call for help. It was all a misunderstanding. My *psychic* stopped in unexpectedly."

Jessi hung up both phones and returned to the bedroom as an irate Lela stormed out of the bathroom wearing the towel, the Chinese tattoo on her shoulder, a lady bug tattoo on her hip, and her wounded pride. "You're the one who was looking for me, remember?"

"Get your naked wet ass dressed, now!" Jessi exploded.

"I can't!"

"What do you mean, you can't?"

Lela tilted her head upwards like many women do when they are caught in an awkward position and use their chin as a shield. "My clothes happen to be in your washer and dryer."

Jessi slumped down tiredly on her bed. It was going to be a very long night.

Five hours and several loads of laundry later, Jessi and Lela were waiting in a Hall of Justice interview room. The lime green walls of the small room seemed to mock the exhausted Jessi. She yawned and checked her watch. It was 6:47 A.M.

"Maybe your friend got lost." Lela said, calmly arranging her assortment of crystals and minerals on a well-used black velvet cloth that she had removed from her ever present carry all.

"No, he'll be here."

"See this green stone right here?" Lela said, holding a polished stone up to catch the light. "It represents mother earth and all living things; it's a healing stone. The blue lapis lazuli here promotes peace and harmony."

An uninterested "Mmmm," was Jessi's only response as she yawned yet again and opening her purse, fumbled around irritably before removing a bottle of Excedrin and dumping three tablets into the palm of her hand.

"I use this one for headaches and tension," Lela said, holding out the polished green stone to Jessi. "Here, hold it against your temple and..."

"No, thanks, I'll stick with three of these little white ones," Jessi shot back, quickly swallowing the pills and chasing them down with a cup of lukewarm water from the gurgling cooler in the corner.

Lela watched her with a studied interest. "You're expending an awful lot of negative ions right now. Put your head back and breathe deeply through your nose. Like this," she said, leaning her head back and inhaling deeply.

"You followed me home the night before last, didn't you?" Jessi asked.

"Did I? I don't recall doing that," she said, picking up her green healing stone and rubbing it against her wrist. "I think I'm getting arthritis. This seems to help."

"You followed me home. That's how you knew where I lived."

"Whatever explanation makes you feel good, go for it," Lela answered.

Jessi could feel her anger growing again. "You know, you're being pretty casual for someone facing a breaking and entering charge."

"I didn't break in. You were looking for me, remember? I let myself in through an open window," she said, retrieving Jessi's business card from her cloth bag and waving it in her face. "How was I to know you were on a materialistic, my property trip. I needed a shower and... I had a...a little laundry to do."

"A little laundry? You did nothing but laundry all damn night!" Jessi shook her head in exasperation. "Do you usually break into someone's home when you feel the need to be clean? How often is that, three, four times a year?"

"Is it my fault your overfed cat was wet and wanted in? Maybe I should turn you in to the animal protection league, poor neglected, fat little cat."

"Hey, listen up. Insult me all you want, but leave my cat out of this. Gussie is not fat."

As the two women moved nose-to-nose, Lela shook her head mockingly. "I really don't bring out your best qualities, do I? Look at you; your aura is all over the place."

Before Jessi could respond the door opened, and Cutler came in juggling three Styrofoam cups and placed one in front of Jessi. "Cream with no sugar for you, and..." He handed a cup to Lela. "Green tea, just like you ordered," he said, removing his jacket and hanging it over the back of a chair. He sat down across from Lela and, removing the lid from his own cup, took a welcome sip of hot black coffee." Now, let's you and me talk about Michelle Sandoval."

Lela took a sip of her tea, but remained quiet.

"Her friends called her Mickey," Cutler continued, watching Lela's eyes for any kind of reaction.

He got it.

Lela choked as she swallowed the hot tea. "Ohmygawd! You guys really found her? She's real, isn't she?" she blurted, turning to Jessi with a sardonic grin that quickly dissolved into tears that welled in her eyes and poured down her cheeks. "I told you she was real! I told everybody who would listen that she was real! I am not fucking crazy!"

Jessi had quickly given up on using tears as a barometer of emotion during interrogations. Over the last year she had met dozens of women, and also a few men, who could pour out emotions and tears like they were turning on a Slurpy machine. Jessi removed a Kleenex from her purse and handed it to Lela while exchanging looks with Cutler. His shrug told her he was thinking the same thing.

"Do you mind if I look at your drawings?" Cutler asked, pointing at the sketchpad sticking out of Lela's carryall.

"Knock yourself out," she said, handing Cutler the pad. She seemed oblivious to them as she dug deeper in the carryall and brought out a stick of incense and a throwaway lighter. After lighting the incense, she pushed her chair back with a *screech* and moved around the room spreading the smoky aroma in what must have been a soothing ritual for her troubled soul.

Jessi's double sneeze brought her back to reality. "Do you mind putting that out?"

"This incense is organically based. Your reaction to it speaks volumes about your immune system as well as your inhibitions."

Jessi was unimpressed.

As the women glared at each other defiantly, Cutler held up Lela's sketchpad at a page where she had written the number "1305" over and over.

"Tell us about this number you saw in your..." Cutler paused searching for the right word, "visualization."

"It's a number. What about it?"

"Where was the number?" Cutler asked. "Was it written on a piece of paper, a license number maybe?"

"I don't know, I ..." Lela retreated inwardly, searching for the familiar thread to follow that would allow her to relive the frightening images that weren't her own. She shrank away, not wanting to subject herself to the pain that both was and wasn't hers, but there was no retreating as her mind unlocked the door, and the terror replayed in her brain for the hundredth time. She saw a featureless silhouette carry a heavy plastic bag over his shoulder and dump it unceremoniously into a trash dumpster!

Lela's eyes rolled part way back in her skull before her head slumped at an odd angle and a series of tortured groans escaped from her throat.

For the next minute and a half Jessi and Cutler leaned back in their chairs, sipped their coffee and watched the strange performance with the same interest as a cat watching a hand moving under a blanket.

"This a put on or does she have some kind of a medical condition?" Cutler asked.

Jessi shrugged. Lela's groans were oddly familiar to her and made her increasingly uncomfortable until she realized where she had heard them before. They were the noises she, herself, made when she woke herself up while trying to flee from a threatening nightmare.

Lela slowly allowed herself to return to the small room, sweating and exhausted and, seeing the skeptical looks exchanged between the cops, retreated again, but this time to her normal bluster. "Skeptics abound on tree lined lanes, but a true believer shall walk through hell to deliver us," she said in a sing song rhythm that seemed oddly incongruent in the cramped room.

"You were about to tell us about the number," Jessi reminded her.

Although her hands were trembling, Lela picked up her pad and quickly sketched a garbage dumpster complete with the number "1305" stenciled on the side and tossed it toward Cutler. "There, is that what you wanted?"

Cutler looked at the sketch and then back at Lela. He let the silence lengthen before passing the pad to Jessi. The stillness in the small room lengthened as Jessi studied the drawing before finally exchanging a look with Cutler. They knew that there was no way Lela could have known that Michelle Sandoval's brutally violated body was found in a dumpster with the number 1305 on it unless she was somehow involved in putting that body there.

Jessi acknowledged Cutler's unspoken message with a subtle nod. This was his case, but it was *her* territory. She'd brought the suspect in, and he was giving her first crack. Jessi decided to try tact.

"Lela, everybody gets into things they can't control. I mean, sometimes we find ourselves in situations where things happen that we don't like and we might feel like we're in danger if we say anything to-"

"What the hell are you babbling about? I wasn't there."

Lela's pronouncement seemed to float around the room like incense smoke.

"Oh, silly me; now I get it. Tinker Bell with a badge and the Sheriff of Nothingham here think I had something to do with Mickey's death? Well you're both full of shit!" Lela blurted, giving her pent-up anger free rein.

Lela was furious as she began stuffing her crystals and polished minerals back into her large carryall. "You think I like being here – that I like being laughed at?" She pointed in the general direction of the squad room. "You think I don't know what those fascist fuckers in there call me? What you two are thinking? And no, asshole, I do not have a medical condition!"

Midway through Lela's tirade, Lt. Sakelaris cracked the door and stuck his head in. "Can I see you folks a minute?"

Lela stood defiantly. "Feel free to see them all you want. I'm done talking. I'm out of here!"

Jessi grabbed the larger woman by the arm and forced her back into the chair. "Sorry to wound your sensitive psychic pride, but you're being questioned in a murder case, not to mention being a suspect in a breaking and entering that took place at my residence earlier today. You're not going anywhere. Now sit down, and stay down!"

Lela glared. "I'm not saying another word without my attorney present."

Jessi looked at her thoughtfully before exiting with Cutler.

Outside the interview room, Sakelaris removed a computer print-out sheet from a file folder. "Running the name Lela Starr I came up with nothing. Running her vehicle tags I got a hit on one Lela *Haley*. She's been through the system for petty theft, shoplifting, defrauding an innkeeper, under the influence, possession of marijuana, driving off without paying for gas, possession of LSD for sale, DUI, and being a public nuisance. I could go on, but listen to this; your psychic's real claim to fame is being a scofflaw. She's got close to twenty grand in outstanding parking tickets on that van of hers."

"Then she's got paper out?" Jessi asked.

Sakelaris nodded. "She's got a no bail warrant just on the parking tickets and five grand on a DUI failure to appear. Have fun," the lieutenant said as he handed the file to Jessi and walked away.

"Thanks, Lieu," Jessi said.

Sakelaris nodded over his shoulder and reentered the squad room.

Jessi pulled back the curtain covering the one-way mirror that afforded them a view into the interview room. Lela was sitting lotus fashion on the floor, her eyes closed, her hands resting palms up on her knees, as the sickly sweet smelling incense wafted around her. Jessi and Cutler watched Lela slowly turning one of the crystals in her left hand before closing her eyes and rubbing it across her temple.

Jessi shook her head unconsciously. "I'll admit she's as weird as they come, but I don't see her as the cold-blooded killer type, do you?"

Cutler was less skeptical. "After some of the things I've witnessed, I'm not surprised by much. All I know is your house guest here is the only lead I have, and I think she's up to her hairy armpits in this. "

Cutler turned away from the glass to look directly into Jessi's eyes. "So, how do we get her to play ball without scaring her away? She's definitely a loose cannon. Any good ideas?"

The two of them exchanged a long look before Jessi raised the file folder Sakelaris had just given them. "Maybe."

When Jessi and Cutler re-entered the room, Lela made a show of standing and extinguishing her incense with her fingertips before carefully replacing it in her carryall. Jessi was expressionless as she opened the file folder and handed Lela two legal papers.

"What's this?" Lela asked, feigning total ignorance of what she was looking at.

"Lela, those documents are bench warrants with your name on them."

"For what?" Lela snapped belligerently. "And I don't think you know me well enough to be on a first name basis. I'm not stupid, you know?" Lela almost spit the words at her.

"Okay, Ms. Starr; I'm sorry, I meant to say Ms. *Haley*. Don't play stupid games with me, and I won't treat you like you're stupid, got it?" Jessi spit back, grabbing the papers from Lela and waving them for effect. "You know what these are as well as I do. And you also know that after you leave this comfy little room here, you are going to the county lockup for quite a long time. I'd suggest a little less smart ass and a little more cooperation. Are we communicating here, or do I have to talk to one of your rocks?" Jessi snapped, snatching Lela's polished green stone from the velvet cloth and offering it a mock greeting. "Hell-ooo in there! Anybody home?"

Lela remained stubbornly mute for a moment before sighing in defeat and holding her hands up in surrender. "Look, I don't want to go to jail. The food is full of MSG and other additives, and I don't sleep well. Besides, they won't let me have my things," she added, pulling the well-worn carryall protectively against her chest.

"Yeah, jail is a bitch alright, but... life's full of adjustments," Jessi said, pulling a set of handcuffs from the leather pouch behind her back. "Let's go."

"Maybe we can work something out?" Lela suggested.

"With me? No way. You're going to jail. With him...?" Jessi said as she nodded toward Cutler, "I don't know. You'll have to talk to the sheriff about that."

Lela turned to face Cutler. "What do you want from me?"

Cutler took a sip of coffee before he spoke. "You like to fly?"

12.

At 5,500 feet the clear air was deceptively unstable, causing Lela and Jessi to gasp in unison, as the Cessna seemed to fall out from underneath them. Lela clamped one hand onto the back of Cutler's seat as the other dug into his shoulder.

"Sorry ladies, the rainstorm last night stirred things up pretty good. Don't worry, we're perfectly safe."

With that said the plane hit another air pocket and dropped sharply, causing Lela to increase the pressure on Cutler's shoulder. "To hell with it! Take me back! I'll do the jail time on the damn parking tickets!" Lela shouted as she leaned forward, nearly loosing her sunglasses as she shrieked in his right ear. "I'm going to sue you for every cent you've got if you don't land this fucking puddle jumper, and let me out!"

"Relax, we're almost there."

Jessi was sitting in the right front seat, next to him, fighting her own growing queasiness with deep breaths. Cutler gave her a reassuring smile. "I'll go higher–try to find some better air." Jessi forced a smile and nodded as Cutler reached down and turned the trim adjustment wheel, giving the small craft a slight nose up attitude.

As the airplane made its gradual assent Cutler noticed Jessi's interest in the passing landscape and smiled proudly. "Everything you see out there is part of my jurisdiction."

"That's amazing, " Jessi said,

Lela shook her head in disgust. "Who came up with the name Grace for this place? There isn't anything down there but mesquite trees."

"There's a story there," Cutler replied.

"I figured there might be. It was only a rhetorical question. You don't have to answer it," Lela said.

"Way I heard it," Cutler said, ignoring her, "the State Legislature had to come up with one more county." He held up his hand. "Don't ask me why, some political thing, probably. Anyway, the folks from Brown, Comanche, Mills, San Saba, McCulloch, Eastland, and Callahan Counties all got together and threw in land from their counties that weren't good for anything. Legend has it that after they made the deal, they all went out to celebrate with a big dinner. Before they commenced eating, someone offered *grace*, thanking the powers that be for letting them get rid of the land."

"Hey, Hermit," Lela snapped, "if you could get your make believe F-18 on the ground before you two join the mile high club, I'd appreciate it."

Lela's offhand, F18 remark went unnoticed by Jessi, but it caused Cutler to stiffen in his seat. When he turned to judge her expression, she had removed her dark glasses, and her eyes locked onto his in a challenge. Feeling slightly unsettled, Cutler turned back to the front, his eyes darting over the instrument panel before spotting the service patch of the 101st Airwing he had removed from his flight suit and pinned to the headliner. That would explain the F18 remark, but the reference to his call sign, "Hermit," unnerved him. A magician's trick, no doubt, but a damn good one.

Two hours and twelve minutes after lifting off from Houston, the Cessna settled down softly on the Grace airstrip and taxied back to Kenny's Flying Service. Ten minutes later the three of them were crammed, along with their luggage, into the sheriff's Blazer heading south on County Road Six.

They rode in silence for a few minutes, Jessi and Lela enjoying the relative stability of the Blazer in comparison with the Cessna.

Lela's voice broke the silence. "By the way, Officer Cole, what'd you do with fat Gussie?" Lela asked.

"Fat Gussie?" Cutler looked curious.

"My cat. And he's not fat, he's just big boned. Aaron, in the apartment above me, takes care of him when I can't make it home. Feeds him fresh catfish. Gussie loves it." She yawned and Cutler noticed.

"You okay now?"

"I'm fine. It's just nice to be on the ground."

"We'll get you checked into Velma's, and you can get some rest."

Cutler pulled the Blazer to a stop at an intersection. He glanced into the rearview mirror at Lela. Her dark glasses hid her eyes from him. Almost on impulse he made a left hand turn onto the on ramp of State Route 12 that ran as a main artery from Brownsville to Grace. The four lane divided highway took the place of the old Route 12. A twisting two lane stretch of blacktop that had earned the nickname "Cemetery Road" because of the dozens of small white crosses scattered along its 72 mile route in memory of auto accident victims. The new roadway was a particular godsend to long-haul truck drivers.

As the Blazer moved swiftly along the highway, Lela felt herself becoming agitated. Her face felt suddenly hot and flushed, and she felt dizzy. She laid her head back in hopes of shaking the growing feeling of dread. Then it hit her. She was looking into Mickey's dead eyes, and reflected in them was a highway road sign that read:

SHILOH ROAD - REST STOP - NEXT RIGHT

159

"Take the next exit," Lela directed. Her voice was flat, emotionless.

Although Cutler was hoping for some reaction, he hesitated, not sure he heard her right. "What'd you say?"

"I said take the next exit. The rest stop."

Cutler's heart rate accelerated. Jessi noticed his tension but didn't react; knowing intuitively that something crucial was playing out.

The Blazer moved past a half-dozen parked trailer truck rigs before pulling to a stop in a row of cars next to the rest room complex. Without saying a word Lela opened the back door, stepped out, and walked slowly away from the Blazer.

"This is where they found Michelle Sandoval's body?" Jessi asked.

Cutler nodded as they climbed out of the Blazer and walked to where Lela had paused next to the rest room. She looked pale and shaken as she clutched her quartz necklace.

"What's going on, Lela?" Jessi asked.

"Can't you feel it?"

"Feel what?" The only thing Jessi felt was the scorching glare of the midday sun and the rumbling of the big rigs speeding past on the nearby highway.

Lela half turned and froze her with a look. "If I have to tell you what, you obviously don't feel it." She walked away and disappeared around the south corner of the rest rooms.

By the time they caught up, Lela was standing in front of a trash dumpster that was sitting on a slab of concrete behind the building. As Cutler and Jessi watched, Lela walked to the dumpster and touched the large numbers 1-2-2-1 stenciled on the side.

"This isn't the same dumpster, but this is where they left Mickey," she said, turning to face them.

Cutler showed little or no expression. This was the first thing she had said that was wrong. He let the disappointment dissipate before responding.

"This is the place, huh?"

Lela nodded. "Yeah, except..." she turned and, looking over Cutler's shoulder, pointed toward the highway. "The dumpster was over there by the fence."

Bingo! At the time of the discovery of Michele Sandoval's body, the concrete pad had not yet been poured, and the trash dumpsters were placed alongside the fence. Cutler was both elated and angry: elated that the thin thread of evidence he had been following wasn't broken and angry that this woman standing so calmly before him had probably participated in the vicious murder of a defenseless young girl. As he looked at Lela, he swallowed the trace of bile that rose in his throat.

"I'm thirsty," Lela said.

"There's a soda machine around the corner. What can I get you?"

"Bottled water."

Lela moved away from them, crossing the lawn and walking toward the fence.

"She was right about the dumpster being over there?" Jessi asked.

Cutler nodded. "There's no way in hell she could have known that unless she was here that night. Now all we have to do is get her to admit it," Cutler said as he turned and started off before pausing and turning back to Jessi. "How about you? You want something to drink?"

"Diet Coke, if they have it."

"You've got it," he said and walked away. As Cutler disappeared around the corner, Jessi crossed the narrow stretch of dry grass and walked the thirty yards to where Lela was standing close to the fence.

"You really think this is the place?"

Lela paused to see if she could detect even a hint of sarcasm in Jessi's tone or her question. She couldn't.

"I don't go looking for these things. They come to me. I...it's hard to explain. I don't exactly *see* things, I... I *experience* things. I don't understand how, and I don't understand why. It just happens."

"Was Michelle Sandoval killed here, at the rest area?

"No. They killed her somewhere else," Lela said, turning in a slow circle as she clutched her quartz necklace tightly. "But it was somewhere around here. I can't really feel something coming from ..." Her voice trailed off, and she shook her head as if confused.

"You said *they*. How many people are involved, Lela? Two, three?"

"I don't know, but I'll tell you this," Lela said as she stopped, turning to face Jessi. Tears were rolling down her face, and she hurried to wipe them away. "It breaks my heart that you think I'm involved."

Jessi watched as Lela hurried back to the Blazer. "It breaks my heart, too," Jessi said softly as she followed.

Cutler was feeding dollar bills into the Coke machine when he saw Charley Weed walk away from his old truck, wheeling a hand dolly of ten-pound plastic ice bags, and approach the shaded alcove. Written on the back panel of the converted milk delivery van was:

SHORT FALLS ICE AND MEAT COMPANY- BANCROFT, TEXAS

"How ya doing, Charley?" Cutler asked as the vending machine took his dollar and dispensed a bottle of water in return.

"Hey, Johnny, good, good," Charley replied, his deep voice a little thick as he took Cutler's hand in a surprisingly gentle grip with his ham sized, rough hands before unlocking the nearby ice storage unit and filling it in silence. Charley was huge, six-foot-five, and despite his expanding midsection, was as solid as a rock. A fact he attributed to hefting ice bags six hours a day, seven days a week, fifty-two weeks a year. Charley Weed stocked every ice machine in Grace County and had done so for as long as Cutler could remember. The big man and his truck were a fixture around Grace County.

"Way this heat's on us I'll bet you're going through a lot of that cold stuff, huh?" Cutler asked, feeding the machine another dollar bill, but it kicked back out. He turned George Washington around, and the machine snatched it away.

Charley was more than just a little slow in most subjects, but ice was something he knew about. "Ice business ain't what it used to be, Johnny. Nowadays folks have got their own ice machine in the door of their refridge. Darn things chunk out cubes faster'n I can count. Even grinds 'em up, for pete's sake."

"I hear that. Got one myself. I love it."

"See, that's my point," Charley replied slowly. "Yes sir, everything's changing now."

"You've always got the meat business," Cutler replied as the vending machine kicked out the second of two Diet Cokes.

Charley's deep, slow, "Har, har, har," carried a trace of bitterness. "Always got meat."

Cutler laughed, but Charley wasn't joking. "How's Kathryn, doing? Hear she got married again." Cutler asked, referring to Charley's niece whom he had gone to high school with.

Charley's tone seemed to stiffen slightly. "I reckon they're doing alright."

Jessi appeared around the corner, and Cutler handed her a Diet Coke. Charley looked at her and nodded, tipping his sweat stained "Short Falls Ice" baseball hat at her. "Ma'am."

"Hello," Jessi said with a smile.

Cutler introduced Jessi, leaving out the fact that she was a police officer, and then turned with Jessi to return to the Blazer. "Take care of yourself, Charley."

"Wait a minute, Johnny," Charley said as he hurried back to his truck, opened a side panel, and quickly returned with a package wrapped in white butcher paper that he pushed into Cutler's hands. "I got some nice knuckle bones for that little dog of yours."

"Thanks, Charley, Henry will appreciate these." Cutler said.

Returning to the Blazer, they found Lela leaning against the front fender, looking off at the never-ending parade of big rigs roaring past on the highway. Cutler handed her the bottled water, and then the three of them climbed back into the Blazer and drove into Grace.

Velma's Motel was located three blocks from downtown Grace. The line of twenty-five freshly painted white with blue trim rooms sat fifty yards back from Center Street, sheltered by a long row of live oak trees. Velma's rooms offered exhausted truck drivers, and an occasional tourist, a warm welcome and a comfortable bed for $45.00 a night. You could find cheaper rooms around but not cleaner ones. Velma's enjoyed a loyal following amongst the long-haul truck drivers and traveling salesmen, and her rooms filled to capacity almost nightly during the summer months, allowing her to flip on her red

No Vacancy, Sorry Friend

sign and turn in early almost every night. Velma hated being woken up in the wee hours and was known to turn on the *no vacancy* sign without a single car or truck being in the parking lot during the slower winter months.

Jessi and Lela yawned, simultaneously, as they waited for Cutler to return from the office. They were leaning against the driver's side of the Blazer, their suitcases at their feet, when an old man and woman drove slowly past in a torpedo tailed 1950 Studebaker and eyed them suspiciously. A scarred, old dog with hairless ears looked out the rear window of the car, staring also.

"What are you staring at, ya old fart?" Lela shouted.

The couple avoided her look and drove away, leaving behind a soft blue exhaust cloud that slowly dissipated. Lela shook her head. "I couldn't live in a hick town like this. Swear to God, I'd go nuts in two days."

Jessi took a deep breath. "Air smells good though, kind of like peppermint."

"That isn't peppermint, honey, that's pennyroyal." The voice belonged to seventy-four-year-old Velma Nash who approached, walking alongside Cutler. "Old Ed Mori is cutting his back field across the way. He let it get plumb full of pennyroyal. The cows hate it, but I don't," she said, removing two room keys from her apron. "You ladies are right here, numbers seven and eight." As she talked Velma moved to unlock the rooms. "Nothing fancy but they're clean."

"Looks like the Houston Hilton to me," Lela said.

Velma was so busy talking she didn't hear Lela's remark. "I know they're clean 'cause I clean every one of 'em each and every day, including the showers and toilets. My husband, Lee, God rest his soul, used to help me, but now I do it all myself, and I've got a stainless steel hip to boot. I ain't complainin', mind you, just sharin'. Ya'll come up to the office if you need anything. I've got some dinner coupons up there if you're interested," she said as she handed Jessi the room keys. Jessi smiled, "Thank you."

"Thanks, Velma," Cutler added as the grey-haired woman turned and walked back to the office. Jessi picked up her bag and started toward room eight when Lela cut her off.

"No you don't," Lela said, grabbing the keys from her hand and confiscating the one to number eight. She thrust the key to number seven back into Jessi's hand and quickly entered room eight before Jessi could respond. "I avoid sevens at all costs," Lela said, closing the door firmly in Jessi's surprised face.

"Don't play craps then!" Jessi said loudly just as the door reopened and a plastic

Do Not Disturb

sign appeared on the doorknob before it quickly slammed shut.

The Sheriff nodded back toward Lela's door. "How should we handle this with her?"

"I think we should give her a good night's sleep and then try to shake something loose in the morning."

Cutler nodded. "Agreed. Well, I'll get going. You must be exhausted."

"Not really, I'm still a little keyed up from the plane ride." Not wanting to admit, even to herself, that she wanted to spend more time in Cutler's company.

"Tell you what. You showed me your office, I'll return the favor and show you mine. Give you a glimpse into the intriguing world of small-town law enforcement."

"Let's go," Jessi said, setting her bag inside room seven and shutting the door before nodding toward Lela's room. "You think she'll be okay?"

"I'll get someone out here to keep an eye on her," Cutler said as they got back into the Blazer and pulled out.

Deputy Kiko Avila looked up from the burglary report he was writing and noticed that Red Cordell hadn't changed positions in over an hour. He just sat at his desk staring at the monitor of the new computer. Every few minutes he'd glance down at the instruction book, then return his unblinking gaze to the screen that displayed a vast and confusing field of program icons.

"You get it figured out yet?" Kiko asked, standing and moving around the desk to look over Red's shoulder. Kiko was tall and thin with an engaging smile that revealed straight white teeth and highlighted his dark, Hispanic eyes and jet-black hair.

"No," was Red's terse reply. In a daring moment earlier in the day, he had attempted to use the mouse to move an icon and the machine had frozen. The blinking cursor had disappeared, and now it refused to reappear, and Red was sure he had damaged beyond repair the brand new machine that the boss had entrusted to his care. Red glanced up at Kiko, an unspoken plea for help in his eyes. "I lost the mouse thing again."

"The cursor you mean?"

"No, I'm the curser here. Want to hear a couple of fucking choice ones?" Red flared.

"Don't look at me, partner, I didn't lose your cursor," Kiko said. "You probably ruined the damn thing. You know how sensitive these machines are. In fact," Kiko said, sniffing the air for effect, "I smell burning plastic. I think you might have over expanded your ROM input lead and burned the rotating RAM accelerator up! God sakes, Red, the boss is gonna *shit!*"

"I don't smell plastic!" Red said, his light skin glowing redder by the second.

Red Cordell had arrived in Grace County with the rodeo thirty years ago this coming September. A brash twenty-six-year-old rodeo clown with two tours in Viet Nam under his Marine Corps belt, entrusted with the responsibility of protecting fallen cowboys from the slashing horns and rock hard hooves of wild-eyed, bucking bulls. He loved the excitement, knew most of the bulls personally, and had saved many a bull rider's butt from a ton and a half of snarling, snorting muscle and flesh coming straight at them. That's when Red would dart in, giving the bull a sharp slap on the muzzle, or a twist of the horns, to distract the enraged animal and give the floundering rider a split second to escape before he, himself, dived into his barrel or scrambled over the high arena fence to safety. Over the years Red had been stomped a dozen times and gored more than once. The young studs could have the spotlight of the eight-second ride; he liked being in the ring face-to-face with the bull. The rodeo was his life, and he could see no further than the next one, until a huge Brahma bull named *Johnny Hawk* entered his life at the Grace County Fair Grounds.

He was in the ring, his attention on a cocky rookie cowboy named Jeremy Hansen. Jeremy had the misfortune of drawing the never before ridden Johnny Hawk in the opening go around. The bull was so mean and cantankerous that even Red and his partner, a wild-eyed clown from Idaho named Cory Romriell, got butterflies as they watched him burst into the chute. Johnny Bumpus, Johnny Hawk's proud owner, didn't think much of rookie Jeremy Hansen's swagger, so he ratcheted up the cinch an extra tug on Johnny Hawk's sensitive, bowling ball sized testicles.

Looking through the slats in the chute gate, Red could see the pain in the bull's eyes condense into pure fury. He had felt a jolt of apprehension in that split second before the gate flew open. It was over quickly as Jeremy guessed wrong and leaned forward. The bull guessed right and went dead left, leaving the stunned cowboy momentarily suspended in air, his hand locked under the cinch rope. A split second later the young bull rider's legs were dangling helplessly under the bull's massive midsection and his head was bobbing precariously close to Johnny Hawk's lethal hooves as the bull whipped Jeremy in a tight circle.

Red flew into action, his foolish clown costume flapping with jangling bells, as he darted in, smacked the bull on the nose, and then, throwing himself onto the back of the bull, managed to free Jeremy's hand from the cinch rope. As Cory Romriell and several cowboys rushed in to pull the stunned cowboy to safety, the inflamed Johnny Hawk turned his attention to Red. He hooked one of his stubby horns behind the clown's knee and flipped him like a limp dish rag over the seven-foot-high fence and onto the soft black dirt in front of the grandstand. When Red opened his eyes he found himself looking into the blue eyes of the then Grace County Sheriff, John Cutler, John's father.

"I'll tell ya this, son, you got enough balls to jump in on that bull like that, you'd make one hell of a cop. What do you say? I need a deputy. You need a job?"

Red still worked the rodeo circuit in his spare time, clowning at high school competitions. It was one of his great enjoyments. Clowning and law enforcement— somehow the two very different activities gave balance to his life. Then the computer arrived.

"All you've got to do is re boot the thing," Kiko said reaching for the computer.

Red's powerful hand grabbed Kiko's wrist. "I'll re-boot you right in the ass if you so much as touch that machine. All it takes is one bad command and your hard drive can blow up and crash in your face."

"Who told you that?" Kiko asked.

"Jimmy."

"Jimmy Parks? The kid that digs ditches for Frank?" Kiko asked, referring to Janie's husband, Frank Cortez, who ran Grace's Water, Sewer, Street, and Park Departments.

Kiko shook his head in mock disgust. "Jimmy knows nothing about computers, Red. He does Play Station or Wii." Kiko laughed. "You're an old thing, Red, a walking antique, mi amigo, a real piece of genuine *Americana,*" he added as he walked to the counter, poured himself a cup of coffee in a misshapen, ugly gray coffee mug, and approached Janie Cortez at her communications console. "When's the Sheriff due back?" he asked her.

"He's back. And he brought two ladies back with him."

"Two ladies? What's that about?" Kiko asked.

Janie shrugged. "Something about the Sandoval case," The phone rang, and Janie took it on the Water Department line. "City of Grace Water Department. Can I help you?" Janie listened for a moment before pushing her swivel chair to the communication console where she keyed the microphone on the CB transmitter. "City Base to Water One, over."

The CB crackled as Frank's voice responded. "Water One, go Janie."

"Sounds like you've got a broken water main at 4th and Benton. Marilynn Davis said water was knee deep in her basement."

"Roger that. We're on the way," Frank responded.

"K.A.H.199 and out." Janie signed off in their usual manner. Nobody in the entire county realized that K.A.H.199 was not an FCC tag but stood for *kiss and hug 199 times*, except Janie and Frank.

As Janie disconnected from her caller, Kiko ambled over to the cloudy window of the trailer and, peering out, saw Cutler's Blazer turn off Main Street two blocks away and move toward the office. Although he would never tell him this, Kiko was glad to see that Cutler was back. Things always seemed to run smoother when the sheriff was around.

Kiko Avila and John Cutler met while both men were attending the law enforcement academy in Austin. Their personalities had complimented each other; both were disciplined, competitive, and dedicated.

After graduation from the academy, the junior college educated, bilingual Kiko had been heavily recruited by a half-dozen law enforcement agencies from all over Texas. Kiko had almost made up his mind to accept the Houston Sheriff's Department position when Cutler had invited his classmate to visit his uncle's ranch the week after graduation.

The city born and raised Kiko had never been on a horse before, but once he had learned how to hold on, he didn't want to let go or climb down. The two men had spent three solid days on horseback chasing cows from one end of the ranch to the other. Kiko rode like a wild man, always scanning the next hill. He was not a man to notice details unless it was at a crime scene, and then he noticed everything. Several times over those three days, Cutler asked him if he noticed the wildflowers, the rare cactus, or the unusual rock formations he had just ridden over. Kiko would look at him blankly before spurring his horse into motion and heading for the next hill.

Cutler rode the hills at a slower pace, enjoying the subtle nuances of the ever-changing landscape. His Uncle Merlin had taught him to appreciate the indigenous wildlife, and he could provide you with the scientific names of most of the plants the horses pounded over. He enjoyed seeing the little bluebonnets in bloom, as well as the deer skittering through the cedar brush and past beautiful oak and pecan trees.

On the last day of his visit to Grace County, Kiko had, at Cutler's urging, applied to the Grace County Sheriff's Department. He was hired on the spot. He then returned to the city only to pack his bags and say goodbye to his mother and father and seven brothers and sisters. In the ensuing nine years, Kiko had met and married a beautiful young Hispanic woman from San Antonio, named Helen Ciseneros. They now had two dark-haired children, eight-year-old Miguel Jr., and five-year-old Angelica. The kids were fussed over by everyone in the office, including Red and Cutler, especially at Christmas and birthdays.

As Kiko stood at the window and watched the Blazer pull in, Henry jumped up and started yapping as he hurried over to the door. Kiko wondered how the dog always knew when Cutler arrived. All cars sounded the same coming through the deep gravel of the parking lot. The little dog could be sleeping soundly, but as soon as the Blazer pulled in he was up and waiting at the door. "The boss is back! With a babe!"

"It's about time he got here," Janie said, turning away from the radio just as the door opened and Cutler and Jessi entered. Henry greeted him with a series of happy yelps. Cutler reached down and, picking Henry up, received a wet welcome as the little dog thoroughly licked his face.

"Everybody, this is Officer Jessi Cole from the Houston Police Department. During her stay with us, she is to be accorded any and all help she needs," Cutler said as he turned to introduce Jessi to the squirming dog. "This is my buddy, Henry. He came with the office."

Janie bristled as she stood and approached Jessi and Cutler. "Of course, you'd introduce the dog first."

"This is Janie Cortez. She pretty much runs things around here."

Janie smiled and extended her large, round hand. "Hardly everything, but I give it a try," Janie said proudly.

"Red Cordell and Kiko Avila." Cutler nodded in the two deputies direction.

Kiko smiled and stepped forward to shake Jessi's hand.

"I almost went to work for the Harris County Sheriff's Department up in Houston, but I decided to come here instead. Best decision I ever made," Kiko told her.

"You don't miss the big city, huh?" Jessi asked.

"Oh, every once in awhile I miss the skyline, but I wouldn't trade places with you now."

Red had stood by patiently long enough. He pumped Jessi's hand and nudged her toward his desk. "Welcome to Deep Texas, little lady. He didn't happen to bring you here to help with the computer did he?"

"Red, Officer Cole is here to assist in the Sandoval homicide investigation. She is not here to work on *your* computer."

Cutler turned back to Kiko. "Anything exciting happen while I was gone?"

"Not really. Had a little incident out at The Oasis. Ed Wells and Pete Small got into a hell of a knock-down-drag-out over some female truck driver from Brownsville. They tore up the place pretty good. Red and I had to set 'em down and let 'em reflect on their behavior awhile," Kiko said.

"Bet Red enjoyed that," Cutler said.

"Definitely. Pete made the mistake of swinging on him. It was over in, what, one, two seconds, maybe three? My buddy over there might not be too good with hard drives, but believe me he still drives hard. Oh, and old Arden Graves' dogs got out again, raised hell with a half-dozen of Dave Madison's sheep. Dave shot both dogs."

"That's too bad. She loved those dogs like they were her kids," Cutler said.

"I know. Now Arden's the one raising hell. I'll stop by and talk to her later today."

Janie moved off to take an incoming call on the police line. All eyes watched her until she turned around and held up one finger, signaling the call was not an emergency. Janie tore a hot pink sticky note from a pad and held it out to Cutler. "Hot pink call from Kathy Garlin."

Hot pink calls had become a standing joke in the trailer. The requests for Cutler's help from lonely, single women, and even a few married ones, came regularly enough that Janie had purchased a pad of hot pink sticky notes to accommodate them. They were passed back and forth among the deputies like hot potatoes.

Cutler took the note and glanced at it. "What is it this time?"

Janie raised her eyebrows. "She wants you to check on the new locks she had installed in her house."

Cutler held out the note to Kiko who immediately pushed it away. "Oh no you don't. I'm a married man. I couldn't handle a 'hot pink' call. It's all yours, boss."

Cutler scowled as he moved to where Red's eyes were locked onto the computer monitor. "Red, take care of this, will you?"

Red looked up from the monitor and winced as he took the pink slip. "No way, no how. Ms. Kathy wants *you* out there, not me."

"Come on Red, help me out on this."

"Do you have any idea how it feels to disappoint somebody by just showing up? No, of course you don't." Red stood up and wagged the note under Cutler's nose. "I'll take care of it on the way home. That way I'll get a free dinner."

"Thanks, I owe you one."

"You owe me at least two dozen," Red grumbled as he returned to the computer.

While Cutler and Red had been talking, Jessi had moved a few steps to where a large map of Grace County, with red tacks scattered on it, was mounted on the wall. She was counting the tacks when Cutler joined her.

"Those tacks represent deputies. We've got twenty-six of them spread out over 4,000 square miles." He nodded toward Kiko and Red. "The three of us try to handle things around Grace. I just got an okay to hire five more deputies," he said, taking a light blue paper flier off a nearby desk and thrusting it at her.

Jessi barely looked at it before passing it back. "I'm kind of a big-city girl, but thanks for the thought."

The police line rang again as Cutler surveyed the inside of the shabby trailer, trying to see it through Jessi's eyes. "I know it's not much, but we're trying to get a bond measure approved so we can build a new facility within a year or two."

"Yeah, and I'm trying to fit into a size eight dress, too!" Janie yelled from her console across the room. "Sheriff, Joe Myler out at The Oasis wants to yak at you," Janie said, again holding up the obligatory, non-emergency one finger.

As Cutler moved away to take the call, Jessi wandered over to where Red continued his ongoing battle with technology and glanced over his shoulder. The frustrated deputy turned toward her and shrugged help-lessly. "I lost my mouse thing. The blinker."

"The cursor, you mean?" Jessi stated.

Jessi followed the mouse cord to the rear of the CPU. It was unplugged. "This might help," she said, snapping the fitting into the port. Red's eyes brightened immediately and then flared as he guessed correctly that a certain party in the office had set him up- again. "Kiko you dirty sonofab...! Thank you, ma'am."

Kiko smiled and ducked into the rest room.

Cutler hung up the telephone and turned to Janie. "We got a 4-1-5 domestic out at the Oasis. I'm going to ride out and see what's up."

"You want me to handle it?" Red shouted from his desk. "I'll *gladly* go to get away from this darn machine."

"No, that's alright. I want to give Jessi here an insider's view of the exciting world of local law enforcement."

13.

C utler spent the ten minute ride to the Oasis pointing out local landmarks and giving Jessi a non-stop local history lesson encompassing everything from the condemned old brick courthouse that housed a dozen jail cells as well as the restless ghost of a local cow rustler named Monty Bauden to Pocatello Pablo's World's Famous Truck Stop.

"They say Pocatello Pablo makes the biggest chicken fried steak in the world."

"Really?" Jessi said, turning away slightly to hide her smile. She had the sudden urge to laugh but she fought it gamely. "So who came in second?"

"I don't rightly know," Cutler answered, feigning seriousness. "You're the first person that's ever asked that. Tell you what, though, when we get back to the trailer I'll call the folks at the chicken fried steak hall of fame and find out for you."

"That's O.K., no big deal," Jessi said before they both broke out laughing.

"I must sound like a complete idiot going on about this place."

"Not at all," Jessi said. "You just sound like a person who takes a lot of pride in where he lives. Nothing wrong with that. And besides, it's so clean here. Doesn't anybody litter?"

"Oh, hell yeah, but everybody else picks it up. Truth is, we got a local ordinance that says if you see someone litter you are within your rights to shoot them dead. "

Jessi nodded. "Sounds reasonable to me."

Cutler was so intent on watching her that he had to brake hard to avoid rear ending a pickup stopped at one of the town's three traffic lights.

"I wreck my new Blazer that wouldn't look too good in the weekly Tribune," he said, feeling his cheeks burn with embarrassment as he made a right turn and pulled to a dusty stop in the half full parking lot of The Oasis Bar and Grill.

As Cutler and Jessi climbed out of the Blazer, Joe Myler, the gravelly voiced owner and bartender walked away from a beat up, white Camaro and approached. As he did he held out his beefy hand to Cutler who shook it warmly.

"Thanks for coming out so quick, sheriff," Joe said as the hard-thumping jukebox sounds of Travis Tritt seeped from the bar.

"Joe Myler, this is Officer Jessi Cole from Houston."

"Ma'am."

Jessi nodded and shook Joe's hand.

"So what's going on with Darlene and Eddie this time?"

"I know they started somewhere else and ended up here. The 'what's' and the 'why fors' I ain't got a clue. Darlene's over there in the Camaro. Eddie's inside pounding down boiler makers. He might be my nephew but he has turned into one mean spirited sonofabitch. If she won't file charges on him I will!"

"Alright, I'll talk to Darlene first," Cutler said, walking toward the dirty, white Camaro parked on the edge of the lot.

"I take it you know them?" Jessi asked as she fell in beside him.

"Yeah, from way back. Eddie works at the Big O Tires over in Slocum and Darlene works at Shoney's Restaurant right down the street. I went to school with both of them," he explained as he approached the dented, passenger side door where Darlene Willis sat, sobbing softly into her hands.

"Hey, Darlene, it's John Cutler. What's going on?"

The woman's frosted blond ringlets hung loosely over her shoulders, covering the Shoney's name tag on her blue uniform, and concealing the left side of her bruised face. She tried to speak, to form words, but all that escaped her puffy lips were exhausted, desperate sobs.

"Hey, it's going to be alright," he said as he kneeled next to the open window and reached in to part her hair and expose the concealed side of her face. Cutler and Jessi both winced. The woman's left eye was a blackened mess, swollen shut and seeping bloody tears. She bore such little resemblance to the cute little blond he had a crush on in the sixth grade that it caused Cutler to shudder.

Leaving Jessi to sooth the injured woman, Cutler retrieved an Insta-Ice pack from the medical kit in the Blazer and hurried back to the Camaro where he popped the blue bag with his fist and handed it to Jessi to place on Darlene's damaged face.

"Are you hurt anywhere else?" Jessi asked as she leaned into the car and placed the ice pack over the woman's eye. Jessi's nostrils tweaked as she caught the familiar whiff of beer mixed with perfume.

Darlene pushed her head back into the well worn head rest. "I think he cracked one of my ribs. I can't breathe too good," she moaned as more sobs raked her heaving chest.

Darlene's words tumbled over each other, broken and disjointed and barely understandable. "I just- don't- know - what to- do, John."

"I do," Cutler answered, turning to Jessi.

"Would you mind staying here with her for a minute?"

"Not at all. Do what you have to do," Jessi replied, opening the car door and kneeling down next to Darlene.

Eddie Willis was sitting at the long bar involved in a loud game of liar's dice with two other men when Cutler entered the semi darkness and made a beeline for him. Eddie, a husky, six foot two former linebacker at Grace High School, saw Cutler coming and hurried to gulp down the remnants of his drink before he started to rise in greeting. As he stood on wobbly legs, his ample beer gut stretched the front of his dirty blue, sleeveless t-shirt that exposed a half dozen faded tattoos.

"Hey, there's my old football buddy!" he slurred. "How the hell you doing, John? I been meaning to stop by the double-wide and say 'howdy' but-"

Without breaking stride, Cutler grabbed Eddie by the back of the neck and propelled him forcefully toward the rear exit. The other patrons were suddenly very interested in their drinks or their fingernails avoiding eye contact with Cutler.

"Hey, man, cool it. What the fuck is this about?" Eddie complained drunkenly, stumbling over his words and his work boots and falling flush onto his face.

"What do you *think* this is about, *man?*" the sheriff replied, dragging the large man through the open rear doorway onto a covered porch that served as a screened in storage area. "Get up, asshole!" Cutler barked as he jerked the man upright and went nose to nose.

"Hey, John, we're buds, right? I mean we go *way* back. You know what a bitch Darlene can be. Hell, all I did was slap her around a lit-"

Cutler's powerful fist exploded into Eddie's gut, expelling all the air in the big man's lungs and folding him over onto his knees. The sheriff retrieved a wooden chair from a stack in the corner and turning it backwards, sat down facing Eddie as he struggled painfully to re-inflate his burning lungs.

"O.K., here's the deal, *buddy*. You know the old saying 'fool me once, shame on you, right? Fool me twice, shame on me?' Well, fool me *three times* and you, my old friend, are totally and completely fucked! You tagged Darlene in the left eye, right?" Cutler asked a split second before his right fist exploded into Eddie's eye with a sickening thud and spilling him over onto his back. Eddie groaned in pain and rolled onto his stomach where he assumed the fetal position. "You just earned yourself thirty days in jail for spousal abuse. When you swung on me just now you earned yourself *sixty* days! Know what that means, Eddie? That means the taxpayers of Grace County are going to support your wife and three kids while you sit around with your asshole cellmates playing hearts and blaming everybody but yourself for your predicament. Am I right?"

"John, I am so sorry. I didn't mean to-"

"You didn't mean to what?"

"To hurt Darlene," Eddie sobbed. "Hell, I love that woman. She's the mother of my babies!"

"And this is how you show your love?" Cutler removed his cell phone from his pocket and called the office. "Janie, have Kiko meet me at the Oasis ASAP. I need him to transport a prisoner."

The Sheriff stood, replaced the chair on the stack, and returning to the prone figure, removed the set of handcuffs from the rear of his belt. Eddie whined as Cutler bent down and winched the big man's arm behind his back to snap the cuffs onto his wrists. The dark smell of sweat and booze rolled off the drunk in nauseating waves and his brazen sobs infuriated Cutler even more.

"John, please! Please don't do this. I won't ever hit her again. I promise on my momma's grave!"

"Your momma ain't dead you dumb fuck!" Cutler barked, jerking Eddie to an upright but unsteady stance.

"Listen closely, Eddie. What I am about to tell you is very important to your long term health. Now I'm hoping that while you're locked up Darlene has brains enough to file for divorce. But if she doesn't, I recommend that you rent a Budget trailer and move out of Grace County for good. Because if you don't, and I hear you've hurt her again, you're going to end up a bloated, maggot-filled piece of shit floating face down in the Brazos. That's not a threat, Eddie, that's a promise. And remember that poem that Miss Reed had us read in senior English? 'A promise made is a debt unpaid and the trail has its own stern code?' Sam McGee I think. Anyway, you think about it," Cutler said as he pushed the big man toward the steps.

Oasis owner Joe Myler stepped out from the bar. "Everything copasetic, John?"

"Under control, Joe."

After leaving Darlene in her mother's care at the hospital emergency room, Cutler drove Jessi back to Velma's Motel. It was dark when he finally turned into the motel parking lot and stopped opposite her room.

"Hell, it's all ready 10:30," Cutler said as he checked his watch. "Sorry to keep you up so late. You must be exhausted."

"Yeah, I am tired," Jessi replied.

"Thanks for your help. You were good to Darlene and I appreciate that. Maybe she'll heed your advise and get a divorce," Cutler said.

"I doubt it," Jessi replied honestly as she opened the car door.

"Yeah, I know. I'll tell you, both of them are treading water in the shallow end of the DNA pool," Cutler said. "I'll have somebody pick you up in the morning. Eight o'clock too soon?"

"Eight's fine," Jessi said, but before she could climb out Cutler reached across the seat and took her hand.

"Thanks for the company."

"Thanks for the tour," Jessi said as she climbed out.

Cutler watched Jessi walk to her room and unlock her door and felt a familiar stirring in the pit of his stomach. "You are one dumb sonofabitch," he mumbled to himself.

Jessi looked back, smiled and waved as she disappeared into her room.

"See ya," Cutler said, returning the wave. His eyes were drawn to the next room as the curtain parted and Lela Starr peeked out. Her eyes locked with Cutler's and she glared openly as he put the Blazer in gear and pulled away.

Cutler looked over at the patrol car parked in the shadows at one end of Velma's parking lot. He motioned to Shaun Peterson, who gratefully started the car and rolled out of the lot behind Cutler.

Jessi woke up with a knot in her stomach. She had spent most the night tettering on the brink of sleep where she carried on long, senseless conversations with John Cutler and rewrote her speech to Darlene Willis a hundred times. In her dream, Darlene's response was always the same. "Would you help me peel the spuds?"

In between dreams, Jessi forced herself to listen for any unusual sounds coming from Lela's room. Like Sheriff Cutler, Jessi was suspicious of Lela's role in the kidnapping and murder of Michele Sandoval. The woman knew something and Jessi was far from convinced that the knowledge came from a sixth sense. It was her responsibility, her job to find out if Lela's visualizations were a mask for evil.

Over the course of the long night Jessie had crawled out of bed several times to look outside, but there was nothing to see or hear, which might have been part of the reason she hadn't slept well. It was too quiet. No sirens in the middle of the night, no traffic, no neighbors. The motel parking lot was virtually empty. Even the patrol car that she had noticed when Cutler had dropped her off was gone. Not a lot of tourists out here in "deep Texas," Jessi thought.

She groaned and rolled over surveying the room from a different angle for a few minutes before she finally forced herself to an upright position. From the edge of the bed she pushed herself toward the inviting promise of a hot shower. The water was only luke warm but it refreshed her and she quickly dressed in a khaki pant suit. Leaving her room, she rapped on the red enameled door to number 8. She waited a full minute before she gave the door a heavy pounding. Nothing!

"Damnit! Open the door!"

"You looking for me?" the voice came from behind and the startled Jessi spun around ready to do battle.

Lela, looking clean and rested, sketchbook in hand stood behind her. "Your aura's all over the place." Lela reflected mildly. "Probably from staying out too late with the sheriff."

"Where in the hell have you been?" Jessi countered. "You may not be in a cell, but..."

"But what?" Lela flared.

"You just need to let me know where you are," Jessi finished.

"You're telling me that you want me to wake you up at 5:30?" Lela arched her brow. "I don't think so."

"What were you doing up at 5:30?" Jessi asked. "I thought I'd have to pry you out of there."

"Go figure. I can sleep with an 18 wheeler rumbling over my head, but that damn chicken brought me right out of a sound sleep."

"Chicken? What are you talking about?"

"The Triplett rooster," Velma said as she pushed her maid's cart toward them. "The Triplett's, just in back of us, keep some chickens. I get my eggs from them. They got Chester to keep the hens happy. Chester's a big old red rooster."

"Lemme guess, good old Chester does this little wake up call every morning when the sun comes up?" Lela asked.

"Every morning. Sometimes he'll sound off in the middle of the day if he nails a particular hen," Velma explained.

"Oh goody," Lela said. "Something else to look forward to."

"By the way the sheriff gave me a jingle a while ago. Said Red Cordell would pick y'all up at eight sharp."

Jessi nodded.

"Before you go, come by the office. I made some apple turnovers for the picnic this afternoon. You can give me your opinion," Velma said as she turned and started for the office. She stopped and turned back to face them. "I've got some strong coffee on, you're welcome to a cup."

"Sounds wonderful," Jessi said.

"French roast?" Lela asked to Velma's retreating back.

Jessi scowled at Lela. "When did you get so particular. You get most of your coffee from half empty cups anyway."

"I hang out in front of Starbucks, and if you must know, I've developed quite a sophisticated pallet. I find that blends from Africa are way too harsh. Columbian is so weak it's immaterial. Actually, I prefer Italian but a fresh ground French Roast will do in a pinch."

Jessi laughed in spite of herself. "Why don't we just rough it today and take Velma's house blend, huh?"

Lela nodded and slowly followed Jessi toward Velma's office.

The sheriff was sitting at his desk sipping his third cup of bitter Folger's, deeply engrossed in the Sandoval murder book when Janie and Frank Cortez arrived at 7:40 A.M. Frank was carrying his usual box of donuts that he opened and set on the water department desk. Janie, carrying the latest edition of *The Grace Tribune*, moved to the radio console where the graveyard shift dispatcher, sixty-two year old Afton Murphy, sat crocheting edging on a flannel baby blanket. Afton was a large woman that dwarfed the ergonomic chair that some traveling salesman had sold to Janie when her defenses were down. Afton used it so as not to hurt Janie's feelings.

"Good morning, Afton," Janie offered, stifling a yawn as she glanced over the older woman's shoulder to check the log book. "Anything exciting?"

"Another snoozer. An 18 wheeler went off 25 right past Hart Road. The driver fell asleep at the wheel."

"Was he hurt?"

"Just some bumps and bruises. Lucky bastard. There was more vandalism calls on Purry Road. Somebody's slamming mailboxes and breaking car windows again. Shelia Ferguson's new Cadillac got it. *She* wants the sheriff to come out personally and have a look. I'll bet the a-hole that's doing it is downright dirty jealous. I'll bet he's driving a beat up old wreck."

"Probably," Janie agreed. "But that would include 99% of our population."

Afton laughed. "Isn't that the truth."

"What's going on with the sheriff?" Janie asked, nodding toward the back of the trailer where Cutler continued studying the murder book.

"He was here at o dark thirty and look what he's wearing," Afton raised her penciled eye brows.

Janie smiled when she saw Cutler had shed his normal white shirt for a softer, short sleeved blue one. He'd also changed from Levis to Dockers.

"Well, I'll be," Janie smiled broadly.

"All that for Founder's Day?" Afton asked.

"I don't think so. There just happens to be a female police officer from Houston that's stirred his nest."

"Really? That's interesting," Afton said.

"How's my blanket coming?"

"I'll have it finished by tomorrow," Afton promised.

Afton spent the bulk of her shift making small receiving blankets in the long hours between midnight and eight o'clock when the telephone refused to ring. She had started making them for her seven grandchildren. She now made them on request, and estimated that over her twelve years at the sheriff's office, she had made close to eight hundred of the small coverings. If the tall, angular Afton looked incongruous with a small hook, crocheting delicate edging, no one had ever mentioned it.

"Good," Janie answered. "Erin Lane's shower is next Saturday. Anybody else giving her one of your blankets?"

Afton pondered. "Nope, I think you're it. Becka Hall bought one but she's in Waco with her momma."

"That's good," Janie answered. "Go ahead and take off, dear."

"I still have fifteen minutes. Are you sure it's okay?"

"Hey, how many times have you covered my butt when I was running late with a sick kid or a dead battery?"

"That's what friends do, Janie."

"Exactly, now get out of here and I'll see you at the picnic as soon as I get off."

"You don't need to tell me twice." Afton removed her headset and gathered up her crocheting.

Janie picked up headset from the desk, slipped it over her neck and carried the newspaper to the rear of the double-wide where Cutler was reading.

The sheriff glanced up when she approached.

"Morning," Janie offered. "You have to have that book memorized."

"I keep hoping I'll see something I've missed."

"Have you seen today's *Tribune?*"

"Haven't had the chance," Cutler answered, taking the paper from Janie.

"Look on page six under Sel Turner's "Local Beat" column."

Cutler opened the paper and traced down the column with his finger. "*Green fees are being increased at Silver Reef Golf Course. The five dollar bump will hurt seniors the most and pro Denny Howell's announcement came on the heels of -*"

"Not that one, keep going," Janie interrupted impatiently.

"*With re-election time right around the corner, local law enforcement officials are dusting off our most infamous cold case file. The murder of Michele Sandoval, the thirteen year old Dallas girl whose tortured body was discovered at a Grace County rest stop in June of last year. I have it from a very reliable source that Sheriff John Cutler is so desperate that he has enlisted the aid of a top Houston P.D. homicide detective and an internationally known psychic in the hunt for the killers of the Sandodval girl.*"

I think your humble reporter speaks on behalf of the parents of Michele Sandoval as well as many of the citizens of Grace County when I ask our amiable sheriff, 'What took so long, John?"

"He is such an asshole," Janie said as Cutler set the paper aside. "Don't let it get to you."

"Well, the man's right about one thing," Cutler offered. "Five bucks is way too much to raise the green fees out at Riverside."

Janie's answer was interrupted when the front door of the trailer opened and Red stepped in. "Come on in ladies, su casa es tu casa."

Henry, who had been sleeping under the desk, immediately rose and trotted in the newcomer's direction, anticipating a greeting and Jessi didn't disappoint the friendly Lapso.

How were your rooms?" Cutler asked, putting the book aside and standing.

"Well, if you really want to know," Lela answered. "I found it very difficult to get to sleep. My mattress was too soft, and everything smelled of pine oil. I'm very sensitive to those kinds of chemicals."

"The rooms are fine and my bed was very comfortable, thank you for asking, "Jessi said, shooting Lela a look as she added, "The only thing I smelled last night was incense–sickly, sweet incense."

"Well, someone got back in the wee hours. Woke me up from the first decent dream I've had in years."

"Didn't you just say you couldn't sleep? Besides, it wasn't the wee hours," Jessi flushed, "It was only 10:30 and besides, -" she started to add before noticing that they were the center of attention. She bit back her reply and glared. Lela crossed her arms with a satisfied look on her face.

Janie waited for the women to finish before leading them to where Frank was rummaging through the clutter on the Water Department desk.

"Janie, where the hell did I put that work order for the fire hydrants?" Frank asked as he continued searching for the wayward work order. Janie approached, retrieved the paper from the in basket and placed it in his hands.

"Right where you left it, "Janie said.

Frank was in the process of taking a bite of a chocolate-frosted, raised donut when Janie led Jessi and Lela over. "This in my better half. Frank, this is Jessi Cole and Lela Starr from Houston.

"Pleased to meet you ladies," Frank said, juggling the paperwork Janie had just handed him as well as the donut and a cup of coffee. He quickly gave up on the handshakes, holding out a plate of donuts instead.

"Bought them fresh this morning."

Jessi shook her head. "I'd love one, but Velma just loaded us up on apple turnovers."

Lela grimaced as she gingerly choose two raised donuts and dropped them in her bag. "Do you know how much refined poison there is in these?"

"Of course we know, we're cops!" Red laughed as he and Cutler each took a donut.

Frank put down the donuts and turned his attention to Lela. "Ah ha, you must be the world famous psychic hotline lady."

"I don't align myself with telephone con-artists and hustlers," Lela snapped.

"No, she's more into crystals and, ahh, 'visualizations,' is it?" Jessi's voice displayed a sarcastic hostility that surprised even herself.

There was a momentary silence before the Water Department phone rang and, as Janie plugged in her head set to answer it, Frank gave Lela a mischievous smile. "Okay, psychic lady. Tell me what the phone call Janie is taking is all about."

Lela gave him an appraising look and waved her arms in a mock ritualistic motion. "Mr. Cortez, my sources tell me you're going to be in deep shit today," she said, folding her arms and turning her back to shut them out.

Janie hung up the phone and called across the room to her husband. "Frank, that was Erin Pence over on Brush Street. Her sewer's backed up again."

The implications of Lela's prediction were not lost on Frank, but he didn't know if he was impressed or not. He looked at Lela's unresponsive back, started to say something to her, and then changed his mind. "Of course her sewer's backed up again, her grandkids flush paper towels down the toilet. What a stinking way to start my day." As he headed for the door, he kissed Janie on the cheek. "I'll see you at the picnic. Save me some of that potato salad of yours."

The phone rang as he left.

"Sheriff's Department. This is Janie. How can I help you?

As Janie moved to her console, she picked up a pencil and started writing on a yellow tablet.

Jessi looked over at the sheriff and reddened to see that he was staring at her. She brushed a hand through her hair and resisted the urge to check her reflection in the small mirror on Janie's desk. She unconsciously straightened her shoulders. She had no idea how lovely she looked in the simple white blouse and khaki pantsuit that hid more than it revealed.

There eyes met again for an instant before Jessi forced herself to approach him.

"So what's on the agenda today, Sheriff?"

"Besides the Founder's Day Picnic?" Cutler smiled and then grew thoughtful. "I'd like to take our guest back out to the rest stop, see if we can get her to open up. All we've got to do is hit the right button, and she'll give it up in a heart beat. I can feel it."

Jessi nodded. "It's your call."

Behind them Janie hung up the phone and approached Cutler's desk. The troubled look on her face was immediately apparent as she handed the sheriff the legal tablet he had been taking notes on.

"What's this?" Cutler asked, glancing at the tablet.

"Clarence Deavers over in Slocum called Louie Adams this morning and reported his thirteen-year-old daughter missing. She's been gone since Monday night, so why he waits until Friday morning to make a report, I can not fathom."

"What's the girl's name?" Cutler asked.

"Samantha, Samantha Deavers, but they call her...?"

Lela turned from across the room, a stricken look on her face. "Sammy!"

Jessi and Cutler exchanged a puzzled look.

"How in the hell did she know that?" Cutler asked.

14.

꩜

Lela was silent and withdrawn during the drive to Slocum. She sat in the backseat of the Blazer seemingly oblivious to her surroundings. Her eyes were unfocused, and she had taken off her quartz necklace. Her fingers wrapped around the crystal, holding it like a lifeline as the 4x4 sped over the undulating road. The highway had been laid over the top of a twenty-mile stretch of ancient sand dunes, and the constant up and down motion could be difficult for anyone prone to carsickness.

"When we were kids we called this stretch Upchuck Road," Cutler said, glancing at Jessi.

"This is worse than your damn airplane! Slow down!" Lela barked from the back.

Jessi glanced over her shoulder at Lela but said nothing. Cutler was driving fast, *too fast,* and Lela looked like she could toss her cookies at any moment. Jessi debated with herself whether or not to speak up. She was so used to being the one driving that it was hard to feel safe with someone else at the wheel. With the speedometer buried, Jessi made a decision.

Cutler sensed her concern. "Don't worry. I drive this road all the time."

"How far is this Slocum?"

"About forty miles." Cutler answered.

"Is it a new town?"

Cutler glanced over at her, puzzled. "No, the courthouse is one of the oldest in the area. Why'd you ask?"

"I just thought you were concerned it would flee the area before we got there."

"Point taken," Cutler said, smiling as he slowed to 80 mph.

They rode in silence. In the back, Lela had put her head back and appeared to be dozing, while Jessi looked out the window and enjoyed scenery totally new to her big city experience. Twenty-five minutes after leaving Grace they passed the

"WELCOME TO SLOCUM"

sign and drove quickly through the older section of the small town, past a half-dozen old buildings that comprised the downtown shopping area and then past a town square that housed the library, the Sheriff's substation and the old brick courthouse that Cutler had mentioned earlier, all resting comfortably under the relatively cool shade of one hundred-year-old live oaks.

Jessi rolled down the dirty window, sacrificing the cool, air-conditioned atmosphere for a better view of the town. As they drove, she noticed that nearly every person they passed waved and that Cutler took the time to return the greeting, stopping in the middle of the street at one point and yelling at an attractive, middle-aged blond woman who was climbing into her car, "Hey, Janice! You're way too young to be a grandma!"

Janice smiled and gave him a thumbs up. "Eight pounds two ounces. A boy. They named him Mike! Nick's got a cigar for you!" she yelled back. Cutler got another block before an attractive, dark haired Latina woman stepped away from her car and flagged him down.

"Hi Johnny," she said, leaning down to look into the car at Jessi and Lela. Her dark eyes were friendly and open.

"Hi, Ellie. Marty still asleep?"

"No, he's got the boys over to the park playing whiffleball. I think he's warming himself up for the big ballgame today."

"I'll see you all later, then."

"At the picnic," Ellie said, again glancing in at Jessi as they drove away.

"Ellie's married to my cousin, Marty Burris. Marty's a highway patrolman."

As they continued driving, Jessi watched Cutler and felt a touch of envy. "If I didn't know better I'd think you knew every person in town."

"He's probably related to them- on both sides," Lela shot from the back.

Cutler ignored her. "I'll bet I know most of them," he said, smiling. "Best people in the world."

On the west side of Slocum, Cutler made a right turn onto Hughes Road, and the Blazer threw up a heavy, choking cloud, forcing Jessi to roll up the window as dust billowed around the fast-moving 4x4. Jessi eyes were drawn to an abandoned drive-in theater.

Cutler noticed her interest. "That's the old Starlight Drive-In. It's been closed for years. You'd be surprised how many people drove over here to see the movie, some from as far away as Grace and Bancroft. In its day it was the place to be." Cutler explained.

"Let me guess," Lela piped up from the back. "You lost your virginity there?"

"No, but I know a few people who did."

"Bernie used to call drive-in theaters 'sperm banks," Lela volunteered. "Bernie said 'he was a regular donor.'" Her laugh died for lack of a second.

Cutler glanced in the rear view mirror at Lela. She certainly wasn't the dull-minded homeless type he was accustomed to dealing with. He knew that she had to be involved in the Sandoval murder, but could she also be somehow involved in this disappearance too?

"I didn't think towns like this still existed. Amazing," Jessi said.

Cutler pulled the Blazer to a stop alongside resident deputy Louie Adams's Ford Bronco patrol unit that was parked in front of the Deavers' house. Louie, an African- American, was sitting inside the running vehicle, enjoying his air conditioner as he finished writing up his missing persons report on Samantha Deavers.

Louie was forty two in age and girth and had an ever present toothpick poking from the corner of his mouth. He had been a senior at Grace High School when John Cutler was in his freshman year. Louie had been an all around athlete, lettering in three sports, and had been named to the small school all state football team as a tackle two years in a row and still had the bad knee to prove it. The knee had killed his scholarship hopes, but he had readjusted his goals, graduating from Waco City College with his AA degree and an interest in criminal justice. He was quickly snatched up by the San Antonio Police Department and spent six years there before running into Grace County's newly elected sheriff and old friend, John Cutler, while visiting his parents in Slocum. Cutler had just fired Slocum's then resident deputy; a mean-spirited bully named Arnie Wasco, and offered Louie the job, which he accepted. Louie moved his wife, Annie, and his three sons home to Slocum and had been there ever since, earning the respect and friendship of the neighbors he served.

Louie rolled down the window and smiled at Cutler. "How was Houston, boss?

"Big and noisy. How're your boys?"

"Big and noisy," Louie replied.

"Do you know the missing girl?"

"Only too well," Louie said, nodding toward the house. "I've been out here a bunch of times about Sammy. A couple of times over shop-lifting at the Payless and the grocery store, another time for busting a radio antenna off a car, another time for having a joint at school, three or four times for truancy. She's run away more than once. She's a hellion, I'll tell you that. The old man and his boys aren't exactly Rotary Club leadership material either. They're always up to something out here."

"I know. I go way back with the Deaver boys," Cutler said as he nodded and pulled the Blazer past Louie's Bronco and drove past the

DON'T WORRY ABOUT THE DOG,

WORRY ABOUT THE 357 IN MY HAND!

sign hanging on the broken-down wooden gate and pulled to a dusty stop in the Deavers' cluttered front yard.

As the three of them sat in the Blazer and looked around, it was immediately obvious that the Deavers didn't believe in throwing much of anything away. The yard was a pack rat's paradise: rusting cars, tractors, stoves, water heaters, televisions, a half-dozen dryers and washers, ranging from old Maytag wringer types to newer models, their motors, gears, clutches, and belts long since scavenged. Here they sat, discarded but still on display, a dusty showroom marking the advancement of the American household appliance. Bedsprings were also part of the landscape along with an old refrigerator that still held rotting lettuce, apples, and several items that defied identification. The smell told the story. Oddly enough, someone had planted pink geraniums in an old toilet bowl in some unexplained attempt to bring a spot of beauty to the clutter.

As Jessi and Lela climbed out, they were immediately surrounded by the mongrel canine trio of Rusty, Dusty and George, who greeted them with a chorus of loud barking. After a moment nine-year-old Nicole Deavers burst out of the house, quieting the dogs as she approached the police car.

"They won't bite you," she said, her voice high-pitched and fragile in its sweetness.

Lela took one look at Nicole and froze. Without conscious effort or control, she saw a flashing mixture of color and jerky, black and white kaleidoscopic images of Nicole walking down the dirt road with Samantha. The girls moved in slow motion, close together, yet not touching. Lela shuddered, as the images broke apart and shattered, leaving her leaning against the Blazer dizzy and nauseated.

Jessi watched Lela's reaction. It was behavior open to any amount of interpretation. Was it a sign of guilt? Was she afraid that Nicole would recognize her and implicate her even further? It was surprising how often police work revolved around being able to read witnesses as well as the suspects. Lela could be both. She was definitely a conundrum.

Cutler was oblivious to the situation being played out behind him as he came around from the driver's side and smiled at Nicole. "Hi there, what's your name?"

"Nicole."

"Are your parents home?" the sheriff asked.

The girl's thin, pinched face looked suddenly hopeful. "They're in the house. Did you find Sammy?"

"Not yet, honey. I'm sorry," Cutler answered.

Nicole reclaimed her pinched expression as she walked to the front porch and slumped down heavily on the worn, wooden steps, a discouraged and sad little girl.

Jessi, Lela, and Cutler all glanced at her worried face as they climbed the steps and paused in front of the once white door that was now blackened around the knob and badly scratched at the bottom from the dogs. As they stood before the door, Jessi noticed a strangely familiar, sour chemical smell that triggered a trace of recollection buried deep in the recesses of her memory.

Cutler knocked.

Lela shuddered visibly. "There is absolutely no good karma coming from inside that house. I'll wait out here," she said, turning away as the door opened and Clarence Deavers stepped out. He was a stocky, powerful-looking man with short, graying hair, wearing filthy bib overalls, worn boots, and an expression devoid of any friendliness. His wife, Glenda, holding her year-old grandson, peered at them over her husband's shoulder. She was a woman who hadn't aged well, wearing her dirty, limp hair in an unattractive ponytail that framed puffy eyes and a dull complexion. Her former attractiveness had come from youth and health, both long lost as she traveled through life cleaning up after Clarence, raising four children, and now a grandson.

Cutler extended his hand. "Mr. Deavers, I'm Sheriff Cutler."

Deavers kept his own hand rigidly at his side. "I know who you are. You helped put my oldest boy in Huntsville State Prison."

Cutler acknowledged the truth of the statement. "That'd be Clarence Junior."

"No, that'd be Spike. Clarence Junior did his time in the county lockup. He's out now. Spike will be released come next June. This is Spike's boy," he added, turning and touching the drowsy baby's arm. The child was sucking on a white pacifier that covered his entire mouth. The baby smiled when Jessi reached out and let him grab hold of her hand, the pacifier dropping from his mouth as his smile widened and then turned into a wail when he realized that he'd lost his security. Jessi bent down and retrieved the pacifier, handing it to Glenda who rubbed it on her dirty skirt before plopping it back into the baby's mouth.

Glenda leaned forward to better see her visitors. "Spike found the Lord in prison."

"That's good to hear," Cutler said. "Let's hope he doesn't lose track of Him once he gets out. Can we come in?"

Clarence looked like he would like to protest but moved aside grudgingly. "We told the colored deputy everything we know about Sammy."

Inside the house Jessi looked around for a place to sit but quickly gave up. The sofa was filled with clean and dirty laundry mixed together in a disorderly heap. Dirty dishes were on the floor, licked clean by the dogs. One chair held greasy wrenches and other tools and what looked like the parts to a four-barrel carburetor. On one side of the room, amidst the squalor, was a splendid, Mitsubishi big screen HD TV, the volume so high they had to shout to be heard over a Jerry Springer rerun featuring an enraged guest who had just discovered that his sexy, new girlfriend had testicles. Glenda turned the volume down but left the picture on, her gaze straying often to the TV screen as their discussion got underway.

"Folks, I know this is difficult for you, and I appreciate your cooperation, but we need to understand everything we can about the situation here," Cutler said.

"Something like this was bound to happen the way that girl tramped all over the place," Clarence's voice was both angry and defensive.

"Did she have any particular boy she might be interested in?" Cutler asked.

Clarence snorted, "She ain't particular; she's interested in all of 'em."

"When was the last time you saw your daughter?" Cutler asked.

Glenda spoke up. "Early evening, Tuesday. I sent her and Nicole to the store for me."

"Nicole's the little girl outside?"

Glenda nodded. "Samantha runs away all the time. That's why we didn't report her missing right off. She takes off, sometimes for a few days and then comes back home, but never this long."

"Do you have a recent photo we can look at?" Jessi asked.

Mrs. Deavers left the room but returned quickly with an unframed eight-by-ten school photograph of the smiling Samantha and handed it to Jessi. "We gave a little one just like that to the deputy."

"You don't need 'em both, do you?" Clarence asked, a hint of accusation in his voice.

"No sir, we don't. I just want to look at it," Jessi said, studying the picture. The resemblance of this girl to the one in Lela's sketch was ambiguous. She would need to compare them, but there was something about it that triggered a memory. Jessi handed the photo to Cutler, and as he continued questioning the Deavers, Jessi watched the couple closely. In her time on patrol she had been in many homes more squalid than this one. Could these parents somehow be involved in their daughter's disappearance? They seemed genuinely concerned about her but angry, too, especially Clarence. Had Samantha fled from this house with just cause? One thing Jessi was sure of; the Deavers weren't pleased to have the law in the house. Maybe the big-screen television was hot. As she looked around the room, Jessi had a sinking feeling that Samantha Deavers would never enter this house again.

As Lela sat down on the steps beside Nicole, one of the dogs approached and plopped his sour, smelly jowls on her knees and waited patiently to have his ears scratched.

"That's George. He don't take to just anybody," Nicole said, impressed.

"I have a way with animals," Lela said, scratching George's neck. "They always like me."

Nicole looked at Lela curiously. "Are you a policeman, too?"

Lela laughed. "No, not even close." She raised her eyebrows questioningly. "Did you really think I was a cop?"

"Not really. You're different than the other two."

"You can say that again." Lela was momentarily thoughtful, but she shook it off, smiling as she took Nicole's hand and gently turned it over. "Would you like me to read your palm?"

Nicole pulled her hand back. "I don't believe in that stuff."

"No? Tell you what. I'll tell you what I see in your future, and then you can decide what to believe."

"I guess that's okay," Nicole said, extending her small hand toward Lela.

Lela took the girl's hand and studied it for a moment before tracing her finger along a crease. "See this line? It means that you'll have a long and happy marriage, and this line here shows that you'll have at least three children. Let's see here. Yup, just as I thought, a boy and two girls."

"Yuk! I don't want kids! I'm only nine."

Lela laughed. "It won't happen for a while," she said, continuing to study Nicole's palm. "I see a lot of happiness in your life."

"Can you really see all that in my hand?"

"All that and more." Lela said as Nicole reached out and touched the quartz necklace that dangled from the delicate silver chain around Lela's neck.

"Sammy had a necklace like that. She wore it all the time."

At that moment Jessi exited the house, and as she came down the steps behind them, Nicole stood up to give her room.

"Are you going to find Sammy?" Nicole asked her face solemn.

Jessi looked at the little girl, and her heart went out to her, but there was no reassurance that she could offer. "I hope so, Nicole. I really do. Look, we really need your help. Your mom said you and your sister walked to the store that night. Would you show us the way you walked?"

"I need to tell Mom I'm going. I'll be right back." Nicole sprinted into the house. After a few moments she returned, carefully tucking a five-dollar bill into the pocket of her shorts. "Mom wants me to get some lunchmeat since I'm going to the store anyway," Nicole said, avoiding their eyes to hide her embarrassment.

Jessi and Lela followed close behind as Nicole hurried out of the cluttered yard and down the dirt road. As they passed Deputy Adams's Bronco, he smiled and rolled down the window. "Can I help you folks with anything?"

"No thanks, we're just taking a walk," Jessi answered, hurrying to keep up as Nicole veered off the road and into a vacant field filled with weeds and littered with bottles, cans, candy wrappings, and fast food containers. Nicole walked purposely through the field, following a smooth path that she and her sister had worn in the dry ground. On the other side of the field, they crossed a dirt road that bordered the old, abandoned Starlight Theater. Nicole scrambled through a hole in the fence, turning briefly to make sure Jessi and Lela were still with her. The women struggled through the narrow opening, and the three of them continued over the packed gravel lot, walking between rows of rusted speaker poles, the huge white screen looming behind them.

"This is the way you came?" Jessi asked Nicole.

"Yes. This is the way we always go to the store,"

"This place is a little spooky," Jessi said, glancing around at the sea of poles as they approached the graffiti covered brick walls of the low building that had housed the projection booth, a snack bar, and rest rooms.

Lela felt suddenly light-headed and a little dizzy. She leaned against one of the speaker poles before kneeling on the hard gravel, holding very still, just wanting to let the feeling pass. She looked up at the huge, torn movie screen and saw Nicole and Sammy walking ahead of her through the deserted grounds. Sammy picked up a speaker and pretended to be listening. The two girls giggled and continued walking as the image faded.

"Lela?"

Jessi's voice pulled her back. "Are you alright?"

Jessi returned and helped Lela to her feet.

"I don't need your help," Lela snapped, jerking her arm away.

"Fine with me," Jessi said as she caught up with Nicole.

Nicole waited at the fence for the two women to climb through the barbed wire. She checked for traffic before leading them quickly across the busy four-lane road that ran past the small shopping mall.

As the unlikely threesome entered the IGA Supermarket parking lot, Jessi reached out and took Nicole by the hand. "I want you to tell me everything you remember. It doesn't matter how small or unimportant. Let's start with what you came shopping for, okay?"

"We had a list: bread, milk, chocolate chips, and dish soap. Mom said we could get a Coke and some M & Ms, too."

"Okay, now you crossed the road like we just did and you walked through the parking lot. Was it right here, where we are now?" Jessi asked as they continued walking toward the store past rows of parked cars.

"Yes. I think so."

What's the first thing you remember?" Jessi asked.

"Sammy starts bossing me around and acting real prissy. She does that just in case there's someone around who'll notice."

"And was there someone around that day?"

"Yeah, over there," she said, pointing off toward the side of the store entrance. "There were two boys in a red truck. They yelled at Sammy."

Jessi paused. "Yelled? Like a 'hello' type of yell?"

Nicole nodded. "Yeah, I didn't know them, but Sammy did. She called one of the boys, Lenny, I think. I'm not sure."

"Was the truck old or new?" Jessi prompted.

"I think it was old, but it was fixed up real cool."

"Did Sammy go over to the truck?"

"Yes, she goes over and starts talking and acting like a big deal, flirting, then she tells me to go in the store. I didn't want to because Mom gets mad if Sammy goes off with boys."

"Mad at you?" Lela asked, bristling. "What the hell for?"

"Mom thinks that if I'm with her, Sammy won't be so wild," Nicole said. "If something happened to Sammy, it might be my fault," she said, her small voice teetering on a sob. "I should have stayed with her."

Jessi kneeled and hugged the tearful child. "You couldn't have known."

"Anything else you remember?" Jessi asked standing and leading Nicole toward the store entrance where a teenaged boy was busy arranging a line of shopping carts.

"No, I just went into the store and got what Mom wanted. When I came out Sammy wasn't out here, so I sat down on the bench over there and waited around. I thought maybe she just went for a ride with the boys in the truck, but they never came back, so I just went home. Mom yelled at me."

Lela abruptly halted next to the entrance. "You forgot something, Nicole."

"No, I didn't," Nicole protested, but stopped when she saw the strange, far away look pass over Lela's face.

"Can't you smell them?"

"Smell? Smell what?" Jessi asked.

"The puppies."

"Puppies?" Jessi was puzzled.

Nicole's eyes lighted up. "I forgot about the puppies. But how did you know?" Nicole looked at Lela curiously.

"It's, a … It's a long story, Nicole, maybe someday I'll, I'll be-" Lela stuttered.

"Never mind," Jessi answered, kneeling next to Nicole. "Tell me about the puppies."

"There was a woman giving away little puppies. She was outside the store at the side of the door, right over here. I wanted to look at them, but I didn't stop."

Jessi's mind raced as she shot Lela a cold look. So she was there the night Samantha Deavers disappeared! There was no other explanation! Hell, for all she knew, Lela Starr might have been the woman with the puppies in some kind of disguise!

Lela sensed Jessi's feelings. She was exhausted to her very core of being a suspect, but more weary of never being able to escape from the hell that dwelled within her brain. She turned away, walking to a nearby wooden bench where she slumped down in the shade of the grocery store, totally spent. She felt instantly queasy as a terrible anguish swept through her.

Jessi studied Lela from a distance of some twelve feet, looking for any kind of tell tale reaction that would somehow clarify her obvious involvement. Jessi had a sudden sinking feeling that Lela was manipulating her, and everyone else, like they were all pawns in some kind of diabolical chess match! With that realization a hard, angry knot suddenly formed in her stomach. She forced herself to let go of the anger and focusing, turned again to Nicole. "When you came back out of the store, was the woman with the puppies still out here?"

Nicole look momentarily puzzled. "I'm not sure, I... No, I don't think so. I'm sure I would have noticed if she was because I waited on the bench for a while. I know I would have looked at the puppies. Can I go in the store now? I have to buy lunchmeat."

"Sure, I'll come in with you," Jessi said before turning to Lela. "I'm going to see if anyone was working Monday when the girls were here. Don't go anywhere."

"Oh, right, like I've got so many places to run off to."

"Lela, this is important. Don't give me any reason not to trust you."

Lela smirked at Jessi, only partially listening, and waved her off.

While Nicole went in search of lunchmeat Jessi spotted an older, balding checker who was taking advantage of the lull in customers to straighten a display near his register. His name tag read "Rich Alrich-Asst't Manager."

Jessi quickly explained who she was to the somewhat suspicious man. His face brightened when he saw her badge.

"From Houston are you? I'll just bet you're the super duper detective that I read about in Sel Turner's column."

"Actually, I'm not a detec-"

"The wife and I took a vacation down your way a couple of years back. We're big Rockets fans. Caught a couple of games. Good seats too. Quite an experience. Quite an expense too, but well worth it. My

God those men are tall. Much taller in person. Even the short guys, the point guards, are taller than me by a good six inches."

Jessi nodded. "It'd be great if the Rockets could get to the playoffs this year."

"If they make the playoffs, you can bet Kathy and I will be there."

"Do you remember if you were working Monday evening?"

"Monday through Friday. I've been here over twenty years and finally get the weekends off."

"Do you happen to remember Nicole and Samantha Deavers coming in on Monday?"

"Their mother sends them all the time. Can't be certain which day. Let's see, Monday I had to help the Budweiser guy set up a 'Monday Night Football' display. I can't say for sure," the checker said, rubbing his bald head before leaning toward Jessi and lowering his voice to conspiratorial level. "Truth is we've had a bit of a problem with the older girl."

"What kind of trouble?"

"Shoplifting, nothing big, a lipstick here and there; candy, nylons, hairbrush, that sort of thing. We definitely had to keep an eye on her. Last time I remember, it was just the young one that came in. Nicole, that's the little one, she's a doll, no problem."

"Was Samantha banned from the store?" Jessi asked curiously.

"She probably should have been, but no, nothing like that. The manager didn't want to tangle with old man Deavers. This goes way back. We had several run ins with old Clarence while his boys were growing up. They were both thieves. Still are. No, the policy with Samantha was just like I said ,'keep an eye on her.' I was glad when Nicole came in by herself. Made my job a little easier."

Jessi nodded. "You recall a woman giving away puppies in front of the store any time this week?"

"Sure I do. That would be Monday. Now I remember because my granddaughter was visiting from Grace and wanted me to get her one," he stroked his chin thoughtfully. "A big woman with long dark hair. I had to go out and remind her not to hassle the customers."

"Was she from around here?" Jessi asked hoping subconsciously that this mystery woman was innocently trying to find homes for a litter of puppies.

"Now that you mention it, no, she wasn't from around here," he rubbed his head again in what Jessi assumed was an unconscious habit. "I thought I knew just about everybody around Grace County. I guess I don't."

While Jessi and Nicole were in the store, Lela sat on the bench clutching her necklace and stared across the parking lot. There was something here that she needed to tap into; some unsettling, free floating energy field that clung to the hot asphalt like a mist and held out a promise of …what? What was it she felt? Apprehension? Terror? Certainly fear! She closed her eyes and gritted her teeth, forcing herself to grasp onto something, anything that would offer her clarity. And suddenly the mist evaporated and she focused. At the edge of the parking lot Lela saw Sammy Deavers, cuddling a puppy, disappear into the night. Lela willed herself to follow but Sheriff Cutler's Blazer pulling to a stop close-by broke her concentration and her vision evaporated.

Cutler climbed out and approached just as Jessi exited. "Where's the little girl?"

Jessi nodded toward the store. "She had to get something for her mom. How'd it go with her folks?"

"They were busy covering their parental ass." Cutler responded. "Anything come out of your walk?"

"Yes. We've got two boys in a *cool* old red pickup truck who she might have gone with."

"Good, now we're getting somewhere," Cutler said, noticing Jessi's troubled look as she looked off at Lela. "Something bothering you?"

"Nicole did remember a woman standing out here giving away puppies but not until after Lela prompted her."

"Prompted her? What does that mean?" Cutler asked.

"Like maybe she had a 'vision' or something."

"We don't have time for more mumbo jumbo stuff," Cutler said, the disgust in his voice apparent.

"I know all that, but the assistant manager confirmed that there was a woman giving away puppies that night. But he didn't recognize the woman."

"This is a farming community, Jessi. People are always giving away puppies and kittens. I've seen folks giving away goats and chickens out here. That doesn't prove anything."

"I know, but..." Jessi's voice trailed off.

"But what?" Cutler asked.

She nodded toward Lela. "I honestly can't figure her out. If she were involved in these crimes, why would she give out information that would only make her more of a suspect? It doesn't make sense."

"Nothing about that woman makes sense," Cutler agreed. "Did he even remember the girls being here Monday?"

He remembered Nicole being here, but claims he didn't see Samantha. Apparently Samantha had been caught shoplifting on a couple of occasions. The management has some history with the whole Deavers family.

"I'm not surprised," Cutler said.

They watched as Lela got up from the bench and joined them. Ignoring Jessi, Lela looked directly at Cutler.

"You can't send that little girl back to that house."

Cutler was bewildered. "Who? Nicole? What the hell are you talking about?"

"Why do you think her big sister kept running away? And why didn't they report Sammy missing the night she didn't come home? If they-"

Jessi interrupted. "Lela, cut to the chase. Just exactly *what* are you saying?"

"We've got to save that little girl. With Sammy gone it's only a matter of time before that asshole father and Junior turn their attention to her."

Jessi and Cutler exchanged a look.

"You're saying she's being sexually abused?" Jessi asked.

Cutler's eyes narrowed. "Did Nicole say something to you in that regard?"

"She didn't have to tell me," Lela answered as she stalked away.

As they waited for Nicole, Jessi tried to sort out her scrambled thoughts.

Cutler guessed correctly what she was thinking. "There's no way that woman could know what's going on inside the Deaver's house," Cutler said finally.

"I know," Jessi agreed. "But are you willing to risk that little girl?"

"Hell no," Cutler growled. "But you just can't make that kind of accusation without some kind of proof."

"So what do we do?"

Cutler was quiet for a few moments. "I'll make a few calls, see what shakes out."

"And in the meantime?"

"In the meantime, let's see if Nicole would like to take in the Founder's Day Picnic. Give her a break from all this crap."

Nicole exited the IGA supermarket and approached carrying a small grocery sack.

"How'd you like to go to the Founder's Day Picnic over in Grace?" Cutler asked.

"I should be getting home. Mom will be mad—I mean, worried—if I'm away too long."

Cutler nodded. "I appreciate you being concerned for your folks. Tell you what, I'll give them a call and let them know that you're on official police business. I need to ask you a few more questions, and we might as well check out the parade and barbecue while I give you the third degree. What do you say?"

Nicole's worried expression dissolved into a bright smile that lit up her face.

Cutler made arrangements to have the lunch meat that Nicole had purchased taken out to her parent's home, knowing that that young girl would worry unless it was done.

He motioned brusquely for Lela to get into the car and the four of them drove the forty miles back to Grace, Nicole with nonstop questions about the afternoon's picnic.

"You've never been to the Founder's Day picnic?" Jessi asked.

"Sammy's been and Clarence and Spike probably, but forty miles is too long a drive for Mom and Dad." Nicole was almost defensive.

"Yeah," Jessi agreed. "It's lucky we're going there anyway."

"Somebody's got to get me back home tonight," Nicole's face pinched. "If I don't feed the dogs, they don't get fed."

Cutler turned around briefly. "Don't worry, you're dogs will get taken care of."

"Maybe Junior will feed them," Nicole relaxed slightly. "Junior likes the dogs. He says they're the best watch dogs in the county."

"Take me back to Velma's," Lela directed when they reached the outskirts of town. "I'm not going to some rinky dink Founder's Day Picnic. I don't know why you people would want to celebrate *this* place being found anyway."

Jessi glanced over the rear seat. "Let's get one thing straight: If I'm going to the picnic, you're going to the picnic."

Nicole's worried eyes met Lela's. "It might be fun."

"When you get old enough, come to Houston, I'll show you a real town, a town *worth* finding."

"Now there's something to look forward to," Jessi said. "Don't worry, Nicole, Lela will be the first one in line for the cotton candy."

Lela looked at Jessi for a long moment before turning to Nicole and smiling. "Now if they would have mentioned the cotton candy up front, we wouldn't even be having this conversation."

"I had cotton candy before," Nicole agreed happily. "It's the best."

"The parade starts at 11 o'clock," Cutler said over his shoulder. "We should just about make it."

"A parade," Lela rolled her eyes. "It just keeps getting better and better."

15.

Deputy Kiko Avila's patrol car was affectively blocking traffic from entering the downtown section of Main Street where the parade route wound its way to the city park.

Kiko stood next to a line of wooden barricades and directed traffic off onto a side street. The handsome Kiko smiled when he saw Cutler's Blazer approach and pull to a stop next to him. While Jessi, Lela and Nicole climbed out of the Blazer, Kiko approached the driver's side as Cutler got out.

"Everything O.K.?" Cutler asked.

"Couple of fender benders. Nothing serious. Aren't you staying for the parade, boss?"

"I'm going to run by the office, make a couple of calls. I got some feelers out on the missing Deaver's girl. I need to check and see if anything's developed."

"You're going to miss Red," Kiko warned.

"Back to his roots again, huh?"

"He spent most of the morning putting on his makeup. Worse than any woman I ever saw."

"Take a picture for me. I'll be back as soon as I can. And Kiko, keep your eye out for a cherry looking red pickup. Probably an older model."

"What's that about?"

"Possible tie in to the Deaver's girl."

Kiko nodded and stepped back as Jessi joined them.

"Hope this is okay with you," Cutler said as he gave her a long look. "I'm not trying to stick you with babysitting, but I've got to do a couple of things."

"I didn't think you were," Jessi looked up at him. "I'm viewing it as a form of surveillance. All part of the job."

Without thinking, Cutler reached out and gently brushed a strand of hair out of Jessi's eyes.

Jessi stepped back, embarrassed by the small act of intimacy in such a public place.

Kiko noticed and quickly moved away, leaving them in an awkward silence.

"I'm sorry, I wasn't thinking, I-"

"Anything in particular you want me to talk to Lela about?"

"Hell, I don't know." He rubbed his eyes tiredly. "I feel like I'm missing something. You've got fresh eyes, just keep 'em open. See if you can get her to open up a bit. Anything she says sounds interesting or catches your attention, call me."

"You got it."

"I won't be long."

"We'll be here."

Cutler climbed back in the car, reluctant to leave. There was something about Jessi that awakened more than just desire, although that was there too. Very much there. When he flipped a U-turn and pulled away, he glanced in the rearview mirror and spotted Jessi standing next to a barricade watching him.

As they waited for the parade, Jessi handed Nicole a five dollar bill and told her to treat Lela to a Snow-Cone at a nearby booth. She watched the two of them move through the long line before using her cell phone to call Houston and bring Lieutenant Sakelaris up to speed on their investigation. His response was short and to the point.

"We've had a dozen calls from the local TV people. They want to interview the female Rambo who did *The French Connection* chase with the city bus."

"You're kidding?"

"I don't kid on duty. Get your butt back here as soon as possible."

"Will do, Lieutenant," Jessi hung up and then immediately redialed asking to be transferred to Records.

"Records, this is Crook."

"Murray, this is Jessi Cole."

"Jessi, you won't believe this but they interviewed me on the six o'clock news. All three stations for crying out loud! I didn't have a clue what to wear or what to say. It was totally unreal. I tried to get you yesterday, and some moron in the squad room said you were out in the boondocks with a cowboy fortune-teller."

"You probably talked to Tyley, right?"

"How'd you guess?" Murray asked.

"Actually, he was half right. I am out in the boondocks with a cowboy *and* a fortune-teller. You ever hear of Grace County?'

"Never. Where is it?"

"Well, let me put it this way. We're way out in *Deep* Texas somewhere. Want to join us?

"What do you mean?"

"The sheriff's office is trying to get their communications system upgraded. Only trouble is they know nothing about computers. They'll pay you seventy-five bucks an hour, plus expenses. Not a bad way to spend a weekend. Interested?"

"Maybe, do they have any good restaurants up there?"

"None that will make you flaming shish kebabs, but have you ever had a foot long chicken fried steak?"

"You're making me curious. Any horses up there?" Murray asked.

"Horses? Good God, boy, we're in *Deep* Texas; they invented the horse three miles from where I'm standing."

It was quite entertaining for Jessi to watch her charges' reaction to the parade. Lela feigned disinterest in everything while Nicole was mesmerized by everything. Nearly a dozen high school and junior high marching bands were interspersed with simple floats from community organizations like 4-H, Big Brothers and Sisters, Little League Association, Bobby Sox, and several local churches. The thirty member strong VFW Post Marching Group hefted their well oiled M1 rifles as they marched sharply past, bringing their weapons to "present arms" as they passed the reviewing stand where Old Glory and the Lone Star hung limply in the growing heat. Following the VFW, a large contingent of very small children from a local preschool, raced past on tricycles and noisy Big Wheels, their proud parents followed close behind providing direction and encouragement.

One very familiar, red-nosed rodeo clown, riding a large, well muscled, quarter horse that sported a straw hat, dipped into his saddlebags and threw pieces of candy into the crowd as the chestnut colored horse clomped noisily along the roadway. The clown, his red wig bouncing from under his sweat stained, well-worn Stetson, guided the horse purposefully to where Jessi and the others were watching, flung himself from the saddle, doffed his hat and personally deposited several pieces of candy in Nicole's hand.

"Deputy Red, I presume," Jessi laughed as Red kneeled and made an exaggerated show of kissing the back of her hand.

Red, his red long johns partially covered by an oversized pair of worn bib overalls, doffed his hat again, before bowing deeply to Lela and swinging himself back onto the saddle and continuing down the street.

"Unbelievable," was Lela's only comment.

After the parade, Jessi, Lela and Nicole followed the crowd and walked the four blocks to the city park where the enticing aroma of barbecue, hot dogs, and corn was wafting through the air from several large, portable grills. Hundreds of watermelons were cooling in huge galvanized water troughs and tables were covered with a sea of potluck dishes. A sign on one of the grills announced:

> *"Meat courtesy of Short Falls Meat and Ice Company.*
> *Good neighbors make the difference."*

Continuing through the crowd, Jessi recognized the large man she met earlier at the highway rest stop. The ice man smiled and nodded in her direction. She returned the smile and watched for a moment as he pushed a heavy wheelbarrow full of ice bags toward a table where members of the Odd Fellow's Lodge dispensed a variety of soft drinks. Jessi returned her attention to the crowd, scanning the faces of teen-aged girls, hoping in vain to spot Samantha Deavers.

The pleasant, familiar sounds of organ music wafted from a brightly colored merry-go-round that was the centerpiece of a small carnival that also featured a Ferris wheel, a miniature roller coaster, and a variety of game booths.

As they paused to get their bearings, the public address system crackled to life and a male voice announced: "Ladies and gentlemen, Grace County's world famous sack race will begin in exactly four minutes and fifteen seconds. It's not too late to join in."

"I've never done a sack race! Can we try it?" Nicole's eyes sparkled with anticipation.

"Don't look at me," Lela said as she turned away.

"Never mind," Nicole said, disappointed. The pinched look around her mouth returning as she looked down at her feet.

"That sounds fun. Of course we can do it," Jessi said.

"We can?" Nicole brightened.

Lela glowered. "I said I wasn't going to make a fool out of myself in front of all these dimwits and if you-"

"Excuse us for a minute, Nicole," Jessi said as she took Lela by the elbow and led her out of the girl's earshot. "Listen up," she said close to Lela's ear. "You're one step from being handcuffed and held in a cell as a material witness. All I need is one excuse because it would save me a hell of a lot of trouble if you were behind bars. That way, I could go back to Houston."

Lela shook her head in disbelief. "Are you telling me that if I don't do this fucking sack race thing you're going to handcuff me?"

"In a heartbeat. Got 'em right here in my purse, ready to go," Jessi opened her purse and showed Lela one loop of the stainless steel cuffs.

"Fascism at it's worse. Un-fucking-believable," Lela spit.

"Unbelievable for sure," Jessi answered.

Lela gave Jessi a sour look before moving to Nicole. "I'll betcha a hotdog we can win this thing," she said, taking Nicole's hand and following the crowd toward an area of grass that was roped off for family games.

As Jessi followed she looked around and noticed Ellie Burris struggling into a burlap bag with two boys, nine and twelve, flanking her. Ellie looked up and waved in recognition. Jessi waved back just as Lela and Nicole hopped over to her.

"Saddle up, partner," Lela said sarcastically tossing a burlap bag in Jessi's direction.

Jessi smiled as she caught the bag.

"O.K.? So what's our strategy?" Jessi said.

"Ahh, gee, let's just try not to fall down and get trampled in the stampede, shall we?" Lela said, fluffing her cheeks in exasperation.

"I think we should just win," replied Nicole.

"That's the spirit." Jessi struggled into her burlap bag and joined the others at the starting line with Nicole in between.

The P.A. voice interrupted any further talk. "On your mark, get set..." The rest was drowned out by the shrill whistle and the laughter of shrieking children and adults alike as they held tightly to their sacks and attempted to jump, hop or crawl toward the finish line, thirty yards to their front. Along the way nearly half of the competitors tripped and fell, while a quarter of the survivors collided, going down in twisted heaps. Nearing the end, Lela tripped falling into Nicole who grabbed hold of Jessi bringing all three of them down just shy of the finish line. Ellie and her boys, still upright, hopped past. Nicole and Jessi rolled on the ground and roared with breathless laughter.

"What the hell's so funny?" Lela gasped as she rolled over onto her back. She tried to remain stoic but the laughter was contagious and she joined in.

"My underwear's wedged so badly I can't breathe!" Lela chuckled.

Jessi rolled over on her side and propping her head up with her fist, watched Nicole wrap herself in the burlap bag and giggle. The pureness of the little girl's joy was warmly familiar and for an instant she was back in a classroom, enjoying the spontaneity of young people's laughter. As she watched Nicole, she wondered briefly if it was the first time she had been able to enjoy just being a little girl.

An out of breath Ellie approached with her two sons. "Hi, I'm Ellie Burris, and these are my sons Emillo and Kyle."

"I won!" Emillo announced proudly.

"Barely," Ellie said, putting an arm around each of her boys who immediately squirmed free. "You were over in Slocum with John this morning, right?"

Jessi nodded.

"I just wanted to welcome you to Grace County."

Jessi smiled. "Thanks, I'm Jessi Cole and this..." she nodded toward Lela who was retrieving her carryall. "...is Lela Starr, she's..."

"She's here under duress," Lela said, joining them.

"Marty's mentioned you," Ellie said.

"Ah, you just made my day," Lela interrupted sarcastically "There's nothing I like more than being the topic of small town gossip."

"You'll have to excuse Lela," Jessi explained. "She's a sensitive...I mean she's *very* sensitive."

Ellie laughed as Lela shot Jessi a withering look.

"She reads palms," Nicole said shyly. "She said I'm going to have a bright future."

"She read your palm did she?" Jessi cocked a brow at Lela.

"Yes she did," Lela acknowledged. "And now, the infamous Lela Starr is going to set up shop and take some of these local yokel's hard earned cash." Lela moved away, pulling out her sketchpad as she headed across the grass.

"Where can I find you?" Jessi asked.

"Gee Mom," Lela shot back over her shoulder, "In the shade. Where else?"

"You don't leave my field of vision, understood?" Jessi warned.

Lela ignored her and continued walking.

"And you do this work on purpose?" Ellie smiled.

"Spoken like a true cop's wife. Makes you wonder about me, doesn't it?" Jessi said, watching closely as Lela hurried across the park and sat down in the shade of a large elm tree where she was soon joined by a large, familiar clown. "Lela definitely marches to the beat of a different drummer."

"She's just sad all the time, but I think she's nice," Nicole said.

The word "nice' spoken by Nicole's bird like voice caused Jessi to shudder involuntarily as she looked at the girl and then back at Lela. "Nice." The word echoed in her mind. Is that what poor Michele Sandoval had thought too?' "Nice," as in reading their palms, gaining trust and intimacy while luring them further into danger until the trap was sprung and it was too late. If Jessi looked at the situation logically, Lela couldn't have had anything to do with Samantha Deavers disappearance. Or could she? The call from her parents came in the day after their arrival in Grace but the girl actually went missing on Monday. She made a mental note to ask Lela where she was on Monday. The logistics seemed impossible, yet...

"You're a million miles away."

Jessi looked up to see John Cutler approaching with a tall man in glasses. The man moved to Ellie and kissed her on the cheek as both of the boys clamored for his attention.

"I'm just trying to inject myself into the mind of a psychic and possible kidnapper," Jessi answered.

"That would make anybody hungry. How about taking a little break and trying some of Grace County's famous barbecue?"

"Actually, I am hungry but I've got to keep a visual on the aforementioned psychic."

"No you don't. Red is taking this shift. We're off duty," Cutler said as he took her hand and placed it on his arm.

Jessi felt the urge to pull back, to withdraw, almost afraid of the warmth she felt from his touch.

"Off duty, huh? You're never off duty. Tell me you haven't been checking the parking lot for red pickups."

"Oh yeah, so tell me you haven't been scanning the crowd in hopes of spotting Samantha Deavers?"

"Guilty as charged," Jessi laughed as Cutler guided her a few steps to where Ellie and the others were gathered.

"I want you to meet my cousin, Marty Burris. We're kissin' cousins on my mother's side, only we don't kiss. Marty, this is Jessi Cole." Cutler said.

Jessi noticed the man standing with his arm around Ellie. "Nice to meet you," she held out her hand and mentally processed his description, a trick Big Deke had passed along in between catching fish while they drifted lazily in "The Bloodworm."

At six feet one, 185 pounds, Marty Burris towered over his wife. He had light brown hair cut razor short, wore heavy, unstylish horn-rimmed glasses ala Buddy Holly, and was between thirty-five and thirty-eight. He had a deep cleft chin and he wore an easy smile. He was either a cop or a Marine, Jessi surmised.

"Marty's one of Texas' finest Department of Public Safety officer. Highway Patrol," Cutler explained.

"Johnny's been bragging to me how pretty you were for the last two days. I had to come and see for myself. He wasn't exaggerating, for once," Marty said.

Cutler laughed, shaking his head in embarrassment. "Thanks, Marty. I owe you one."

"Hey, it's the least I can do for my favorite cousin. You ready for the softball game?" Marty asked.

"Yeah, guess it's time to pull a hamstring or two," Cutler replied.

Ellie stepped forward. "How about if Nicole comes with us for a while?"

"The boys and Nicole go to school together over in Slocum," Marty added in way of an explanation. "And they would just love Nicole's company. Isn't that right, boys?" Marty asked, grabbing each of his sons in the crook of his muscular arms and pretended to squeeze. "I can't hear you!"

"Yes, Dad," the embarrassed brothers answered in a well practiced unison.

Jessi took Nicole aside. "Does that sound fun?"

Nicole hesitated. "Yeah, I guess so."

"You can say 'no' and I'll cover for you," Jessi said.

"No, I'm O.K.. They're nice." Nicole answered.

"The boys want to ride the Ferris wheel and try some of the carnival games," Ellie said, holding out her hand toward Nicole. "How are you at ring toss?"

"Pretty good, I think," Nicole answered, taking Ellie's hand. She looked back at Jessi who gave her a reassuring smile.

"We'll see you in a little while," Jessi said.

Jessi and Cutler walked slowly through the park, past groups of chattering families, friends and neighbors sitting on lawn chairs or blankets spread out on the thick grass, taking advantage of the cool shade offered by long lines of oaks, elms and a few maple trees. It seemed to Jessi as if every group they passed greeted Cutler like he was a member of their family and he responded in kind. Questions like "How's that new baby doing?" to condolences like "Sorry to hear about Grandmother Reese passing. Grace County won't be the same without her," to playful warnings like "Hey Larry, don't forget the sunscreen this year, huh?" to explanations like "Poor Larry had a little too much to drink last year and fell asleep with his shirt off. He got so sunburned all of his buddies were pouring beer on him just to help him cool off. He almost drowned."

They hadn't gotten very far when Cutler paused and reluctantly relinquished custody of Jessi's hand. "I'll be right back. There's someone I need to talk to."

Jessi watched with growing interest as Cutler cut across the grass to intercept a tall, very attractive brunette who was hurrying through the park, scanning the crowd. She assessed the woman critically: Five foot seven, thirty to thirty-five, a hundred and forty, brown hair, wearing jeans and a red top. Jessi ticked off the statistics as if writing a report. Adding mentally, hair color from a salon; jeans, *tight* fitting jeans; top, cut low and snug to accentuate large breasts (probably real). Damn!

As Jessi watched the couple talking, she felt a strange stirring in the pit of her stomach. "What the hell are you, jealous? You don't even know the man," she mumbled to herself. The woman suddenly leaned in close to Cutler, speaking confidentially. Jessi, embarrassed by the flush she felt in her cheeks, turned away, and as she did she bumped into a tall blond man.

Excuse me," she said stepping back.

"No harm done," the man smiled, his white teeth accenting a tan, movie star handsome face. "I'm Sel Turner and I'm betting you're Jessi Cole, Houston P.D.'s finest homicide detective."

"Ah ha, the fearless reporter," Jessi said, the name clicking into place.

"Sometimes fearless, sometimes not," he replied, pleased that Jessi knew who he was.

"Tell me something. Do you ever check your facts before you publish?" Jessi asked.

Turner laughed. "You read my articles; you'll find all my facts are quite accurate. However, in my column I do tend to take just a bit of poetic license."

"Just a bit, huh?" Jessi shook her head, smiling in spite of herself. " I'm a patrol officer. I'm certainly not a detective. And I'm sure not a 'Female Rambo.' I read that as *a lot* of exaggeration, don't you?"

"Tell you what. Have lunch with me. We'll discuss the column line by line," Sel coaxed. "You and your psychic are the biggest story I've had in a long time."

"She's not my psychic," Jessi bristled for a moment before relaxing. "Oh, oh, I can just see the headline now. 'Rambo denies psychic influence.'"

Sel laughed. "Perfect. You're not only a female Rambo you're a natural lead writer. You can go to work for me any time."

"Not a chance, she doesn't work for minimum wage," Cutler said, deftly interjecting himself and the brunette between Jessi and Turner. "No one deliberately works for you, Sel."

"Hi, I'm Rose Lawson," the brunette held out her hand as she stepped toward Jessi, effectively shutting off any further exchange between the sheriff and the reporter.

"Jessi Cole," Jessi said shaking Rose's hand.

"Welcome to Grace," Rose said warmly, the genuineness of her smile disarming Jessi.

"So what's the Child Services Department doing here?" Sel asked curiously.

"What, a social worker can't enjoy the picnic?" Rose asked.

"If I'm not mistaken, this is the first Founder's Day you've been to in ten years," Turner said.

Rose chuckled. "You keep track of who goes to the picnic? Maybe you should get a life. I'm here because John promised to introduce me to Houston's female Rambo," Rose winked at Jessi. "Nice to meet you, Jessi. Let's get together soon."

"I'd like that," Jessi replied.

Rose linked her arm through Sel's and drew him away. "Now, let's leave these folks alone and go get ourselves a big bowl of Janie Cortez' potato salad. I'm famished."

Cutler looped his arm casually around Jessi's shoulders arm and they continued toward the barbeque area. "I called Rose about the situation with Nicole Deavers. She was interested because she had a pending file on Samantha Deavers, which she'll make available to us, unofficially of course, since it's a juvenile investigation and off limits to us."

"Let me guess: Accusations of abuse at home?"

"I can't legally say yes or no to that," Cutler answered.

"You just did. Thanks."

Jessi looked off at the departing social worker. "I like her," Jessi said as they continued walking.

"Yeah," Cutler agreed. "After high school she went off to Dallas to college, but came back when her mom got sick. She's top drawer. If there's anything going on out at the Deaver's place, she'll find out." Cutler explained. "She'll make sure Nicole's taken care of too."

Jessi stopped and shook her head.

"What's wrong?" Cutler asked.

"My first year of teaching was a real eye opener. Like most people, I just assumed all kids were loved, valued and cared for, like I was."

"Yeah, I learned the hard way too," Cutler answered. "Lots of sadness in the world," he added.

"And it never ends, does it?"

"Not when your job's *people,* I'm sorry to say. Sometimes you just have to go with what your instincts tell you."

"What do your instincts tell you about Samantha Deavers?" Jessi asked.

"I don't know if the Deavers girl is a kidnapping or a runaway, but looking at the family, who would blame her if she did run away?"

"You don't really think so, do you?"

Cutler unconsciously combed his fingers through his hair in frustration. "No, I don't think so, but there's no reason to link her disappearance with Michele Sandoval's murder either."

"No reason but there's something that's bothering you. I can hear it in your voice," Jessi stated.

The sheriff pointed off. "I can't help but feel that she's the key to this whole thing," Cutler nodded his head in Lela's direction.

Jessi looked over to where Lela sat on the grass, busy with her sketchpad, as a loose line of over a dozen locals waited to have their caricatures done by the world renowned psychic from Houston. Lela was wearing an enormous pair of Mickey Mouse sunglasses and on the trunk of a nearby tree she'd tacked a caricature of Red in all his clown regalia as the real life clown stood guard a few feet away watching, but not interfering.

"John!" A woman dressed in baseball attire and carrying a canvas bag with glove, bat and cleats strode purposely toward them. Jessi turned and saw a big woman, not fat, but tall and big boned with short hair setting off angular cheekbones and striking dark eyes. Her nose was underlined by thin lips.

"Hi Kathryn," Cutler greeted her with a smile.

"We've got a problem, Johnny. Lloyd Harris is on vacation and Jim Park sprained his wrist changing a tire this morning. He's out for the game. We've got eight people. I've been beating the bush but nobody will play." Kathryn said as she turned abruptly toward Jessi and gave her a quick head to toe inspection. "You're in good shape and you're certainly not the cheerleader type. I'll bet you know how to play softball, right?"

"I do, but I haven't played for a long time," Jessi shook her head. "I'm a bit out of practice."

"Kathryn, I want you to meet Jessi Cole. Jessi, Kathryn Weed," Cutler said.

"Nice to meet you, Jessi. Look, I'll be honest. We're desperate. We really need a first baseman. Say you'll do it. Otherwise we have to take an automatic out."

Jessi looked down, sweeping her hand to indicate her pantsuit. "I'm not dressed for softball."

Kathryn looked stricken.

Cutler stepped in. "After we eat I'll take you back to your room to change, that is if you're willing to play for us."

"Jessi shrugged. "I'm not promising I can even hit a ball anymore."

"But you'll try," Kathryn brightened. "I'll round up an extra mitt. What size of cleats do you wear?"

"Seven."

"So when are we going to meet that new husband of yours?" Cutler asked.

"Soon," Kathryn promised. "He's up in Comfort on business this week." With a wave, she hurried off in what Jessi assumed was a search for size seven cleats and a mitt.

"I can't believe I'm doing this. I haven't picked up a mitt since high school." Jessi said as she removed her key from her purse and opened the door to room seven, leaving it ajar as she entered.

"You might enjoy it," Cutler said as he lounged against the wall outside the door waiting as Jessi rummaged through her suitcase before finding a pair of shorts and a t-shirt that she had intended to use as night wear.

"I never enjoy making a fool of myself," Jessi said loudly as she disappeared into the cramped bathroom and closed the door, emerging a few minutes later with her clothes changed and her hair brushed up and held in a ponytail. She grabbed a pair of Reebok running shoes off the bed and joined Cutler. "I guess I'm as ready as I'll ever be," she said closing the door and turning to face him.

"Anybody ever tell you that you're gorgeous?" Cutler said.

Jessi couldn't tell from his tone whether the question was frivolous or momentous and simply looked at him.

Their gaze locked as he covered the few steps between them before leaning down and kissing her lightly on the lips. Instinctively her arms went up around his neck and pulled him closer. It was a long moment before she pulled away and walked toward the Blazer.

"We'll be late for the game."

"This isn't finished," Cutler promised.

They were both quiet on the ride back to the park. Jessi glanced at Cutler's face. He appeared to be scowling, a look she couldn't interpret.

"This isn't finished." She repeated his words several times to herself, each time a little surprised at the frankness of the pronouncement, but at the same time excited by it. She wasn't sure she wanted this complication, and yet...

The slow pitch softball game was a mercifully short and sweet contest for the home team. The Grace Rejects held the visiting Slocum Shysters scoreless for the first five innings and ended up winning 10 -3. The Rejects dominated the game start to finish with a stacked lineup that included American Legion star Marty Burris at shortstop, Jessi on first, Janie Cortez pitching, Frank Cortez on second and Cutler anchoring the infield at third. The hands down MVP however, turned out to be the Rejects catcher, Kathryn Weed. The large woman successfully nailed two Slocum runners at home, blocking the plate so effectively that one of the Shysters had to be helped off with a bloody nose and a possible cracked rib. Kathryn had a rifle for an arm and proved it by twice throwing out runners trying to advance on overthrows. It was Kathryn's hitting, however, that wowed the crowd. Weed launched two homeruns, booming shots that cleared the Little League left field fence by thirty feet and accounted for nearly all of her teams ten runs.

Jessi, who started the game with the simple prayer of, "Please don't let me make too big of an ass of myself," enjoyed herself. The act of concentrating on something as simple as where and when the white ball would come her way, freed her for an hour and twenty minutes from the weight of worrying about missing girls. She had a good day at the plate as well, going two for four. Her first hit was a blooper, but her second was a line drive that rolled nearly to the fence and allowed her to reach third base.

Jessi and Cutler couldn't keep their eyes off each other. Marty Burris noticed, leaving the dugout to give his wife inning by inning updates of the developing relationship. Ellie had also noticed from the grandstand and wasn't surprised.

"I told you he had that look," was her only comment.

The game went by quickly and when Jessi returned the borrowed glove and cleats Kathryn Weed gave her a big hug.

"You're welcome on my team anytime, girl."

"Thanks, Kathryn, it was fun."

Lela Starr was a hit with the Grace County crowd. At one point, Deputy Red Cordell counted 22 people waiting to fork over seven dollars for one of Lela's sketches. So many people wanted the colorful caricatures that Lela had soon exhausted her limited supply of sketchpads and had tacked up a new sign that read:

"Intimate Palm Readings - $10."

"Ain't everyday you can get your palm read by an internationally known psychic," Red heard Delores Fry, a Wal-Mart clerk from Slocum, explain to her sister, Pat, about the article in the paper.

As darkness came and the palm reading slackened, Lela quickly broke out her supply of quartz crystal necklaces and peddled them from a low of seven to a high of twenty-two dollars. An hour later, the necklaces were gone and Lela broke out her Tarot cards.

Red could only shake his head in amazement as the parade of customers continued.

"So what's that big hard looking thing poking out from your baggy pants? Let me guess. It's a big ol' 44 magnum like Dirty Harry carried, huh?"

Red refused to be baited.

"You know, you can talk to me. I mean, it's not like you're one of those fucking Buckingham Palace guards or something, Jesus. I mean you stand there in all your stupid get up and I know for a fact that you want to light up one of those extra long Pall Malls you got stashed in those baggy pants of yours. Am I right, or not?"

Red was silent for a full minute before he spoke. "Clowns don't smoke while clowning. The two things don't go together."

"Oh, right, the Happycratic oath? I get it. Bad for the image. So sit there in silence and die of a nicotine fit for all I care," Lela said as she stood and stretched her legs. "But I'll tell you this, every clown I have ever known has serious mental problems."

"Bullshit." Red stated flatly. "And besides, *bag* lady, I'm a rodeo clown, not one of those circus freaks."

"Ohhh, the clown talks. This clown is not only mentally ill like the average sad assed clown, but he throws himself in front of gigantic bulls crazed by having their balls crushed. That's normal is it? Hell, you're even crazier than the other clowns are!"

"And you know all this because you were on staff at the Walter Reed Psychiatric Unit before you started driving your shopping cart?" Red asked.

"I know this because I am an astute observer of people. I've seen the neurotic pleasure that clowns get in losing themselves in poorly applied greasepaint and tacky costumes."

"An astute observer of people my ass..."

"Let me get this straight," Lela angled her head and looked at Red thoughtfully. "You won't smoke because you don't want to spoil the happy, wholesome clown image, but profanity doesn't seem to be a problem."

"Will you just get the hell off my back," Red countered, turning away to watch the large crowd heading across the grass toward the fireworks display.

Lela started to laugh. "Get off my back? Get off my back? Hell, clown boy, now you know how all those bulls felt. That's what they were trying to say to you and your crazy friends all those years. Get off my damn back!"

The last thing Red Cordell wanted to do was encourage Lela by laughing and he tried gamely to stifle the urge, but in the end he threw in the towel, erupting in a deep, rumbling, embarrassed laugh that drew Lela in as well. Thirty seconds later they were finally winding down.

"You got me there," Red chuckled.

"So here's the deal, I'll get off your back if you tell me about being a rodeo clown. What was your most memorable moment? I mean the one absolute best experience you had."

Red studied Lela for a moment, trying to decipher her words and her body language. Was she making fun of him. He decided that she wasn't, and for some reason he couldn't explain to himself, he opened up to her.

"Bob's Your Uncle. Old 22."

"That was his name?"

"Yup. 'Bob 22' for short. Meanest bull I ever saw. The Cowboys didn't like him 'cause he didn't give 'em the kind of ride they could get a big score on. He wasn't big, hardly even average in size; mangy looking hide; stubby little horns; one shorter than the other; sharp little hooves. Nothing to him, really, except, for some reason, he hated clowns. He didn't give a crap about the cowboy riding him. That was just some dead weight on his back that would eventually fall off. No, he wanted the clowns, he wanted us, and by God, from the time he left the chute until the pickup men wrangled him back into the pens, that S.O.B. ran us from one side of the arena to the other. I'll bet he put ten clowns in the hospital and retired four of us that I know of. You know the barrels, right? We jump in a big old heavy barrel and the bull rolls us around the ring. The fans love it. Personally I never liked the barrels 'cause I got motion sick in 'em a couple times."

"I went to a rodeo once. I know the things you're talking about," Lela said.

"Well, with Bob's Your Uncle 22, we didn't dare crawl in the barrels 'cause that old sonofabitch would try to crawl in there with us. Seriously, he'd stick his big 'ol head in there and use it like a Mix Master. Oh, boy, that bull hated our guts. I must have fought him twenty times and in those twenty times he never left the ring until every damn one of the clowns were out of breath and up on the fence looking down on him. Then he would allow them to shoo him out."

Red was silent for a moment as he stared off, caught up in the memory.

"That's it?" Lela asked.

"One night a cowboy named Karl Evans draws Bob 22 and he does his eight seconds pretty good but when he tries to get off, his hand gets hung up in the bull rope and Bob 22 just starts to spin him around like he's a helicopter rotor. I jump in, do about five revolutions before I get Karl's hand loose and he falls clear but not before he takes a hoove above his eye and it knocks him cold. So while my partners are packin' and draggin' Karl out of the way, I swat old Bob 22 on the nose to distract him and try to run him away from the others. Well, Bob 22 goes for the fake and I can just feel him on my ass as I high tail it for the fence so I make a quick cut. Well, I'm wearing baseball spikes for traction, right, so when I make my cut, one of my spikes hits something and I go down flat on my back, spread eagle, right in front of that bull."

"Don't stop," Lela prodded as Red paused.

"Bob 22 jerks to a stop, dust and mud from his hooves fly all over me, I got dirt in my mouth and I'm looking up into his ugly, mean face, his hooves are right here t'ween my legs, and I simply froze. We just look at each other for at least two or three seconds. Then I cover my face and I roll up in a ball to protect the jewels, 'cause I'm dead certain he's going to give me the stompin' of my life and then the damndest thing happened. Bob 22 just raises his right hoof, places it very gently on my rib cage, about right here," Red said, patting himself on his left side. "Then the damn thing let's out with a huge bellow. Scared the holy crap out of me, I'll tell ya. Then that bull looks me straight in the eye and I'll be damned if he didn't smile before he turns and trots out of the arena."

"That's it?"

"They retired Bob after that."

Lela looked at the clown and slowly shook her head as a deep smile spread across her face. "I got a one word response. *Bull!*"

They laughed hard, enjoying the silliness.

"So here you are. What happened to the bull?"

"Well, a couple of weeks later I'm riding down Stony Point Road out south of town here and I pass Miller's Slaughter House and there's Bob's Your Uncle 22 in a holding pen waitin' for the grim reaper. So I stop, bail him out for 1200 bucks, and now he's out at Sheriff Cutler's ranch terrorizing every heifer he can find."

"Nice touch, clown. Now I'm going to the nearest restroom and hide while the fireworks scare all the wild creatures half to death and poison the air of our mother earth. If I were you I'd step behind the tree there and light up," she said as she gathered her belongings and stuffing them in her carryall, hurried off. She paused after a few steps and yelled back at him. "And quit calling me a bag lady! I am a perfectly normal human being with a lack of money who happens to carry a bag. There is a difference you know!"

"Yeah, yeah, whatever." Red's scowl was camouflaged by the outline of his painted red clown lips. He pulled a Pall Mall from his baggy pants and lighted it as he watched Lela walk toward the restroom.

The cinderblock restrooms were located on the southern fringe of the park, next to the field where the pyrotechnics crew had set up the launching mortars for the Rotary Club's annual fireworks display. As Lela entered the women's side of the squat building the deep "thump" of the first launched skyrocket shook the stall doors, startling her.

"Good god, can't a person even go to the bathroom in peace?" she said as a crushing "boom" sent a huge flowering circle of super heated magnesium expanding outward in an beautiful burst of red before expiring, leaving only a ghostly white outline that quickly evaporated.

"Anybody around here ever hear of air pollution?" Lela shouted before moving purposely to the middle of three stalls. Closing and locking the door she sat on the toilet and opening her bag, removed a large stack of paper currency. Lela quickly sorted the bills, mostly ones, fives and tens and counted them.

"Mmmm, "$378. Not bad for a couple of hours," she purred, stuffing the thick stack of bills back into the carryall as the lone light globe in the room went dark.

"Hey, I'm using the toilet, O.K.! Turn the damn light back on!"

The room remained in darkness, lighted only by a dull glow from the open doorway.

"Oh, this is just great," she barked as another "thump" shook the stall and the ensuing "boom," spread a silver glow over the room. A heavy sense of dread brushed her heart as she realized she was not alone.

"Is someone in here?" She recognized the fear in her voice and it startled her. "This isn't very funny, you know." Her heart raced as she left the stall and hurried toward the door. As she moved she heard the "squeak" of tennis shoes. Turning toward the sound, her eyes caught a blur of motion before her head exploded inward from a blow that dropped her facedown on the cool, polished cement that reeked of Pine-Oil. The warm saltiness of her own blood dripped over her lips and onto her tongue. She was aware of exploding fireworks but she couldn't tell if they were going off outside, or inside her head.

Lela teetered at the edge of darkness, fighting the powerful urge to sleep, struggling to escape the numbing pain in her head and neck and make some sense of her predicament as a cat with red eyes crossed in front of her. She suddenly felt hard hands encircle her throat and begin to tighten like an iron vice. She struggled in vain for a breath, fighting with all her will to inhale just as she heard sharp voices from somewhere off in the distance. The pressure was removed from her throat before another vicious blow exploded into her skull and pushed her over the edge into the safety net of unconsciousness.

"Where's Lela?" Jessi asked as she cut across the grass and approached Red.

Red gestured toward the restroom. "She just went to the can."

Jessi nodded and veered off toward the rest rooms. As she walked toward the small building, she noticed the women's end of the cinderblock structure was dark in comparison to the well lighted men's side where an assortment of flying insects played an endless game of tag.

Jessi paused and came alert, feeling a familiar knot rise in her stomach. "Lela!" Jessi shouted, her voice muffled by two "wumps" from the launching mortars. "Lela!" Jessi called again. She covered the remaining ten steps and was entering the rest room when a large person burst past her roughly, knocking her hard against the outside wall. The person disappeared into the darkness but not before their long blond hair caught the light of the exploding airbursts, and there was a lingering aroma of cologne in the night air.

She watched the fleeing figure for a moment longer before turning and entering the darkened room. "Lela, are you in here?"

The silence was shattered by a triple "wump" as a trio of airbursts rocketed upwards and exploded 800 yards overhead, bathing the room in an eerie red white and blue glow that exposed Lela's prone figure and the growing pool of blood under her head.

"Oh my god, Lela..." Jessi said as she dropped to her knees and felt for a pulse.

16.

❦

"It was my fault, boss" Red pronounced. He was visible standing at the mirror in the small restroom attached to the hospital emergency room.

"You're fault? How's it your fault?"

"I should have gone with her," he said, using a moistened Handy Wipe to remove the heavy circle of red greasepaint from around his mouth. He had shed his clown suit and was again dressed in his uniform.

"To the rest room? No way."

"I was having a smoke. I should have been closer. I might have at least heard something," Red said.

"I had you watching her because I didn't want her to run away. How in the hell were you supposed to know that somebody would attack her with 700 people walking around?" Cutler said, the worry lines above his eyes deepening. "No, Red, it's not your fault."

Cutler sat in silence for a moment thumbing through a well-worn back issue of "*PEOPLE*" magazine before tossing it on the table and standing up. "I honest to God don't get it. Of all the people walking around that park today, who'd choose that nut to bop on the head? And why? Somebody didn't like the sketch she did for them?"

"She's a hell of an artist, I'll give her that," Red mumbled. "I think she was robbed, plain and simple," he said.

Cutler shook his head. "Rob her of what? Her sketchpad?"

"Hey boss, that broad took in some serious bucks today. I couldn't say how much but she had a big old wad in that bag of hers. I saw her stash it."

"Well, Jessi went through the bag and found nothing. No money at all," Cutler said.

"I'm thinking she had to have close to $300 on her," Red said.

"And one of our upstanding citizens mugs her for it. That makes sense," Cutler agreed, nodding.

Red continued wiping his face. "Or maybe somebody didn't appreciate their palm reading? I mean, some of that stuff she was saying was pretty racy. Lots of sex talk and stuff like that. I heard her tell one woman to slip some Viagra in her husband's beer," he said as he tossed the Handy Wipe in a garbage can and stepped out of the restroom.

"Or maybe..." Cutler's voice trailed off.

"Maybe what?"

"Did you notice anyone hanging around, watching her during the day? Anybody you didn't recognize?"

"No, not that I recall, but hell, there was lots of folks out there, and believe me, she did get lots of attention. What are you thinking?" Red asked.

"I'm thinking that maybe her accomplice in the Sandoval homicide wanted to shut her up, permanently, and they were interrupted when Jessi came in."

"I don't know, boss, the more I'm around her, I...Good god, she wants to save the Spotted Owl for pete's sake. She wants to save the salamanders and the whales and the friggin' sea turtles and the old growth redwoods and the Polar ice cap and the Bolivian rain forest and all sorts of shit. Hell, kinda hard for me to imagine her killing anybody."

"Lela's O.K."

The two men turned as Jessi entered from the hallway. She was still wearing the white t-shirt she sported for the softball game but she had stopped at her motel room and retrieved a pair of blue sweat pants.

"It took ten stitches to close the cut on her lip and twenty-two more for the gash on her head. The doctor thinks she might have a concussion so he wants her to stay, at least overnight."

"How's she doing other than that?" Cutler asked.

"She's madder than hell. Say's that whoever hit her stole $378.00 cash."

Cutler looked at Red and nodded. "Guess you were right."

Red simply shrugged.

"Can I talk to her?" Cutler asked.

She just got an injection of something. She's gone for the night," Jessi answered.

"Anything else she tell you that could help?" Cutler asked.

Jessi shook her head. "Not really. It happened so fast. It's my fault. I should have stopped the person when they came out."

"Why is everybody blaming themselves? It wasn't anyone's fault but the asshole who beat her up. And Jessi, you probably saved her life," Cutler said, glancing at his watch. "It's ten-thirty. I don't want her alone tonight so we're going to have to bring in Shawn Peterson to take first watch."

"Shawn took his family to San Antonio for the weekend, remember? I'll take first watch," Red said.

"I'll stay," Jessi volunteered. "I can sleep in the bed next to hers. I don't mind."

"I'll stay," Red restated. "I feel like I owe her that."

"You don't owe her anything," Cutler countered.

"Maybe I'm doing it for myself then," Red said. "Either way it's settled!" Red set his jaw in the fully locked position that Cutler recognized oh so well.

The sheriff simply shrugged and turned toward Jessi.

"I need your help on a stakeout," Cutler said, guiding her toward the door.

Jessi waited in the darkness of the parked Blazer and watched Cutler leave the Shell Mini Market across the street with two Styrofoam cups of steaming coffee. He had a purposeful way of walking that radiated confidence, and she liked the way he looked in jeans.

As Cutler slid into the Blazer, he handed her the coffee before removing his hat and tossing it onto the back seat.

"Thanks," Jessi said as she tasted the strong, slightly bitter brew.

"You're welcome," he replied.

They sat for a moment before Cutler spoke again. "So, did you ever get a hold of that computer guy in Houston?"

"Murray Crook? Yes. I had to promise that we'd take him horseback riding," Jessi said as she took the lid from the cup and sipped the hot coffee.

"Now a horse ride is something I *can* manage."

They sat in silence, drinking coffee, watching the cars and pickups coming and going from Scotty's Snack-Out Drive-In across the street and down the block.

"You think our boy in the cool red truck will show up?"

"Come the weekend, every kid in Grace County will bust their butt to make it over here. It's been that way for as long as I can remember," Cutler replied.

"This ranch of yours, do you go out there every night after work?"

"No, it's quite a ways out, thirty-two miles, actually. Most nights I sleep at the office. We've got a couple of cots there we can pull out. I go out to the ranch most Sundays–spend a couple of days. My Uncle Merlin bought a half-dozen Longhorns from an auction house in Laredo. We've built up a small herd over the years. Longhorns have quite a history you know. They first came here from…"

Cutler was suddenly embarrassed. Maybe he was sharing too much with this woman. He couldn't expect her to possibly understand the love and passion for the land and animals that he had shared with his uncle. To her, Longhorns were probably nothing more than smelly animals that kicked up dust and attracted flies.

"Sounds like a nice life."

"Yeah, I guess it is. Maybe I could show you the ranch before you leave," Cutler replied.

"Yes, I'd like that," she replied as Cutler's cell phone rang.

"This is Cutler…Oh, hi Rose, what's going on?" He listened in silence for a few moments. "Good, they're good people… Thanks for calling… Yeah, I'll tell her." Cutler returned the phone to the dashboard. "That was Rose Lawson from Child Services. She decided to place Nicole Deavers in a temporary foster home pending her investigation."

"What kind of a foster home is it?" Jessi asked uneasily.

Nick Dunn and his wife, Cathy, They're great people so there's no worry there."

Jessi came alert, pointing off. "Look at that pickup!

Lenny Price's cherry-red 1955 Chevy pickup pulled into the Snack-Out Drive Inn, idled noisily past several parked cars, and then burned a ten-yard patch of rubber as it spun around to repeat the drive through, only to come grill to grill with the sheriff's Blazer. As Cutler and

Jessi climbed out and approached, Lenny leaned out and offered a weak smile.

"Sorry about the rubber, Sheriff, but my accelerator stuck."

"Could I see your driver's license and your registration please?" Cutler asked as he checked the inside of the cab, noting that Jessi had automatically moved to the other side of the truck and was doing the same thing from the passenger side window.

"I hope you're not going to write me up, Sheriff. I'm married with a kid, and my wife's pregnant again. I can't afford another ticket." Lenny's voice carried a heavy dose of "poor me" as he handed Cutler his papers.

Cutler scanned the license and registration. "Lenny Price? You wouldn't be any relation to Lavar Price, would you?"

Lenny beamed, sensing a glimmer of hope. "That'd be my daddy."

Cutler smiled, "That'd make your momma Kami Evans?"

Lenny's smile broadened. Maybe there was a God after all, he thought. "Yes sir. That's my momma. You know my folks?" Lenny prayed.

"I went to school with both of them. In fact, I sat in a car with your momma on this very spot probably twenty years ago. Man, where does the time go?"

"I hear that." Lenny was a tad bit cocky as his confidence came trotting back.

"Step out of the truck, Lenny."

"Yes, sir." A note of disquiet sneaked back into his voice. "Something wrong, sir?" He asked as he opened the door and climbed out of the cab.

"Put your hands on the hood," Cutler directed as he quickly patted down the puzzled Lenny.

"What's going on, sheriff? I ain't had nothing to drink. Swear to God, sir."

"Did you hear that Samantha Deavers is missing?"

"Who's Samantha Deavers?"

"Oh, I'm sorry, I thought you knew her."

As Lenny turned, Cutler moved eyeball to eyeball with him. "In fact, I was told you were the last person to see her."

"No sir, swear to God, I don't know her. I never heard of her."

Cutler's expression froze the young man in place. "Lenny, there are two things in this world I truly hate: phone solicitors and liars! Of the two, I hate liars more!"

Lenny's Adam's apple bobbed and weaved as he debated his next course of action.

Jessi gave him a slight push. "There was somebody with you when you picked Samantha up at the IGA Food Store on Monday night. Who was it?"

"Ray Larson, ma'am, but we didn't pick her up. We just talked to her, and that's God's honest truth. I swear."

"You just told us that you didn't know her, which makes you a damn liar. Now, you're saying that all you did was just talk to her, and we're supposed to believe you because you say 'honest to God?'" Cutler said.

"Ask Ray, he'll tell you. We didn't pick her up. Hell, she wouldn't get in the truck."

"Okay, listen up," Cutler said reaching behind his back and taking a set of handcuffs off his belt. "And think hard before you answer me because you have the right to have an attorney present before you answer any more of my questions."

"I don't need no lawyer," Lenny blurted. "I didn't do anything!"

Cutler stared at him in silence for a few moments. "When the state crime lab people go through this pickup, are they going to find any trace of Samantha Deavers in here?"

"Hell no!"

"You're 100% sure of that?"

Lenny hesitated. "Well, they might find something on the window or the door frame. She leaned in to talk to me."

Cutler moved back to the Blazer, reached in, removed his cell phone from the console, and, turning it on, handed it to Lenny. "Call your friend, Ray."

"I can pick him up if you want me to." Lenny volunteered.

"That's nice of you, Lenny, but you're going with me, and your pretty red truck here is going to be towed."

"Awe shit," Lenny whined as he placed the call.

"Why?" Kitty was seething. "What the hell were you thinking?"

Pinky shrugged. He had taken off his shirt in the cool room, exposing the crude, faded blue tattoos that covered half his chest and most of his back as he used a combination toothpick, flosser to clean his back teeth. "Another ten seconds and they'd be planning a funeral for that bitch. If I would have had more time, I could have gotten that female cop too. It was just bad luck she came up when she did."

"The way I heard it, the female cop might have gotten you," Kitty said, waiting to see if the jab struck home. Pinky was under the impression that no one was capable of getting the upper hand on him – especially a woman.

"There isn't a dike bitch cop in the world that could get me, *ever*," Pinky spit.

"You just made things more complicated, you know that?"

"I get rid of complications," Pinky answered.

"There were no complications until you decided to dress up in my wig and beat up an old woman," Kitty's anger rose again.

"I think the wig was a nice touch," Pinky said smugly.

Kitty gave him a look. "Fortunately, they think it's a simple mugging." Kitty thumped her open hand on the stack of rumpled greenbacks that lay on the Formica table between them. "At least you were smart enough to take the money."

Pinky looked at Kitty and shook his head. "You really don't get it, do you? These people see things we don't."

"What people? What the hell are you talking about? "

"Psychics."

"Psychics? You mean that old hippie. She's a joke." Kitty looked at Pinky. It dawned on her that just for the briefest of moments she'd seen an expression on his face she never expected to see – vulnerability. It was gone quickly, but it gave Kitty a fresh insight, and a new weakness she might be able to exploit.

"In the joint I read every book on psychics I could get my hands on. They do far out things."

"Like what?" Kitty asked, her voice dripping skepticism.

"Like there's a woman in France that solved a twenty-year-old homicide case by looking at a pair of shoes. Another woman in England solved a murder by just touching a bloody shirt. The third eye's no joke. I'm telling you that old hippie just might be seeing things that –"

"Don't believe everything you read in books," Kitty interrupted. "She's here because the sheriff is desperate. Besides, if she's such a great psychic, why didn't she see you coming?" Kitty chuckled at her own humor. "She could have spared herself a headache and some bruises."

Pinky shook his head slowly, deliberately. "You know something, bitch? You're brain's in a fucking tiny little box. You're thinking's way too narrow to comprehend this space we all occupy, let alone a whole 'nother dimension. Take in new ideas. Grow a little. Maybe you need a lesson. Maybe I need to expand your box." He reached across the table to grab her.

"Not now," Kitty said avoiding his grasp. "All your lessons begin and end with your crotch."

"Nothing wrong with that." Pinky's eyes were flat as he assessed her. "If you're not going to fuck me, I've got things to do," he said as he stood and snatched the money from the table.

"Listen to me. For our sake you have to stay away from that old hippie. She's no threat to us, I promise."

"You haven't been listening to me, bitch! As long as she is alive she is a threat! Don't you understand that?" Pinky exploded, slamming his rock hard fist on the table, eyes narrowing in a deadly warning that Kitty instantly recognized. Her mind raced trying to diffuse the explosion she knew was close.

"Maybe it's time to go trolling again," she said.

Kitty wasn't anywhere near ready to go back out, but she had to keep Pinky distracted. He was becoming a dangerous liability. "We'll try again tomorrow night."

Pinky nodded slowly as a part smile, part smirk spread across the hardened, leathery skin of his face. "I'll make sure the van's ready."

Wesley James "Pinky" Covine was born on January 10, 1974 at the Washington County Hospital in Panama City, Florida to a twenty-eight-year-old woman named Leona Covine. There was no father of record listed on the birth certificate of the four pound, one ounce boy who came into this world missing the little finger on his left hand. The screaming, heroin-addicted "preemie" had been given the nickname "Pinky" by a nurse in the county run facility, little realizing that the tag would follow the boy his entire life. Pinky had spent two warm months in one of the nursery's incubators before being discharged to join his deadbeat mother and three siblings in the cold reality of southern Florida's county's welfare system. Over the coming years Pinky and his two sisters and a brother would be bent, folded, and spindled through dozens of foster home situations that ran the gamut from good, to adequate, to bleak. While her babies, none of whom shared the same father, were left to fend for themselves, Leona would take to the streets, selling her fast deteriorating body for anything and everything she could possibly inject in a vein, snuff up her nose, or otherwise smoke or drink. Leona would eventually die of AIDS at the age of thirty-seven.

For her son, Wesley, Leona had been, for all intents and purposes, dead and gone by his sixth birthday. That day was remarkable because it had heralded the youngster's first of many encounters with the law. At that time Wesley and two of his siblings had been living in a highly regarded rural group foster care facility. The morning of his birthday he had wandered away and entered a neighbor's chicken coop where he methodically wrung the necks of over two-dozen prized Rhode Island Reds. The owners had heard a commotion, discovered the boy covered in blood and feathers, and called the police.

Pinky's next official encounter with county authorities came when he was eleven and was reported to have sexually abused an eight-year-old girl who shared the same foster home. Wesley was transported to the County Juvenile Detention Facility. Over the coming years, "Juvvy" would become the most influential environment in Wesley's life, a place where he would spend thousands of hours in the company of the county's worst role models. He was in some ways, a fast learner.

Pinky's known criminal résumé grew quickly, showing repeated entries for petty theft and vandalism, graduating to selling drugs, grand theft auto, and finally a felony rape. The rape was so vicious a crime that it landed him, at age seventeen, in Florida's Youth Authority Facility at Tallahassee, where he remained until his twenty-fourth birthday.

His stay at "Tally" gave the budding psychopath ample opportunity to reflect on his past mistakes and improve on them. Pinky soon came to the realization that every time he found himself in serious legal difficulties, it was because his victims would sit in court, sobbing, and point their accusing fingers at him. Pinky reasoned that if these women were not there to point the finger, then he had a much better chance of indulging in his fantasies without concern of punishment. Emerging from "Tally" seven years later, and having lost all contact with his siblings, Wesley became a sea gypsy, taking low paying seasonal jobs on fishing boats along the Florida Keys before working his way north into the Gulf States. He made few friends and was described as a "lone wolf" by many of his coworkers. The "wolf" description was quite accurate. Pinky had become a vicious and dangerous sexual predator. Through his low-key jobs he succeeded in making himself almost invisible, allowing him to grow bolder as he stalked females in every city where he worked. Over the next eight years the battered bodies of over a dozen females, ranging in age from thirteen to fifty-six, were discovered in Gulf State cities where Wesley Covine's boats happened to dock.

It was in Galveston, Texas that he made a critical error in judgment. After getting rip-roaring drunk, Pinky "borrowed" a 357-magnum handgun from the skipper of a deep-sea trawler he was working on, and he used the weapon to hold up an all night grocery store. During the course of the robbery, which was all captured on videotape, the young female clerk managed to trip a silent alarm before being savagely pistol whipped and dragged into a back room. Police units arrived on the scene within minutes, and Pinky was taken into custody, literally with his pants down. Galveston Police authorities had no idea that the bearded seaman they had in custody was a huge fish caught on a relatively small hook. Pinky was certainly not going to share with them the fact that they had one of the most vicious serial killers in the history of the southeastern United States sitting in their jail.

The pragmatic Pinky, well versed in jailhouse law, struck a plea bargain that dismissed the kidnapping and attempted rape aspects of the case, as well as the felon in possession of a firearm charge, and pleaded guilty to armed robbery and assault. He was sentenced to Huntsville Prison to serve a term of no less than eight, no more than twelve, years.

Like many convicts with an abundance of time on their hands and their eye to an early release date, Pinky developed a keen interest in establishing pen pal relationships, sending out dozens of correspondences to desperately lonely women he met through letters provided by the prison Christian Outreach Program. The closer Pinky got to his release date the more critical it became for him to snare someone who would provide a temporary haven where he could reacclimatize to the outside world before resuming his predatory ways, and on one Sunday morning in December, fate intervened in the form of Kitty Reece.

In a letter later found in his possession, Pinky described the meeting:

Huntsville State Prison
Huntsville, Texas

Dear Ms. Lucas,
I know you said I should address you as Kitty, but I have a slight problem doing that with such a well-educated and proper woman as yourself. I hope you don't think this letter too forward of me, but after meeting you and the others from the Whole Gospel Ministry of Peace at

the prison this morning, I wanted to write a personal "thank you" for taking the time to come to this awful place.

I know this sounds crazy, but one minute I sat in that hot little chapel elbow to elbow with 33 other sweaty cons, and the next minute I saw you stand and give testimony to the power of Jesus Christ our Lord and Savior and when our eyes made contact I felt a jolt hit me. For the rest of the meeting I felt that you and I were alone in the chapel and that you were getting your message from ABOVE and passing it directly to my ear. Being able to shake your hand and talk to you for a few precious seconds has lightened my load considerably, and for the first time in the 2,584 days I have been here, my spirit is free.

I sincerely hope you will come again. Maybe if you have the time you could drop this sorry repentant a note, and tell me more about your life.

Sincerely,
Wesley Covine

Kitty's reply came within a week:

Bancroft, Texas

Dear Wesley,

Thank you so much for taking the time to write that kind and wonderful letter. I have read it over and over. I, too, was moved by our Sunday prayer meeting. I have to confess that when Pastor Dillis first approached me about traveling to Huntsville Prison to give testimony, I agreed, but with dread in my heart. I remember looking out over a sea of blurred faces before the Lord Jesus Christ entered my body and soul and swept away my fear, leaving me with a confidence I have never previously experienced. My heart felt ready to burst with happiness, and it was at this moment I saw you smiling up at me. I knew in that instant that I was sent to Huntsville Prison to share with you my simple message. In all those faces I saw no one but you.

As I related in my testimony, my life has been full of sadness and tragedy, beginning with the untimely passing of my mother when I was seven years old. Mother died after giving birth to my little sister, Molly, leaving my father and I to do our our best to give our precious baby a proper Christian upbringing. My father died of a heart attack when I was nineteen, leaving me to raise Molly and run the family business alone. Molly disappeared on her thirteenth birthday and her uncertain fate has haunted my life ever since. It was not until I accepted the Lord Jesus into my life as a constant presence that I truly felt blessed.

If you would like me to, I would be honored to visit you at the prison and continue our Bible study on a one-to-one basis. I anxiously await your reply.

Warmest regards,
Kitty Reese

To Pinky, Kitty Reese was a gift, the perfect pawn for the ultimate con. He had no way of knowing, however, that *he* was the pawn, but he'd soon learn.

It was one-thirty in the morning when Jessi left the small interrogation room and poured herself another cup of coffee. Night dispatcher Jill Richards watched her with interest from the communications console.

"I can order you something to eat from Pocatello Pablo's if you want, dear. They'll deliver for us."

"That's nice of you to offer but I'm not hungry. I stuffed myself at the picnic."

"I did too," Jill replied, shaking her head in awe at Jessi. "It must be awfully exciting, I mean, being a woman and being able to be out there with all the fellas," she gestured toward the outside. "Me, I just sit here and answer the phone. Sometimes I get excited just to be part of that."

Jessi smiled. "Sometimes it is exciting. Most of the time, it's not." She glanced into the small room where Cutler continued the interrogation of a frightened Ray Larson.

The eighteen-year-old auto parts clerk had a chronic case of acne that had left his complexion pockmarked and perpetually inflamed.

"We didn't do anything to that girl," Jessi heard him say through the door.

She turned and continued through the office, pausing where Lenny Price was sitting under the watchful eyes of night deputy Stan Denno.

"Let's hope your buddy in the other room has the same story, my friend, because if he doesn't...?" Stan pulled a finger across his throat.

Lenny shuddered and turned away, looking for a more sympathetic audience, his pleading eyes settling on Jessi. "I'll tell you this, ma'am; it wouldn't surprise me at all if something did happen to Sammy. She's like thirteen, going on twenty-five, if you know what I mean?"

"I don't know what you mean. Explain." Jessi replied.

"Hell, she's balled half the guys in town."

Jessi shook her head. "And since you were trying to score with her, that makes you what, twenty-five going on thirteen?"

Lenny looked mortally wounded as he looked at Jessi, realizing there was no sympathy forthcoming.

Jessi turned away from him in disgust. "What a self-serving little prick," she thought just as Cutler exited the interrogation room and directed the confused Ray Larson to the rest room in the corner.

Lenny Price was immediately on his feet. "Sheriff, I've got a wife and baby waiting for me at home."

Cutler didn't bother to make eye contact with Lenny as he brushed past.

"Maybe I should be calling me a lawyer then," Lenny blurted to Cutler's back.

The sheriff froze and turned. "You really think you need a lawyer, do you?"

"Ahh, no, I mean, ahh, I guess not, but I got a wife and child to consider. Don't I?"

"Then, by all means, call your wife and tell her you will be a little longer," Cutler answered. "And while you're on the phone, you might try and explain to her that you're being detained because you were dicking around with a thirteen-year-old girl. Or maybe you'd like me to call your folks? You know what they'd say, don't you? They'd tell me to take you out back and kick your stupid ass which I would surely love to do!" Cutler roared as he turned and approached Jessi.

"How'd it go with his friend, Ray?" Jessi asked.

"So far their stories are just different enough to be believable, but we'll wait for the lab results on the pickup before we write them off. Stan, keep those two guys apart. I don't want them exchanging alibis any more than they already have."

It was nearly two-thirty in the morning before the sheriff released the two boys with the admonition not to leave the area and with the understanding that they would return the next day if the situation warranted.

"So, you ready to call it a day?" Cutler asked Jessi.

"Definitely."

They made the five minute drive to Velma's Motel in total silence, each lost in the day's events and the unspoken promise of what was about to happen.

"Well," Cutler said as he pulled to a stop in front of Jessi's room and turned the engine off. "Been quite a day."

"Yes, it has been," Jessi answered.

Cutler reached out and covered her hand with his own. The simple gesture causing the butterflies to rise in unison and flutter through her stomach. As their eyes locked across the darkness Jessi felt a warmth flowing up her arm and into her breasts before spreading through her neck and flooding over her face. They kissed lightly, Cutler touching her cheek ever so gently and stroking her hot cheeks with the tips of his fingers.

"You know that if I go in your room with you, it'll be all over Grace County by tomorrow morning," Cutler said.

Jessi brushed her lips softly over his. "Is that a problem for you?"

"Not for me," Cutler responded. "I just wanted you to know how it would be."

"I can live with that," Jessi said opening the door and climbing out of the car.

As they entered the dark room, Jessi turned to face him. "It's important that you realize I don't do things like this lightly."

"Neither do I," Cutler said, fastening the chain lock on the door.

They came together slowly, their lips parting as their mouths tasted each other for the first time and their nostrils took in the intimate potpourri of skin, hair and clothing.

Cutler's hands quickly found her breasts, stroking their roundness, deliberately trying to slow his own excitement as he felt Jessi's body respond to his touch. Her arms circled around and under his shirt as she ran her fingers down his back. The simple act sending ripples of excitement through his body. He stepped back and pulled his shirt over his head. The skin of his muscular chest and wide shoulders glowed white in contrast to his deeply tanned arms and face.

"I want to watch you undress," he whispered, setting on the edge of the bed and pulling off his boots.

Her eyes held Cutler's as she moved back and stepped out of her shoes, slipped her pants down over her hips and pulled them off followed by her top. She moved close to him, wearing only her bra and panties. She slipped her panties off and let her bra fall to the floor leaving herself exposed. His eyes took her in slowly, completely before rising to meet hers. They looked at one another as if trying to read each other's heart before he reached out and pulled her willingly down to join him.

17.

Jessi woke up early, arms and legs entangled with Cutler's. She held still, enjoying the closeness of the moment, noticing the gray light of early morning pushing through the gaps at the end of the plastic backed curtains. She was surprised at how good it felt to wake up and have him there and for a moment she listened to the evenness of his breathing. Jessi turned her head ever so carefully so as not to disturb him and closed her eyes.

"I thought you'd never wake up," Cutler said softly as his arms tightened around her and their lips met, desire taking over.

"You sure you want to do this?" Cutler asked as he pulled the Blazer to a stop in front of the Grace County Medical Center.

"I'm sure. I've got a report to write, and I want to talk to Lela again anyway. She was in no condition to be questioned last night."

Cutler nodded. "I'll send someone over with the Sandoval file and my notes on the Deaver interview."

"I'll compare them with mine. Maybe something will jump out."

They exchanged a long look that had nothing to do with the job.

"This isn't finished," Cutler said as Jessi got out of the car.

Jessi laughed. "I've heard that before." She closed the door and walked toward the entrance.

Jessi was still smiling when she approached Lela's room, nodding at the middle-aged deputy who looked up as Jessi walked past him and entered the room.

"Do you know what time it is?" Lela barked watching Jessi set her purse down on the nightstand.

Jessi checked her watch. "Yeah, it's 9:30 in the morning. So what?"

"So it's well past high time you got here," Lela snapped. "I'm going nuts. The clown left about three hours ago and Deputy Nash here, a foot washing Baptist if I ever saw one, has chosen not to delight me with his scintillating conversation." Lela pointed to where an uncomfortable Deputy Lee Nash had taken refuge behind a newspaper. His chair was angled by the open doorway so that he had a visual of both Lela and of the hallway.

"Sheriff Cutler's instructions were to watch anyone entering, but to definitely keep an eye on her. He said diddly squat about carrying on conversations," Nash explained, his voice dropping to a near whisper. "That is not a restful woman."

"I hear that," Jessi said, her eyes taking in the thin, vulnerable woman on the bed. The top of Lela's head was bandaged, her face battered, angry bruises were visible on her neck and arms. Jessi unconsciously tightened her lips and shook her head.

"Don't be giving me any of your pity," Lela scolded. "I suppose you expect thanks for saving my sorry ass last night?"

"I didn't know you needed saving, or maybe I would have gotten the bastard." Jessi shook her head again. "And I'm not pitying you. Well, maybe I am feeling just a wee little bit of pity. Have you looked in the mirror lately?"

Lela gave her a glimmer of a smile which caused her to wince as a trickle of blood oozed from her split and swollen lips. "You're just feeling guilty," she said numbly.

"Guilty? Why should I feel guilty?"

"Because the minute you and the Sheriff of Nothingham entered that motel room and shut the door, you didn't give me another thought."

Jessi felt her face redden as Deputy Nash quickly gathered up his paper and stood awkwardly by the door.

"Why don't you go get a cup of coffee, I'll take over here," Jessi said, releasing the embarrassed deputy to beat a quick retreat down the hallway. Jessi turned back to Lela.

"Just what makes you think the sheriff and I spent the night together?"

"Maybe *you* should look in the mirror," Lela countered. "You don't need to be a psychic to read that satisfied glow. And besides, Deputy Nash there is Velma Nash's nephew. These people communicate. So tell me, was the sheriff average, good, super, what?"

"None of your business. And I don't need to explain myself to you or anybody else," Jessi said, blushing in spite of herself.

"No, no you don't. Susan B. Anthony won that for us, right?" Lela said, smiling through her swollen lips. "I'm just envious, that's all." Lela reached out and picking up a droopy, straw gardener's hat off the nightstand, placed it gingerly on her head, covering her bandages. "I don't do bandages well."

"Cool hat. Where'd you get it?" Jessi asked.

Velma brought it up to me. She brought me some chicken soup no less. So how do I look?"

"Smashing."

"Smashing or smashed?"

"Take your pick," Jessi said, sitting down on the edge of Lela's bed and pushing the movable table aside. The table held a breakfast tray that Lela had barely touched.

"You need to eat, you know?"

"I know it sounds a little strange coming from someone who shops in garbage cans but I don't have much of an appetite. But please, have all you want. Enjoy this wonderful free food. Bon appetite."

"No thanks," Jessi said, noticing that Lela had burned several sticks of incense in a glass ashtray that sat on her nightstand. She had also laid out her assortment of healing stones in an arrowhead pattern pointing toward the door. "Looks like you got your security system all set up."

"You can never be too secure," Lela responded tiredly lying back in the bed. "I'll bet it beats sleeping with a 357 under your pillow."

"Mine's a nine millimeter. So, did you remember anything that could help us track this person down?"

Lela simply shook her head. "Happened so fast, and I got clobbered so hard. I think it had to be a man."

"He must have been wearing a wig then because when he pushed past me I saw long blond hair," Jessi explained. "And he smelled like-"

"Old Spice. I know it was Old Spice because Bernie wore Old Spice. And there was another odor too. Something under the cologne that I've smelled before. Something that I..." her voice trailed off as she drifted to sleep.

Jessi spent the rest of the morning sitting in an uncomfortable, burgundy colored Naugahyde chair pouring over the Michelle Sandoval murder book reading the detailed statements of the truck driver who found the girl's body and the first law enforcement officer on the scene, who, ironically, turned out to be Sheriff Cutler's cousin, highway patrolman Marty Burris. She paused briefly over the photos of the corpse as it was discovered in the trash dumpster and then read the lengthy autopsy report, scanning quickly two full pages of grisly pathology photos before pausing on the posed, junior high photo that highlighted the girl's innocence and natural beauty. She read with interest the dozen or so interviews with Michelle's classmates, teachers, friends, family and neighbors; each reflecting on the warm personality of a beautiful girl who simply loved life.

It was close to five in the afternoon before Dr. John Corollo, the slender, graying, amiable man who had delivered nearly eighty percent of Grace County babies for the past forty years, entered the room and began giving Lela a head to toe inspection.

"Good afternoon, ladies. D'all get some sleep last night?" he asked, his voice dripping a deep Texas drawl.

"I slept like hell, she slept like a baby and just where the hell have you been, playing golf for Pete's sake?" Lela complained.

"Actually," he said, shining his pen light into her eyes, "Golf doesn't interest me. I've been playing tennis." He placed a blood pressure cuff on her arm and inflated it.

"Gee, Doc, that makes me feel so much better," Lela quipped sarcastically as the doctor listened to her heart beat through his stethoscope.

"I'm pretty damn good, too. Grace County senior's champ as a matter of fact," he said.

"Really? I thought you rednecks spent your spare time shooting beer bottles off each other's heads and having demolition derbies and tractor pulls, that sort of thing," Lela said as the doctor rotated her neck.

"That hurt?"

"Every muscle in my body hurts."

After five full minutes of bending elbows and knees, listening to heart and lungs, checking the soreness around Lela's kidneys, the doctor released her and Deputy Lee Nash drove them back to the office.

Sheriff Cutler was sitting at his desk, buried between foot high stacks of files and half finished reports, when Jessi and Lela entered the double-wide trailer that served as both the City of Grace municipal offices and the Grace County Sheriff's Office. Lela made a beeline for the sheriff.

"Hey!" Lela rapped her knuckles on the edge of his desk.

"Hey what?" Cutler grunted.

"So who did it?"

"Good day to you too. Glad to see that you're up and around. Did what?" Cutler asked, closing a file.

"Twenty-two stitches in my head, bruises over 50% of my body, my personal space shattered, and my aura totally decimated. That's *what*!"

Cutler raised his eyes, unconsciously wincing at the black and blue circles around her eyes. "Don't know. We're looking into it."

"Looking, huh? How about mug books. You got any mug books I can look through?"

"We've got some mug books. But seeing as you didn't see the person who attacked and beat the crap out of your aura, what good would it do?"

"You're not much into the finer points of law enforcement are you? Where's Jack Webb and Joe Friday when you need them?"

Cutler ignored her. "Since you're finally up and around, I'll tell Clyde to go ahead and get his machines set up."

Lela was instantly on guard. "Machines? What kind of machines?"

Cutler studied her face. "Polygraph."

"You want me to take a lie detector test?" Lela asked, turning to include Jessi in her icy glaze.

Cutler nodded.

Lela shook her head slowly. "I'm taking a lie detector test because I got mugged?"

Cutler stared at her for a moment, measuring his response. "It'll only take an hour or so."

"Oh, now I get it. This is about Mickey Sandoval," she shook her head sadly, turning her attention to Jessi. "How could you think I would be involved in the death...the murder...of that little girl? How could you!?!" she exploded, her voice trailing off into partially stifled sobs.

Jessi watched her for a moment before speaking. "Lela, if you have no involvement in Michelle's death, then this can prove it."

Lela took a Kleenex off a nearby desk and wiped her eyes.

"Yeah, O.K., whatever. I've been hooked to machines all night, might as well hook me up to some more. Bring on this Clyde because I'm going to kick his ass!"

Cutler stood as Janie Cortez approached. "Janie, take Ms. Starr back and introduce her to Clyde, will you please?"

As Janie led Lela toward the interrogation room Cutler, came out from behind his desk and approached Jessi.

"How you doing?" he asked.

Jessi nodded and smiled their eyes locking for a long moment.

"Your friend from Houston's here," he said.

Jessi was puzzled. "Friend? Who?"

Cutler pointed across the room to where Murray Crook sat at a computer with Deputy Red Cordell looking over his shoulder. Murray looked up and waved at Jessi.

"Murray!" Jessi hurried across the room to exchange hugs. "How'd you get here so fast?"

Murray was wearing a pair of faded jeans and a brightly decorated Hawaiian luau shirt he had purchased at Hilo Hattie's on the Island of Maui. "Tell you what, girl. After you called me last night I developed a bad case of flu so I did the responsible thing, called in sick, and damn well hit the road. You know that dented old BMW of mine? It just went over three hundred miles in just under five and a half hours and I only got one speeding ticket that my pal Red here is going to take care of. Isn't that right, Deputy Red?"

"Done deal little buddy. I'll pay for it out of my own pocket if I have to." Red stood and slapped Murray solidly enough on the back that the smaller man nearly lost his balance. "This little fella's done more with these computers in the last two hours than I've done in the last two weeks."

"I told you Murray was a computer geek, err, *genius*. Sorry," Jessi joked, also giving Murray a playful swat.

"What is it with you people? You show affection with body blows?" Murray complained.

"So how's it going, Murray? Can you bring these folks into century 21?"

"Does God love Texas?" Murray sat back down in front of Red's computer and taking a CD from a stack, inserted it into the processor. "Let me put it this way, Jessi. By this time tomorrow, Deputy Red here will not only be using Windows, he'll be talking terabytes, megahertz, gigabytes and flash drives like he invented the language."

"Never happen, little buddy," Red pointed across the room to where Deputy Kiko Avila talked on the telephone. "My friend over there says I'm what you college boys call a Luddite, whatever the hell that means." Red laughed, almost giddy at having the responsibility for setting up the new computer system taken off his broad shoulders.

Murray stifled a smile as he took one disc out of the processor and inserted another. "Well, hang onto your tattoos, Deputy Red, because you're about to enter cyberspace!"

According to many, sixty-two-year-old Clyde Briscoe not only had the best string tie collection in the State of Texas, but was the best lie detector man in the state, as well. Clyde was so good, some said, he didn't even need to hook his subjects to all that fancy machinery. He could just hold their wrist between his thumb and forefinger and look into their eyes to ascertain the veracity of their answers.

Clyde was a skinny six-foot-three, and a two-pack-a day Camel Lights habit had kept his weight under 170 pounds and his voice deep and gravely. Clyde, himself, explained his success as his ability to make his subjects relax.

"You've got to put your clients at ease," he would explain to his students. "For all they know, all these wires and needles could electrocute them."

Clyde's method to help his *"subjects...*not suspects " relax was to engage them in casual, good old boy conversation for the four or five minutes it took him to attach the sensors and cuffs and then to inform them that "This here machine ain't going to tell me whether you're lying or not; it's just going to tell me how confident or nervous you are about your answer." He would continue this good old boy routine, and by the time the subject realized it, he or she was giving answers to questions that could have potentially disastrous effects on their futures. Lela Starr, however, was one subject who seemed immune to Clyde's charm.

"Do you like ice cream?" Clyde asked her in a tone which a grandfather might use to address his granddaughter.

"I used to like Ben and Jerry's, but not any more. They sold out to a corporation too, just like the rest," Lela responded and then added, "Of course I like ice cream. What kind of horseshit question is that? Do you think I'm un-American or something? Take control of your subject, Clyde, show her the ropes!"

The ever patient Clyde simply smiled and continued. "If you don't mind, little lady, I think it might be a bit easier on the old machinery if you could just answer yes or no. Let's try another one. Do you drive a car?"

"Only when it's running," Lela shot back.

"Do you own a car?"

"No, I don't own a car. But, I do own a van. Does that count? Oh, excuse me. The answer is no, but depending on your response, it could be 'yes'. That make sense?"

Clyde, unruffled, made a scribble on the graph paper, noting mentally the rhythmic swing of the needles as they traced their relentless patterns of peaks and valleys.

"Were you present when Michelle Sandoval was killed?"

"No! Absolutely not!"

"Did you see Michelle Sandoval's body being placed in a trash dumpster?"

"Yes I did, but I wasn't there, I..."

"Do you take sugar in your coffee?"

Lela waited a good ten seconds before responding. "I drink tea."

"Was the sky blue today?"

"I certainly think that depends on where you were standing. In the Azores, I couldn't say. Jamaica, probably. Here in boonyville, yes."

Jessi glanced through the closed glass door into the back office of the trailer. From her vantage point she couldn't see Lela at all and only part of Clyde Briscoe's back. She checked her watch and noted that the polygraph test had been going on for over two hours and it was getting dark outside. She walked to where Deputy Red Cordell and Murray Crook were huddled in front of the computer. Night dispatcher Jill Richards stood behind them, her headset dangling as she watched, fascinated, at the ease at which Murray worked at the computer.

Jill shook her head and smiled. "Red, honey, this is the first time I've seen you smile in a month of Sundays."

"Life is suddenly good again," Red replied, again poking Murray good naturedly on the shoulder. The police line rang and as Jill plugged in to a nearby outlet, Red glanced up to see her flash one finger at him before looking back at the monitor.

Murray looked perplexed. "Don't think me too forward, but that's about the tenth time one of the dispatchers have flashed you the finger. What's up?"

"One finger, the call is business as usual, go back to work. Two fingers mean the call is police business that has to be handled, but it's not critical, maybe I'll stick you with it, maybe I won't. Three fingers mean grab your gun and your car keys and hit the road, all hell's breaking loose."

Down the hallway behind them, Lela suddenly exploded from the small office fleeing the trailer like a caged animal released from captivity, slamming the door so hard on her way out that the screen insert popped out onto the tile floor. A tired looking Clyde Briscoe exited the office behind her, rolling down the sleeves of his wrinkled western shirt, and lighting up his first Camel in over two hours, he took a deep drag as he approached Cutler's desk.

"So what do you think, Clyde, she worth hanging on to?" Cutler asked as he rose from his desk.

Clyde let the smoke linger in his lungs for as long as possible before surrendering it. "Johnny, swear to God, that woman's so off the wall I can't get a clear reading on her one way or another," he said, grabbing another drag off the cigarette before continuing in his gravely tone. "Hell, half the time in there I got the feeling she was testing me."

"You think she might have been sandbagging you?" Cutler asked.

Clyde shrugged. "Maybe. Hell, who knows? Tell you this, I'm glad it wasn't a fist fight; she'd a kicked my ass good. Maybe it's time I hung it up and went fishin', permanently."

Cutler frowned. "So where do we go from here?"

"I can try it again later tonight or tomorrow, but right now I don't know what to think. You got any hard stuff in here? "

"Yeah, in the bottom cabinet where my cot is," Cutler said, pointing across the office to a small side room.

As Clyde headed for the Jim Beam, Jill disconnected from her call and, standing, handed Cutler a yellow sticky note.

"That was Louie. He just talked to another clerk and two grocery baggers at IGA Supermarket who also saw a woman with long dark hair giving away puppies outside the entry the night Samantha Deavers disappeared."

Cutler looked at the three names on the note and recognized two. "Is Eddie Huerta still the manager at IGA?"

"As far as I know, he is," Jill said.

"Call the store and tell Eddie I need Rich Alrich and these other people over here to give a formal statement ASAP. If we can find the woman who had the puppies, we just might have a witness to what happened."

Jessi moved to the window of the trailer and looked out, spotting Lela sitting sullenly on a large boulder next to the flagpole. Cutler joined her.

"I honestly don't know where to go with this right now," he said. "She just about drove poor Clyde into retirement."

Jessi simply shook her head. "I don't know either."

"Play good cop, bad cop. Put it all on me. Tell her I think she's lying and..."

"She's way too bright for that," Jessi responded.

"Give it one more shot, will you?"

Jessi exited the trailer and approached Lela, her feet crunching noisily as she moved through the deep gravel of the parking area. "Mind if I join you?"

Lela shot her a cold look. "Did I pass your fucking test, or not?"

Jessi swept her hand in front of her in an ineffective attempt to clear away a thick column of noseeumms that were barely visible in the growing darkness. She raised her eyebrows.

"It wasn't my test."

"Okay, let me be more precise. Did I pass Sheriff John Cutler's fucking test or not?"

Jessi gave her a long look before she sat down on the rock next to her and took a deep breath. "Look, you're tired, I'm tired, and I'm sorry if all of this has upset your sensitive psychic soul, but this isn't the kind of situation cops are accustomed to dealing with. You see, Lela, people who come to the police with the kind of information you presented to us are, ninety-nine and nine tenths percent of the time, involved up to their eyeballs in the crime and are usually trying to cut a deal or otherwise save their own sorry ass. So look, if you want to cut a deal, let's do it, but don't bullshit me anymore. Like I said, I'm tired too."

As Jessi turned away she felt Lela's eyes burn into the back of her head.

"Well, I'm not trying to cut a deal, but I would very much like to save my sorry ass, and I'd like to know if I passed the fucking bullshit lie detector test! Jesus, is that too much to ask?"

"I don't know. You've got poor old Clyde so rattled he's in there drinking straight up shots of JB and chain smoking Camel Lights. Poor old guy can hardly talk," Jessi chuckled and thought she may actually have heard Lela laugh as well. She reached down and scooped up a handful of gravel. The stones were still warm from the sun and felt good in her hand. "You've got to admit, you're not the usual kind of witness," Jessi added as the women exchanged a look that resulted in a flicker of camaraderie. They both turned away. After a moment Lela broke the silence.

"So what happened with Nicole Deavers? Is anyone going to help that little girl?"

"The sheriff notified Child Protection Services. They put her in a foster home until they're finished with their investigation."

"Good. But I'm surprised. I figured the sheriff would think I'd had another psychic revelation and ignore me."

"Nicole's safety is too important not to follow up on it. I'll admit it's not a great environment she's living in, not even a good one, but what makes you think something of a sexual nature might be going on?" Jessi asked.

"I told you. That dump reeks of bad karma. Besides, I looked at old man Deaver. His aura tells it all."

"His aura?" Jessi's tone slipped to skeptical.

"I know the symptoms."

"How do you know them?"

"Let's just say I know them and move on, O.K.?"

"Are you talking from personal experience?" Jessi asked softly.

Lela's eyes flashed fiercely. "I'm a survivor. I won't let some pathetic bastard take my identity. No matter what is done to my body, my soul is my own." Lela paused. "I'm afraid Nicole isn't as strong as I was, err, *am*. She's so young." Lela's voice trailed off.

Jessi could feel tears pricking the back of her eyes and fought them back. She put her hand out to comfort Lela but drew it back, unsure of her welcome.

Lela turned back to face her. "I'm not some kind of freak."

"Is that what started your visualizations?"

"*That?*" Lela gave her a disgusted look. "You really are closed off emotionally, aren't you? The politically correct term for *that* would be child abuse. It has the right tone without giving offense to the more sensitive among us. No, *that* gave me nightmares, hives, and difficulty in maintaining relationships, or at least that's what the psychiatrist said. It did not make a psychic of me." Lela looked at Jessi.

"I'm sorry, Lela." Jessi didn't know what else to say.

"Don't start getting all soft and schmaltzy on me. And don't worry about *my* childhood. I didn't have one. I was born old, like Athena from Zeus's head."

"I think the mythology was that Athena was born full-grown, not necessarily old," Jessi corrected.

"Thanks so much for bringing that to my attention, Ms. Cole, but you'll have to admit, it's a great image," Lela paused, staring openly in to Jessi's face. "You look a lot like your mother, you know? Was she like you?"

Jessi returned her stare with a startled look that slowly dissolved into a mischievous smile. "You're the psychic, you tell me."

"I'm tired of talking. Your friend, Clyde, wore me out. You talk for a while. I'll correct you if you're wrong. Go ahead, tell me about your mom."

Jessi was silent for a moment. The memories of her mother were almost out of focus, blurred around the edges. As a child she hadn't thought of her mom as pretty, but later, looking at pictures, she saw a dark-haired woman with laughter in her hazel eyes and an easy, friendly smile—an attractive woman, surprisingly small in stature. It surprised Jessi that she was now three inches taller than her mom had been.

"Mom died when I was nine. I don't really remember a lot. She taught third grade and loved it." Jessi's voice trailed away as she remembered her mom bringing home ideas for class projects. They would spend hours cutting paper, pasting, coloring, and painting. Her mother, Dorothy, always asked her opinion, saying, "If it doesn't pass the Jessi test, it doesn't get in my classroom." Jessi especially liked it when her mom was doing a science unit. They would try out endless experiments in the kitchen, many of them ending in disaster and leaving them helpless with laughter. The plaster of Paris volcano was her favorite. When Dorothy lit the fuse for the simulated eruption, they watched, fascinated, as the mixture began to bubble, then suddenly exploded, hitting the ceiling and sending them both running for cover.

She thought of her mom and dad together almost in slow motion—the way they looked at each other, Deke coming through the door and wrapping his strong arms around her mom, hugging her closely to his chest. At night, when they thought she was asleep, she would lie in bed hearing the intimate, quiet laughter coming from their room. After her mom died, she missed that laughter.

Jessi came out of her reverie to see Lela watching her. "You might not remember much, but you were smiling, so what you do remember must be pretty good."

Jessi smiled. "Yes, I guess so... Well? Are you going to tell me?"

"Tell you what?"

"How long you've had these visualization things?"

Lela's eyes brightened, and a hint of a smile formed on her lips. "That's the first real question you've asked. Does that mean you accept me as a fellow human being? My heart is suddenly a-flutter."

Jessi ignored the sarcasm and scooped up another handful of gravel.

"The first time I really remember was after my twelfth birthday. I got a new bike, and I took it out for a ride," Lela said.

"I thought you were born full grown."

"You want to interrupt, or do you want the story?"

"Sorry," Jessi said meekly.

"I was riding along with Rebecca Hall and Leslie McKinley. I fell off somehow and slammed my head into the curb. Fifty stitches and two days later I started having seizures. Not the grand mal type but bad enough to scare my parents and friends. I still have to take medication."

"The visions started after that?"

"I was sitting in class one day, Brookhaven Junior High, worrying about my small breasts, when *zap!* I felt like somebody hit me with 220 volts right between the eyes, and I had a picture of a young girl, someone's hands around her throat. Her eyes filled with terror. Just a flash, and then it was gone."

Jessi waited for the conclusion, but Lela wasn't going to volunteer it.

"Well, did it actually happen?"

"I don't know, didn't know how to find out. I went home and sketched what I remembered. I have dozens of sketchpads. Now I see frightened little girls, and I feel their terror."

Jessi gave her a speculative look. "It's just young girls? Around the age of twelve? About the same age you were when you had the accident, right?"

"Yeah, I guess so. What's your point?"

"I don't know, but it's odd."

Lela was silent for a moment. "The people that are doing this are out there, somewhere close, hunting. I can feel them. They're predators. They are absolute evil," Lela hissed, feeling chilled despite the 94 degree heat. "I want to show you something," she said, leaning down and removing her sketchpad from her carryall. She quickly thumbed through the pages before handing it over.

Jessi set the pad on her lap and studied the pencil and charcoal sketch depicting a faceless woman with long black hair. Jessi had no way of knowing that the rendering was a lifelike depiction of Kitty wearing a wig that she had donned for Samantha Deaver's abduction.

Jessi continued studying the sketch for a moment longer before she noticed at the bottom of the page a small drawing of what appeared to be a dog or wolf with strikingly red eyes. Jessi pointed at it. "This animal, is it part of the same vision?"

"I really don't know. I just drew it for some reason. I put it on the same page, so maybe it was."

"Your ability to feel and see things, this gift you have is..."

Lela laughed sarcastically. "You sound like Oprah, 'This *gift* you have, dear.'" Her voice suddenly hardened. "You call what I go through *a gift?* How about *curse?* Gift my ass. If it was a gift, I'd return it."

Jessi turned the page in the sketchpad and was surprised to see a caricature of herself leaning out of a city bus and grabbing a fleeing felon by the nape of the neck. The drawing captured the essence of Jessi's face, including full lips and freckles. "Lela, you're really good at this."

"I should be. It's helped pay my bills for the last twenty years. You can have that if you want it," Lela said as she tore out the page, exposing the drawing under it. It was another caricature depicting Cutler behind the yoke of his airplane while a sick looking Lela hangs her head out the window, and another frightened woman, presumably Jessi, dangles from a rope underneath the plane.

"Have you shown this to the sheriff? It is absolutely adorable!"

"Adorable!" I haven't heard the word adorable since the movie, *Pillow Talk,* for hellsakes! How somebody like you became a cop, I will never know."

"Yeah, well, right now I'm a cop with dirty underwear and a headache," Jessi said, standing and brushing the rock dust from the back of suit pants. "I'm going to find a Laundromat. Want to come?"

"I've got a sack full of laundry back at Velma's," Lela answered, also standing and following Jessi toward the trailer.

When Jessi asked Cutler for the use of a county car to go to the Laundromat, he automatically reached for the keys to his Blazer. On second thought, he opened a drawer, removed another set of keys and, standing, told Jessi and Lela to follow him outside.

Cutler walked to the back of the trailer and opened the unattached garage where a custom-made tarp covered the vintage green 1957 Chevrolet Bel Air convertible. As the women watched, the sheriff quickly removed and stowed the tarp neatly in the trunk of the car. He climbed in behind the wheel and smiled as the 327 cubic inch V8 fired on the first crank and murmured smoothly. Cutler climbed out and gestured for Jessi to climb in. "My first car."

Jessi was impressed. "How long have you had it?"

"My Uncle Merlin and Aunt Stella gave it to me when I was a sophomore in high school. Runs like a top."

Lela looked at each of them in turn, shook her head, and climbed in the passenger side. "Home, James!"

Jessi pulled the Chevy away from the county office trailer and headed for Velma's Motel to pick up their laundry. As she guided the car down Third Street, she rubbed her temple, trying to massage away the oncoming headache that was bad enough to make her ears ring. Lack of sleep and food was beginning to catch up with her.

"I need a donut fix," Jessi mumbled. She felt Lela's eyes boring a hole through her. "Do you want to say something to me?"

"Yeah, I do as a matter of fact. I'm not real thrilled to be running around in a dead woman's car, you know?

"What are you talking about?" Jessi asked.

"You didn't see the picture in his desk?"

Jessi was perplexed and a little angry. She tried to remember when Lela had been left alone in the office long enough to sort through Cutler's desk. "What were you doing looking in the man's desk, for hellsake?"

"For a cop, you're really not very observant," Lela commented.

"And what does that mean?" Jessi asked, irritated.

"The first day we got here, there was a picture on your sheriff's desk. It was of a young woman standing next to this car."

"And?"

"And I asked Janie about it. She's awfully protective of him, ya know."

"Lela!"

"It's a picture of his wife, now deceased."

"He told me about Angie," Jessi was defensive. "So what is *your* point?"

"And it's not on his desk anymore. That's all," Lela explained as Jessi turned off of Third and drove down the mostly deserted Main Street. Nearly all of the businesses were closing up or already shuttered.

"Hell, it's not even seven o'clock and it's dead. I'll bet they roll up the damn sidewalks when the sun goes down," Lela said, cupping her hands to her mouth and screeching "Wake up and get a life, you pencil-neck hicks!" She turned back to Jessi. "God, I hate this burg!"

"Do you have to scream like that? I've got a splitting headache."

"It helps for me to yell. It makes it so I don't get emotionally constipated like you are."

Jessi shot her a dirty look but kept quiet.

"You know what your problem is?"

Ignoring her, Jessi popped three aspirin into her mouth, swallowing them without water. "Yes," Jessi snapped. "I'm tired, I'm hungry, and I've got an aspirin stuck in my throat."

"That's the least of your problems. You're boiling with turmoil, but what's worse, you're supercharged with positive ions."

"Oh shit, here we go again. Positive is good, right? So why do I have a headache?"

"No, positive is not good; positive is bad. Negative ions are what you want. Here..." Lela said, opening her floppy carryall, taking out an eight-by-ten inch piece of cardboard that had a dozen quartz necklaces stapled to it, and removing two of them. "These are just the thing." She hung both crystals from the Chevy's rearview mirror. "The green one will help you relax. Sleep with it under your pillow tonight. It will draw off a lot of the destructive positive ions and give you a good cleansing."

"A spiritual enema, so to speak?" Jessi deadpanned.

Lela shot her a cold look. "Swear to God, cops have to be the most cynical creatures on the planet."

"Tell me something I *don't* know," She ran her hand through her hair, suddenly enjoying the *almost* cool night air whipping through the open car. "Okay, so the green one will give me a spiritual cleanse, what will the other one do for me?"

"This one is rose quartz. You need this one a lot more than the other," Lela replied, reaching out and gently touching the crystal. "This will help you and your sheriff with your love life."

The women's eyes met across the darkness and for just the briefest of moments, there was a flash of understanding, a hint of friendship. "Tell you what. If that necklace will improve my love life, I'll take three of them," Jessi said, laughing. Out of the corner of her eye, she saw Lela join in her laughter.

18.

The movie ended at 7:07P.M., and a few minutes later a covey of seventh-grade girls from Waco's Rincon Middle School breezed out of the Cinema Six Theater complex lobby and hurried to the curb where Mrs. Jeanette Mathews was waiting in her Ford Taurus station wagon. The girls were giggling self-consciously, sure that they were the center of attention as the other movie goers jockeyed around them. Like most teenagers they made every attempt to be different from the crowd – but not from each other, dressing in look a like shorts, flip flops and the latest fashion of crop tops, the colors different, but the styles the same. Four of the girls were spending the night at the Mathews' house for a pizza party and sleep over that Mrs. Mathews' daughter, Lauri, had planned as part of her 13th birthday celebration. One of the five girls, thirteen-year-old Julie Abbot, would not be attending the sleep over. Julie had to depart with her family early the next morning for a weekend trip to her uncle's home in San Antonio. As the four girls climbed into the station wagon, Jeanette Mathews talked to Julie over the roof.

"Julie, honey, I'm sorry you can't come with us."

"Yeah, me too," Julie answered.

"I think I'd better wait until your mom comes."

"No, that's okay. She'll be here any minute. You go ahead," quickly adding, "There she is now," as she pointed off.

Jeanette Mathews nodded and, climbing back into the station wagon, pulled away as Julie walked toward the white Nissan that had just turned the corner. Instead of stopping, the Nissan continued past, and Julie could see clearly that it wasn't her mom. "Oh, well, she'll be here soon," Julie thought as she moved back to the theater and leaned against the stucco wall. Her mother, Terri, was never late, and Julie felt slightly uneasy that something might have happened to her.

Julie had no way of knowing that a worn-out fuel pump on her ten year old Nissan had stranded her mom halfway to the theater. Terri had used her cell phone to call her husband, Gary, at his shop and asked him to swing by and pick up Julie at the theater before coming to get her.

As Julie waited, she thought of all the fun she was missing. The four girls were her very, very best friends in the whole world, but she was glad she was going to San Antonio. She loved the trips to her Uncle Joe's house, mainly because of Caitlin, her fifteen-year-old cousin. Caitlin was pretty and smart and treated her like an equal. The biggest plus of all, that made the four-hour drive bearable, however, was Shaun David, Caitlin's fifteen-year-old neighbor, whom Julie referred to as *"The Bomb"* in letters to her cousin. Julie had met Shaun the summer before and had developed a crush that distance, time, and half- dozen exchanged emails had swelled into Herculean proportions. Julie was thinking of Shaun when she heard Kitty's voice.

"Excuse me, dear, but have you seen a little puppy?" an obviously distraught Kitty asked as she approached, adding quickly, "I lost him over by the park. He's tan and his name is Rusty." Kitty's tight blond curls and tear filled eyes gave her a vulnerable appearance which caught Julie off guard.

"No, I haven't, but I've only been out here a couple of minutes. Sorry."

"I've got to find the little guy. He's just barely weaned," Kitty said as she frantically scurried off and disappeared around the corner.

Julie had been leaning against the building for less than a minute when she saw the man approach. He was in his thirties, stocky, with short hair and a goatee. In his arms he was carrying an adorable tan puppy, and as he approached the theater, he stopped and looked around as if he were either lost or looking for someone.

"Excuse me," Julie said, "but did you just find that puppy?"

Pinky turned and approached Julie. "Yeah, he was wandering around the park over there. Is he yours?" he asked, holding the squirming puppy out to her.

"No, but the lady who lost him was just here."

Pinky again held the puppy out to Julie. Her defenses were melting, and she took the puppy. She was so taken with the small dog that she didn't notice the wolf head tattoo on the back of his right hand.

"Did you see which way she went?" Pinky asked.

"No, but she turned the corner over there. We can probably catch her if we hurry," Julie said, quickly covering the thirty yards; and turning the corner, she spotted Kitty halfway down the block approaching a van. "Hey, lady, here's your puppy!" Julie yelled as she hurried to catch up.

Kitty looked up, smiled in relief, and waved, but rather than walk to meet the girl, she waited at the van. Julie hurried up to her with the lost puppy.

"Rusty, you little brat," Kitty scolded. "Don't you ever do that to Mommy again," Kitty cooed, giving the puppy a kiss on the nose before looking up at Julie with a warm smile. "How can I ever thank you?"

"It wasn't me. This man found him," Julie nodded at the approaching Pinky.

Kitty turned toward Pinky. "Thank you so very much."

"Hey, I'm glad it worked out for you."

Julie nuzzled the puppy one last time and held it out to Kitty. "I have to go now."

"Hold him one more second, could you?" Kitty asked as she opened her purse and removed a heavy ring of keys. "Let me get this door open, and then I'll take the little brat from you." Kitty giggled as she unlocked the door and slid it open with a smooth, fluid motion. "Just set him in there with the others, okay?"

"Others?" Julie said, puzzled.

Pinky's eyes made a final sweep of the street and sidewalk to see if they were being observed and then closed on Julie, timing his movements perfectly so that as she reached into the van to place the puppy in the box, he slammed into her, simultaneously cupping his hand over her mouth and driving her into the van. Lying on the stunned girl's back, he brought his legs up just as Kitty hopped in, slid the door shut, climbed in behind the wheel, and pulled out.

While Julie lay in stunned terror under Pinky's two hundred pounds, her father, Gary Abbott, a thirty-six-year-old sheet metal contractor, drove by the white van as it pulled away.

Gary had approached the theater from the backside. He had pulled his dark blue Ford F150 to a stop at the corner to the east side of the entrance, beeping his horn and scanning the sidewalk in front of the Cinema Six for Julie's familiar form. He saw a dozen people, several of them teenagers, standing in small groups. He sounded his horn again, but his daughter was nowhere in sight. Gary checked his watch and then drove around the block looking for an empty parking space, assuming that his wife might have been wrong about the time the movie ended and that Julie was probably still in the theater.

In one of the cruelest ironies of the night, Gary circled the entire block before parking his pickup in the exact spot Kitty's van had vacated less than two minutes before.

After driving away from the theater, Kitty headed toward Interstate 35 by the shortest possible route. She was meticulous about her speed, keeping the van at, or below, the limit, forcing herself to be calm, stopping at all yellow lights. She passed one Waco police cruiser going in the opposite direction, certain the cop could somehow spot her nervousness. "There's a cop."

"Relax, will you? Why would he stop you?" Pinky barked from the back.

Kitty's heart pounded in her chest as she watched the police cruiser disappear through the outside mirror. "He's gone!" she said, turning her attention back to the road. As she drove, her eyes were drawn to a dark haired, attractive woman leaning against a parked, white Nissan on the opposite side of the street.

Terri Abbott leaned against the door of the disabled car and scanned the traffic for her husband's familiar truck. She glanced at her watch and tried not to worry. She knew that Gary should have picked Julie up at the theater by now and been there to help her. She had *never* been late to pick up Julie. It was an obsession with her. Julie was their only child, still her precious baby, and she worried constantly about her. Terri looked down the road again and unconsciously tapped the cell phone on her front teeth. "You worry too much," she told herself out loud and continued waiting for her husband.

Gary Abbott went into each of the six theaters looking for Julie, and when he couldn't find her he quickly located the theater manager who had flashed Julie's name on the corner of all six screens. When this didn't produce his daughter, Gary called Terri's cell phone number, trying to fake calmness to his already nervous wife, and asked her to telephone Jeanette Mathews to see if Julie might have gone with the other girls to the sleep over.

After hanging up he hurried outside to again scan the sidewalk. Nothing. As his uneasiness continued to grow, he approached the ticket booth where two clerks sat behind Plexiglas windows.

"May I help you?"

"I hope so. I was supposed to pick up my daughter out here after the movie but she's not here. I talked to the manager and checked all the theaters. She wasn't in any of those."

The older of the two clerks, a forty-year-old mother of three, Jean Campbell, responded immediately to the sound of panic in Gary's voice. "What movie was it, sir?"

"I'm not sure. All I know is my wife was supposed to pick her up a little after seven, but she had car trouble, so I came. I got here about twenty-five after."

Jean scanned the show times on the placard above her head. "*Incredibles* ended at 7:07."

"Yeah, that's the one she was going to. Look, maybe you saw her. She's thirteen, dark hair, pretty, green eyes, and she was wearing shorts and a blue top. She has braces on her teeth."

Jean Campbell and Sandy Peck exchanged looks and shook their heads. "Sorry."

Gary turned away from the booth and questioned a half-dozen teenagers who were standing in a group waiting for rides. None of them could recall seeing his young daughter.

Gary quickly returned to the pay phone and dialed his wife's cell phone.

Terri answered with an anxious, "Did you find her?"

"No, did you call her friends?"

"Yes, they left her in front of the theater. Jeanette said it was about ten after seven."

The unspoken panic in their voices chilled each of them to their core.

"I'm going to come and get you."

"No," Terri said. "Stay there in case she shows up. I'll come there."

"You sure you'll be alright?"

"I'll be fine, Gary. I'll be there as soon as I can." Teri struggled to sound calm.

"I'm going to call the police then," Gary said, not believing what he had heard his own voice just say.

Terri pushed the END button on the cell phone and, grabbing her purse through the open window of the car, she turned and started jogging toward the theater. As she ran, tears flowed freely down her face, and she started praying out loud.

"God in heaven, please don't let anything be wrong! Please, dear Jesus, help me! *Please!*"

A taxi pulled alongside and slowed to keep pace with her. The small Latino driver leaned across the front seat and smiled out at her through his open window. "Buenos noches, senora. Do you need a ride?"

Terri jumped in the rear seat and the cab sped away. As she rode, her eyes were drawn to the mounted identification placard that displayed a picture of the driver with his name. It read "Jesus Flores."

Terri then saw the magnetic Jesus on the dashboard and crossed herself. "Thank you," she said softly.

"Da nada," Jesus answered.

Gary called 911. Forcing himself to sound calm, he explained the situation to the operator and then returned to the sidewalk in front of the theater to await the arrival of the police. Gary saw the ticket clerk, Jean Campbell, knock on her plexiglass window and wave him over to the booth.

"No luck?"

Gary shook his head.

"Did your daughter happen to have a puppy?"

"Puppy? No, why?"

"I do remember seeing a young girl walk past carrying a puppy. I think she was wearing a blue top, but I'm not sure."

"A puppy?" Gary asked, puzzled.

"Yes, she was with a man."

Gary was instantly alert. "What man?"

Gary's hard tone scared her, but the implications of what she might have seen frightened her even more. "I don't know. I...I think he was about your age. He had a goatee."

Gary Abbott turned and saw the police car pull to a stop, he was as close to panic as he had ever been in his life.

Pinky sat on the floor studying Julie as she lay next to him. He had duct taped her mouth immediately before tying her hands behind her back and then taping them to her ankles.

"Be careful with her," cautioned Kitty, glancing over her shoulder as she guided the van westbound on Highway 84 at exactly fifty-five miles an hour.

Julie lay trussed up, fighting for air and trying desperately to make sense of her situation, the scent of Pinky's cologne mixed with body odor began to overpower her. In her 13 year-old mind she was smelling pure evil and as he continued staring at her, hot tears spilled down her cheeks. When he touched her she thought of home, and she cried harder and then threw up, blowing vomit out her nose and gagging.

"Don't let her choke," Kitty said, glancing nervously over her shoulder.

"Shut the fuck up and watch the road!" Pinky bellowed as he ripped the tape from Julie's mouth and let her continue to regurgitate, choking and coughing loudly until she was left watery eyed and gasping for breath. Pinky mopped up most of the vomit with a roll of paper towels, which he crammed into a plastic sack. He grabbed Julie by the shoulders and jerked her around so that she was forced to look into his flat, expressionless eyes. The terror in the girl's face filled him with a familiar sense of power, and he felt a sudden surge of pleasure. He reached into his pocket and pulled out Samantha Deaver's quartz necklace and placed it over Julie's head, letting the sparkling crystal dangle loosely from her thin neck. Julie shut her eyes tightly and forced her mind to carry her away from the van and the evil man. Her hands were useless, and as she strained against the duct tape that bound her wrists together, her fingers felt a wire that was running along the floorboard. A memory suddenly came to her of her father sitting on the tailgate of his pickup using black electricians tape to cover a wire. "What are you doing, Daddy?"

"My taillights shorted out. If I don't fix it, the police will pull me over and give me a fix-it ticket," he had explained. The sound of her father's voice faded and Julie turned her thoughts and energy to the wire. As she did, she heard the puppies for the first time. They must have been crying the whole time, but she had blocked everything out until now. The puppies were somewhere close behind her, their small voices whimpering in the darkness.

In that moment Julie understood perfectly why they were crying.

Jessi fed quarters into the washing machine and closed the lid as heat from the wall of dryers made the room not only hot but also uncomfortably humid. She opened the mini-box of Cheer and dumped the soap into the open chute at the top. She was glad she had only one load. The Laundromat was busy, and she and Lela had access to only one regular-sized machine. Lela had done her load first and was now tossing her wet clothes into the last available dryer at the end of the row.

Two Latino men chatted softly in Spanish as they sorted through piles of dirty work clothes next to her and pushed them into their washer before retreating outside to the parking lot to smoke cigarettes and retrieve cold beers from their beaten up Datsun pickup. Jessi could hear their truck radio that was tuned to the Houston Astros game. She knew the Astros were hosting the Giants for a three-game home stand, and she was tempted to go out and check the score but decided not to. Since arriving in Deep Texas, she had lost track of not only the Astros but the entire free world as well.

Several women with small children were attacking huge piles of laundry in what was obviously a weekly routine. One mother had brought a box of graham crackers and generic sodas to appease her three preschoolers. Pulverized crackers were now scattered over the top of the long folding tables and on the floor where cans of soda had spilled, leaving sticky puddles on the cracked linoleum. The women were sipping sodas and gossiping as they ignored their children and sorted and folded clothes. A small boy named Delmar, wearing an official, and duly licensed, rainbow colored *NASCAR* jump suit that marked him as one of the famous "Rainbow Warriors" pit crew, clutched a pint size model of Jeff Gordon's Chevy in his sticky right hand and zoomed in a circle around the room making popping engine noises. He zoomed his Number 24 past the other children and anyone else on the high-banked oval of his imaginary racetrack that got in his way. Jessi sidestepped quickly to avoid a collision as Delmar completed the twenty-third lap of his never-ending main event.

"Delmar, watch out for the lady!" his heavyset mother yelled from across the room. Jessi had no illusions whether the future speeding ticket holder was paying any attention to his mom. So far he had totally ignored nearly forty-five minutes of her threats. "Delmar, I'm going to count to three..."

"And four, and five, and six, and seven, and eight, and..." Lela mumbled tiredly as little Delmar dropped out of the chute and roared down the straightaway toward where she was folding clothes. The Monte Carlo suddenly left his hand and, loosing traction, hit the wall, spun crazily out of control, and slammed hard, burying itself in the warm skirt that Lela had just removed from the dryer. Delmar squealed with delight and was just about to put his sticky, dirty hand on Lela's clean skirt when he found his round little bottom firmly deposited on a chair.

"Delmar, I'm going to count to one. One! Now would you like your little butt whacked, or will you mind your manners?" Lela hissed, glaring into the eyes of the perplexed child. The tiny Rainbow Warrior looked at her with stunned disbelief before he hopped off the chair and scurried back to the protection of his oblivious mother, willing to write Number 24 off as a total loss.

Jessi made her way over to Lela, handing her a brown paper grocery bag. "Did I just witness an example of Texas road rage?"

Lela picked up a pile of clean, folded clothes and carefully deposited them in the bag. "I had the right of way, officer, plus he was speeding," she said, sniffing a clean blouse. "People take clean clothes for granted. They don't realize what a luxury they are."

"People take a lot of things for granted, myself included, " Jessi agreed, watching curiously as Lela sniffed, fluffed, folded, and caressed each item of her worn, but now clean, wardrobe before placing it in the bag. "How long have you been living on the street?"

"I don't live on the street. I live in my van. There're a lot of people worse off than I am," she snapped defensively.

"I didn't intend to insult you, Lela. I simply asked a question."

"Well, it's obviously an emotionally charged question, said the homeless old bitch," Lela glared at Jessi.

"Forget it. Sorry I said a word," Jessi raised her hands in mock surrender as she started to back away.

Lela hit herself on the forehead with the heel of her hand. "There I go again. Everything I say comes out wrong. I'm sorry, I... I haven't always been like this–not that there is anything wrong with the way I am," Lela said, giving Jessi a look that dared her to make a comment.

"Are you going to tell me about the 'way you were,' or not?"

"Yeah, well, at least I'm not the only smart ass here, am I?" Lela said. The metallic taste was suddenly in her mouth, but she tried to ignore it, push it away. "Not now, please," she thought as she fought to stay in control. "Now, where were we?"

"You were about to tell me the way we ..."

"The way we were, right. Well, it goes like this. Bernie Butts and I..." The DING of Lela's dryer finishing its cycle interrupted them. "You were saved by the bell, kid."

"Come on, I want to hear it," Jessi protested.

Lela gave her a dismissive wave over her shoulder. "Later," she said, opening the dryer door and pulling the last of her laundry out.

Jessi moved to check on her washer before stepping outside for a breath of warm, fresh air.

As Lela turned and carried her dry clothes toward the folding table, she suddenly slowed and stiffened. A second later it *hit*, sending a shower of blinding sparks into her eyes. She was totally helpless. She dropped her clothes and staggered against a running dryer turning in its relentless circle of tumbling clothes and what sounded like shoes thumping off the inside of the hollow cylinder. Lela forced her eyes open and found herself peering through the round dryer window. Amidst the tumbling clothes was the face of *Julie Abbott* her hands pounding against the Plexiglas; she struggled to scream through the duct tape that covered her mouth! The words seemed to explode from her terror filled eyes:

Help me! Please, help me! Oh God, please send someone!"

Julie's face tumbled past the opening again and again, disappearing momentarily before reappearing and pounding on the window in a futile effort at escape.

Lela screamed, jerked open the dryer door, and started tossing shirts, socks, towels and underwear in a blind, sobbing frenzy.

"I'm coming. Don't give up. Please, I'm trying to find you. Please!"

Everyone in the Laundromat watched, open-mouthed, as Delmar's mother approached, stunned by what she was witnessing. "Hey, those are my clothes! What in hell are you doing?" The heavy woman turned on Jessi as she hurried in from outside. "What's the matter with her? Is she crazy? Can't you do something?"

Jessi watched helplessly as Lela continued tossing clothes out onto the floor until the dryer was bare. "It's empty, Lela. There's nothing left to toss."

Lela was suddenly overwhelmed by exhaustion. She turned and looked helplessly at Jessi.

"Why? Why did you do that?" Jessi asked her, bending to pick up a warm Levi shirt which she handed to Delmar's, baffled, if not frightened, mother.

Lela was sweaty and ashen and looked terrified as she buried her head on Jessi's shoulder. "She was there, Jessi! In the dryer! I saw her! My God, I saw her! Please, I can't look. Tell me she's not in there! Please, Jessi, look. Just look."

"I did look, Lela. It's empty."

Lela took a deep breath and shuddered. "She was in there. I swear."

"Who? Who was in there?"

"Julie!"

19.

✑

Grace County night duty dispatcher Jill Richards received the fax from Waco P.D. at 20:48 hours, and after reading it over quickly, she keyed her microphone. "All Grace County units, Waco P.D. has gone statewide with a possible two-zero-zero-three, child abduction, that occurred on this day at approximately 19:30 hours. Victim is a thirteen-year-old female, five three, brown and brown, 102, last seen at a Waco theater complex. Details to follow. G.C.B. 471."

After finishing the broadcast, Jill placed the fax in the log basket before moving to the coffee counter where she filled two oddly shaped cups to the rim with steaming, fresh coffee which she carried across the room to where a disheveled Murray Crook and Deputy Red Cordell were firmly ensconced in front of the new computer. Jill, her light-weight headset dangling from her neck, handed one misshapen cup to a grateful, tired-eyed Red and held out the other to the strange, intense young man from Houston. Murray shook his head and waved her off.

"Thank you, dear, but please, not here," Murray said, standing and moving to where the slightly startled Jill had retreated. He took the misshapen mug from her, savoring first the sip and then the moment, before kissing the puzzled woman on the cheek and hurrying back to his place in front of the computer, but not before turning on Red. "Never, and I mean *never*, drink anything when you are working with your equipment. You can screw up your entire system with an accidental spill," Murray said with enough authority that the chastened Red handed his misshapen mug back to Jill before joining Murray alongside the keyboard. Jill set Red's coffee down very gently and moved in close, watching over Murray's shoulder as his well-manicured fingers flew over the keyboard writing batch files and initializing printers and faxes and modems and scanners and installing graphics and fonts and on and on and on.

Jill smiled and laughed, an infectious laugh that hinted of her boundless energy. She was taking classes in pottery at the Slocum Community Center and had proudly supplied the office with heavy, misshapen coffee cups that everyone used.

"You really like this computer stuff, don't you?" Jill asked Murray.

"My dear, this is not only my line of work, it is my passion. You are looking at a resource that was totally unimaginable a mere twenty years ago. And ten years from now...? The possibilities blow my mind," Murray answered with feeling.

Red shook his head, and a look of worry sent a deep crease across his forehead. "Well, if you can't spill a little java on the damn things, you got problems. This thing's more temperamental than my 1950 Ford pickup sitting out there in the parking lot," Red complained.

"Ford truck, computer, think of them both as beasts of burden. The computer has been trained to perform repetitious, mundane tasks rapidly, correctly, and with absolutely no complaints."

"Sounds like me," Jill said, laughing loudly.

"This machine is going to make both your lives a whole lot easier. It is going to allow you to get information and eliminate the middle man. You'll be able to access State Records instantly, Local Wants and Warrants instantly, the National Crime Information Center instantly, Bureau of Missing Persons instantly, DMV, FBI, ATF, the possibilities are endless."

"I'll tell you this, partner. If this thing here can do all you say it can, then you just might have a convert on your hands."

From the Laundromat, Jessi drove out into the desert, as Lela told her, "to allow the crystals to do their calming work unfettered by civilization." Lela rebuffed Jessi's attempt to talk more about her latest "vision" choosing instead to zero in the radio on the 50,000 watts of KTEX moldy-oldies radio station. With the old Chevy's dual Glass Pac mufflers providing a deep-throated, harmonious backup, the sounds of "Crystal Blue Persuasion" serenaded them on their wind-whipped journey through the darkness. Jessi found an old Texas Rangers baseball hat on the back floorboard, which she pulled down low over her forehead in hopes of keeping her hair from turning into a worse mess than it already was. She steered the old convertible down a deserted stretch of dusty road, trying to form questions that might get Lela to open up.

Lela tilted her head back, closed her eyes, clutched her crystal necklace tightly in her hand and let the warm wind whip her long, graying hair.

"The Summer Triangle is right above us," Lela said, her eyes still shut.

Jessi looked over at her, curious. "What's the Summer Triangle?"

"Daneb, Altair, Vega. Stars?"

"How can you see stars with your eyes closed?"

"I don't need to see them to know they're up there. It's August. They're up there, trust me. So's the Northern Cross right above your head," Lela said.

Jessi slowed the purring Chevy and pulled to the side of the road, stopping on a short rise where the scattered lights of Grace were visible behind and below them. Turning off the engine, she was struck by how well the silence went with the surroundings. She pulled off the hat and, laying her head back on the seat, looked up, drinking in as much of the vast night sky as her eyes and mind could hold. It had been years since she had seen the night sky away from the ever-present brightness of Houston. Sometimes when Big Deke took her fishing, they would see the sky like this, and he always would point out the Big Dipper and The Milky Way. "I keep forgetting how beautiful the sky is." Her voice sounded intrusive, and she was sorry she spoke.

Lela opened her eyes and pointed up. "There, see the stars right there: four across, three down? That's the Northern Cross. Same stars going the other way are Cygnus, The Swan. I had an Indian friend who called the same stars 'Goose Flying South.'"

"I don't see them, but I'll take your word for it."

Lela continued pointing. "And right below it is Aquila, The Eagle; and the little one over there is Delphinius, The Dolphin. Down there is Capricornus."

Jessi was impressed. "Where did you learn so much about astronomy?"

"Bernie Butts, and, don't laugh, that was his God given name."

"Come on, you promised." Jessi sang a few words "The way we were...!"

"Okay, but no singing, and no smart-ass remarks, agreed?"

"Agreed."

"Well, 'Once upon a time...' I owned a funky little gift shop in downtown Houston, right off Lockwood by the University. I sold Tarot cards, incense, crystals, beadwork, a little tie-dye—astrology stuff, you know? It wasn't a gold mine or anything, but it paid the rent. Then Bernie Butts comes from Alaska and rents the little flat upstairs while he does graduate work at the university. Life was sweet, at least for a while. Bernie was…how do I describe him? He could be good. He could be bad. He was incredibly intelligent; at least he told me he was, and I believed him, or at least I did most of the time. He was also a drunk, a doper, a thief, a cheat, and, quite frankly, the most sexy, precious man I've ever met. Bernie and I had some good, no, correct that to read *great*, times!" Lela laughed, a natural, head-back laugh that brought a curious smile to Jessi's lips and seemed to transport Lela far away from the car for a moment. "Where was I?"

"You and Bernie…good times, no, *great* times."

"Oh, and they were. Lord did we have fun." Lela let the sentence just sit there waiting for Jessi's curiosity to get the better of her:

"So, don't stop now."

"Tuesday, September 21st, 1990," Lela said.

"I went out grocery shopping, and while I was gone Bernie got doped up, climbed into the tub, lit some candles, passed out, and burned everything up."

"What about Bernie?" Jessi asked.

"He was boiled. A two hundred and fifty pound rump roast. I lost everything, of course. After that I got strung out pretty good, and here I am in deep fucking Texas chewing out a six-year-old stock car driver named Delmar, of all things, and telling a cop my life story. Go figure."

"I don't want to sound callous, but didn't you have any fire insurance?"

"Jesus, I tell you the saddest story you'll ever hear, and you ask about insurance? That, my dear, is what separates cops from real people. You will not allow yourself to personalize the rest of us poor bastards. Well, damnit, I, for one, am a real live person. Deal with it, and hell, no, I didn't have insurance. It may have been 1990, but we were '60s children. We wore flowers in our hair and lived on idealism and love and named our kids Groovy Scrotum and Pink Nipple and the like. We didn't need insurance."

Lela's look defied Jessi to contradict her. She didn't. "I'm sorry about Bernie, Lela."

"Yeah, me too."

They sat there on the bluff for another few minutes, not talking, just enjoying the view and then drove slowly back to Velma's Motel where Jessi surprised Lela by offering to sit with her for a while…"If you want to talk about anything."

Lela's smile faded immediately. "Oh, so that's what all this good buddy stuff is all about. You think I'm going to get all warm and cuddly and run off at the mouth, name my co-conspirators, confess, or some such shit like that, huh?"

"Lela, I said nothing about confessions, or co-conspirators, or anything else. *You* did! Right now I'm not trying to do anything," Jessi said tiredly.

"Bullshit!" Lela snapped, opening the Chevy's door and clambering out. "The Sheriff of Nothingham is afraid I'm going to flee his jurisdiction, and he wants you to baby-sit me." She leaned into the back seat, grabbed her carryall and the brown paper bag filled with clean clothes, and stormed toward her room.

Jessi also got out. "Actually, my motives were a little more sinister than that. I just thought you might need somebody to talk to."

"Need? You know what I need?" Lela said as she unlocked the door to number eight. "I need a hot shower, my crystals, my incense, and…" She entered the room, slammed the door shut and then quickly reopened it to scream, "and I need Bernie Butts!"

Jessi used the phone in her room to call the sheriff's office and learned from night dispatcher Jill Richards that Cutler had left explicit instructions for her to meet him at Pocatello Pablo's Truck Stop, right off Highway 12 at the top of Main Street.

"What about Lela? I can't leave her here alone," Jessi explained to Jill.

"Not to worry, dear," Jill replied. "I'm going to dispatch Deputy Lee Nash over there to keep an eye on her. Sheriff's orders."

"O.K., tell him I'm on my way," Jessi said as she hung up and hurried into the bathroom. She quickly brushed her teeth, pulled on her favorite pair of snug fitting jeans and a clean blouse, shoved her holstered 9MM in her purse, and was nearly out the door before having second thoughts. She struggled out of the jeans and traded them for a pair of loose-fitting khaki pants. "Coward," she said as she turned out the lights and hurried out.

Six minutes later she guided the old Chevy into the parking lot of Pocatello Pablo's, pulling slowly past a block-long double line of idling big rigs, and parked close to the restaurant between the sheriff's Blazer and a black and white Texas Highway Patrol Mustang. As she climbed out and approached the entrance, she passed a large man who was removing bags of ice cubes from the back of a covered truck and stacking them inside an ice dispenser unit next to the gas pumps. He glanced at her and smiled pleasantly as she passed.

"Ma'am, how you doing tonight?" He continued stacking ice bags.

"Fine, thank you."

The way he said it, placing the emphasis on 'ma'am,' gave her the distinct feeling that he somehow knew her. She paused and looked back, remembering. "Charley. Charley Weed. Am I right?"

"Yes, ma'am, you remembered."

"So did you," she replied, smiling. "Charley, you must work harder than any other man in Grace County. Every time I see you you're working."

"My daddy said hard work never killed anybody but the lazy," Charley smiled turning back to the truck.

"That makes sense, I guess," Jessi turned and opened the door to the restaurant. As she did she was instantly swallowed by a cacophony of CB radio chatter, a ringing cash register, a jukebox blaring out a twangy symphony of hard drivin', hard drinkin', gear jammin', back-slappin' "Here's A Quarter, Call Someone Who Cares," Travis Twitt tune. In the background, Jessi heard clattering coffee mugs, banging plates, ringing telephones, a hardened squad of fast talking, fast walking waitresses shouting out orders sounding like codes from secret military operations—like, "Poky one dry spud with eyes, tubes, sour on wheels, and no fire!" —but which, when translated, sounded much less romantic, like "Pocatello Pablo's hearty breakfast special served 24 and 7 consisting of a pound and a half of hash brown potatoes, hold the gravy please, three eggs sunny side up, sausages, sour dough toast, and please make it to go, and hold the burn-your-mouth hot salsa." With a shout of "Order up!" a steady flow of steaming plates shot onto a stainless steel counter from the small, bunker like kitchen where Pocatello Pablo and his two sweaty Latino assistants moved in a well-choreographed ballet over and around a huge, smoking, red hot grill.

Jessi walked through the dining room and found herself surrounded by a squirming platoon of loud truck drivers, laughing farmers in bib overalls, and cowboys trading good-natured insults over the heads of an elderly couple dressed in their best clothes. They smiled quietly at each other as if the madness around them was only part of the decor like the red plastic tulips resting in a cloudy water glass on top of the black napkin dispenser on their table.

Jessi spotted Cutler sharing a window booth with Marty Burris and headed for them.

Cutler's eyes lit up when he spotted her, and he stood as she approached. Marty, wearing his highway patrol uniform also rose and greeted her with a smile.

"I'm glad you could make it," Cutler said.

"Thanks for asking me. Hi, Marty."

"Hi, Jessi. Thanks for coming. I've actually been babysitting him. He's been a nervous wreck waiting for you to show up," Marty said with a smile.

"What are you talking about, boy?" Cutler barked at Marty before turning to Jessi. "Don't mind poor Marty here. He got dropped on his head as a child."

"True, and he's the one that dropped me," Marty replied. "Hey, Jessi, how's that old dog of a Chevy of his run, anyway?" Marty asked, picking up his straw trooper hat off the seat of the booth.

"Nice. It's fun to drive. I'm not running you off, am I, Marty?" Jessi asked sliding into the booth next to Cutler.

"No, not at all. I should have been out the door ten minutes ago, but I was afraid to leave him by himself," Marty said. He then shook Jessi's hand. "Thanks again for playing softball with us yesterday. You're the classiest first basemen we've ever had."

"Thank you. I enjoyed the game and I have muscle cramps to prove it," Jessi said, rubbing her sore thighs and adding. "I really enjoyed meeting Ellie and your boys. I'd love to see them again sometime."

"You will tomorrow afternoon," Marty said as he pulled on his hat and started out, pausing for effect. "Let me guess," he said, turning to John. "You haven't asked her yet?"

"Goodbye, Marty!" Cutler said, waving him off like a bad dream. "Go get yourself some new glasses, boy. Those make you look like Buddy Holly."

Cutler's teasing reference went back a long way with his cousin, but the remark was right on the money. Marty did favor the long since dead rock and roller, and the glasses cemented that resemblance. Marty had bought them during his junior year of high school because his other glasses kept getting knocked off his face and broken during basketball games. He had switched to contact lenses but quickly developed an intolerance for them, so the heavy, black plastic frames filled the bill nicely. Marty had become so accustomed to wearing them, so comfortable with their weight and the snug feel of the elastic strap that held them tightly to the back of his head that he refused to give them up. He just had new lenses put in the old frames whenever the need arose. He had other glasses at home—light wire-framed ones that Ellie liked because they made him look rather bookish— but when he went out the door to go to work, the "Buddy Hollys" went with him, a part of the "Texas Tan" uniform he was proud to wear. They were his good luck charm.

Marty shook his finger at his cousin and lifelong friend saying, "Hey, Hermit, don't knock the peepers," and went out the door leaving the two of them to fill the sudden void.

"So what's happening tomorrow afternoon?" Jessi asked.

"Oh, yeah, that. I... I was supposed to ask you to a barbeque kind of thing over at Marty and Ellie's tomorrow. It was Ellie's idea... well, maybe Janie started it and then Ellie picked it up and ran with it. Ellie is Janie's little sister."

"Janie being Janie Cortez from the office?"

"Yeah. Janie and Frank will be there. Kiko and Helen Avila are going. So's Louie Adams and his wife and family from..."

"Slocum?"

"Right. So, would you like to do that?"

"Sure, sounds fun," Jessi said, watching through the window as Marty Burris backed his black and white highway patrol Mustang away from the cafe and pulled off into the darkness.

A harried, thin waitress approached the booth juggling four huge platters of food and deposited them heavily on their table. Her name was Annie Pizer, and although she was sixty-one, her frizzy wig was jet black. Nearly fifty years worth of Marlboro cigarettes had helped her to lose not only her hair, but her larynx as well. Annie now spoke and smoked through a button-sized hole in her throat. Her speech was brought to life with the aid of a small, battery-powered amplifier that she carried in her uniform pocket and brought out to place over the hole. The amplifier gave her voice a mechanical tone that sounded strangely like a robot with a southern twang. "There you go, Johnny."

"Thanks, Annie. Bring me some coffee, too. Jessi, what do you want to drink?"

"Diet Coke, if you have it."

Annie raised her amplifier. "I got it," she said and moved off.

Jessi was overwhelmed by the food in front of her. "What on earth is this?"

"Oh, I took the liberty of ordering for you. I hope that's okay. What you're looking at there is the world famous chicken-fried steak."

"Red told me about it. He was right. Incredible," she said, looking down at a piece of meat just slightly smaller than a large size pizza. On platter number two rested two dinner rolls, a half cup of peas, and a year's supply of mashed potatoes and gravy heaped so high it reminded her a little of the plaster of Paris volcano she and her mother had made for a third grade science experiment.

Pablo claims it's the biggest one in the world."

"And who's to argue with Pablo, right?" Jessi asked as Annie Pizer returned with her Diet Coke and poured Cutler a refill on his coffee. "Enjoy," she said through her amplifier.

As Annie moved to the next booth, Cutler dug in, savoring each bite. Jessi cut off a small piece and pushed it around the plate until Cutler finally noticed. "Something wrong?"

"Actually, I'm a vegetarian. Not strict or anything, but..."

Cutler's face fell. "How thoughtless of me. I apologize. I wasn't thinking, I..."

"It's no big deal, O.K.? I can eat the potatoes and..."

"Annie! Bring back the menu!"

Annie was back in a flash, laying the menu out and standing there with her pencil poised for action."

"Do you have any quiche?" Jessi asked.

"Sorry, hon, not on the menu," Annie answered.

"O.K., just give me the quesadilla, cheese, no meat."

"Coming right up," Annie answered and hurried away.

"I'm sorry. I really am," Cutler said.

"Don't be silly. Don't let your food get cold. Go ahead, eat."

Cutler took a bite of steak. "So'd you get your laundry done?"

"Yes, and more. Lela went bonkers."

"What do you mean?"

Jessi shrugged. "She just went berserk. One minute she's perfectly normal, folding clothes, and the next, *boom,* she's out of control. She claims she saw a face in one of the dryers. She started screaming and throwing clothes all over. She thinks another girl by the name of Julie has been kidnapped and is asking her for help."

"Sounds like she's the one who needs help. Maybe she's on drugs. Maybe LSD or something like that. She has a history with acid, right?"

"Yes, she does. I suppose she could be having residual hallucinations from the LSD. I really don't know. Her visualizations are pretty specific."

"She back at Velma's?"

"Yes, she's totally exhausted."

"So's Clyde Briscoe, but he wants to take another shot at her Monday. He said he wanted to try a different polygraph machine on her or something."

"Brave man. Have you heard from the crime lab on Lenny Price's red pickup yet?"

"They're going bumper to bumper. Nothing so far."

They stopped talking while Annie deposited the quesadilla in front of Jessi and refilled her diet Coke.

"Thanks," Jessi said.

"Sure thing," Annie smiled.

As they ate, Jessi glanced out the window and noticed an animal control truck pull in and park in the spot Marty Burris' Highway Patrol Mustang vacated only a few minutes earlier. A heavy woman, with close-cropped brown hair and wearing a khaki shirt and green uniform pants, climbed out of the truck and, entering the cafe, made a beeline for their booth. "You got a minute, Sheriff Cutler?"

"Sure, sit." Cutler patted the seat next to him and slid over to make room.

"Marie, this is Jessi Cole, from Houston. Jessi, Marie Sisco's our A.C.O.

Marie gave Jessi an enthusiastic handshake. "Woof! Woof! I'm the dogcatcher. They gave me the Animal Control Officer title so they won't have to give me a raise, but that's a whole other story. So," Marie said, smiling at Jessi, "you're the lady everybody's talking about driving Johnny's Chevy around?"

Cutler interceded. "What's going on, Marie?" he asked, taking a large bite of his steak.

"I've been going out to Arden Grave's place every day since her dogs killed those sheep and had to be put down, just to talk, you know, but she won't even open the door for me."

"Poor old gal's pretty upset. Those dogs were like her kids, you know," Cutler said, breaking a dinner roll in half and covering it with a thick layer of butter.

"So I go out there again today, and she finally opens the door up just a crack to talk, and I can see she's got an old shotgun sitting right inside the door. Said she won't talk to anyone except Johnny Cutler. I don't think she'd do anything to anybody with it, but I think you might want to stop by and talk to her first chance you get."

"Kiko was going to stop by and see her. If he doesn't do any good, I'll check on her tomorrow."

"I'd appreciate it," Marie said, sliding out of the booth. "I'll get out of your hair now and let you enjoy those chicken-fried sides of beef. Nice to meet you, Officer Cole."

"Nice to meet you, too."

As Marie walked to the counter and slid onto a stool, Jessi looked down at the untouched chicken-fried steak. Using her fork to hoist the meat, she flopped it over the pile of mashed potatoes, the limp steak covering the entire plate like a deep brown throw rug. She rolled her eyes and laughed. "My father would have loved this place."

"My dad sure did," Cutler said with a smile, turning away slightly so she couldn't see in his eyes that he was falling in love with her.

20.

❦

Highway Patrolman Marty Burris left Pocatello Pablo's Truck Stop at 22:35 hours and was about to pull onto the northbound Highway 12 ramp from Taylor Road when he saw the red BMW streak past southbound at what he estimated was 100 mph plus! Quickly flipping a U-turn, Marty pointed the black and white down the southbound ramp, and by the time his seatbelt was fastened, he was in pursuit at 100 mph and still had an inch of accelerator left. Two minutes later Burris pulled up behind the speeding BMW, clocked it at 120 mph and flipped on his light bar. The car slowed instantly and pulled to a stop on the shoulder of the two lane roadway.

At precisely 22:41 hours Marty radioed central dispatch in Waco that he was out of his car on a code 10-38 traffic stop and gave the location as five miles south of the Taylor Road exit on State Highway 12.

The driver of the BMW turned out to be a young, attractive Beaumont orthodontist named Dr. Colleen Mace who, with her husband Tony dozing cozily by her side, was on her way to Austin for a three day orthodontic convention. She was speeding because, as she explained to the nice officer, she didn't want to miss the kick off seminar on the hottest new braces that were soon to be gracing the teeth of America's youth and depleting the savings accounts of their parents. On this long day of ironies, Marty and Ellie had just made their final payment on a set of glittering mouth jewels for their angel-faced teen-age daughter, Alexa.

"Well, next time you go to Austin, fly. You'll get there later, but you might see more of the country," Marty said, watching his favorite joke zoom right over her head.

Colleen was apologetic and didn't complain, or laugh, or even blink when Marty cited her for driving 115 mph in a 75 mph zone and said, "Brace yourself, Doc," as he removed the $725 ticket from his booklet and handed it to her.

"Why should she blink," Marty thought as he returned to his Mustang. "She can make that much off me in about an hour and a half."

The puppies were starting to get on Pinky's nerves big time. Starved for their mother's milk and warm protection, they had been bawling nonstop for two solid hours. The longer they drove the more frantic their whining became, until, finally, they were yapping and Pinky was pulling his hair. "Shut up, you little bastards!"

Kitty had bought a-half-dozen cans of evaporated milk, but that had succeeded only in giving the dogs severe diarrhea which was filling the back of the van with an overpowering stench.

"Smells like a fucking dog pound back here! We have got to get rid of these damn dogs!"

"Well, just what do you want me to do?" Kitty asked from behind the wheel.

"Either take the next off ramp, or I'm going to start tossing the stinkin' little bastards out the window!"

Kitty swung the van off Highway 12 at the Hawkes Road Exit and drove along the frontage road for a half-mile before stopping in a grove of trees that concealed them from passing traffic. While Pinky slid the door open and pulled the box toward him, one of the puppies popped out the other side and crawled, unnoticed, into the shadows where it came face to face with the softly weeping Julie Abbot. As the girl wept, the little runt licked her tears before snuggling up close to her neck and closing its eyes.

Kitty moved behind a tree to relieve herself as Pinky carried the box of puppies through the darkness and down a short path before dumping them unceremoniously into a dry flood control culvert. The puppies squealed in alarm as they landed hard, but the sandy bottom of the ditch cushioned their fall.

Pinky stood over the culvert and urinated before hurrying back up the path where he dropped the Fort Howard Paper Company box on the ground and stomped it flat, folding it quickly and shoving it into a litter barrel. He quickly set the box on fire with a plastic lighter and watched until flames flared up the side before hurrying to the van and climbing in the back.

Kitty was already behind the wheel. "Maybe we should let her pee if she has to," she said.

"We'll be there in half an hour. She can pee then," he replied before spotting the wayward puppy curled close to Julie and, grabbing it by the scruff of the neck, flung it out of the van. The force of the landing knocked the wind out of the runt, leaving him dazed. The rear wheels of the van spun out, missing him by two inches as it pulled away and disappeared into the night.

At precisely 23:06 hours Officer Marty Burris radioed Waco dispatch that he was clear of the traffic stop and was resuming normal patrol duties. He drove for three miles before taking the Hawkes Road turnoff and was circling back to re-enter northbound Highway 12. As

Burris' Mustang approached the ramp, he slowed to allow a white Ford van to proceed ahead of him.

Inside the van, Kitty was instantly alert, involuntarily tensing as she spotted the patrol car following her down the ramp. "I see him," Pinky said from the rear as he glanced back at the Mustang. "Don't panic, just watch your speed. Let him pass you." His tone was calm and flat.

On the floor, under Pinky's feet, Julie resumed twisting and pulling the strand of wire. The blisters on her fingers had long since popped, leaving them sore and throbbing, but she sensed what was playing out above her and, gritting her teeth, continued.

Marty Burris signaled as he swung the Mustang into the fast lane to pass the van when he noticed the vehicle's left taillight begin to *blink*. Slowing, he allowed the van to pull ahead before he changed lanes and moved in behind it. The taillight continued to flash on and off randomly. Marty flipped on his flashing lights and followed the van onto the highway apron where it pulled to a stop.

At 23:07 hours Officer Burris keyed his microphone and informed Waco dispatch that he was making a routine traffic stop two miles north of Hawkes Road at highway marker 130. He asked for a DMV check on a Texas plate number Adam Sam Adam four zero seven four.

At 23:10 hours, supervising dispatcher Trudy Brigham, came back with the requested information. "Texas plate Adam Sam Adam four zero seven four comes back clear to a 1996 Ford Econoline van registered to Robert and Deborah Motta, 2291 Maple Drive, Waco."

In fact, Pinky and Kitty had spent over two hours earlier in the day driving around Waco looking for a van similar in color and age to their own. They had found it parked on the third level of a Waco shopping center garage. Pinky had slipped out of their own van and had quickly unscrewed the plate, attaching it to their van before they had staked out the theater that night.

Pinky had learned from a Huntsville cellmate named George Gomes that by stealing a plate with a similar vehicle description, he might buy himself a second or two if a crisis developed and they were stopped by a cop. George had been right.

"Roger that, Show me out on a 10-38 equipment check." As Marty Burris climbed out of the Mustang, he noticed a large, blond female exit the driver's side door and approach his vehicle. Burris met Kitty next to the front fender of the Mustang where the flashing lights from his Mustang bathed them in a dancing halo of red, yellow, and blue.

"Is something wrong, Officer? I'm sure I was going the speed limit."

"Your speed's fine, ma'am. It's your left taillight."

Kitty turned and looked at the rear of the van, keeping her face averted. The left taillight glowed as brightly as the right one did. "Looks okay to me."

"It was blinking off and on while you were driving. Looks like you might have a short. I'd have it checked out as soon as you can. There's a truck stop up the road a couple of miles, Taylor Road exit. You can get it fixed there.

"Thanks officer," Kitty mumbled. "I appreciate your help."

In the rear of the van, with the flashing light bar from the police car illuminating it like a rotating disco ball, Julie heard the policeman's voice right outside, and her heart leaped! He sounded so much like her daddy, she let go and peed her pants. Pinky was lying behind her on the floor, his rock-hard arms wrapped around her like a steel snake as he hissed in her ear, "You want to fucking die right here, you try

315

something." Julie sensed correctly that she was going to die anyway, so when she again heard Marty's voice again outside the van, she slammed her head against the carpeted side panel as hard as she could.

Marty was just turning away from Kitty when he heard the muffled *thump*!

Kitty smiled and nodded toward the van. "My husband was sleeping. He probably fell off the seat," she joked, hitting the rear door of the van with the ball of her fist. "Go back to sleep, Wesley. It's okay." She turned to Burris. "Thanks again, officer. We'll get the light fixed at Pablo's," she said as she turned and moved toward the front of the van.

Marty watched Kitty closely. Seventeen years and thousands of traffic stops had left him keenly aware of what might seem like trivial details to others. If the van was registered to Robert Motta, why did she call him Wesley? It seemed a little far fetched to think that Wesley was a nickname for Robert. And another thing, trivial also, but why would somebody from Waco know the truck stop was named 'Pablo's'?

"Yup," Marty thought, "something is amiss," and as he followed Kitty to the front of the van, his right hand moved automatically to rest on the butt of his holstered 9mm pistol. The scenario was beginning to feel just a tiny bit like a dope smuggling stop to him.

Highway 12 was a well-used corridor for smugglers bringing controlled substances, usually marijuana, hashish, or cocaine, into the United States from Mexico. Marty had made dozens of such stops; the most memorable had occurred, ironically, exactly one year ago tonight. He had stopped a station wagon for speeding six miles south of his present location and discovered $400,000 in cash and over two million dollars worth of neatly packaged cocaine resting comfortably under an army blanket in the back of the car. He had spread-eagled the two suspects on the ground, cuffed them, and then radioed cousin Johnny for a backup.

"Ma'am," Marty said loud enough to be heard over the roar of a passing 18 wheeler, "Would you mind getting your driver's license and registration for me? Just routine."

"Certainly, officer," Kitty replied, opening the driver's side door and reaching into the interior for her purse. She caught just a glimpse of Pinky's back as he slipped soundlessly out the slightly ajar side door.

Kitty set the black leather purse on the seat and started sorting through its contents. "I have it here, somewhere."

The way she stood, looking down at her purse with the lights from the Mustang illuminating her features triggered something in Marty's brain.

"Here it is," Kitty said turning and holding out her driver's license to him. In that instant of recognition, Marty smiled.

"Hey, Kitty, what are you..." he took one step forward before he caught a flash of movement behind him. The flash was from the Mustang's headlights reflecting off the thick, razor-sharp blade of Pinky's knife as it slashed into the patrolman's neck with such force that it sliced cleanly through five inches of skin and muscle and severed both Marty's carotid arteries and his trachea.

Marty pitched forward onto his knees, feeling nothing but warmth rushing to his cheeks like thousands of pinpricks that instantly enveloped his entire face and shot down his side.

Marty's last thoughts were of his son, Kyle's, first walking experience. With Ellie standing behind him, the boy had taken three, tiny, unsure little steps, arms out, and then pitched forward, squealing with delight as Daddy caught him and kissed his warm neck, and then there were no more thoughts.

A deep gurgle escaped Marty's destroyed throat as Kitty brought her heavy shoe down on his head *again* and *again,* crushing the skull and splattering drops of blood up onto the rear door and window of the van and onto the hood of the Mustang, giving instant payback to the hot shot athlete sonofabitch who never once gave her so much as a simple look!

Pinky noticed the headlights coming up behind them. He pushed Kitty aside and grabbed the dead officer by his boots and dragged him, face down, to the passenger side of the Mustang, leaving a wide, slick blood trail over the pavement and on the gravel. He opened the door and quickly lifted the body onto the seat and slammed the door closed. Marty's head flopped against the window, and his vacant, puzzled eyes seemed to stare out at Pinky, freezing him in the light for just a split second as the 18 wheeler roared past, kicking up miniature dust devils that swirled around Kitty's bloody shoes as she stood alongside the van like a statue.

Pinky, his shirt drenched in Marty's blood, grabbed Marty's straw cowboy hat off the ground and pulled it down low over his eyes. He hurried to the driver's side of the police car and barked "Follow me!" at Kitty as he dove behind the wheel of the Mustang and started flipping toggle switches until the flashing colored lights were extinguished. He took a deep, steadying breath and, jerking the car into gear, sped off with the white van close behind.

They were each carrying Styrofoam doggy boxes as they came out of the restaurant and paused next to the old Chevy. Cutler rubbed his stomach and groaned.

"How can you stuff yourself like that and be so thin? It's not fair," Jessi said.

"I only ate half of it. The rest..." he held the tray aloft, "is for Henry's dinner."

"And breakfast, and lunch, and a snack. Here, he can have mine, too," Jessi said, placing her box on top of his. Cutler carried the boxes to the Blazer and placed them on the floor behind the passenger seat.

They stood in silence for a moment before Cutler worked up enough courage to finally ask her. "You've got two choices: you can plead exhaustion, which I will respect and concur with, or we can get a beer at the Oasis."

"What's the attraction at the Oasis?" Jessi asked.

"Other than my company? It's got one of the loudest, raunchiest cowboy bands that you've ever heard."

"This is that rowdy cowboy bar we went to the other day?"

"It is."

"Let's go," Jessi replied.

"Good, I'll lead the way. We're just going about a mile down the..." Cutler was interrupted by the *long trumpeting blast* of the shiny blue Freightliner as the driver laid on the horn and then hit his jake brake, gearing down a little too fast before hissing to a skidding stop behind them. Both doors of the cab popped open and the agitated husband and wife driving team of Betty and Blair Wilcox hopped down. Fancy gilded lettering declared their CB handles, *"Bitchin' Betty"* on the door below the passenger-side window and *"Panda Bear"* on the driver's side.

Cutler sensed correctly that something was wrong, most likely a car wreck.

The heavyset Blair spoke first, a little unsure as he unconsciously stroked his thick mustache. "Officer, I think something might be wrong back down the road there a piece."

"What's the problem?" Cutler asked, noticing the exchanged look between Betty and Blair.

"We're not sure," Blair said as he half turned and pointed back toward the direction from where they had just come.

Betty cut in. "There was a patrol car stopped alongside the road with it's red lights going," she shrugged and held her arms out, palms up.

"We couldn't see the cop anywhere, I mean the officer."

"What kind of a patrol car was it?"

The question confused Blair for a second. "Highway Patrol. Mustang."

Cutler was instantly aware that his heart was racing.

Betty continued. "There was this big woman just standing there alongside a white car like she was..."

"Van! It was a white van, and there was this other guy, too, but no cop!" Blair explained.

"And this guy, he..." Betty shuddered at what she might have seen, deathly afraid to say it.

Blair moved in and touched her neck in a gentle show of support. "Tell the man what you saw, babe."

Tears welled in Betty's eyes as she blurted out the terrible word, "*Blood*! I think the man might have had blood on him, but I'm not sure." Her voice trailed off into soft sobs that told Jessi and Cutler she *was* sure.

Cutler was frozen.

Jessi jumped in, her voice calm but firm. "How far down the road? Can you remember the nearest exit?"

"It was this side of the last exit, not more than five miles," Blair answered as Jessi and Cutler bolted for the Blazer and scrambled through the doors.

The Oklahoma City bound truck drivers watched as the Blazer backed out and then fishtailed out of the parking lot, bouncing crazily over a line of potholes before it screamed down the southbound ramp. Panda Bear and Bitchin' Betty exchanged a look, and then Panda Bear held his sobbing driving partner of twenty-two years and watched until the flashing lights disappeared in the distance and the eerie sound of the siren faded away.

Inside the speeding Blazer, Cutler and Jessi had already learned from a concerned Trudy Brigham at Waco Highway Patrol dispatch that Officer Marty Burris had radioed her at 23:10 hours that he was out of his vehicle on an equipment check at sign marker 130. Since it was only 23:22 hours as they spoke, she hadn't been concerned that he hadn't cleared the call yet. Trudy immediately tried to raise Officer Burris on the radio, but he wasn't responding, and when she came back to give Cutler the vehicle description and license number of the van, she asked him to advise her immediately upon his arrival on scene.

Less than a minute later Cutler did just that, barking "On scene!" into the microphone. He shouted "Hang on!" to Jessi as he slowed the Blazer only slightly and barreled into the hard-packed and sloped median strip, throwing up a cloud of dust and sand and scattering tumbleweeds before bouncing roughly back onto the southbound lane where he quickly pulled to the side of the highway and squealed to a stop! He grabbed his portable high beam off the floor and, stepping out, swept the roadway and borrow pit with a bright halo of white light, quickly picking up the mile marker post with the luminous numbers "130" reflecting back at them.

No white van! No Mustang patrol car! Nothing moved in the darkness but the dancing lights from the Blazer's flashing light bar. Jessi opened the door and was standing with one leg still in the Blazer as Cutler aimed the light further up the road. An eighteen wheeler bore down on them from the rear, and when the driver spotted Cutler's flashing lights, he immediately hit his jake brake and swerved the truck and trailer into the fast lane, blowing past with such force that the wash nearly took Cutler's hat off and left the air heavy with the smell of diesel exhaust.

"What's that down there?" Jessi asked from the other side. Something lying on the side of the road had reflected light back at her. They jumped back in and covered the seventy-five yards to the marker in the longest five seconds of Cutler's life.

Jessi was out first with the Mag light and saw at once that the reflection had come from a pair of eyeglasses that were lying in a pool of oil at the edge of the road. When Cutler saw them he knew instantly that they were Marty's *Buddy Holly's*. He automatically reached for them. Jessi grabbed his hand first. He nodded his acknowledgement bleakly. In that instant they saw that the sticky puddle was not oil at all, but blood, lots of blood. Surrounding the blood puddle were red footprints and unmistakable crimson drag marks and even more blood splattered on the highway. Both of them knew that whoever was dragged away had suffered a severe, if not fatal, injury, and judging from the level of coagulation, they also knew it had just happened!

"Leave the glasses there," she said, softly. Helping the trembling Cutler to his feet, they both retreated from the obvious crime scene, not wanting to contaminate it any worse than they already had. Cutler reached in through the door and brought out his portable radio. Before he could broadcast, Jessi raised her hand. "If they have your cousin's patrol car, they're also listening to the radio."

Cutler nodded, surprised at his lack of professionalism and embarrassed by it. He quickly grabbed his cell phone and informed the Waco Highway Patrol dispatcher of what they had found, asking that a helicopter be dispatched to their location. After ending that call, he was about to call his office when he saw Jessi look off. "Look, over there. What's that?" she asked, pointing off into the distance where a red glow seemed to grow in intensity. "A fire? What's out there?" Jessi asked.

"Nothing," was Cutler's response. "Let's go." They hurried back to the Blazer, roared back onto the highway and headed for the closest turnoff. As he drove, Jessi used the cell phone to call the office.

Night dispatcher Jill Richards was standing beside Deputy Red Cordell, both watching over Murray Crook's shoulder, mesmerized as his fingers raced over the keyboard of the computer. Jill and Red exchanged a look and a shrug that confirmed what each of them was thinking: they were watching pure genius at work.

The police line rang, and Jill moved back quickly to the nearby console to plug herself in.

"Sheriff's Office, can I help you?" As Jill listened, her sudden intake of breath caught Red's attention and he turned slowly, troubled by her odd body language. She seemed to slump slightly before steadying herself. In the eighteen years they had worked together in this office, Red had never seen her chin quiver during a call. She was as professional as they came—rock solid.

Murray noticed Red's concern and he, too, rose to his feet. Jill made eye contact with Red, holding up three fingers as she continued to listen. Red jerked open the bottom drawer of his desk and pulled out his holstered 9MM and quickly strapped it on, pushing his black baton into its holder on the wide belt and grabbing his four-cell Maglight and portable radio. He had done it all in less than five seconds.

"What? Is it?" Murray asked in a soft, frightened tone.

"Something's up-something bad."

Jill listened for a moment longer jotting down information, and then closed the connection. When she looked up her voice was deliberate and controlled.

"There's been some kind of incident out at the end of Tubbs Road. Marty Burris is involved. Sheriff said stay off the radio."

Red asked no questions. Moving quickly, he grabbed his keys and was out the door before either of them saw his tears. Murray and Jill heard his Bronco start up and explode out of the parking lot, sending a shower of pea gravel ricocheting noisily off the tinny trailer, followed by the piercing wail of his siren. Murray and Jill exchanged looks before Jill slumped down wearily behind her console and struggled to hold back her tears as she realized that things might never be the same in her office again. She took a deep breath to control herself and called Janie Cortez at home. All she got was her machine. She disconnected without leaving a message, and as she did, the police line rang. Jill cleared her throat and took the call like a pro. "This is the Sheriff's Office, can I help you?"

"Jill, this is Janie. What's the siren about? What's going on?"

As Jill talked on the phone, Murray picked up Henry, the dog, and stroked his head.

Cutler took the turnoff and covered the mile and a half quickly, in spite of the bone- jarring potholes that kept Jessi on the edge of her seat.

They found Marty Burris's Mustang fully engulfed in flames at the end of Tubbs Road. Cutler skidded to a stop, retrieved the fire extinguisher from the floor in back, and approached the fire. As they got within thirty yards, they had to stop, raising their hands to shield their faces from the intense radiant heat that had melted the light rack on the top and blistered the paint.

Looking into the flames, Marty's dead eyes were clearly visible against the background of blackened flesh, open wide, as they were that day long ago when he and Cutler had exchanged high fives and leaped off the cliff to plunge fifty feet into the Nueces River! Cutler started toward the flaming car again, but Jessi had a firm grip on his forearm. She said nothing; it was obvious that Marty was beyond their help. Cutler let out an agonized, painful groan and hurled the useless fire extinguisher as far off into the brush as he could. They stood there, watching the car burn and listening to the wailing sirens of incoming emergency vehicles growing louder. Cutler turned away from the flames and wept.

21.

The experience at the Laundromat had left Lela shaken and exhausted, and she welcomed being back at Velma's. She closed the door on Jessi thinking that all she wanted to do was to climb into bed and escape into sleep. As she turned the key in the lock, she was surprised at how familiar and comfortable the small room was beginning to feel.

Crossing the room, she set her clean laundry and carryall on the bed before slipping off her sandals and entering the bathroom. She quickly slipped out of her long dress and underwear and stepped into the shower. Fifteen minutes later she was still under the steaming hot cascade, letting it pour over her. Only when the water started turning cold did she reluctantly turn it off and step out to dry herself with the soft, fluffy towels.

She lit incense and laid her crystals on the nightstand before climbing into bed. The cool sheets soothed her sensitive skin. She fell asleep almost instantly.

She slept soundly for almost two hours before she jerked awake, the familiar pain in her temples twisting her face into painful contortions, all accompanied by the usual metallic taste and smell. As she succumbed to the vision, she saw Julie staring into her eyes, the girl's face bruised and dirty.

"Help me, please. Somebody, please help me."

Lela struggled furiously, but her constricted throat wouldn't give her breath enough to ask the simple question: "Where are you?" Lela was helpless, and then the wolf's head came again, its red eyes burning into her spirit as it pulled Julie away from her.

"Nooo!" Lela cried as Julie was jerked from her grasp. Lela wanted to retreat from the image. She wanted the safety of the familiar motel room, but she had to see where they had taken Julie. It took all of her willpower to stay in the vision, to follow the wolf. She climbed up and looked over the edge of a dark structure, catching just a glimpse of figures entering it. There were letters on the building, but they were fading even as she saw them. She struggled to hold onto the vision, but it retreated, leaving her in a cold sweat and fighting for breath. She lay in the darkness for a long while before finally sitting up and turning on the lamp next to the bed. She removed her sketchpad from the carryall and, sitting cross-legged and naked, started sketching furiously. First the shadowy outline of a large, dark building appeared, and then across the bottom of the page in block letters, she drew in *CECOM*. She turned to a fresh page and continued drawing with heavy, intense strokes.

By midnight word of officer Marty Burris's murder had spread to every law enforcement agency in the State of Texas, and the normally deserted Tubbs Road turnaround was bumper to bumper with nearly two-dozen police vehicles. Four were Highway Patrol Mustangs identical to Marty Burris's unit that now sat charred and smoldering, dripping in a soupy, black slurry created by water from the Grace Volunteer Fire Department's lime green pumper. Arriving in two trucks and three pickups within twelve minutes of Jill Richards's first call out, the seven volunteers and one full-time fire captain, adrenalin pumping, had quickly doused the burning car and now stood, or sat, on the running board of the truck, talking in hushed tones as they removed their heavy, yellow, soot covered turnouts and helmets and hung them from the pumper. Among the firefighters were fire captain Bob Maddocks, volunteers Frank Cortez, part-time city worker Jim Park, flight instructor Kenny Braren, and Pocatello Pablo from the truck stop. Each of them had counted Marty Burris as a friend.

The remainder of the vehicles were Grace County Sheriff's Blazers and Broncos and a sprinkling of cars from other agencies, including sheriff's cars from nearby San Saba and Mills Counties, and two unmarked cars from the FBI field office in Waco. A Highway Patrol Bell Jet Star Ranger shared the sky with another police helicopter from San Saba County, their muffled "whump-whump-whump" echoing in the distance as they relentlessly crisscrossed the seemingly never-ending labyrinth of gulleys, washes, and rutted, dusty backroads of Grace County. The choppers' thirty million candle power searchlights sliced through the early morning darkness like laser beams from UFOs as they looked in vain for the killers' elusive, and now infamous, white van.

A battery of powerful floodlights brought in from a nearby highway construction project illuminated the burnt Mustang for a pair of crime scene technicians. Dressed in blue jumpsuits and wearing latex gloves, they inched, heads down, over the ground, pausing periodically to snap flash pictures of an object before dropping it into a bag to be carried to their portable crime lab. The custom-made Winnebago RV was parked unobtrusively away from the scene.

Three TV news remote units with their easily recognizable portable satellite dishes had been kept back, set up alongside the road, close to a barbed wire fence, well over a thousand yards from where knots of uniformed Texas Highway Patrolmen stood shaking their heads periodically as each, in turn, came to the sobering realization that the *crispy critter* in the car was not one of the usual faceless civilian casualties they were trained to process but was one of their own. Even more sobering was the realization that the pile of carbon was someone most of them loved like a brother. The familiar pounding of an incoming helicopter caused them to turn and watch as it arched into a tight circle and then settled into a nearby field that had been marked by a circle of burning road flares. The powerful turbine engine quieted and the rotors slowed, the door slid open, and the head of the Texas Department of Public Safety's Traffic Law Enforcement Division, Commander Mike Cleary, stepped out. He was met by the Sixth District supervising officer, Major David Albright, who led Cleary through the field, over a barbed wire fence, and past the line of cars to where John Cutler was standing with Kiko, Red, Louie Adams, and other deputies inspecting a map spread out on the hood of his Blazer. Cutler looked up from the map as Albright and Cleary approached, Albright taking Cutler's arm.

"Commander Mike Cleary, this is Grace County Sheriff John Cutler. He's the OIC. He'll bring you up to speed."

As the two men shook hands, each recognized the gravity of the moment reflected in the other's eyes. "Welcome to Grace County, sir. Right now we're working two crime scenes: this one and the other back on Highway 12 where Marty, err, Officer Burris made the traffic stop." Cutler tapped the map for emphasis.

"What do we have on the vehicle he pulled over?" Cleary asked.

"The tag Marty ran, Adam Sam Adam 4-0-7-4, came back as a 1996 Ford Econoline registered to Robert and Deborah Motta of Waco. Those folks are currently sitting at the Waco Police Department and appear to be totally unrelated to any of this. Their van, however, is missing its rear plate. They weren't aware it was gone until tonight. They think the plate had to have been stolen sometime within the last two days, probably while they were shopping."

Cleary let the information filter and percolate for a moment before responding. "So our perps stole a plate that matched their own vehicle. Drug runners?"

"That's my guess. That way, if an officer asks for a rolling ID, it will at least *look* like the right car," Cutler said.

"But if an officer stops them, they know they're had once he checks their ID against the information radioed on the plate."

Cutler nodded in agreement. "Yeah, but there's a gap in there of a minute or so when the officer is unaware, offguard. I think that's when they got Marty."

"Was he shot?"

"We don't know yet. There was an awful lot of blood spilled up there—possibly a knife. I..." Cutler's voice broke slightly. He took a deep breath and continued. "A couple of long-haul truck drivers, a married couple, alerted us to the situation. The woman was riding shotgun and caught a glimpse of a man and a woman standing by the patrol car with no officer visible. The witness thought she saw blood on the man. They also confirmed seeing a white van.

"It fits with the evidence. There had to be at least two perpetrators. They left two distinct sets of bloody footprints on the road. After they killed him they put him back in his car, and one of them drove the Mustang down here. The other one followed in the van. At that point they poured gas all over it and lit a match, probably to cover any prints they might have left."

"No other witnesses?"

"Another officer and I were the first unit down here. Nobody passed us going out. I figure they had to take the road over there," Cutler said, pointing off to where a dusty fire road crossed a metal cattle guard and then snaked out to interconnect with a thousand other narrow fire roads that crisscrossed the back country. "That means the people we're looking for could possibly be locals who knew they could cut back onto Highway 12 about three miles over there," Cutler said, pointing northeast.

"Or maybe they're still out there," Cleary offered.

Major Albright spoke up. "I hope so, because if they are, those choppers will nail them. Plus we've got three, First Team Army choppers enroute from Ft. Hood loaded with state-of-the-art heat seeking equipment. If they're holed up out there, we've got 'em."

Commander Cleary nodded toward the smoldering Mustang. "What do we do now?"

"We're not going to remove the body out here. We'll cover the car and put it on the back of a tow truck and take it to the state lab in Austin. That way the crime specialists will get first look along with the medical examiner," Cutler explained.

The meaning of Cutler's words were not lost on Cleary or Albright. Marty's body had been so totally consumed by the fire that it was almost impossible to separate it from what remained of the fabric of the Mustang upholstery, and attempting to do so could further destroy what little evidence might remain.

"What's the family situation? Cleary asked.

Two boys, Emillo and Kyle. His wife's name is Ellie."

"How's she holding up?" Cleary asked.

"Our dispatcher, Janie Cortez, is Ellie's sister. She's over there now. I talked to her a few minutes ago. It was pretty solemn. All the family's been notified, and they're on the way," Cutler said.

"Somebody said you were related to him, a cousin?" Albright asked.

"Kissin' cousin on my mother's side," Cutler said, feeling hot tears springing into his eyes as his voice quivered. "Only we don't kiss."

"I'd like to go over and pay my respects. Should I wait until morning?" Cleary asked Albright, who used his eyes to pass the question on to Cutler.

"Janie said they were just getting the boys settled down, so probably tomorrow would be better," Cutler answered.

Cleary nodded and extended his hand to Cutler. "Thanks for all you've done, sheriff. I'm sorry for your loss. Anything we can help you with, you've got."

"Tell you what. If you'd go down the road and take care of briefing the TV people, I'd appreciate it."

"You got it," Cleary said, turning to Albright. "Where are they?"

As Albright lead Cleary to a waiting car, Cutler turned and scanned the area for Jessi, easily spotting her standing with a Highway Patrol officer, Val Smith, a tall, handsome bachelor that women in the Grace City Offices swooned over every time he stopped by. Janie Cortez swore Val looked like Robert Redford. As Cutler watched Jessi and Val talk, he was surprised by the nagging sensation in his stomach. It had been so long since Cutler had felt jealousy that for a moment he mistook it for hunger. "Jesus, I am not that old." He refused to go over to them and instead returned to studying the map.

Jessi had met a lot of Val Smiths in her seven years on the force. Most guys she knew put on uniforms because it was a requirement of the job, but a few of them wore uniforms because they thought they looked great in them. Val was one of the latter, a man who viewed life from a totally self-centered perspective.

Jessi soon tired of Val's "And after I graduated from JC, I did..." mentality and found herself simply nodding and saying "uh huh" to everything he said. She wondered if Val was giving much thought to his friend, Marty Burris. If so, she hadn't heard or seen it. As Val droned on, she watched Cutler across the parking lot. The difference in the two men was striking. In the two days she had known Cutler, she couldn't recall him volunteering information about himself. She smiled inwardly because, in that respect, he reminded her of herself, or at least of how she liked to view herself.

When Jessi spotted Animal Control Officer Marie Sisco's familiar truck pulling to a stop close-by, she found the opportunity to escape, flashing Val a brilliant smile. "Excuse me, Marie was supposed to check on something for me. Nice talking about you, err, with you."

As Jessi approached the truck, Marie stepped out. "Did Val give you one of his Highway Patrol trading cards?"

"You're kidding, right?"

"No joke. He even signed mine. I used it to scoop poop." Marie nodded toward the line of patrol cars she had just passed. "Pretty grim, huh?"

"To say the least."

"Marty Burris was one of the good guys, you know? Always had a smile for you. Always interested in what you were doing. Great sense of humor. This has got to be killing Johnny. They were like brothers. What kind of a fucking asshole would do something like this?" The big woman's voice dissolved into soft sobs, and she turned away in embarrassment, wiping away tears with the cuff of her shirt."

Jessi patted Marie's shoulder as they stood in silence for a moment. She heard the puppies before she saw them, their high-pitched whining leading her to the rear of the truck where all six were standing on their rear legs scratching at the wire cage. Their yellow coats were dulled from excrement, and dirt and dust they had picked up from the culvert.

"What beautiful puppies," Jessi said, moving close enough to the cage that one of the small dogs was able to lick her face through the wire. "Can I hold one?"

"Sure," Marie said. Releasing the bar that held the cage shut and holding the other squirming animals at bay, she retrieved the runt and handed it to Jessi.

"What a precious little thing," Jessi said as the happy little animal eagerly licked her chin. "Poor little thing acts like he's starving."

"He is. Somebody tossed them out like so much garbage. I'll feed them as soon as I get back to the shelter."

Jessi snuggled the dog under her chin and smiled at the memory the puppy smell evoked. She had been seven years old and the puppy had been a white Cockapoo named Tasha. She had slept in her room for the next eight years. "Are they too little for a helping of the world's biggest chicken-fried steak?" Jessi asked.

"Probably, but in their condition, I say 'go for it.'"

Jessi handed the runt back to Marie and quickly retrieved the plastic doggie boxes from the rear floorboard of Cutler's Blazer. Marie removed a Swiss Army knife from her belt and used it to chop the two steaks in small pieces before placing the boxes in the cage where the famished puppies attacked them voraciously.

"How anyone can abandon sweet little puppies, I'll never know," Jessi said.

Marie shook her head. "Well, when you pick them up several times a week, you get used to it. Most times when they're dropped off close to a road they end up as speed bumps. These little guys were lucky."

The women watched the ravenous puppies devour the food, licking the plastic trays until they were spotless. The small animals, dirty and exhausted, then quieted quickly as they cuddled in a squirming ball and went to sleep. The runt snuggled deep down in Jessi's arms, closed his eyes, and gave a tired sigh. He was safe.

"Well, I'd better get them back to the shelter," Marie said as she took the puppy from Jessi and gently set it next to its siblings.

Marie walked back to the driver's side of her truck before pausing and looking back at the surreal scene. "I'd like to talk to Johnny, but he looks pretty busy. Tell him I'll stop by the office tomorrow, would you?"

"I will."

Marie climbed back into her truck her eyes blurring with tears. "I can't believe this has happened. You just... just never know." She closed the door and drove slowly down the road. Jessi watched her tail-lights as she turned onto the highway headed for Grace.

Cutler was going over the maps with Kiko, Red, and Louie, breaking the highway down into grids that would be assigned to four-man search parties at first light. The men looked up as Jessi approached, Cutler noticing Jessi's tired expression. "I think that we've done as much as we can tonight. I'm going to take Jessi to pick up the car.

The men nodded their agreement.

Cutler left Kiko in charge of both crime scenes and then drove Jessi back to Pocatello Pablo's to retrieve the Chevy.

As they pulled up and stopped next to the green convertible, Jessi popped the door open and then paused. "Let me know if anything breaks."

"I'll do that," he said, and then added quickly, "Thanks for keeping me on track tonight. I appreciate it, Jessi."

"John? I'm sorry about Marty. I'm here if you need me."

Cutler nodded as Jessi got out. "Jessi, I wish... I wish right now that I could lie down next to you and fall asleep in your arms."

"I'll give you a rain check."

"Promise?"

Jessi smiled. "Promise."

He waited until he heard the Chevy start before pulling away.

It was four o'clock in the morning when Jessi pulled into Velma's lot and parked in front of number seven where she sat for a moment trying to make sense of what had happened. She couldn't. Violence never made sense, but it was the one true constant of her job. She got out of the car, noticing that Lela's room was dark. As she removed her room key from her purse, she pictured Lela sleeping soundly and envied her. Across the street she saw Deputy Lee Nash sitting behind the wheel of a Sheriff's Department Blazer, patiently watching Lela's room. He gave her a tired wave before starting the car and pulling away.

Jessi entered her room, locked the door, and adjusted her curtains to let in a little light. She hated the pitch-black darkness; she felt like she was in a cave, and it made her feel claustrophobic. At home she slept with both her draperies and her window open. Yawning wearily she pulled off her clothes and collapsed on the bed. An endless supply of hot coffee had left her with a sour stomach. She removed her watch, set it down on the small nightstand, and flipped the lamp off. She was sound asleep within thirty seconds.

After dropping off Jessi at the truck stop, Cutler returned to the city trailer to find several deputies and a highway patrol sergeant seated at various desks, talking on phones or filling out reports. Murray Crook huddled over the computer as Jill sat in front of the radio console monitoring the unusually heavy traffic on the normally silent band. Everyone looked up and nodded when Cutler entered, but no one spoke. He needed to get some rest. He was mentally and physically exhausted, and he knew that the hard work was just beginning. The killers had somehow avoided detection by over a hundred police officers and had been swallowed up in the vast country. They'd find them sooner or later, but it was obvious to him from monitoring the helicopter radio traffic that it would most likely be later. "Wake me up if you hear anything," he said to one of the deputies, and as he passed Jill he reached out and gave her shoulder a squeeze, just a gentle reminder of their shared grief. He disappeared into the small side office to lie down on the cot with Henry at his feet and fell into a fitful sleep.

For Lela there was no hope of going back to sleep. She had moved off the bed when Jessi had driven up and watched her through a slit in the shutter. After Jessi had disappeared into her room, Lela had returned to bed but couldn't force herself to sleep. The dreadful feeling of lurking evil and horror wasn't going away. It was close, too close, and kept invading her mind, refusing her even a moment's peace. She sat up, turned on the light, and studied the blurry images she had drawn in the sketchbook. Tossing the sketchbook aside, she got up and paced around the small room wearing Julie Abbott's fear wrapped around her shoulders like a heavy blanket.

In the past, after experiencing a visualization, Lela had always been content to lay the responsibility for action on someone else, usually the police. She rationalized that if they chose to think she was a crackpot and someone suffered as a result of their inaction, then at least her conscience was clear. She had tried her best. She momentarily considered banging on Jessi's door and telling her of her latest vision, but she wasn't in the mood to see the look of suspicion and disbelief, if not pity, in the younger woman's eyes. No, she had to do something on her own.

The realization came to her like a blow. She had to act.

Relieved that she had made a decision, Lela quickly dressed, putting on a clean skirt and blouse from her stack of fresh laundry, and headed toward the door. She opened the door and paused, returning to retrieve her crystal necklace from the nightstand. She carefully put it over her head, her long fingers caressing the crystal for its reassuring comfort. She set the key on the nightstand and looked around the tiny room. In many ways it contained everything she wanted, and she realized with regret that she would probably never see it again. She pulled the straw gardener's hat on, eased it over her painful wound, and quietly closed the door. As she turned, she noticed the old Chevy parked in front of Jessi's room. "Great. A dead woman's car in front of room number seven," she thought, shuddering at the combination. "Not a good omen."

Lela wasn't sure of the time because she never wore a watch. The gesture was a futile, '60s-inspired protest against arbitrary rules imposed on her by the fascist Big Brother state. She knew it was foolish, but it had become a habit. She even went so far as to unplug the standard issue motel clock next to her bed.

It was still dark outside, but she sensed it was close to dawn. Lela had no idea where she was going. She quickly walked away from Velma's and made her way toward the center of town. Ten minutes later she was walking down Grace's deserted Main Street toward the old Bancroft highway. There was no hesitancy in her steps. She was a woman possessed, allowing Julie's terror to show her the way.

The old highway was dark and deserted, and as she walked down the middle of the narrow road, the early morning air chilled her and she rubbed her arms for warmth. Off in the distance she could hear the drone of helicopters sounding like airborn tractors as they tirelessly plowed back and forth above the back roads. The relentless *thumping* increased her anxiety, and Lela considered turning back. She wasn't a brave person, and she longed for the comfort of her little motel room. She had nearly convinced herself to turn around when she heard the rumbling approach of a diesel, heard the *blast* of an air horn, as the truck swung out to avoid hitting her. Lela scrambled to the side of the road as the 18 wheeler slowed and hissed to a stop.

"Where ya headed?" The driver called out the window.

Lela hesitated, looked ahead and saw a sign:

Bancroft - 22 miles

As soon as she heard herself say the name, she knew she was right. "Bancroft."

"I'm going right through there. Climb in."

Lela stepped onto the running board of the noisy, black Peterbilt and, opening the door, climbed into the warm cab to be met by a cloud of cigar smoke. "Thanks, I appreciate your stopping," she said, wondering if she really did.

The truck driver, a short, jocular cigar smoker named Ozzie Neff, never once stopped talking, first about the "Smoky" that was murdered the previous night, followed by a stream of other topics—like his bowling average (188), his horses (he had owned six), his wives (he had had three)—all the while puffing like a steam engine, blowing smoke at her for the thirty minutes it took them to cover the 22 miles. Lela was relieved when the big, noisy "Pete," as Ozzie called the Peterbilt, thumped over a railroad crossing and slowed to a hissing stop next to a sign that read:

- WELCOME TO BANCROFT -

Population 4,344

- Deep in the Heart of Texas-

Lela climbed down from the cab and waved at Ozzie, waiting for the big rig to pull away before she crossed the quiet, two-lane highway and measured her surroundings. Now what? She couldn't ask directions because she didn't know where she was going. She looked at the railroad tracks and, hesitating only briefly, followed them west, away from town, as they paralleled Short Falls Road. It was Sunday morning, and the eastern horizon was starting to glow.

She covered nearly a mile before she spotted the group of buildings looming in the distance. Just seeing them caused a chill to move past her heart. She slowed and then stopped as the cold reality of her situation hit home. What did she expect to find out here? And if she did find something, what could she possibly do about it? She should have told Jessi or Cutler, put the burden on their shoulders. She had never felt so alone or frightened in all her life, and cursing herself for her weakness, she turned around and hurried back toward Bancroft intending to locate a pay phone and call Jessi at the motel. She made it a hundred yards before the familiar metallic taste filled her mouth and signaled the oncoming spell. She looked around for a place to go, somewhere off the tracks where she could lie down until it passed. In a blind panic she took a step off the tracks and stumbled head over heels into the deep borrow pit that separated the rusty tracks from Short Falls Road. As she pulled herself to her knees, she felt an electrical jolt stiffen her body and thrust her face into the powdery dirt.

Julie Abbott's frightened presence filled her head and pleaded: "Help me, please. They're going to kill me!"

Lela lay in the borrow pit for a long time before she was able to roll onto her side and pull herself to her knees. Remaining on her knees she crawled up the steep side of the pit on all fours, dragging herself over the sharp rocks and onto the track bed before staggering to her feet.

Ignoring her scratched and bleeding knees and elbows, she again looked back toward the sleeping village of Bancroft, then spun and faced the buildings looming in the distance. There was not time to go back. She had to go to Julie.

22.

Ɔ⊙

It was an odd, unsettling dream. Jessi was trapped, somehow stuck in a narrow crawlspace. The harder she tried to free herself, the more firmly she became wedged between the cold, damp walls. She was aware that the air had thinned, and she was struggling for breath. She began to panic as she realized that she was dying and was strangely fascinated by the simplicity of it. She struggled to scream, but the only sounds that came out were muted, guttural groans that were swallowed by the strange buzzing sound close to her head.

Jessi opened her eyes and looked at the strange room. It took her several seconds to remember where she was and that the buzzing sound was the radio alarm clock. She sat up, unable to find the on/off switch. She finally located the plug and yanked the cord from the wall socket. It was six A.M. and just getting light out. She lay back down for a moment and, without intending to, dozed.

She woke up the second time to light pouring through the opening in the drapes. Jessi stumbled out of bed, closed the drapes, and made a beeline for the shower, where she closed her eyes and let the hot water stream over her body and wash away the remnants of last night's fatigue. She dressed quickly and went outside, made a hard right, and hurried to the office where Velma always had a pot of fresh coffee brewing. Velma wasn't in the office or her quarters, but the coffee looked hot. Jessi poured herself a Styrofoam cupful and went back outside, sipping coffee as she returned to Lela's room number eight. Her curtains were drawn tight. Jessi wanted to get to the city trailer as soon as possible. She decided to let Lela sleep. Jessi dug through her purse and wrote Lela a note letting her know where she would be and leaving her cell phone number as well as the number at the sheriff's office. She wedged the note in the door jam and gave one last look at the drawn curtains before heading the Chevy toward the city trailer.

There were no parking spaces available in the usually-empty, gravel parking lot. Jessi could see Cutler's Blazer parked in front surrounded by several other Blazers carrying the Grace County seal. Cars and trucks from other agencies were crammed into the small lot, as well as a satellite equipped van from a TV station out of Waco. Jessi finally parked the Chevy a long block away and walked back to the trailer, making her way past several groups of people gathered in the parking lot discussing in hushed tones the night's stunning events. A reporter from KRTV was conducting interviews with local residents for background insights on Marty Burris.

Inside, the double-wide was teeming with uniformed personnel. Jessi remembered the sheriff telling her that he had thirty deputies in the county, and it looked like they were all there, gathered around the large map, listening intently as Cutler went over their individual patrol assignments. The daily work of the county had to go on, and it was his job to give these men direction. He was their compass. He spoke calmly and with authority as he sent his men, one by one, back out into the field. He didn't see Jessi come in, and she wasn't going to intrude.

As Jessi moved past, Deputy Louie Adams from Slocum smiled and nodded a greeting. Jessi returned the smile and continued through the trailer, past two Highway Patrolman, the state crime scene investigators, and two men who were, no doubt, FBI agents in suits and ties sitting at the Water Department desk talking on the phones. She spotted Janie Cortez, Afton Murphy and Jill Richards manning the constantly-ringing phones. The older Jill had gamely finished her shift and steadfastly refused to leave.

As Janie disconnected from a call, Jessi made her way over and gave her a hug. Janie's eyes were puffy from spilled tears, and she clung to Jessi tightly before moving away to answer another incoming call.

Murray Crook was sitting listlessly at the computer and Jessi assumed, correctly, by his five o'clock shadow and wild hair that the usually meticulously groomed records clerk had been working all night.

"Where's Red?" Jessi asked.

"He's still out at the scene," Murray answered. The two friends exchanged looks. "God, Jessi, this is absolutely awful."

"I know, I… You always hear cops talking about how close death is but no matter how many times you hear it, or say it, you're never really prepared to deal with it when it happens."

"How's the set-up going?" Jessi asked, nodding at Murray's dwindling stack of compact discs.

"We're getting there. I've got the statewide bulletin up and running. Look," he said, pointing at the screen. "This is the follow-up to the Waco kidnapping from last night."

"What kidnapping?" Jessi asked, puzzled as she leaned down to read the screen.

"I'll print it out," Murray replied, keying in a command. The brand new laser printer hummed into action quickly printing the two-page report, Murray rubbed his whiskery jaw. "I feel like crap. I'll bet I look like crap, too. I do, don't I?"

Jessi's expression confirmed his fears. "Tell you what. Here's the key to my room at Velma's place. If you want to go over there and grab a shower, get a little rest, feel free," she said as she removed the key from her purse and held it out.

"I accept," Murray replied, taking the key from her hand and standing.

As Murray yawned and stretched, Henry, the dog, was suddenly at Jessi's heels trying to get her attention. She knelt, scratched the dog's ears, picked him up, and slumped down in the chair Murray had just vacated. Murray removed the pages from the printer tray and handed them to Jessi.

Jessi scanned the report, while absentmindedly stroking the dog's back.

"That is one great dog. He kept me company all night. Didn't you, old boy?" Murray cooed, leaning over and patting the dog's head. Henry licked his hand in appreciation. "Look at that. He's known me all of one day, and he's licking my hand like I'm a king. That's the kind of friendship and loyalty I need in my life. I might get me a dog. It would be kind of nice to have someone happy to see me when I come home at night."

"Hey, Marie Sisco's got a whole litter of puppies you could take home. Cute little things," Jessi said.

"Who's Marie Sisco?"

"The dog catcher," Jessi said, her body stiffening as she read the kidnap victim's name for the first time. "Ohmygod!" her mind seized on the possibility. "Julie! Her name's Julie!" she blurted, setting Henry gently on the floor and standing.

"I know that look," Murray said. "You're on to something."

"I don't know if I am or not, Murray. Sometimes I second-guess every thought I have," Jessi said as she walked away and approached Cutler, who was finishing up a conversation with an FBI agent.

Cutler's smile was welcoming. "Good morning. I didn't see you come in."

"You were pretty involved. I thought I'd wait until things calmed down a little before I intruded," Jessi said, adding quickly, " I don't know if this means anything or not, but I wanted to run something by you." She handed him the kidnap report.

"What's this?" Cutler asked, glancing at the pages.

"That's a kidnap report out of Waco."

"Yeah, I heard the broadcast last night," Cutler said, continuing to scan the report.

"Do you remember I told you that Lela went nuts at the Laundromat last night?"

"Right. The face in the washing machine."

"It was the dryer. She said the girl was named Julie."

The light tone of Cutler's voice darkened as he read the name on the report. "Julie Abbott." He looked up from the pages. "Hell of a coincidence?"

"I think we might be beyond coincidences by now but listen to this," Jessi said as she took the report from him, turned to the second page, and pointed at an entry.

"...A cashier at the theater ticket booth reported seeing the victim in the company of an unknown male. Victim was reported to be carrying a small puppy..."

"A puppy? Is that important?" Cutler asked.

"I don't know if you saw her or not, but Marie Sisco stopped by the Tubbs Road scene last night."

Cutler said nothing, letting Jessi get to the point in her own way.

"She was coming back from a call and came across a litter of puppies that somebody had dropped off," Jessi explained. "She saw the fire from there." Jessi let the statement hover in the air as she looked at Cutler and waited for a response.

She could almost see the light go off in his brain. "Where'd she find the animals?"

"I'm not sure. She said something about a frontage road, but it must not have been too far from Tubbs Road."

"What time was the kidnapping reported?"

Jessi scanned down the report. "Seven thirty."

Jessi and Cutler exchanged a long look before Cutler turned to Janie. "Get Marie Sisco on the phone. Find out where she found those puppies, and tell her to meet us there."

Janie was already dialing before Cutler finished talking.

Cutler and Jessi reached the Hawkes Road turnoff and had just stepped out of the Blazer when Marie Sisco pulled her animal control truck to a stop behind them.

"What's up?" Marie asked as she approached.

"Is this where you found the dogs last night?" Cutler asked.

"Yeah. I was coming back from a call out on Mantelli Road. Old Joe Van Seters had a lamb tangled up in some barbwire and needed a little assistance. I helped him cut the lamb out and decided to come back on the frontage road rather than the highway. It's habit, I guess. I'm always on the lookout. The little runt was right there in the middle of the road. I almost hit him. I figured that if there was one, there were probably more, so I looked around. I heard them before I saw them," she explained as she made her way through the grove of trees and down the narrow path that led to the culvert. "Watch your step."

Once they were at the bottom of the path, Marie pointed over the edge of an eight-foot drop at the gravel-and-sand lined, dry flood channel. "The other five were running around down there."

Cutler slid down the embankment on his butt, utilizing the heels of his Tony Lama's as brakes. He searched the sandy bottom, and then used his flashlight to peer into an eight-foot-wide cement pipe, illuminating discarded beer cans, wine bottles, and other trash. "Looks pretty calm now, but I've seen an eight-foot wall of water shoot through this pipe," he shouted up to Jessi and Marie. He moved in a deliberate, slow circle, looking for anything that seemed out of place.

"See anything?" Jessi asked.

"Not yet, but they had to carry the dogs down here in something," he said, continuing to poke around the culvert.

Leaving Marie to watch Cutler, Jessi retraced their steps back up through the grove of trees, her eyes sweeping the litter-strewn ground. She smelled it before she saw it. It was the familiar, acrid smell of burning paper mixed with garbage that alerted her to the litter barrel, and as she stood next to it she saw a trace of smoke curl up. "John!" she shouted.

Cutler and Marie were there quickly, watching as Jessi poked a long stick into the smoldering barrel. "What you got?" Cutler asked.

"I don't know, but somebody burned something here recently. You got any latex gloves in the Blazer?" she asked Cutler.

"I got a whole box of 'em!" Marie hurried back to her truck and returned within half a minute with the gloves.

Jessi pulled a pair of the tight-fitting gloves on before removing a charred piece of cardboard along with segments of still-damp newspaper. Jessi sniffed the paper before holding it out to Cutler. They both shrugged.

"Gimme a toke, err, a hit of that," Marie said, sniffing the charred paper like a Sonoma County wine snob. "No doubt about it. Dog piddle. And I'm an expert on that."

"Just to be on the safe side we should probably cordon off this whole area," Jessi said.

"I've got a roll of crime scene tape in the Blazer," Cutler said, then added "They'll want to go through this barrel piece by piece."

"You've still got the puppies?" Jessi asked as she turned to Marie.

"Yeah. They're out to the shelter."

"You haven't bathed them yet, have you?" Jessi asked.

Marie raised her eyebrows. "No, I haven't sent for the groomer yet. It's on my B list. *Way* down on my B list."

"Don't adopt them out just yet," Jessi said.

Cutler nodded, keeping pace with Jessi's thought. "We'll send a technician over to the shelter. They'll have to be combed for trace evidence: hair, fiber, secretions."

Cutler hurried to the Blazer, returning quickly with the roll of yellow, crime scene tape and a large garbage bag. As Jessi slid the remnants of the burned box into the plastic bag, their eyes met. "Good find, Jessi. Looks like I owe you another chicken fried steak."

As Lela gazed at the buildings in the distance, a sudden wave of panic swept over her heart and settled heavily in her stomach. She wanted to turn away, run, but she forced herself into motion instead. Staying on the railroad tracks, she covered the remaining mile in just over twenty minutes. The closer she came to the buildings, the larger they loomed, especially the three-story tower. From a distance, shadows on the tower's east side resembled the head of a skeleton, but as she grew closer she could see that the skull was actually three sets of broken windows: two on the third floor and one on the second floor.

Lela was within a hundred yards of the buildings before she realized that the railroad tracks she was following led directly into the maze of buildings, disappearing behind a massive galvanized metal door at the rear of the compound. As she approached the door, she found it secured with a heavy, rusted chain and a large padlock. The sheet metal around the lock had long ago been shredded by countless 22 bullets and shotgun rounds fired at close range. Plywood had been inserted into the damaged area, but it, too, bore the scars of dozens of bullets that had tried, but failed, to penetrate the chain or damage the lock.

Dropping to her tender knees and putting her eye to the door, Lela tried to peer into the building through the bullet holes. All she saw was darkness, but a stream of escaping air cooled her cheek. The only sound she could make out was the steady drip, drip, drip of several water leaks. Suddenly she froze as the sound of metal striking metal echoed somewhere deep within the building. Someone was in there!

Hugging the rear of the building, Lela hurried along to the end of the east wall, passing a willow-lined holding pond, where she paused and peered cautiously around the corner. The north side of the compound was as deserted as the east, and she hurried past piles of discarded wooden pallets, dozens of empty 55-gallon drums, piles of rusted machinery, long strips of torn conveyor belts, and sheets of galvanized roofing that had blown off the high roof. Coming to the end of the north wall, she again paused and peered carefully around the corner and into the center of the compound. The first thing her eyes were drawn to sent shivers up her back. Halfway up the front of the old cement building, spelled out in faded, three-foot-high letters was:

CE COM

As Lela stared at the sign the rest of the painted lettering slowly became visible; bleached by decades of direct sunlight and washed by nearly a century of rain, it was still there:

SHORT FALLS ICE COMPANY

The original concrete slab for Short Falls Ice and Meat Company was poured in 1904 and, for its time, was huge. Covering nearly three acres, the cement provided a foundation for a company that would provide block ice and cold storage which enabled the local cattle growers to move their beef by rail to major distribution points in Waco, Dallas, Abilene, or even Kansas City and Chicago. World War I had erupted in Europe, and the demand for high-quality beef skyrocketed. That demand lasted until well after World War II, but with the introduction of refrigerated railroad cars and long-haul trucks, the need for block ice had slowly melted away, and in 1951 the icehouse had finally closed its doors.

Since that closure the old ice house had been bought and sold over a dozen times to various groups of investors and individuals who found out the hard way that the menagerie of crumbling cement buildings were far too expensive to maintain, let alone renovate. The buildings, especially the three-story water tower, had continued to disintegrate, becoming wonderful, albeit dangerous, playgrounds for generations of Grace County youths who, according to their age, walked, bicycled, or drove the two miles to the deserted buildings. Once there, they spent long summer hours playing on the railroad tracks that cut through the buildings past vast loading docks where cattle cars once disgorged a never-ending stream of overheated, mooing, manure-stained cattle. The animals were shooed and prodded up a long, narrow, wooden chute until they disappeared into the building to meet their fate on the waxed killing floor at the hands of a tireless swarm of strong, sweaty butchers who rendered them into sleek, naked sides of beef to be hung by hooks and moved by overhead tracks into vast cold storage rooms to await shipment out.

Once the terminally ill buildings were abandoned, the youth of Grace County spent their days trying to put them out of their misery: tearing down walls, prying the heavy wooden doors off the freezer rooms, setting fires, and breaking out windows. If they weren't destroying the buildings, they were scrambling up wooden ice chutes to play hide-and-seek in the cavernous, dark interior pockmarked with countless cold storage rooms and long stairwells leading to moss-covered, foul-smelling, cement brine tanks. The young, daring trespassers "surfed" on top of long metal conveyors using cardboard sheets or pieces of rough plywood to glide down the rollers. In order to prove their courage, boys were expected to scramble to the top of the covered water tower and then step gingerly along the rotting wooden walkway, seventy-five feet over the killing room floor, while their frightened girlfriends covered their eyes and sobbed, begging their heroes to come down. These same girls would have been terribly disappointed if their boyfriends had honored their requests instead of conquering this heart-stopping rite of passage. Girls who attempted the same feat were thought of as crazy and were never asked to return.

In 1965, the property had been purchased by a humorless local butcher named Harold Weed. A widower, left with two young daughters to raise. Harold had boarded off most of the buildings and had borrowed twenty thousand dollars to convert part of the original ice house into Spartan living quarters for himself and his girls. The loan also funded a retail custom meat business that offered his customers over-the-counter service as well as cold storage lockers they could rent. Harold had worked for the original Short Falls owners, spending twenty-five years on the killing floor before being laid off. Buying the property had been a *fait accompli* of sorts for the hard-working, tight-fisted man. Working eighteen-hour days alongside his slow-witted brother, Charley, the business slowly expanded. Pouring his profits back into the company, the butcher obtained another twenty-thousand-dollar loan and used it to rehabilitate part of the old ice house, soon having it up and producing again. The ice production was not on the grand scale it had been in 1925, but it was enough to provide local businesses with all the cubed and crushed ice they could sell and keep over a hundred Short Falls ice dispensers stocked and, in the process, make a small fortune that Harold Weed would not live to enjoy. The butcher died of a heart attack while driving a portable slaughter rig home after dressing out a beef for a local farmer, leaving his daughters, nineteen-year-old Kathryn, and thirteen-year-old Molly, as co-owners and protectors of the historic Short Falls Ice Company. Tragically, Molly would disappear within six months of her father's passing. Investigators would eventually determine that the beautiful little girl had apparently been abducted while waiting for the school bus on Short Falls Road. Her older sister, Kathryn, reported to investigating officers that she had accompanied the girl from the icehouse to the bus stop, a distance of three-eighths of a mile, and had left her there and returned to work. Suspicion was immediately directed toward Molly's slow-witted uncle, Charley Weed, who lived on the premises in a small camping trailer. Authorities eventually determined that Charley was away from the county on a deer-hunting trip at the time of the disappearance. A massive search had been conducted throughout Grace County, but no trace of the girl was ever found.

Lela tensed as she heard the sound of a door opening somewhere within the compound. She wanted to stay where she was, frozen against the wall, but she was exposed and her instincts told her she was in terrible danger. She forced herself into motion, moving quickly, but quietly, across the fifty yards of open ground to the alcove of what appeared to be a long storage shed. Glancing out she saw the lumbering Charley Weed step out of a broken-down, teardrop-shaped camping trailer that was parked close to the storage shed and stride purposefully across the compound to where his delivery truck was parked next to the loading dock, under a long conveyor belt. As Lela held her breath and watched, the big man climbed a set of steps, his large boots thumping loudly against the polished cement as he moved across the loading dock to the building where he opened an electrical box and pulled a switch. The sound of the conveyor belt starting echoed through the compound and, within seconds, a steady stream of ten-pound ice bags appeared from a metal chute on the second floor of the building and were carried down to where the muscular Charley expertly caught them as they dropped off the end of the belt and stacked them in neat rows in the back of the insulated truck. As Lela watched him load the vehicle, she was torn. She had seen him talking to the sheriff at the rest stop on the first day. Could she call out to him? Ask him for help? Explain her strange mission? What if he was involved? No. She didn't dare.

In less than twenty minutes the truck was loaded and Charley moved back to the building to turn off the empty conveyor belt. He then retrieved a brown clipboard from a hook next to a glass door, returned to close the rear of the truck, climbed into the cab, and drove out of the compound.

Lela watched the truck disappear, her stomach filling with a heavy dread. Any hope of gaining an ally had faded when the man in the truck left. She wanted desperately to find a safe place where she could hide and wait out whatever awful thing was about to happen, but one thing was certain: Julie was in that building. Lela knew it. She could feel the girl's fear.

Pushing herself out of the alcove, she moved quickly across the graveled lot and kneeled, shaken and breathless, under the loading dock for a few minutes. Still on her knees, she forced herself to peek out at the glass door. Mounted on the cement wall next to the door a sign read:

SHORT FALLS ICE AND CUSTOM MEATS

Monday-Saturday 8AM to 5PM

Closed Sundays

Lockers Available

Hurrying up the cement steps, Lela sprinted across the loading dock. Hugging the smooth concrete wall, she crept to the door and glanced under the red "CLOSED" sign dangling from a peg on the inside of the glass. Venetian Blinds blocked most of her view, but she could see a glass display case stocked with long rows of freshly sliced steaks, roasts, chops, and ground beef. A cash register sat on a low counter away from the meat display, and a stainless steel door led off into the rest of the building.

Lela cautiously turned the knob, but the door was locked. The familiar silver tape of a burglar alarm system was clearly visible lining the plate glass. She retreated from the door and moved along the loading dock where a series of retractable, metal garage doors closed off different entrances to the old section of the original packing plant. Each of the doors was firmly bolted down with an eight-foot metal bar that ran through metal loops set in concrete and secured on each side by heavy locks.

She scanned the building looking for an open window or another door that might allow her entry but saw nothing. Looking up she spotted several open windows on the upper floors, but there was no way she could scale the sheer, smooth front of the building. Her eyes searched frantically for some way in, and then like hundreds of teenagers who came before her, her eyes fell on the answer: the ice chute.

Lela moved quickly to the conveyor belt that Charley had used earlier and swung herself onto the two-foot-wide rubber belt. She clutched the metal sides, slowly pulling herself up the steep incline to the second floor where the metal framework disappeared into the building through a small, square opening in the cement front. The opening was shielded by a square flap of heavy black rubber that swung open as a bag or block of ice passed through and then closed back up, keeping to a minimum the loss of valuable frigid air.

Lela lifted the flap and felt the rush of cold air wash over her sweaty face. She peered inside, finding her view blocked by a line of ice bags. The actual opening into the building looked too narrow for her to get through, but she knew she had to try. Rolling over onto her back and bracing herself with her legs, she lifted the flap with her left hand and, reaching inside the opening, grabbed hold of the conveyor frame, pulling herself slowly into the building. Halfway through she found herself tightly wedged. The feeling of panic was almost overwhelming, and she began hyperventilating. Forcing, willing, begging, praying herself to calm down, she slowed her breathing and started to squirm, moving an inch at a time until her hips cleared the sides.

Once inside, she rolled off the belt and squinted into the darkness, her eyes slowly adjusting to her surroundings. The room was a twenty-foot square lined with blocks of ice that stood in ghostly rows in front of a large crusher. To the right of the crusher was a table where the pulverized ice was bagged.

Lela moved along the wood-lined wall, her footsteps cushioned by a deep layer of sawdust, until she felt the heavy metal door. Touching the cold metal, she was suddenly aware that she was shivering and her breath was vaporizing. Her hand located the narrow metal plunger that opened the door. It was locked. She retreated back to the conveyor and, crawling onto the belt, pulled herself through another rubber flap into the next room, which turned out to be darker than the room she just left. She could see nothing, and as she climbed off the conveyor, she extended her hands in front of her to feel her way, brushing against something heavy and cold. She withdrew her hand and felt the object sway ever so slightly. She froze, trying somehow to take measure of the form she was brushing against. It was a foot taller than she was, and as she reached up to touch it she dislodged something with her hand that fell to the floor with a loud, hollow "thud!"

She clutched her crystal necklace for security. " Please don't let anyone hear that. Please."

She stood motionless for as long as she could stand it before starting to move forward again. As she took a step, her shoulder brushed against another object, then another, until she had counted ten of them. Locating a wall, she moved slowly along, using her freezing hands to sweep lightly over the smooth, wooden surface until she struck the door plunger hard enough to sting her numb fingers. She continued feeling the wall around the edges of the door until she felt the familiar nub of a light switch and flipped it on, blinking against the sudden intrusion. As her eyes adjusted to the dim yellow light, she glanced around to see that she had moved through several rows of frozen beef carcasses dangling from heavy metal hooks that allowed the carcasses to slide freely along a series of channels suspended from the ceiling. Lela turned back to the door and was reaching out to try the handle when she heard the muffled sounds of approaching footsteps! Without thinking she flipped the light switch off and, dropping to her knees, scrambled back into the frigid darkness, the clumps of sawdust sticking to her knees and flimsy skirt, effectively muffling any sound of her movement. Reaching the far corner of the room, she realized too late that she had moved away from the conveyor belt that offered her only possible route of escape. She took refuge under a hanging side of beef, cowering in the darkness as the door opened with a loud metallic "snap!"

Although Pinky hadn't heard anything himself, Kitty was sure something had hit the floor above their heads, something unusual. As far as Pinky was concerned everything about the old icehouse was unusual. It was as big as some of the prisons he had lived in, but unlike the cellblocks, it was empty and silent. The building seemed to have a life of its own, though, especially at night when it groaned and creaked like a damn old woman; a cold old woman.

Pinky, wearing Marty Burris's straw cowboy hat, entered the carcass room and, flipping on the light switch, moved quickly through the frigid room, impatiently pushing carcasses aside to scan the floor under the rows of hanging beef. As he moved relentlessly toward her, she was afraid he could hear her heart pounding in her chest! She watched hopelessly as the black army boots moved unerringly closer. Her eyes dropped to the floor, seeking an escape route, when she spotted the fallen meat hook sitting within a foot of her trembling knees. Pinky's hand entered her field of vision to retrieve the hook, and as it did Lela saw *the wolf* on the back of his hand, its *glowing red eyes* seeming to seek her out.

"Here's your fucking noise," Pinky mumbled to himself as he retrieved the cold hook and replaced it in its seat on the overhead channel. Retreating to the door, he turned out the lights and closed the heavy door with a "swoosh," leaving the terrified Lela shivering in the darkness.

Lela stayed still, barely breathing, for as long as she could stand it, before she crawled out from under the carcass and forced herself to stand. Her legs were cramped, and her back throbbed as she stiffly made her way back to the door. She placed her ear against the smooth metal, straining to catch the slightest trace of movement. She was shaking uncontrollably from a combination of fear and the heavy cold that was seeping into her skin. She pressed her frozen hand against the round plunger and pushed it slowly until the lock *snapped* open. She forced herself to wait a full minute, counting slowly to sixty before she pushed the door open and a stream of warm air welcomed her into a dimly-lit hallway. At one end of the hall, a flight of stairs rose to the top floor of the icehouse, while at the opposite end of the hall, a set of steps led downward. Lela rubbed her cold hands, blowing her warm breath on them as she turned toward the down staircase, moving quietly across the squeaky wooden flooring. Approaching the stairwell she paused and looked down. A half-dozen steps led to a small landing, and then the stairwell made a 90-degree turn and continued down. Lela descended slowly, trying in vain to keep her steps quiet. She reached the landing, and turning the corner, found herself six inches from Pinky's face.

"Looking for somebody?"

Lela screamed, pushed him off, and tried wildly to retreat up the stairwell. Pinky grabbed her right ankle and jerked her back to the landing. Lela lashed out with her feet, in a desperate attempt to flee, but Pinky only laughed at her ineffectual efforts.

"You like to kick, huh?" He spit the words at her, and raising his right foot, stomped down full force with his heavy army boot on Lela's diaphragm, leaving her clutching her stomach and gasping for air. Then he took hold of her hair and jerked her frightened face close to his."What are you looking at you old bitch?"

Lela could only gasp and struggle to breathe as she looked into Pinky's hard, flat eyes. The heavy odor of Old Spice mixing with a heavier smell made her instantly nauseous.

"I should have slit your fucking throat the other night! I knew you would cause me trouble!"

Lela groaned in response, causing the enraged Pinky to spike his fist hard into her mouth, snapping her head back and splitting the stitches in her already damaged lip .He grabbed her by the ankles and dragged her down the remaining steps to the cement floor below. Lela felt each step banging the back of her skull, opening the deep wound and releasing a steady flow of warm blood that poured over her face and joining with the crimson flow from her split lip, poured into her mouth, causing her to choke. Reaching the bottom, Pinky opened a heavy wooden door and dragged her across a large room, leaving a heavy blood smear on the waxed cement floors. Lela had glimpses of solid wooden tables with racks of large boning knives, cleavers, and rolls of white butcher paper mounted on overhead spindles, and then the *odor* hit her like a blow. The smell of death was everywhere, seeped so deeply into the floor and walls that not even large doses of pine oil could mask it.

Pinky stopped abruptly, and Lela heard a door open nearby and the sound of heavy footsteps approaching.

"Ohmygod, there *was* somebody there! Who? Who is it?"

Pinky turned his captive over with his boot.

361

Lela forced her eyes open and as her eyes focused she found a large female looming over her. The woman was wearing a blue, print dress and something about her was oddly familiar.

"Who do you think it is! I told you the third eye was trouble!" Pinky screamed. "She crawled in through the fucking ice chute!"

"But why?" Kitty demanded, directing her question to Pinky before turning to Lela. "Why would you come here?" Kitty lashed out with a foot, kicking Lela in the ribs. "Answer me damnit! Who sent you?" Her voice betrayed a hint of panic.

"Sent her? What the fuck you talking about, woman? Who'd send her, the fucking C.I.A? She's a fucking psychic! She's been chasing me for twenty fucking years and I'm going to cut her up in pieces!" he yelled, touching the large, sheathed knife on his belt.

"No!" Kitty raised her hand for silence. "Wait here with her and don't do *anything* to her. Not yet. I'm going to check around outside, make sure she's alone. She might have a car or something." Kitty turned and hurried out, leaving Pinky alone with the terrified Lela.

"Yeah, right. Anything you say, you fat, ugly bitch," Pinky mumbled sarcastically to the departing Kitty as he darted to a heavy cutting table where he opened a drawer to retrieve a roll of silver-colored duct tape. Pinky returned to Lela and, dropping to his knees, soon had her wrists bound behind her back and her ankles taped together.

"How about drawing a sketch of me?" Pinky laughed. "Or telling my future. Yeah, you want to read my palm? Read *this*!" he barked, slapping her so hard across the face that a misty spray of Lela's blood splattered off the wall ten feet away. Pinky quickly climbed astride her heaving chest and plastered a strip of the silver tape over her bloody mouth. His eyes hardened as he looked down at her. She was utterly helpless, totally under his control. The familiar feeling of absolute power flooded his senses, giving him an instant erection. Pinky ripped off the top of her flimsy blouse-exposing her white breasts.

Lela willed herself somewhere else. Tears blurred her vision as she struggled to construct images of clean, warm air and soaring eagles, and her small room at Velma's. She thought of her long-dead mother, but she could not keep a soft whimper from escaping her constricted throat. She was looking into the eyes of Satin, at the absolute center of the strangely familiar evil that had poisoned her spirit for so long. The realization filled her with an overwhelming dread that she knew led to her impending darkness and death. She prayed to God that it would be over quickly.

Pinky leered down at the weeping Lela. "Shut the fuck up, bitch." He reached for his belt and removing his large buck knife from its sheath, held the sharpened blade to her nipple. The sound of Kitty's returning footsteps caused him to stand and put his knife away. "Hope that was as good for you as it was for me," he chuckled as Kitty entered.

"I couldn't see anybody outside. No cars, nothing," Kitty said, her tone at once both excited and laden with worry. "Put her in the killing room for now," she snapped.

"But I want to have some fun with her," Pinky said.

"Not now. You have to wait. I have to find out why she came, and then you can do what you please." Kitty removed the key from around her neck and hurried across the room to a large, stainless steel door.

Kitty fumbled with the old key, finally inserting it into the heavy brass padlock. As the lock unsnapped it dawned on Kitty that Lela showing up might be enough of a distraction to Pinky that it would work to her advantage.

Pinky grabbed Lela roughly by the hair, dragging her across the smooth floor and into the other room. Lela braced herself against the pain as she was pulled and yanked across a grated drain and deposited, face down, into a darkened corner.

"Let's hurry. I have to go to town," Kitty said, hurrying back to door.

"Don't go anywhere," Pinky laughed as he left her there on the floor and retreated from the room. Kitty swung the heavy door shut and Lela could hear the lock snap closed. She heard footsteps and finally silence.

The smell of death was stronger in here, and as Lela's eyes slowly adjusted to the darkness, she could make out a pattern of streaks and dots of a deep brown color that faded the higher up the wall her view went. She was sure it was dried blood! Lela moved as close to the wall as she could, and pushing her knees against the cement, she was able to turn herself over onto her back. Above her was a large trapdoor where thousands of dead cattle had dropped down onto the floor. Across the room she spotted a huge, stainless steel tub where slaughtered pigs had been cleaned. A series of metal channels holding a dozen sharp meat hooks ran along half of the ceiling. The other half was open and rose three stories into the darkness from which drops of water appeared, streaking to the floor like lasers with a steady, hypnotic, "tic-tic-tic."

"Ahhh!"

Lela stiffened. The sound came from behind her, somewhere in the darkness, but very close. She strained to listen.

"Ahhh."

Lela gritted her teeth and strained, rolling herself over onto her other side, and stared into the terrified eyes of Julie Abbot.

23.

❦

The Texas Department of Public Safety helicopter circled Pocatello Pablo's Truck Stop twice before it set down in the huge parking lot, throwing up a cloud of dust and litter. Jessi waited at the Blazer as Sheriff Cutler carried the plastic bag holding the remnants of the recovered box to the chopper where the observer opened the door and took it from him. Cutler shook hands with the helmeted observer and then, bending slightly, returned to Jessi. They watched the rotors gain speed and the Bell Jet Star lifted, nosed over, and blasted over their heads. Within a minute, all trace of the helicopter was gone, the whine of its turbine replaced by the constant rumbling of passing cars and trucks.

"They'll have it at the crime lab in Austin in less than an hour," Cutler said, looking off as a familiar voice called him.

"Hey, Johnny!"

Charley Weed was standing next to the ice machine, to the side of a group of onlookers that had exited the truck stop to watch the helicopter land and depart. As the people returned to the diner, a worried-looking Charley lumbered across the parking lot and approached Cutler. "Is it true? Marty's really dead?"

Cutler nodded. "Yeah, Charley. I'm afraid it is."

The big man looked down, awkwardly, and shook his head. "Marty stopped me once for speeding over on the old highway. I said 'You going to give me a ticket, Marty?' He said, 'Charley, you're the iceman.

You're *way* too cool to get a ticket,' Charley said as tears welled in his eyes. "This ain't right, Johnny!" he added, throwing out his hands and walking away. Half way back to his truck, he stopped and looked back. "I don't like this!"

Jessi and Cutler rode in silence back to the doublewide, pulling into the parking lot to find dozens of colorful flower arrangements sitting in a semicircle at the base of the flagpole. A group of townspeople was gathered close-by, talking in hushed tones, while on the other side of the trailer, the Grace County Rotary Club fired up their portable barbeque to feed the small army of law enforcement officers with steaks graciously provided by The Short Falls Ice and Meat Company.

Climbing out of the Blazer, the Sheriff spotted Kiko Avila's wife, Helen, being consoled by Kathryn Weed. Kathryn was wearing the dress she normally reserved for Easter Sunday church services, and she was holding a spray of white gladiolas. A tearful Helen approached Cutler and gave him a hug.

"Oh, John, I'm so sorry," Helen said, choking back sobs as Cutler held her against his chest for a few moments.

"Thanks, Helen. I know you are," Cutler answered, knowing instinctively that she was not only crying for the death of Marty Burris, but for the simple truth that she could just as easily be shedding tears now for her precious Kiko. The possibility of instantaneous death was the daily, subconscious companion of every wife or husband of a law enforcement officer. Cutler's eyes met Kathryn Weed's and he nodded.

"Johnny, I wanted you to know my heart goes out to all of you at this time," Kathryn said.

"Thanks for coming down," Cutler answered.

"I brought three dozen steaks over for the Rotary folks to cook up. After Charley finishes up his route, he's going to bring over some more."

"That's very kind of you," Cutler responded.

"It doesn't seem possible that something like that could happen in our wonderful little community. I didn't know Marty real well, but my Uncle Charley did. He's just heartsick about it, the poor soul," Kathryn said, her curious eyes moving to Jessi. "Hi Jessi. Sad time for all of us," she said, taking Jessi's hand and pumping it forcefully several times.

"Yes it is, Kathryn," Jessi replied.

"Well, I'd better get going now," Kathryn said, nodding to the group as she turned and walked to the flagpole just as Janie Cortez exited the trailer and approached, a look of deep concern etched across her expressive face.

Cutler picked up on her look immediately. "What's the matter, Janie?"

"Ellie called," she replied, dabbing her eyes with a Kleenex. "I guess the boys have been sobbing ever since they woke up. They want their Uncle Johnny to come over and tell them what happened to their dad."

The words hit Cutler like a blow to the stomach. "Oh shit." He shook his head and turned to watch Kathryn Weed place her white flowers among the others and bow her head to offer a short, silent prayer.

"If you want to go over there, everything here's pretty much under control," Janie added.

Helen Avila stepped forward. "I'll go out with you," she said.

Cutler nodded and looked back at Janie. "Call Ellie back. Tell her we're on the way," Cutler said, turning to Jessi. "Clyde Briscoe wants a shot at giving Lela Starr another lie detector test. He'll be here in about half an hour."

"She's still sleeping," Jessi said. "I'll go back to Velma's and get her."

Jessi pulled the Chevy into Velma's parking lot and came to a stop next to Murray's dusty BMW that was parked in front of her room. Climbing out of the Chevy she found the note she had placed there earlier still wedged in Lela's door. Surely Lela would be up by now. She moved to the window to look in, but the curtains were still drawn tight. Jessi couldn't understand how anyone could keep their room so dark. "Oh well, everyone's different," she thought. "And Lela is *very* different." She knocked loudly on the door of number eight, and as she waited she noticed the "Do Not Disturb!" sign hanging on the knob of her own room. "Murray must still be resting," she thought and turned her attention back to Lela.

"Come on, Lela, up and at 'em! Let's get that old crystal ball of yours warmed up," Jessi said. rapping her knuckles hard on the door.

Velma's cleaning cart was close by, parked in front of number ten. Velma stuck her head out of the door. "If you're looking for your friend, she's gone."

"Gone? How? I thought I was her only transportation?" A feeling of unease knotted Jessi's stomach. "Gone? Where?"

"Now, that I couldn't tell you. I wouldn't have even known she was gone except I couldn't sleep this morning. My arthritis was acting up, so I was up walking out the kinks. That's why I'm so late getting my rooms cleaned up. It was right close to 4:30 or 5:00."

"Four-thirty in the morning?" Jessi's tone expressed both surprise and anger.

"Yeah. I was looking out the window and saw her leave her room and walk down the highway over yonder," she said as she pointed off. "It was pretty close to the time you pulled in," Velma explained.

Jessi was immediately on guard. She didn't want to believe it and tried Lela's door. Finding it locked, she turned to Velma.

"Did she take her stuff with her?"

"Now, I couldn't tell you that. I haven't made her room up yet. I thought I'd get my other rooms cleaned up first," Velma explained.

The knot in Jessi's stomach tightened. "Would you mind unlocking the door for me?"

Velma hesitated. She didn't like the idea of violating the privacy of one of her guests. "I don't know if I should do that. Is this official police business?"

Jessi accommodated Velma's sense of rightness and pulled out her badge. "It is now."

Velma used her passkey to open the door and watched as Jessi conducted a quick, frantic search of the room. The bed was unmade, the blankets and sheets in disarray as if Lela had slept badly. In contrast, her laundry was still folded neatly in the brown grocery bag. Jessi noticed the room key on the bedside table and the incense. Why hadn't Lela taken her clothes if she was leaving, and if she planned on coming back, why hadn't she taken her room key? She looked back into the room. Her eye caught something covered by the rumpled bedding. Pulling back the blankets, she saw the carryall and the sketchpad. Jessi couldn't imagine Lela leaving without it. She sat down on the bed and opened the pad, flipping quickly through pages filled with Lela's unique view of the world. She had sketched everything and had done it well. Jessi recognized caricatures of Janie with her headphones on, Red and Murray at the computer, the computer mouse actually looking like a mischievous, real mouse as it tangled Red up in confusion. Jessi smiled in spite of herself. She turned the page, and her eyes locked onto the red eyes of the vicious-looking wolf's head. She flipped to the next page and noticed a new sketch revealing the distorted face of a girl tumbling in a dryer. Jessi looked hard at the face, betting that she was looking at a likeness of the kidnapped Julie and wondering if it contained enough detail to fax it to Waco PD. She continued flipping pages, unsure in her own mind what she expected to find.

Jessi closed her eyes and took a deep breath, exhaling ever so slowly, trying to dispel her anger and confusion. She couldn't believe she'd been so stupid, lulled into thinking that Lela was anything but a suspect—or at the very least, a willing accomplice? Had she considered her a friend? No, at least she hadn't been that naïve.

The next sketch showed a decaying old structure, bathed in deep shadows, with a three-story tower rising from the center of it. Lela had penciled in "CE COM" on the bottom of the page.

The curious Velma had followed Jessi into the room and was now peering over her shoulder at the sketches. "For an artist she draws some real weird stuff, don't she?"

"Tell me about it." Jessi tapped the sketch. "This building, does it look at all familiar?"

Velma pursed her mouth and rubbed her chin. "Ummm. Maybe a little, but no, not really. "

The last drawing in the pad was a sketch of Samantha Deavers, not a caricature but a beautiful rendition of the girl sitting on the steps in front of her house.

"She must have drawn these after I dropped her off last night," Jessi said.

Velma was watching the young woman with concern. "I wish I could help you out, dear. I'm sure she'll be back. I told her I was going to make my homemade cinnamon bread today, and that lady surely does enjoy my baking."

Jessi smiled and patted Velma's arm just as Murray stuck his head through the open door.

"I thought I heard a familiar voice," Murray said as he entered and smiled at Velma. He looked rested, his hair slicked back and wet from showering.

"Velma, this is a colleague of mine from-"

Velma interrupted her. "We've already met. I got this nice young man some towels. Did you decide on the room?" she asked Murray.

"Yes, I'll need one for myself. I'll be here at least another day," Murray responded.

"Good. I'll put you in number ten. I'll have it spiffy in no time. Would you folks like a cup of fresh coffee?"

"I'd kill for coffee," Murray said.

"Be right back," Velma said as she hurried out the door.

"Thank you," Murray called after her. "What a nice lady."

"Murray, I want you to look at something," Jessi said, opening the sketchpad to the drawing of the building and pointing at the CE COM lettering. "What do you think?"

"CE COM? What about it?"

"Is it familiar at all?"

'No, should it be?" Murray responded.

"CE COM sounds like one of those dot com companies."

Murray shrugged. "We can sure find out in a hurry. All I got to do is go on line and ask."

"Here you go," Velma's friendly voice filled the small room as she hurried in carrying a brown Melmac tray ladened with steaming cups of coffee in large Styrofoam cups and freshly baked cinnamon bread.

Murray smiled, helped himself. "Thank you, gracious lady."

"I'm having mine to go, Velma," Jessi said, quickly wrapping a piece of coffee cake in a napkin and grabbing one of the Styrofoam cups."

"Are you going back to the office?" Murray asked.

"I'll meet you there later. Right now I'm going to try and track down Lela," Jessi said, grabbing the sketchpad with her free hand and sticking it under her arm. "For some reason she did another sketch of Samantha Deavers last night. Maybe she went back out to the Deaver's place for some reason. Is that the highway to Slocum?" Jessi asked, nodding toward the road.

"That'll get you to Slocum. Bancroft too. I hope Lela didn't go out to the Deavers' place. Them folks are a bad lot," Velma volunteered as she and Murray followed Jessi out to the Chevy.

"Velma, if Lela happens to come back, call my cell phone number or the sheriff's office," Jessi handed the cup and coffeecake to Murray and quickly scribbled her cell phone number on the napkin.

Velma nodded as she took the napkin. "I sure will, dear."

Jessi climbed in behind the wheel of the classic Chevy and started the engine. Murray handed her the coffee and coffee cake. "You want me to go along?"

"No, that's alright, but I would appreciate it if you'd run CE COM for me. Try to figure out what it is,"

"I'll have the answer for you within an hour," Murray said.

Jessi nodded her thanks. As she started backing out, Murray slapped the hood of the Bel Air to get her attention. "What? What's the matter?"

"You look great with the top down, but by the time you get there, your hair will look like hell. I'd put the top up."

"He's right, dear," Velma offered, nodding in agreement.

"Thanks, folks," Jessi rolled her eyes, forced a smile and reached for the baseball hat that was sitting on the back seat. Pulling it down over her hair she backed out.

Charley Weed's last afternoon stop was the Texaco Mini Mart in Bancroft. The big man quickly and efficiently filled the ice machine with bags of crushed ice, block ice, and cubed ice. He opened the vending machine box cover, emptied the one-dollar bills and quarters into a coffee can, relocked the box, and returned to the truck. Climbing into the cab, he picked up the clipboard, and using a stubby pencil that Kathryn had tied to the clipboards with a shoelace, he methodically counted out the money he had collected. He sorted the paper dollars with George Washington facing front, then carefully paper clipped the bills together before counting out the quarters. Making the entries was Charley's favorite part of the job, and he took pains to make each of his numbers as perfect as possible: eighteen bags of ice, nine paper dollars, fifteen dollars in quarters, for a total of twenty-four dollars. Kathryn would always compliment him if the numbers were neat, and that made him feel important. If he completed an entire page in neat rows, she would sometimes reward him with a ten-dollar bonus or a dinner in town.

His entries finished, Charley started the truck and pulled out of the gas station, made a left turn on Short Falls Road, and drove slowly back to the ice house, never allowing the speedometer to pass thirty-five. He was in no hurry to return and spend the rest of the afternoon cooped up in his trailer with nothing but his small, black-and-white TV for company.

He would check on his sunflowers that he'd planted outside his trailer. He planted them every year, and yesterday he had noticed that the big heads were drooping, heavy with seeds. Charley dried the seeds every year, salted them, and roasted them in his small oven. He'd seen the jays coming around, but he wasn't too worried; he'd put netting around the flowers to protect them from the birds. He'd share with them, but in his own time. He reached in his pocket, brought out a handful of last year's crop, and chewed on them slowly, spitting the shells out the window as he drove. He did enjoy his sunflower seeds.

He was hoping that Kathryn would let him run the crusher and bag the ice for his night deliveries. Since Pinky had come to live at the plant, he didn't get to run the crusher much anymore, and he missed the simple satisfaction he got from filling the bags. His nieces's previous boyfriends hadn't been interested in running the machinery, but Pinky liked it. The unsmiling Pinky didn't even like Charley to be in the plant, even made him ring the buzzer every time he wanted something, like *he* was the outsider.

As Charley approached the plant, he felt the familiar emptiness rise in the pit of his stomach. The feeling came each time he passed the spot where little Molly used to catch the bus. It'd been a long time ago, but Charley couldn't stop dredging it up.

Today was even worse. His friend, Marty, was dead, and it made his stomach feel sick. "Too bad, Marty," he said loudly as he turned onto Short Falls Road and drove the hundred yards into the plant. As he pulled the truck to a stop next to the loading dock and got out, he hoped Kathryn would ask him to clean up the butcher shop. She always fed him dinner after he cleaned the meat coolers. Charley grabbed the clipboard and the can full of quarters and started toward the office.

"Where the fuck you going, numbnuts?"

Charley turned to see Pinky walking across the loading dock from one of the outside storage rooms where he stored his set of weights. Pinky was sweaty and shirtless, exposing his defined "pecs," rock-hard arms and washboard stomach, all camouflaged under dozens of cheap, faded, blue prison tattoos. Charley noticed fresh blood on Pinky's army boots and was puzzled. They never butchered on Sundays.

"I'm giving my money and delivery sheet to Kathryn," Charley said, turning sideways ever so slightly, his body language signaling a subtle message of submission that Pinky's finely honed, dog-pack instincts recognized and acted on.

"No, you're not. Give 'em to me, asshole, I'll give them to her. She's busy today," Pinky barked, pulling the heavy can and clipboard out of Charley's reluctant grip.

"I wanted to ask her if I should clean up the shop today," Charley said, for the first time noticing something familiar about the straw hat Pinky was wearing.

"I'll clean it today. You go rest that massive brain of yours."

"I can help you clean it. I'll do the coolers. Kathryn might want me to have dinner with her," Charley argued.

"Hey, shit head, make yourself useful. Go beat off in your trailer like you usually do on Sunday. Then reload and do it again." Pinky sneered as he unlocked the door to the shop and started in.

"Why are you wearing Marty's hat?"

Charley's question froze Pinky in the doorway. As he turned back, his cold eyes locked onto Charley's. "You know something? If you want to clean up in here, have the fuck at it, my man," Pinky said, holding the door open and gesturing for the big man to enter.

As Jessi drove the forty miles to Slocum, her mind raced—leaping from Sammy Deavers' disappearance...to the puppy lady...to Marty Burris's violent death...to the abandoned dogs...to the abduction of Julie Abbott...to Lela's disappearance... and what Lela had said to her about the car. "A dead woman's car," she had called it. Why hadn't John mentioned anything about his wife?

The afternoon heat radiated off the asphalt as the Chevy turned onto the dirt road that led to the Deavers' property. A minute later she pulled to a stop next to a broken-down cement mixer in the cluttered front yard. The dogs sprang from under the steps and barked nonstop as they circled the car. Jessi left the windows up and the engine running, waiting in the air-conditioned coolness for someone to come out of the house and check on the noise. After two minutes Jessi guessed, rightly, that no one was home. It was obvious that Lela wasn't on the premises, and it looked like Nicole was also gone. She was disappointed and instantly regretted wasting the time it took to drive out. She looked at the silent house again.

"Maybe they're taking a nap."

She lowered the driver's side window and turned off the engine. Reaching into her shoulder bag, she came up with three dog biscuits and tossed them out the window.

"So easily bribed," she said as the dogs pounced on the treats, swallowed them in one gulp, and sniffed at her legs as she climbed out.

Jessi slung her bag over her shoulder and picked her way through the clutter past the toilet bowl planted with geraniums. She noticed that the flowers were drooping from the oppressive heat and briefly thought of finding a hose and giving them some water.

"Right, save the flowers, dummy," she thought to herself climbing the porch and knocking on the front door. She didn't expect an answer and she didn't get one.

She walked off the porch and made her way along behind the house as a dust devil grabbed a dirty paper plate and whirled it away.

The back of the property was a continuation of the front, every available square foot covered with one form of salvage or another: piles of broken-down washing machines and clothes dryers, dozens of worn tires, tables heaped with scavenged plumbing parts and copper wire. A smoldering, fifty-five gallon drum sat away from the rear of the house, bringing the smell of burning garbage to her nose. Bags of refuse had been ripped open by the dogs and strewn throughout the yard as they foraged for anything edible. Amongst the litter, she noticed dozens of Sudafed wrappers and several empty Muriatic acid jugs.

Jessi continued to move past and through a half-dozen rusted, partially dismantled cars that were resting on oil-stained blocks. Toward the rear of the property, she spotted two ram-shackle chicken coops. The wall of the closest coop was covered with hubcaps and old license plates.

"Anyone home?"

The silence bounced back at her. She was suddenly aware of how isolated the Deavers' property was. There were no close neighbors.

She paused and looked around catching a whiff of something odd—a chemical odor, familiar, yet out of place. Paint thinner? No, much stronger. She sniffed again, waiting for her brain to put a name to the scent.

Jessi turned back toward the house and noticed an orange-colored extension cord protruding from a slightly raised window in the back. The cord snaked its way through the garbage and across the back of the property and disappeared into the rear coop. As she made her way cautiously toward the building, her ears picked up the faint sound of music coming from a radio.

"Hello!"

The dogs barked and quickly rejoined her, hoping in vain for another treat. "Sorry, guys, but you cleaned me out," she said, approaching the shed. The door had been boarded shut, and the windows were covered in cloudy plastic. Crouching down, she peered through a crack in a splintered board. As her eyes slowly came into focus, she followed the orange extension cord to a dirty counter where it was plugged into to a clock radio and a two-burner, electric hot plate. A large Pyrex dish simmered on the small stove, giving off a strange, potent-smelling steam. The counter was littered with plastic tubing, mason jars, plastic gallon jugs, coffee filters with a telltale purple stains, and various sized funnels. Below the counter Jessi could make out several stacks of blue, five gallon buckets. Jessi smiled as her eyes and olfactory nerve made the connection. It was Toulene, a solvent used to extract methamphetamine! The Muriatic acid bottles and the Sudafed wrappers in the trash now made perfect sense. She was looking at a crude meth lab.

"I'll be damned."

"You looking for somebody?"

Jessi stiffened as she slowly got to her feet and turned to find herself looking into the unfriendly eyes of a heavy-set man in his mid-twenties. He was wearing a filthy Oakland Raiders t-shirt and his arms and neck were plastered with crude tattoos.

"Yes, as a matter of fact, I just came out to see if you've heard anything from Samantha." Jessi's brain raced over alternatives. She guessed the man's weight at close to 230 pounds, way too big to fight.

"We ain't heard nothing," the man said.

Clarence Deavers Jr. was taller than his father and out of shape. His soft stomach and flabby arms gave evidence that not all prison inmates spent their days lifting weights.

His pockmarked, ruddy face turned hostile as he moved close and put his hands against the shed on either side of her head, effectively pinning Jessi's back to the wall.

He was so close she could see his rotting teeth and feel his hot, tobacco-laced breath on her face. She needed to buy time. "Is Nicole here?"

Clarence's eyes flattened. He moved closer, pressing his body against her. "You know damn well Nicole ain't here."

"How about your parents? Are they around?"

"No. They're in town, trying to get my little sister back from you assholes," Clarence answered as he pushed harder, his hands moving to Jessi's neck. "You fucking social workers piss me off. You people need to mind your own fucking business!"

Jessi didn't like what she saw in Clarence's close-set, pig-like eyes. She realized she was going to have to fight him, and she wasn't going to get a second chance at it. She looked beyond Clarence's shoulder and stiffened.

"Lela, thank God."

It wasn't much of an opening, but it was enough. Clarence Jr. hesitated, turned slightly just as Jessi jerked her knee upward, knifing it hard into his groin! As he gasped and folded, she brought the heel of her shoe down hard on his instep. Clarence stumbled and tried to reach for her, but Jessi's thumbs found his eyes, simultaneously digging her fingers hard into the soft tissue of his temple, causing the lumbering man to bellow like an enraged bull as he staggered backwards, covering his throbbing eyes.

"Bitch!" He started to lunge toward her, but Jessi stepped behind him, grabbed his hand and, locking onto his thumb, twisted it painfully, forcing him heavily to the ground. With her free hand she grabbed her shoulder bag that was lying nearby and quickly removed her pistol from its holster and placed the barrel of the gun to the back of his head.

"Listen up, creten! That hard thing poking you in the back of the head is a nine millimeter Sig Sauer. You want to see how it works?"

"Fucking bitch!"

"No doubt, and you hardly even know me!" Jessi pulled her handcuffs from her bag and slipped them over the big man's thick wrists. Clarence pounded his head on the ground in helpless frustration as Jessi snapped the cuffs in place.

"Fucking cop! Fucking bitch cop dyke bastard!"

"Don't go anywhere, Clarence," Jessi stood, dusted off her pants, and took her cell phone out of her shoulder bag.

24.

Cutler sat at his desk and looked out at the limp flag flying at half-mast. The impromptu flower memorial to Marty Burris had more than tripled since morning and was threatening to spill over onto the parking area as more arrangements continued to arrive. The flower deliveries were made not only by florists but by farmers in bib overalls driving dusty pickups, youngsters on bikes, truck drivers in their noisy eighteen-wheelers, teenagers in hot rods, long-haired bikers on their Harleys, cheerleaders, and lowriders.

Inside, a heavy silence had settled over the double-wide. Most of the deputies, their shiny badges marked by a narrow, black band, had returned to their normal patrol duties leaving only three officers on the "extra board." Those deputies, Tim Lane, Danny Parks, and Bobby Koontz, would handle all calls for service in the town of Grace and would cover Kiko and Red's normal patrol routes, freeing the duo to devote themselves exclusively to the Burris investigation. A Highway Patrol public affairs officer named Ron Anderson had taken over the Water Department desk and was serving as the official press officer, as well as the laison between each of the five agencies that had an ongoing involvement in the investigation.

Janie Cortez was sitting at the console, talking in hushed tones to her husband, Frank, when the door opened, and Kiko and Red entered. Both men looked exhausted.

"Where's the boss?" Kiko asked.

Janie nodded to where Cutler was sitting quietly at his desk, staring out the window. "He's been over with Ellie and the boys. I guess the medical examiner from Austin called while he was there and recommended that they finish the cremation over there and just send Marty's ashes back."

"Probably the best way to handle it, don't you think?" her husband, Frank answered.

"Yeah, I suppose." Janie said, sharing a hopeless shrug with Kiko and Red before they walked away.

Cutler looked up as the deputies approached. "How'd it go out there?"

Red shook his head. "We covered every square inch of that damn highway from marker 130 all the way to where the car was torched."

Kiko spoke up. "We picked up every beer can, pop top, paper bag, cigarette butt– you name it, we bagged it–but I'm afraid all we got was a bunch of bags full of trash. Nothing."

"I'll tell you this, boss, if the sonofabitch that did that to Marty gets away, I'll..."

Red's unfinished thought hung in the air as each of them struggled with their own words to finish it.

Cutler looked at the sunburned Red and shook his head. "You guys look like hell. Go home and get some rest."

Red shook his head. "I'd just lay there and worry. Hell, I can do that here."

"I'm not going anywhere but the can," Kiko headed for the rest room. Red walked to his desk where Murray was working on the computer. Murray looked up, forced a smile. "Not so good, huh?"

Red shook his head and slumped down heavily into his chair, absentmindedly massaging his aching, red forehead with both hands. "How's it going in mystery land?" Red asked, pointing at the computer.

Murray looked at the stocky deputy and smiled. "We're on line. We're *there*."

Red sat up straight and stared at the monitor. "Cyberspace?"

"You got it."

A hint of a smile crossed Red's lips. "What are you working on?"

"Jessi asked me to search a name for her. Have you ever heard of a company named CECOM?"

"Not around here," Red answered.

Both men froze and looked toward Janie as the distinctive ring of the police line reverberated through the double-wide. Everyone in the trailer turned and watched Janie take the call. She held up two fingers and smiled as she wrote down the particulars. After disconnecting from the console, she carried the note to Cutler.

"What you grinning about? What's going on?" Cutler asked.

"That was Officer Jessi Cole. She's out in Slocum. She just found a meth lab at the Deaver's place and busted Clarence Junior!"

"I'm on the way!" Cutler barked, his heart racing as he headed for the door with Red in close pursuit.

"Whoa! Slow down. Before she called us, she called Louie Adams on his cell phone and asked for a transport. Louie's out there, and Junior's now cooling his heels in the back of Louie's car, and he's none too happy about it, either. Jessi also asked for a Hazardous Waste Team to handle all the chemicals!" Janie said, roaring with laughter. "She's code four, baby! No help needed!"

"Good for her," Cutler said, smiling in relief. "Then she's alright?"

"She's fine, but Junior is asking for medical attention. Claims he was brutalized."

"That's my girl," Murray shouted from across the room, jumping to his feet and pumping his fist in the air.

"Everybody can relax. She's on her way back," Janie said, just as the police line rang again. Janie plugged in next to Cutler's desk. "Sheriff's Office… Hi, Aaron. Yeah, he's right here," Janie said turned to Cutler. "It's Aaron Butler at the state crime lab. He's got some information on that cardboard Jessi found in the trash barrel."

Kiko burst out of the rest room fastening his pants and hurried to join the group as Cutler picked up the phone. "Aaron, we could really use some good news about now…" Cutler listened intently, not interrupting. "I appreciate you getting on this so quickly." He turned to Red. "They got a print!"

Red gave him a thumbs up as Cutler turned back to the phone. "I'm gonna need that stuff ASAP. Could you fax it up to me?"

Murray cleared his throat, loudly. "Sheriff Cutler?"

Cutler covered the mouthpiece of the receiver as he looked at Murray.

"You can have the information sent here now. We've got the system up and running," Murray said.

Cutler looked at Red for confirmation; Red looked to Murray. Murray nodded, and Cutler passed the phone to Red. Red, in turn, passed it to Murray. "Here you go, little partner. Do your thing."

Murray held out his hand, pushing the phone off. "This is all yours, my friend. You know what to do."

Red nodded and cleared his throat, flexed his fingers for good measure, and raised the phone to his ear. "This is my maiden voyage, Aaron.

Be gentle with me." Red cradled the phone between his ear and shoulder typing in the commands that Aaron was giving him. Red cleared his throat. "Let 'er rip!"

Within seconds the mug shot of a hard-looking biker type appeared on the monitor. Murray took over the keyboard, typed a command, and the mug shot began printing out, followed by a rap sheet.

"Goddamnit, boss. We could have had this capability all along? I guess I just didn't understand the necessity before. Now I do," Red said, solemnly.

"Yeah, I know what you mean." Cutler clasped Red's shoulder for a moment, both men thinking of Marty Burris. Cutler retrieved the sheets from the printer and quickly scanned the rap sheet. "Our guy's J.D. Decker. He's got a history: did some time at youth camp, couple of DUIs, one robbery conviction put him in Huntsville for six years. That was nearly twelve years ago. Looks like he's been clean ever since. Says here he's married."

"I know this guy, "Red said. "He runs that diesel repair shop over in Bancroft. Somebody broke in and stole some parts from him a few years ago. I took the report."

Cutler clipped his holstered 9mm to his belt. "Let's find out why a diesel mechanic is abandoning puppies right next to our crime scene."

As the three officers hurried out, Cutler paused next to Janie. "Tell Jessi what's going on. Tell her to wait here. I'll call as soon as I know something."

Janie nodded as Cutler hurried out. She crossed herself.

Jessi missed the sheriff by ten minutes, entering the office to be met by good-natured applause from the skeleton crew remaining. The attention both embarrassed and pleased her. When Janie told her about the fingerprint found on the cardboard, she felt elated. "God, I hope it's him," she said as she walked back to where Murray was packing his computer discs away in a small case. Murray stood and gave her a hug. "Jessi Cole strikes again! I knew I should have gone with you. We could have pulled our old shish kabob trick on him!"

"I don't think the shish kabob would have worked on Clarence Junior, Murray. He isn't as sophisticated as the Braxtons. Have you heard anything from Lela?" Jessi asked.

"Not a word. In fact, Velma called here a few minutes ago to see if you'd heard from her," Murray said, noticing Jessi's look of concern. "Jessi, don't worry about her. She's a flake; you told me that. That's why it's so hard to help people like that. They can't be counted on to stick to anything. Forget it. She took off."

"Yeah, you're probably right, but I just don't think she'd leave her things," Jessi nodded toward the computer monitor. "Did you have any luck with CE COM?"

Murray picked up a notepad. "I don't know if I did you any good, but I got a few hits. CECOM is the abbreviation for the United States Army Communications Electronics Command at Ft. Monmouth."

"Is that close by?"

"Not exactly. It's in New Jersey."

"What else?" Jessi asked.

"There's a CE COM telemarketing company, a CE COM electronics store, but it's located in Miami. There's a CE COM group that puts on ballet performances all over Europe. Right now they're performing in London. There's a CE COM trucking company in Sydney, Australia. There's an importing company named CE COM in my favorite city in the whole wide world, San Francisco, and there's a C.E. COMPANY nutritional supplement mail order house in St. George, Utah. That's about it."

Jessi was silent as she scanned the notepad looking in vain for some clue, so much as even a *hint* of a connection. Not finding it, she shook her head in frustration and sat down in a nearby chair. Henry rose from his basket and trotted toward her.

"Sorry, Jessi."

"Thanks for trying," Jessi replied, leaning down to part the hair that hid Henry's dark eyes and to scratch his chin. "Hi, little buddy, how you doing?" Jessi scooped the dog into her lap and held him as she opened Lela's sketchpad and studied the drawings, landing once more on the page that contained the rendering of the building and the CE COM reference. There was something on the page, something she was missing; and she could almost taste it.

Jessi picked up a pencil from the desk and wrote the letters CE COM on a note pad. "Murray, if we were playing Scrabble and you had the letters CE, what could you build on it?"

"I'm not good at Scrabble, but I do know how to use a dictionary," Murray said, retrieving a thick Random House from a nearby shelf and quickly thumbing through it. "Ce... here we go. Great. Three, no, four, five and a half pages of ce. That's what, 500 words? Good luck."

"Okay, let's try something else. Let's assume for a minute that COM stands for company. Let's also assume that CE is the first part of the company name. What then?" Jessi asked.

Murray's finger moved down the row of words, "Center, central, century, ahhh, ceramics? That's a possibility. So's cement! Ah ha! I vote for cement. No? How about cereal, or certitude? Certitude, freedom from doubt. I've never had that. Good name for a dot.com company. Wonder if it's registered? Maybe I could make a few bucks."

"Cement's good, but it's not placed right. Look at the way Lela drew it. No, the ce would have to be the last letters, not the first," Jessi, explained.

"Okay, I'm up for the challenge. How about dice? Mice? Rice? Lice? Price? "

Jessi penciled in the letter I. "How about ice?" She asked, setting Henry on the floor and reaching for the phone book on Kiko's desk. She opened the thin book to the yellow pages, thumbing quickly to the section on ice. "Here we go. There's only one listing for ice. Short Falls Ice Company." Something about the name triggered a memory.

"Got something?" Murray asked.

"I don't know," she replied as she stood and carried the sketchpad to where Janie Cortez was sitting at the console, engrossed in a report. "Janie, could I ask you a question?"

"Certainly, ask away," the big woman replied pushing the report form to the side and looking with interest at the sketchpad Jessi placed in front of her.

"Lela drew this. I think it might be a building around here. Is it familiar at all?"

Janie squinted as she looked long and hard at the drawing. "I think so, but I'm not sure. I…"

"What if I said *icehouse?*"

Janie hit the sketch with her palm. "Of course! That's the old Short Falls Ice building. Hell, when I was a kid we'd cut class and go out there and raise hell. Look!" Janie pointed at the sketch, tapping her finger on the tower. "There's the water tower. I've walked right across the top of it. Wooo!" she said, rubbing her arms. "It gives me chills just thinking about it. Scary old place. "

"It's still open, though, right?" Jessi asked.

"Part of it. Kathryn Weed and her uncle-"

"Charley Weed! The iceman. I knew there was some reason I remembered it," Jessi said, pleased she had made the connection. "I know Kathryn from the softball game."

"Besides the ice, they run a little butcher shop, cold storage lockers, that kind of thing." Janie added, "She's had a terrible go of it."

"What do you mean?" Jessi asked.

"You know how it is in some families. Just one thing after another." Janie ticked off on her fingers. "First her mother died giving birth to her little sister, Molly. Kathryn raised that little girl. 'Course Molly was a little rascal." Janie smiled at the recollection. "Had a mind of her own, that one did. Then their dad died of a heart attack, and not six months later, *boom,* Molly disappears. That was what, nearly twenty years ago? Poor Charley still drops in occasionally to see if we've turned up anything. He and Kathryn were both pretty broken up."

"That's odd. I wonder why John didn't mention that to me?" Jessi said, perplexed. "I'm not sure how any of this relates to Lela." Jessi looked at the sketchpad again. "I wonder why she drew the old ice house?"

Janie shrugged.

"Well, maybe Kathryn can help me figure it out. Is this place hard to find?" Jessi asked.

"Not at all," Janie said, scribbling out directions on a sticky Post-It note. "Instead of going straight to Slocum, make a left at the four way stop and follow the arrows to Bancroft. Once you get there, go across the railroad tracks, past Butler's Drugs—it's got a big ice cream cone in front—take a left at the stop sign on Short Falls Road. It's about five miles out. Trust me, you can't miss it," she said, ripping off the note and handing it to Jessi.

Jessi hurried to where Murray was once again engrossed in the computer and grabbed her purse.

"Have any luck?" he asked, not able to pull his eyes totally away from the screen.

"Yeah, maybe. Want to go for a ride?" Jessi asked.

"I'd love to, but I promised Janie I'd help her set up a records program."

"I'll see you later then," Jessi headed for the door.

"Maybe we can all have dinner?" Murray called after her. "Remember, you promised me the world's biggest chicken-fried steak at Pocatello Pablo's!" Murray yelled across the room.

"Bring your doggy bag! No, on second thought, just bring the dog!" Jessi tossed back, pausing next to Janie. "I'm going to drive out to the ice company. If anything happens, call me on my cell phone."

"Will do," Janie said as she answered a call on the Water Department line. "Grace Water Department, this is Janie."

Deputy Leo Beasley had parked his full-size Ford Bronco at the corner of First and Kansas Streets in Bancroft, directly in front of Butler's Drug Store, and was waiting when Cutler's Blazer pulled to a stop next to him. Kiko's Blazer pulled to a stop behind the Sheriff's.

Leo rolled down his window. "Hi, boss."

"How you doing, Leo?" Cutler asked.

Leo shrugged as Red leaned over and nodded at his old friend. "You look like shit, Leo."

"Look who's talking, you redheaded old fart."

"J. D. Decker, you know him? Cutler asked, handing the mug shot through the window.

Leo took the photo and studied it carefully. "Not real well. I see him around. He pretty much stays to himself at his shop. His wife seems nice. They've got a little boy, I think."

"Did you drive by the garage?" Cutler asked.

"Yeah, as near as I can figure, he's there. They live in a little trailer house behind the shop, but I thought I saw somebody walking around inside the garage about fifteen minutes ago."

"Okay, while you and Kiko cover the back, we're going to pull in like nothing is up. I don't want to start sneaking around; somebody might do something stupid. And no radios. We never did find Marty's portable. If you need to call, use your cell phone."

Leo nodded and, starting his Bronco, pulled away from the curb with Kiko close behind.

Without saying a word, Cutler pulled his pistol from his holster and checked the chamber for a round. Red removed the Ithaca 12-gauge shotgun from the floor rack and chambered a round with a hollow *thump,* then laid it on the floor beneath his feet and checked his own pistol. He then nodded and Cutler slipped the Blazer into gear and drove the half-mile to the diesel shop.

J.D Decker's Diesel Service was located on the outskirts of Bancroft, set in from the road on a dusty, two-acre plot where an assortment of broken-down Peterbilts, Macks, and Kenworth trucks awaited parts, service, or the wrecking yard. The garage was housed in a high-roofed metal building. A faded, fifty-foot-long, single-wide trailer house sat on rotting tires on the west side of the garage, taking advantage of the only shade on the property.

The sheriff's Blazer pulled to a stop in front of the garage, and stepping out, Cutler and Red approached the large, open bay door. Red kept the shotgun held close to his leg. "Anybody here?" Cutler called, taking a tentative step into the building as Red moved to the far side of the doorway and slipped silently into the shadows on the inside of the garage.

"Whatcha need?" A man's voice answered from inside the recesses of the building.

As their eyes adjusted to the dimly lit interior, a man's legs came into focus, protruding from under the front end of a bright red Kenworth tow truck. The spotless paint job and elaborate pinstriping combined with the highly polished chrome, marked the "K-Whopper" as someone's prize.

"If you need a tow, my rig's out of service. If you need anything else, I'm closed, come back tomorrow," the man said, continuing to work.

"J.D. Decker?"

There was a short pause before the man rolled himself out from under the truck on a low wooden dolly. The sight of the two uniformed cops, one with a shotgun, standing over him brought him uneasily to his feet. "I'm J.D. Decker," he said, still holding a seven- eighths open-end wrench in his grease-covered, beefy hand. Decker was six-foot-three and weighed in excess of two hundred and sixty pounds, very little of which was fat. A graying flattop had replaced the straggly ponytail he had displayed in the mug shot.

"I'm Sheriff Cutler and this is Deputy Cordell," Cutler said, extending his hand in an effort to diffuse not only the man's obvious nervousness, but also his potential to act violently if aroused.

"I know who you are," Decker said as he looked blankly at Cutler's offered hand before tossing the heavy wrench onto a littered workbench. Retrieving a red shop towel from under the counter, he used it to wipe the grease from his hands. Only then did he take Cutler's proffered hand and give it a firm shake.

"What can I do for you, sheriff?"

Jessi sped down the old Bancroft Highway, and as she rounded a curve, the quartz necklaces Lela had hung from the rearview mirror the night before spun and caught the sun, the crystals sending a prism of light swirling around the interior of the car. Jessi reached out and, lifting the necklaces off the mirror, placed them over her head and around her neck. Was she hoping for some kind of psychic connection, she wondered? Was she getting superstitious, or just trying to cover as many bases as possible? She decided the latter was true and, adjusting her dark glasses, floored the Chevy, surprised by the sudden surge of power as the four-barrel carburetor kicked in with a loud *whine.*

Entering Bancroft, Jessi slowed, passing Butler's Drug Store with its giant ice cream cone suspended on a sign above the sidewalk where, just fifteen minutes earlier, Cutler, Red and Kiko had rendezvoused with Deputy Beasley.

As Jessi drove past the drugstore with its old fashioned soda fountain, a memory of her mom and dad ordering lemon and cherry cokes came to her. She could almost picture them sitting at the counter, which was pretty silly, she thought, since it was her dad's memory retold to her as a child.

The Chevy thumped across the railroad tracks, stopped at the stop sign, and turned left onto Short Falls Road. Jessi didn't have long to wait before she saw the three-story water tower silhouetted against the stark landscape. It was the only building around, and seeing it gave her a strong feeling of deja vu. She glanced at the black-and-white sketch on the seat beside her, the three-story water tower mirroring the one visible through the windshield.

She drove the remainder of the way trying to decide what she was going to do when she got there, especially if Lela had come out here. Judging from the number of new sketches in her pad, she obviously had

had another vision. Was Jessi beginning to believe her? "Damn you, Lela!" Jessi mumbled. What was she thinking coming out here alone?

Jessi turned into the parking area of the Short Falls Ice and Meat Company and pulled to a stop next to the loading dock, facing the office. As she got out she looked around the maze of old structures and immediately spotted the faded "CE COM" lettering on the main building. "This is the place," she told herself. There was a starkness that emphasized its isolation, and it was obvious that much of the facility was abandoned. She looked up at the empty windows, but they told her nothing. As she climbed the steps and crossed the smooth concrete of the loading dock, Jessi noticed the little camping trailer set off to the side, the heavy sunflowers drooping westerly in the afternoon sun. She approached the office door, knocking a few times in spite of the drawn blinds and the closed sign hanging in the window. She knocked again, not really expecting a response and getting none. She rang the delivery bell and heard it echo from deep within the building. Jessi looked around, hoping for inspiration, and seeing another door at the end of the loading dock, quickly walked toward it.

Cutler sat on one side of a desk cluttered with greasy engine parts and open repair manuals. Across from him a worried J.D. Decker sat alongside his troubled wife, Caitlin.

"I don't know how you can think that my J.D. could harm anyone, let alone kill somebody," she said, choking back tears. She was a surprisingly petite woman, appearing even smaller next to her large husband. She wore her sandy blond hair in a tight bun that accented the freckles on the light skin of her forehead. Her worried blue eyes darted between her husband and Cutler. "Sheriff, my husband is a good man, and he never left here last night. He was with Devin and me all night. I swear to the Lord above."

J.D. reached out and patted Caitlin's arm, a silent thank you for her support, but he was clearly worried.

Cutler watched them both, noting their body language, their tonal inflection, looking desperately for some sign they were lying. "I didn't say he killed anyone."

Caitlin spoke up, her voice close to cracking. "We heard about what happened, and I'll tell you true, Marty Burris went out of his way to give J.D. tow calls. J.D. would never harm that man."

J.D. shifted nervously in his chair. "Sheriff, eight years ago I walked out of Huntsville Prison a free man, and this little lady was waiting for me. I made a vow to her, and I made a vow to Jesus Christ, to mend my ways, and I have. Hell, I haven't even gotten a speeding ticket. I'm sure as hell not a cop killer, and that's the honest truth. I considered Officer Burris a friend."

Cutler's and J.D.'s eyes locked, as if each of them could somehow read the truth and intentions of the other.

"Sheriff?" Red's deep voice broke the silence as he stuck his head in the small room and nodded for Cutler to join him. Cutler excused himself, and the two of them moved away from the office a few steps to where Kiko and Beasley waited.

"We're finding nothing. At least nothing, as the judge says, in plain sight."

Kiko gestured toward the shop. "You want us to take it apart?"

"No, not without papers," Cutler replied.

"You don't need a search warrant." J.D's voice caused Cutler to turn. The big man was standing in the doorway behind him. "Take the damn place apart, piece by piece. We ain't got nothing to hide here."

Cutler nodded to his deputies and they moved quickly back into the shadowy recesses of the darkened building. A worried-looking boy streaked into the garage on a knobby-wheeled bike and, skidding to a stop, laid the bike against the wall and pushed past Cutler to enter the office and join his parents. A yellow lab followed at a measured pace, going immediately to a dirty plastic bucket in the corner and lapping up water.

When Cutler entered the office he saw the look of concern on the boy's face as he spoke in hushed tones to his father. "Why they here, Dad? What's the matter?"

Cutler quickly stepped forward and extended his hand to the boy. "I'm John Cutler. What's your name?"

"Devin." The boy's response was so soft, Cutler could barely hear him.

"That's a great bike you've got out here. Bet you've put a lot of miles on it."

Devin nodded as J.D. put his muscular arm around the boy's shoulder.

"Devin and I put it together ourselves. He's a good boy."

"He looks like it. You're what, Devin, ten?"

The boy nodded.

"That makes you a fourth grader at Rio Nido. Mrs. Campbell?"

The boy smiled and nodded. "How'd you know that?"

"I'm a detective in my spare time," Cutler replied as the lab nudged his knee, giving him a good sniffing.

"Lady, leave the man alone." Caitlin grabbed Lady's collar and pulled her away.

"Don't worry about her. I've got a dog of my own." Cutler dropped to one knee and stroked the dog's head. My Uncle Merlin used to say that if a dog don't sniff you, you're boring." Cutler's hand dropped to Lady's underbelly and immediately felt her swollen teats. "She's all bagged up. Where're her pups?" Cutler asked, again locking eyes with J.D.

"We sold them all, didn't we Dad?" Devin volunteered.

"Yeah, we did," J.D. said, fidgeting ever so slightly as he exchanged a quick, worried look with his wife.

Cutler stroked the dog for a moment longer and then rose. "J.D., step outside with me a minute, will ya?"

"Sure," J.D. replied, leaving the office ahead of Cutler who paused in the doorway, turning to the obviously worried Caitlin and Devin.

"Sorry for intruding on your Sunday, ma'am."

"No intrusion; we already went to church."

"Nice to meet you, Devin. You take care of that dog."

Devin nodded as Cutler turned to leave.

"Sheriff?" Caitlin's voice carried a hint of a plea. "Is everything okay?"

"Yes, ma'am, everything's fine. I'd appreciate your and your husband's help watching out for that stolen truck and trailer we talked about," Cutler said, looking over at Devin who was petting Lady.

Caitlin smiled and nodded. "Thank you, sheriff. We'll watch for it."

J.D. Decker was waiting by the open doors when Cutler and the other three officers came out of the garage. As Red, Kiko, and Leo Beasley returned to their 4x4s, the sheriff put on his sunglasses and walked with J.D. toward his Blazer. "J.D., next time you've got a litter of puppies you want to get rid of..."

"I know, Sheriff," J.D. overrode him. "But you saw how Devin was with that dog. It would have broken his heart if he knew what I did.

I can't barely afford to keep food on my own table. I sure as hell can't feed five more dogs."

"I understand that, but next time take them out to the shelter so Marie can take care of them, maybe get them adopted. Or better yet, have the animal spayed. Becca Hall, the vet over in Grace, will do it for next to nothing." Cutler opened the door of the Blazer and climbed in before continuing his reprimand. "But it isn't right to drop them off out in the middle of nowhere to be hit by a car or be food for the coyotes," Cutler said as he started the Blazer and put it in gear.

J.D. looked puzzled. "But sheriff, I didn't get rid of the pups myself. I didn't have the heart."

"What do you mean?"

"I asked Pinky to do it for me."

"Who in the hell is Pinky?"

25.

❦

The door opened with a "swoosh," taking Jessi by surprise. She stepped back, her hand going involuntarily to her shoulder bag, and just avoided getting soaked by a pail of soapy, dirty water being flung out the door. Pinky smiled. "Didn't mean to scare you. I'm just doing Sunday clean up." Pinky finished emptying the mop bucket and looked at Jessi questioningly.

"Is Kathryn around?" Jessi asked.

"There's no one here. The meat counter is closed on Sundays. Come back tomorrow, she'll be here then. We'll open at eight."

Jessi smiled brightly. "Actually, maybe you can help me. I'm looking for a friend of mine. She said she was coming out this way. She's tall, dark hair with gray streaks that's a little on the wild side."

"What the hell would she be doing all the way out here?" Pinky asked as he wrung out the heavy mop.

"We think she's in the early stages of Alzheimer's. She's starting to wander away from the group home."

Pinky looked genuinely apologetic. "Sorry, haven't seen anyone like that. In fact, like I said, there's no one out here but me. I'd sure like to help you out though." He leered.

"That's funny, I'm sure she was walking out this way. Well, thanks anyway." Jessi hesitated. "This is sure an old building. I'll bet there's a story behind this place."

"Yeah, well if there is, I'm not the one to tell you. Hope you find your friend," Pinky finished wringing out the mop and hung it over a railing. As he did, Jessi noticed the wolf tattoo on the back of his hand, its red eyes seeming to search her out. The man's arms were heavily muscled, and the way he carried himself, she guessed, correctly, that he was a prison yard rat who had spent most his time in the exercise yard, lifting weights and flirting with the other weightlifters.

"Sorry to bother you."

"No problem," Pinky said, re-entering the building and closing the door.

Jessi sensed she was being watched as she made her way back to the Chevy and got behind the wheel. She reached over and glanced at Lela's sketchpad, opening it up to the drawing of the wolf's head. "That's it," she said under her breath backing away from the loading dock. Driving back toward the road, she caught a glimpse of the icehouse office in the rearview mirror. A slight movement of the blind caught her attention. Somebody was definitely watching her.

"What did she want?" Kitty asked, her tone laced with worry as she parted the window blind and peered out.

"She asked for you. She had some bullshit line, something about looking for her friend who was crazy and walked away from some group nut house. I'll tell you this: her nutty friend wandered into the wrong fucking place because they ain't ever going to see *that* woman again. That bitch is tallow," Pinky smirked.

Kitty continued watching the Chevy as it pulled onto Short Falls Road and disappeared from view.

"Cool ride, huh?" Pinky said.

"That Chevy she's driving is John Cutler's car. *Sheriff* John Cutler." Pinky's smirk dissolved.

"Something's going on. We can't wait any longer," Kitty said, obviously upset, as she took two hits off her inhaler before hurrying out of the room.

Jessi remembered crossing a dip in the road a quarter of a mile from the icehouse and quickly drove to it, pulling the Chevy off the road and into the head of a wash where it was out of sight. Climbing out of the car, she grabbed her cell phone off the seat and quickly punched in the number of the sheriff's office, hit the SEND button, and waited. Nothing. There was no signal strength marked on the phone.

Jessi hurried to the top of the rise and, shielding her eyes against the sun, looked off. The water tower loomed above the surrounding countryside, stirring a flood of uneasiness that quickened her pulse. She hurried back to the Chevy, slid behind the wheel, and inserting the key in the ignition, hesitated. Every fiber of her being sensed something was wrong and that the icehouse held the answer. She had to get help, but if she drove all the way back to Bancroft to a phone, it might be too late. She removed her holstered pistol and small Mag-lite from her shoulder bag and then locked the purse in the trunk. She slid the pistol out of the holster, quickly checked the clip, chambered a round, and stuck the holster over the top of her belt on her right side. She then placed the key under the front floor mat and, cell phone in hand, hurried away from the car, moving briskly along the wash until it met the railroad tracks. Without realizing it, Jessi was soon retracing Lela's earlier route, jogging along the hot, metal tracks until they disappeared behind the huge metal doors of the icehouse. There was obviously no entry here; the doors were secured by a large chain and lock. She raised her cell phone and saw that the signal strength vacillated between one bar and no bar. It was worth a try, but when she punched in the Sheriff's Department number the phone only buzzed, and she got a "Low Battery" warning message.

"Damn!"

Jessi hurried along the back of the building, but instead of following the wall around to the front as Lela had done, she paused when she noticed a well-worn pathway snaking away from the rear of the building and cutting thirty yards down a steep side hill, leading to a small water hole. The stagnant, half-acre holding pond was lined with a stand of green willows that looked out of place in the stark landscape. Looking around, Jessi noticed that the ground close to the icehouse was dry and lifeless except for an occasional patch of dry brush. Jessi again looked at the pond and the thick green willows. Where was the water coming from? Following the pathway down the side hill, she quickly found the source of the water. A three-foot-wide cement drainpipe jutted out of the ground, and from it came a steady dribble that fed the small pond. Jessi followed an imaginary line from the pipe to its source. It had to come from within the plant.

Wading into the foot-deep water, Jessi's shoes sank up to her ankles in mud. She used her Mag-lite to look into the pipe and saw only cobwebs and darkness. She sloshed through the tepid water to the edge of the pond and broke off a willow branch. Returning to the pipe, she tossed the branch in and pulled herself up into the opening. Dropping on all fours, she crawled forward into the darkness using the willow to sweep cobwebs away. She estimated that she would have to crawl at least forty yards before she would be inside the building.

As she sloshed further and further into the dark pipe, the rough cement scrapped the skin on her hands and knees. The closeness of the walls of the pipe terrified her, and the rancid air seemed to heighten her oncoming claustrophobia. Inching forward her eyes slowly adjusted to the darkness, and she saw a fuzzy glow twenty yards ahead. As she sloshed toward it she shuddered as a spider skittered across her neck. Finally reaching the end of the pipe, Jessi found herself looking up through a large steel grate that separated her from the interior of the old plant. Water dripped onto her face as she reached up and tried to lift the grate. Jessi strained until the veins in her neck threatened to explode, but the heavy piece of rusted metal was stuck fast and wouldn't budge. She adjusted her angle, positioning her body in order to increase her lifting power, but the grate proved too much for her arms and shoulders. Defeated, she exhaled loudly and sat back to catch her breath. The heels of her hands stung and oozed blood.

Lying there, panting, hardly able to even move her shoulders, she remembered back to her academy training days when she was told to grab a 250-pound dead-weight dummy, nicknamed "Partner," and lift him to safety onto a raised platform. Partner was named after the wounded partner he represented and also represented the nemesis of many female officers. Jessi, like most of her classmates, had tried grabbing "Partner" under the armpits and hoisting him up, but no matter how hard she had tried, she couldn't maneuver the dead weight. After being disqualified once, she had been determined not to let it happen again. She had mentally wrestled with the problem and had decided to try to use her own body weight to help her out. With her male counterparts curiously watching, Jessi had grabbed "Partner" under the arms, dragging him backwards to the platform. Once there, she'd sat on the edge of the raised structure and, hugging "Partner" to her chest, literally rolled herself and the dummy up onto the wooden platform where they'd both collapsed in a breathless heap to the hoots and whistles of her appreciative fellow trainees. She had passed the test.

Jessi realized she had to get closer to the grate; she had to somehow hug it. Moving directly under it, she squatted on the balls of her feet and placed her left shoulder against the cold metal. As she tried to stand she felt the metal give slightly. Readjusting her feet and then using more of her back, she took a deep breath and stood. The grate lifted completely off its seat, and as Jessi tilted, the heavy cover slid off, leaving her a gapping hole to crawl out of. She was covered with cobwebs and mud, and the knees of her pants were shredded and bloody from the cement. As she looked around, her hand felt the butt of her pistol for reassurance.

She was standing next to the long loading dock where, years before, a steady stream of railroad cars had disgorged countless thousands of smelly, noisy cattle into a series of holding pens. Looming three stories above her, the old water tower leaked droplets of water from a hundred holes which fell softly all around her, a perpetual cool shower that time had converted into a slimy blanket of slippery moss. Jessi followed the railroad tracks along the loading dock for fifty yards before she spotted a closed door that appeared to lead off into another part of the compound.

She tried the door, and finding that it opened easily, she stepped inside what appeared in the dim light to be a large garage or maintenance shed. Tools and various pieces of machinery were scattered on a workbench, and further in, an old Ford pickup that had been converted into a portable butcher rig was parked in one of several bays. At the rear of the truck bed, a seven-foot-tall, four-sided wooden structure housed an electric winch that allowed the operator to hoist freshly killed animals off the ground so that the butchering could proceed at the operator's eye level.

As Jessi passed by the rear of the truck, a putrid stench filled her nostrils and made her gag. She had accidentally stumbled into the same aroma once before while traveling in Mexico. She and a friend had been walking through the meat section of a vast Guadalajara open-air market where the heads, innards, tongues, and brains of freshly killed animals were displayed in blood-filled pans under a moving sea of flies. The unmistakable smell of death had been overwhelming and had sent Jessi and her friend, Janel, fleeing to the street. Since that time, she had suffered through numerous encounters with corpses in various stages of decomposition, but she never got accustomed to the stench.

As Jessi moved away from the pickup, she bumped into a small forklift parked close to a sliding metal door, which she pushed open and slipped through, finding herself in total blackness. Jessi removed the tiny Mag-lite from her pocket and, flipping it on, found herself looking at the rear of a white Ford van! Her heart raced, and she breathed in sharply as the light beam danced over the rear of the van to settle on the license plate: B-L 46009. That wasn't the tag! Above the plate, on the door, her eye picked up thin streaks. Red streaks! Looking closer she realized she was looking at blood splatter. Switching the Mag-lite to her left hand, Jessi removed her pistol from the holster and, moving ever so cautiously toward the front of the van, tried without success to see through the smoked windows. She carefully opened the front passenger-side door and was startled when the interior light popped on. The van was empty, but concealed behind the driver's seat was another license plate! Her heart raced as she used the barrel of the 9mm to nudge the plate out where she could read it: The letters A-S-A came into view followed by the numbers 4074! This was it! This was the van Marty Burris had stopped! She quietly closed the door of the van, replaced her pistol in her holster, and removed her cell phone from the pocket of her mud-splattered jacket. As she entered the number of the sheriff's office, the phone display again registered no bars and also gave her a low battery power signal. As Jessi moved back to the door and started out, she picked up the outline of another vehicle parked in the bay next to the van. The beam from her Mag-lite swept over it, and she clearly saw the familiar lettering of the Short Falls Ice Company recognizing it instantly as Charley Weed's delivery truck. Taking out her weapon, she moved slowly past the front of the vehicle and noticed that the hood was still warm to the touch. Her light swept over the empty cab and then danced along the side panels. Moving past the rear compartment, several pigeons exploded from the rafters directly above Jessi's head, causing her to spin and jerk the pistol skyward. She stood motionless for a few seconds, willing her heart to stop racing. As she started back toward the door, she glanced down and saw that her shoe was drenched in blood! Turning around, the beam of her light picked up a large pool of blood where she had been standing, next to the compartment at the rear of the truck. Looking closely, she saw a slow, steady drip coming from the underside of the vehicle. As her hand reached out for the handle to the compartment, she paused, briefly considering retreat as a viable option. Taking a deep breath, she turned the handle and opened the compartment! Her Mag-light illuminated three cases of wrapped meat thawing in a corner opposite a half-dozen bags of melting ice. Jessi breathed a sigh of relief and, after shutting the compartment, turned to find herself staring into the dead eyes of Charley Weed!

Her gasp propelled her backwards, where she stumbled hard into the wall. Shining the light upwards she saw that the huge corpse was hanging upside down, suspended from the rafters by a thick, brown rope.

To Lela, there was only one thing colder than the floor she was lying on, and that was the colder reality that she and Julie would be dead in a very short period of time. The insane notion that Julie and Lela would both die here, in this awful place, at the hands of these monsters, so infuriated her that her earlier fright and terror dissolved into a growing rage. All of the years of frightening, unexplainable visions came crashing together, and she suddenly knew beyond any doubt that these two people were the personification of the evil that had been invading her mind all those years.

Lela's anger spurred her mind into motion, and her eyes skittered over the darkened room for the hundredth time. "There has to be a way out!" she thought. "There has to be a way to escape, but how?" For the hundredth time she saw no hope.

Julie gasped, audibly, as the sound of angry shouting drifted in from somewhere outside their darkened prison. As Lela listened, the audible mix of male and female voices–charge, counter charge, slamming doors, heavy footsteps–took her back to her childhood bedroom where she had hid under the covers for agonizingly long, dark hours. Lela could feel Julie's muscles tensing until the girl was quivering, and her shallow gasps signaled she was hyperventilating.

The tape covering their mouths made speech impossible, but they communicated through eye contact. Julie would moan, and their eyes would lock, allowing Lela to see when Julie's terror was building out of control. When she saw the girl's panic, she would move close, rocking awkwardly side to side, until she could touch Julie's cheek with her own. The simple act of contact seemed to soothe and calm the girl, and Lela could actually feel some of Julie's tension dissipate. An unfathomable fear would be triggered by the simple sound of a door opening or closing somewhere in the shadowy labyrinth that surrounded them, and they strained to pick up the sound of footsteps. Footsteps meant the possibility that one of the monsters was coming and triggered uncontrollable sobs from Julie. If they were lucky, and Lela was beginning to measure every moment that they were alone as lucky, the footsteps would recede, and she would make soft purring sounds until she could feel Julie's choppy breathing slow, and she knew that the girl was escaping into an uneasy sleep.

The ringing buzzer awakened Julie with a start and sent Lela's heart leaping with hope! They held their breath and prayed for a miracle. They heard only heavy footsteps growing closer. This time the footsteps didn't pass them by, and the sound of the key turning in the lock flooded Lela with dread. Kitty burst into the room, turning on a piercing overhead light that left Lela momentarily blind, blinking against the intrusive brightness.

Seeing Lela lying close to Julie enraged Kitty. Her jaw clenched as she set the small suitcase that she was carrying down and grabbed Lela by the feet, yanking her roughly back across the room. "Don't you dare contaminate her! You have no right to even touch her. She is mine!"

Lela's head thumped painfully over the cement, and she gritted her teeth to keep from groaning. She would not give this psycho bitch the satisfaction of knowing she had inflicted pain. As Kitty flung her into the corner, Lela's head flopped to the side causing part of the tape to pull away from her mouth! "What kind of a monster are you? Leave this child alone!"

Kitty backhanded Lela hard across the mouth, reopening the jagged cut for the second time that day. Kitty used the heel of her hand to press the duct tape firmly over Lela's swollen, bloody lips as she hissed, "I hope you like my friend, Pinky, because he sure likes you. He *loves* whores!" Kitty's eyes flared with hatred as she stood and rammed the toe of her shoe into Lela's side.

Unfortunately, Lela realized only too well that it was not she who was the focus of Kitty's attention, and she watched helplessly as Kitty opened her bag and carefully arranged make-up, a comb and brush, ribbons, a mirror, and a Polaroid camera on a small table. Lela watched, puzzled, as Kitty picked up Julie and sat her in a chair in front of the mirror. As Julie wept, Kitty slowly, almost lovingly, began brushing the girl's long hair, oblivious to Julie's terror.

"What in the hell was going on?" Lela could not even fathom of what depths of depravity this woman was capable.

Leaving the enclosed garage, Jessi continued along the tracks until she spotted a staircase leading to a second-story doorway. Hopping up onto the loading dock, she quickly climbed the steps and found herself looking at a closed door with a faded red sign nailed to it that read simply:

Co2

The room contained long rows of rusting, empty carbon dioxide tanks fixed in place with metal straps. In the shadows, they reminded Jessi of dark green soldiers with silver heads lined up for inspection. Over the years, some of the straps had rusted through and many of the tanks had tipped over, forming an uneven jumble that Jessi gingerly picked her way across. She exited through an open doorway on the far side of the room and found herself on a raised metal walkway. The metal platform led directly to a heavy, insulated wooden door with a stainless steel handle which was held in place with a large padlock. Jessi's eyes darted over the platform seeking out anything that might be used to break the lock. Finding nothing, she remembered the workbench and hurried back through the Co2 room, down the stairs and into the maintenance shed. Forcing herself not to think of the dead man dangling from a rope in the next room, she searched the counter from end to end before locating a pair of rusted bolt cutters in a drawer. Retracing her steps, she placed the jaw of the bolt cutters over the loop of the lock and squeezed. Nothing. She willed herself to squeeze harder, but again, all of her strength was not enough. In exasperation, she placed the cutters between herself and the door and then grabbed the door handle and pulled with all her might, the heavy handles biting painfully into her chest. Just when she thought she couldn't squeeze any harder, the loop snapped, and the broken lock dropped to the floor. Opening the door, Jessi felt a rush of frigid air that stung the exposed skin on her hands and knees and vaporized her breath. Flipping on her Mag-Lite, she stepped into the frigid darkness to find herself surrounded by dozens of huge ice blocks. The beam of her light picked up a large block and tackle that was mounted to an overhead dolly that allowed the frozen squares to be hoisted onto a thick, wooden counter where a large saw blade would quickly turn them into smaller blocks and send them sliding down a chute to a room somewhere below. Off in a corner a large canvas partially covered another row of blocks.   As Jessi crept through the wintry room, she had to turn sideways, flush to the wall, to push past a maze of bone-chilling blocks. The rough wood that lined the room pulled at her clothing. As she pushed her way toward the far end of the room, she failed to notice a small nail sticking out of the wall and as she slid past it, her holster snagged, pulled from her waist, and fell to the sawdust- covered floor with a muffled "thump." Jessi stood frozen in place. Could anyone have heard it? She snapped off her flashlight and forced herself not to move, willed herself not to even breath. For more than a minute she stood in the shivery darkness as the skin on her hands and face started to burn from the biting air and listened for the sound of approaching footsteps. Finally, convinced that no one had heard her miscue, she turned on the flashlight and pointed it at the floor close to her feet. Her heart raced as the familiar shape of the holstered pistol failed to materialize. Due to the closeness of the huge blocks of ice, she was unable to position herself on her hands and-knees. Bracing herself against the wall she allowed herself to sink to the floor between two blocks of ice where she ran her frozen fingers through the sawdust. Nothing! It wasn't possible! She reached behind an ice block as far as she could extend her arm and desperately swept the flooring with her hand. Still nothing! Fighting a growing feeling of dread she let her fingers trace along the wall where it met the floorboards and felt the sting of slivers jabbing into her numbed fingertips. Tilting her head against the wall and straining against the unyielding wood, she pointed the flashlight behind the block of ice and saw it. The gun had fallen through a narrow grating and was now resting on a conveyor belt six feet below her. Her eyes darted around the room in panic, unwilling to accept the reality of her predicament. Unless she could somehow lift a 1,000 pound block of ice, the gun was gone As she cursed herself she felt the overwhelming urge to weep and it angered her.

"Yeah, have a goddamn good cry you idiot." She took a deep breath of frigid air and coughed as it tore at her stinging lungs. The reality of the lost weapon was quickly replaced by a more pressing reality: she was freezing! Fighting panic and painful leg cramps, Jessi pushed her-self against the wall and willed herself upright. Using the flashlight to reorient herself, she crept silently to the corner of the room where a wooden staircase led to an insulated exit door. A faded, red sign above the door reminded her that:

"Safety is no Accident."

Jessi pushed the heavy plunger handle and felt a welcoming rush of warm air as she stepped out onto another raised metal walkway. Her eyes sought out an opening where the conveyor belt entered the room. If she could find the belt she might possibly follow it to her pistol. But there was no sign of a conveyor belt, nothing but the walkway that led off into the darkness. As she picked her way slowly across the grated metal, her freezing left hand sought out and found a rusted handrail while her right hand pointed the flashlight. To her left was the water tower, to her right, a 75-foot drop to the floor where she spotted the open grate she had entered through. She moved cautiously along the walkway for twenty feet before descending ten steps to a darkened second story landing. The landing contained a series of brine tanks that were connected by a labyrinth of rusted, three-inch pipes to the ghostly water tower looming behind her. Moving gingerly along the pipes, Jessi came alert as she picked up the sound of a voice somewhere ahead. As she stopped to listen, her hand unconsciously moved to her belt and sought out the reassuring lump of the pistol. The cold reality of her vulnerability froze her with indecision. With the gun, she was a force to be dealt with; without the gun, she had only her wits to help her. She wasn't sure that was enough.

Again she heard the voice somewhere ahead.

Jessi strained to listen, trying desperately to figure out where the sound was coming from. The building was a labyrinth, a puzzling, interconnected maze of rooms, stairways, and walkways that seemed to distort sound and camouflage its origin.

She had to make a decision. Should she retrace her tracks in hopes of recovering the pistol, or should she go ahead without it? If she went back, there was no guarantee she'd succeed. Only one thing was certain, she was wasting precious seconds by her indecision.

The sound of the voice drew her forward along the pipes to one of the cement brine tanks that was brimming with brackish, sour-smelling water. In order to cross it, Jessi had to climb four metal steps and then maneuver herself carefully across two, twenty-foot planks that had been laid side by side across the rim of the tank. The sagging planks were waterlogged and coated with a blanket of slippery moss. As Jessi inched over the three-foot-deep moat, she heard the voice again, and she could tell instantly that it belonged to a woman. The cadence was singsong, while the timbre sounded almost soothing. Negotiating the last foot of the planks, she descended four steps and then moved cautiously to where a metal handrail marked the end of the brine room. Ahead she could see a yellow glow and slivers of shadowy movement along the wall in the large, open-roofed room below. As the female voice grew louder, Jessi dropped to her knees and crawled close enough to the edge to peer over.

Twenty feet below, she saw Kathryn Weed on her knees in front of a girl, intently applying what appeared to be a liquid foundation make-up to the girl's flawless skin.

"The color is perfect for you." Kitty leaned back admiring her work. Then frowning, she took Julie's face in her hands. "Your tears are smudging my work. You really need to stop crying."

The sounds of Julie's soft sobs carried up to Jessi's ears.

Jessi was stunned. Could it be possible that the girl was Julie Abbott?

Jessi only half listened to the woman's ramblings as she scanned the room below, taking in the large trapdoor, the huge stainless steel tub, and several 55-gallon drums that were lined up against one wall. A circular metal staircase descended steeply from near where she was lying, ending abruptly on a narrow landing ten feet above Julie and the woman. As Jessi continued surveying the room, her eyes caught a slight movement off to the side. In a corner, hidden in shadows, a body was half lying, half sitting against the wall. It was *Lela!* Her desperate eyes locked into Jessi's as she struggled in vain against the duct tape restraints.

Jessi raised her finger to her lips, letting Lela know she saw her and to signal for her to remain quiet.

As Jessi watched from above, Kitty stood, obviously pleased as she admired her handiwork. Julie's hair was adorned with lavender ribbons, and the makeup had been applied so heavily, the girl resembled a mannequin.

"Perfect, you're just perfect." Kitty said as she picked up the Polaroid and stepped back a pace. "Smile." The flash went off. "One more for luck." Kitty snapped the shutter again and then set the photos aside to develop as she cleaned up the make-up, quickly stuffing it back into the small bag along with the mirror. She looked at the photos again. "Just beautiful. I don't want you to ever change. I'll be back soon with your dress. I think you'll like it." Kitty smiled at the whimpering Julie as if they were co-conspirators. With her smile intact, she left the room and locked the heavy door behind her.

Jessi wasted no time. She hurried to the circular stairway and moved down the slippery metal steps as rapidly and quietly as possible. Reaching the landing, she quickly removed her shoes and, dropping to her knees, crawled under the rail. Dangling over the edge, she swayed back and forth as her hands fought the slippery metal.

"Please God, don't let me break my leg."

Releasing her grip, she dropped to the cement floor. She got quickly to her feet and moved to Lela. "Be quiet," she whispered, as she unceremoniously ripped the duct tape from Lela's mouth wincing at the injuries she exposed.

"Of course I'll be quiet!" Lela whispered, irritably.

"Shhhh! Where's the other one, the man?" Jessi asked urgently, moving behind Lela to undo the tape binding her wrists together.

"I don't know. Where's your gun?"

"I lost it," Jessi replied with a shrug, pulling the duct tape from Lela's ankles.

"You lost it? What? What kind of a cop are you?"

"A dumb one, okay? Now shut up and help me," Jessi snapped as she hurried to Julie.

Lela was stiff after so many hours of lying on the cold cement; and had difficulty pulling herself upright. Her numb legs throbbed as she forced them to carry her across the floor to where Jessi was ripping the duct tape off the terrorized Julie's ankles and wrists. The quaking girl was trying not to cry, but she couldn't hold back the involuntary sobs, and they raked her thin body. Jessi knelt next to her and, grabbing the girl's head, clamped her hand firmly over her mouth and hissed in her ear. "Listen to me. I know you want to cry, but you can't. Not yet. Not a sound. I promise, we'll all have a good cry just as soon as we're out of here. Understand?"

Julie nodded weakly as Jessi forced a smile, removed her hand from the girl's mouth, and brushed the tears away. "Come on, let's go," Jessi said, standing and pulling the girl to her feet.

As Jessi had watched from above, she had noticed several 55-gallon ammonia drums lined up against the wall. She moved quickly to the drums and attempted to move one. The first two were full and wouldn't budge. The third was empty, and she carefully rolled it under the landing she had dropped from. Jessi and Lela grabbed Julie under the arms and hoisted her onto the drum. Julie reached for the staircase landing but was a foot short.

The teenager looked terribly vulnerable standing in her underpants and bra, thin legs and arms a mass of bruises, and shaking uncontrollably as she choked back sobs.

Jessi's and Lela 's eyes met. "If they come back, we're dead," Lela pronounced.

Jessi nodded at Lela, and the older woman quickly climbed onto the drum alongside Julie. The sudden shift in weight made the barrel tip slightly, but Jessi steadied it. Lela grabbed Julie around the waist and slowly lifted her until she could reach out and clutch the edge of the landing. Julie fought and strained to pull herself up, but her ordeal had left her weak, and she hung there, seconds away from giving up.

"Come on, sweetie; give it a try," Lela coaxed softly. Reaching up, she took Julie's feet in the palms of her hands, lifting her as high as possible and gritting her teeth as her aching muscles screamed out in protest!

In desperation, Julie seized at the railing and, catching it, swung her foot up onto the landing where she lay motionless, totally spent.

Lela looked down at Jessi from her uneasy perch on the drum. "Now what?"

"We're going to have to help each other," Jessi said softly, reaching up for Lela's hand.

"Watch our balance or we'll tip it over," Lela whispered, watching with concern as Jessi raised her bare left foot over the metal rim of the barrel and pulled herself up to where she was nose to nose with Lela, their arms around each other. "I didn't know you cared," Lela said without cracking a smile.

"Shut up! You first."

Lela nodded and reached for the railing. She was six inches shy. "I can't reach it."

"Yes you can. Very slowly raise your foot," Jessi instructed, interlocking the fingers of both hands and forming a stirrup for Lela to step into. The method had helped her climb the infamous "wall" at the academy, and she prayed it would work here.

"What do you think this is, Cirque Du Soleil?" Lela raised her right foot and placed it in Jessi's hand. The drum started to teeter, and they froze in place, afraid to even breathe. Jessi slowly spread her feet apart to stabilize the barrel.

"Is that the best you can do? Hell, you'd better start pumping some iron, girl!"

"Yeah, and maybe you could drop a few pounds," Jessi hissed, straining against Lela's weight. "Okay, on three. One, two, three! "

Lela reached out for the railing and missed, hitting against something soft. Looking up she saw Julie's determined face above her. The girl reached down, grabbed Lela's hands, and guided them to the railing.

"Climb, damnit!" Jessi urged, as Lela's foot slammed into her chest, scrambling for a toehold before settling onto Jessi's shoulders.

With Julie tugging and pulling, Lela managed to scramble onto the metal landing. Once there, she turned and reached back down with both hands for Jessi.

A gap of three inches separated their fingertips.

There was only one way Jessi could bridge it. She would have to jump. Jessi's eyes locked with Lela's, and they realized simultaneously that they'd only get one chance at it. It was a low-level trapeze act without a net, and their lives depended on the outcome.

Jessi braced herself and prepared to jump.

26.

❧

As the hot water came, Kitty bent over the sink and deliberately scrubbed her face with soap and a white washcloth until every inch of her skin was bright pink. The make-up case was sitting on the counter, and as she opened it she felt a rush of excitement sweep over her, warming her face and making her cheeks tingle. She dried her face thoroughly before applying the liquid foundation, smoothing it out with powder from a small compact. She put on black eyeliner, and looked at her eyebrows critically, tweezing out a stray hair before tracing over her brows with a dark pencil, then expertly applying blue eye shadow to match her dress. She finished her eyes with black mascara. A thick overlay of dark, pink lipstick highlighted her effort and, as she stood back from the mirror to admire her work, she smiled. She was pleased, oblivious to the garish picture she had just painted.

Moving out of the small bathroom, Kitty kneeled and reaching under the bed, pulled out a plastic K-Mart bag. Standing, she opened the bag and took out a frilly, size five, blue dress, removed the price tags, and laid it carefully on the bed. It would be perfect for Julie. She slipped out of her jeans and pulled her loose-fitting blouse over her head, exposing her thick waist and massive arms. Sitting down on the edge of the bed, she ripped open a new package of panty hose and pulled them on. Moving to the closet, she opened the door and ran her hand down a long row of dresses. As she looked for the right outfit, her fingers moved to her neck and sought out the comforting feel of the heavy brass key that hung between her massive breasts. A smile flitted over her lips as she removed a blue, half-length, silk paisley print and stepped into it. It would be perfect for the party. As she buttoned the dress, Pinky's voice startled her.

"You really get into this shit, don't cha?"

Ignoring the remark, Kitty opened a polished, wooden jewelry box that was sitting on top of her oak chest of drawers and, taking out a string of imitation pearls, fastened them around her thick neck before turning to face the leering Pinky. "Is Charley back yet?"

"Haven't seen him," Pinky lied. "Tell you what, though. Seeing as you're all dressed up, what do you say we make a little nasty before we do them, huh?" He reached out and caught both of her wrists. The look in Kitty's eyes caught him by surprise. There was something there, something he'd never seen before.

"Let me take off my dress, I don't want to wrinkle it" she replied, her voice strangely flat as she moved back to the closet. Her decision was made in a millisecond: Just like the others, Pinky had outlived his usefulness and would *never* touch her again. Reaching into the closet between two of her coats, her hand quickly located the butt of her father's ten-inch hunting knife that was hanging from a wooden peg. As she started to slide the razor-sharp knife from its leather sheath, she heard the crash!

"What the fuck was that?" Pinky said, starting toward the door.

"Check the front!" Kitty commanded, pulling the knife and concealing it next to her leg as she followed Pinky out of the bedroom.

"I wouldn't mind if the bitch in the convertible came back," Pinky said over his shoulder, disappearing into the meat shop as Kitty rushed through the maze of hallways until she was standing in front of the killing room. Taking the key from around her neck, she quickly turned the key in the lock, pushed the heavy door open, and stepped in. Kitty's eyes strained as they darted over the cavernous room.

"What on earth?" Her stunned voice echoed back at her.

Failing to see Julie or Lela where she had left them, she turned in a slow circle, searching the shadows until she spotted the empty ammonia drum tipped on its side. Looking up at the landing and stairway, she caught just a flash of movement as someone disappeared into the old brine room.

"There's no way out of here!" Kitty shouted.

Kitty darted to a side door and opened it to reveal an assortment of mops, buckets, and a ten-foot aluminum stepladder, which she quickly unfolded and set up directly under the landing.

"You're going to make me very angry!" she shouted as she clutched the hunting knife in her bulky fist, unconsciously feeling the razor-sharp edge with her thumb as she carefully climbed the ladder, stepping onto the platform and striding purposefully up the metal stairs that vibrated noisily under her ample weight.

Reaching the top of the staircase, Kitty had to pause to let her eyes adjust to the dark, and the familiar shadows of the brine room came into focus. She smiled inwardly. This building was her life, her playpen. She knew each room, every hallway, every staircase, and every shadow.

"There's no place to hide from me. Don't you see that? There's no way out. No escape."

She scrambled up the four steps to the planks that bridged the brine tank and started across, holding the knife at her side, hidden in the loose folds of her dress.

"Don't you see, that whore wants to take you away from me. She's not your friend. I am. I'm your friend. I went shopping, and I bought a new dress for you to wear and everything. It's blue, like mine. Don't you see I'm simply taking care of you? Nobody else will. It's so silly to hide like this! "

Kitty caught a darting movement on her right. She sensed instantly where they were hiding even before she saw the bottom of their feet below the wooden shelves stacked haphazardly against the wall. "I used to hide behind there, too."

Lela and Julie were pressed against the damp cement wall behind one of the shelves. Julie buried her head in Lela's chest and tried, unsuccessfully, to choke back her tiny sobs.

"Oh, you're scared, aren't you? I understand. I really do," Kitty cooed as she continued across the plank.

Three feet below Kitty, and immersed in the brine tank, Jessi silently raised her head above the foul water and let the cool air rush into her empty lungs. As Kitty raised her foot to take another step, Jessi put her back against the plank and lifted with all her might. The plank jerked out from under Kitty's feet and sent her tumbling into the water where she slammed against the side of the cement tank, splitting her forehead open in a nasty gash that exposed her skull. Kitty flailed wildly, clawing at the water to regain her balance as blood gushed from the gaping wound into her eyes.

Jessi pounced on the larger woman's chest and, with adrenalin pumping into her bloodstream, held Kitty's bloody face under the brackish water. Kitty bucked like an enraged bull, striking out with her balled fists, but Jessi held on, her legs closing tightly around Kitty's thick sides, mustering every ounce of her strength to keep the infuriated, gasping woman under water. Kitty continued thrashing, using her strong legs to propel her knees into Jessi's back.

Kitty had dropped the knife in her fall and as the lack of oxygen made her light-headed and panic started building in her heaving chest, her hands darted over the floor of the tank around her; blindly groping, she felt the familiar shape of the knife brush against her fingertips. In desperation, Kitty clutched the heavy knife and swung wildly with all her strength, feeling it sink deeply into her attacker's flesh.

Jessi felt like she'd been hit with a ball bat; her wind was instantly gone. The sharp, splitting pain in her side forced her to release her grip as the infuriated Kitty exploded out of the water, choking and gasping for breath. Kitty's eyes flashed with hatred as she watched the wounded Jessi flounder in the water.

Jessi felt the sting of the water hitting her lungs, and it brought her to her knees where she gasped, ineffectually, for oxygen. The crazed woman slogged toward her, and Jessi saw her own death reflected in Kitty's wild eyes. If this was her death, so be it, but she refused to die in this awful, smelly water! Jessi lunged at Kitty's knees, but the larger woman simply brushed her aside and raised the knife for the kill. As Jessi moved to the side and raised her arms to ward off the blow, she caught a glimpse of motion off to the side. In the next instant she saw a wild-eyed Lela swing a four-foot length of metal pipe with such force that it impacted with a sickening 'crunch" against the back of Kitty's head! The big woman staggered, took an awkward step to the left, and then collapsed. Lela raised the pipe and hit Kitty again, leaving her face down and still in the bloodstained water.

Jessi pulled herself out of the tank and removed the pipe from Lela's stiffened fingers. "That's enough," Jessi said, her voice sounding oddly strained as she clutched her injured side.

Julie emerged from the shadows and touched Jessi's hand that was covering her wound. Blood was oozing from between Jessi's fingers.

"You're hurt," Julie said, her voice sounding as fragile as a bird's.

"I'll be okay. We've got to keep moving. Come on." Jessi dropped the pipe with a loud clang and, grabbing Julie's hand, jerked her along the slippery feeder pipes. The terrified threesome moved quickly past the smaller brine tanks and rushed up the steps to the metal walkway that led past the water tower. Looking back, Jessi waited for Lela to catch up and, pushing Julie ahead of her, grabbed Lela's arm and yanked her up the steps. "Come on!"

They moved quickly along the walkway, their bare feet strumming against the perforated metal, making the rusted handrail vibrate noisily. The walkway dead-ended at the freezer door where Jessi grabbed the handle and pulled. It opened with a rush of cold air.

To the already terrorized Julie, the thought of entering such a room was like entering hell itself, and she froze in place. "No, please. I can't go in there."

Jessi grabbed Julie's face between her hands and pleaded with her eyes. "Julie, you have to trust me. There's no other way out."

"*Kitty*!"

Pinky's angry voice exploded from the nearby brine room like a gunshot, sending the three women plunging into the ice room. As Jessi pulled the door shut with her right hand, she heard the unmistakable sound of heavy boots charging up the steps and pounding down the metal walkway toward them. She felt her dripping-wet jacket for the Mag-lite. It was gone, lost somewhere in the brine tank. She flipped on a light switch next to the door and the room was bathed in a dim yellow glow from a lone, 40-watt bulb hanging from the ceiling.

"He's right behind us. Keep moving. There's a door on the other side," Jessi whispered, her breath vaporizing as she pushed Lela and Julie down an aisle between rows of huge ice blocks.

As Lela and Julie scurried ahead, Jessi's eyes darted from side to side, looking for anything she could use as a weapon. She should have hung on to the metal pipe, but it was too late now. She spotted an old-straw broom resting against the wall and, snatching it up, hurried toward the center of the room. Raising the broom to smash the light bulb, she ran directly into the 150-pound block and tackle that dangled from the overhead track. The force of the blow knocked her to her knees. Her ears rang, and she swayed dizzily as she fought back an overpowering urge to vomit. She stumbled to her feet, picked up the broom with hands sticky from her own blood, and smashed the burning light bulb just as the door snapped open twenty feet behind her.

Pinky stood highlighted in the doorway, the blade of his knife catching the light and sending a thin reflection flashing through the darkness. He flicked the light switch several times.

"You like the dark, do you? I do my best work in the dark," he said, closing the door and inching his way along the wall. "You did a number on poor Kitty," Pinky said with a chuckle. "How much do I owe you?" As he spoke, his hand worked along the rough, now familiar wall, searching for the secondary switch. "Aren't you girls chilly in here? I am. Hell, I can only work in here about fifteen minutes before I need a break, and I wear a big old parka and gloves."

Pinky's hand found the secondary switch, and as he flipped it on, the room was instantly bathed in the iridescent glow from a light globe burning somewhere beneath the flooring. Shafts of soft, blue light stabbed the darkness, illuminating a large table saw in one corner.

"Ollee, ollee oxen free," Pinky said softly, his cold, flat eyes scanning the room. As he looked down, a smile flattened his lips and exposed his crooked front teeth. A neat trail of blood drops led toward the front and then disappeared behind a block of ice.

Lela and Julie were huddled, shivering, on the floor in the far corner of the side room, wedged between the wall and a line of ice blocks that had been covered with a large piece of canvas. Julie's teeth started to chatter, causing Lela to pull her tightly to her chest and whisper, "Shhh!"

In order to cover the freezing girl, Lela pulled the canvas away from one of the ice blocks and tried to arrange the rough, stiffened material over Julie's shivering body. As Lela held the quivering girl, she realized a face was staring at them from the block of ice. For a moment, Lela assumed she was looking at her own reflection in the glassy ice, but when she looked closer, her heart stopped! She was gazing at the lifeless face of Sammy Deavers, her dead eyes highlighted with eye shadow, frozen in a perpetual expression of puzzled confusion. In the block to their left, Lela could barely make out the silhouette of another frozen face. She closed her eyes and kept Julie's head turned away from the blocks.

Pinky followed the blood trail to the front of the room before he saw it turn back toward the rear. They were no longer just crimson drops, but now were thick red smears. He could tell the prey was weakening. His heart quickened as he remembered that as a fourteen-year-old he had gut shot a big doe that had done precisely the same thing. "Getting tired, are you? A little cold? Why don't you just stop, and I'll put you out of your misery. I'm not such a bad guy."

He was almost to the rear door before he noticed, suddenly, that the smears had crossed the original blood drops. For some reason she was going in a circle. He heard a slight stir ahead and raised his eyes from the floor just in time to catch the swinging 150 pound block and tackle flush in the face, pulverizing the bones in his nose and cheek and dislodging a half dozen teeth. Pinky fell backwards, bouncing off a block of ice before flopping heavily to the floor, unconscious.

Jessi started crawling, frantically forcing herself to concentrate on moving one leg, one arm, one leg, one arm, until she was wedged tightly between a block of ice and the wall, hidden from the predator's eyes where she struggled gamely against the terribly overwhelming urge to give up. She leaned her head back for just a moment.

She opened her eyes and saw she was lying in the front of her dad's boat. She turned her head slightly and watched Deke cast his line out in a looping half circle that landed forty yards from them, sending out concentric circles that raced away, spreading faster and faster.

Deke looked down at her. "Let the line play out a little then reel 'em in."

Lela and Julie hovered behind the block of ice, listening with growing panic as Pinky moaned in pain.

Julie clung desperately to Lela, her teeth chattered noisily.

"Shhh," Lela soothed, pressing the girl's chilled flesh as close to her as she could.

Julie's eyes dropped to the floorboards and she saw something odd in the lighted gap between the flooring. Julie tugged at Lela's arm and pointed down. Six feet below them, Jessi's 9mm pistol rested on a conveyor belt. Lela's eyes darted over the floor and settled on a small, metal grate. She pushed herself silently along the floor, following the grating, the sawdust masking the sound of her movement until she spotted the metal inspection plate that served as cover. Her cold fingers traced the round outline of the frozen metal, desperately seeking a finger hold. When she found a notch, she strained to lift it free of its flush seat, but it wouldn't budge. She tried again, prying and lifting, ignoring the shooting pain of her fingernail ripping away from the quick until the heavy lid moved slightly. Lela took a deep breath and forced herself to lift it free of its seat, and suddenly Julie was with her, pushing the awkward inspection plate aside. The opening the lid revealed was barely sixteen inches in diameter and Lela knew instantly she couldn't fit into it. At exactly the same instant, Julie realized she could fit, and without a moment's hesitation, lowered herself into the hole.

As Pinky lay on his stomach, groaning, a mixture of blood and saliva bubbled from his nostrils and mingled with the sawdust. He raised his bloody face from the floor and looked around the room.

"Fucking bitch!" The words were slurred, barely understandable as his mashed tongue found the holes where his teeth should have been. Grabbing his knife off the floor, he pulled himself onto his hands and knees and followed the heavy smears of blood. When he moved, his head and neck exploded with pain and a gut wrenching bellow erupted wetly from deep in his throat. "Ahhhhhhhrrrrr!"

Jessi, blood seeping from her side, was lying less than six feet away, watching him. Pinky's hand closed on her ankle in a vice-like grip and slowly dragged her backwards. Jessi's fingernails searched in vain for even a crack to stop her slide as the crazed Pinky hauled her across the sawdust-covered floor and flipped her onto her back. As she looked up, his mangled, bloody face loomed over her and a reddish vapor vented from his shattered nostrils.

"You're fucking bitches and I'm going to kill all of you!" he screamed as he raised his knife.

"Jessi!"

Lela's terrified voice came from somewhere behind her. She turned slightly to see Lela push something along the floor toward her and in an instant, Jessi's pistol was within a foot of her hand.

Jessi reached out, blindly clutching at the smooth wood for the familiar shape. At the precise instant she knew all was lost, her fingers found it.

The *boom* of her first shot blasted in her ear and caught Pinky in the throat! The second *exploded* directly into his right eye, and her third round missed him altogether, but it didn't matter. Pinky's lifeless body slumped heavily to the floor where it was surrounded by a fast-growing pool of steaming blood.

Jessi's ears roared as she forced herself upright and looked across the room to see Lela and Julie, their faces ashen, rise from behind the ice blocks. "I think I'm going to need your help."

Lela and Julie rushed to where Jessi stood on wobbly legs. Blood from her wound was seeping through her blouse and running freely down her side.

"She's hurt real bad," Julie said.

Jessi clutched Lela's arm tightly. "I can't walk. Leave me. Go get help."

"I'll stay with her." Julie said, her voice quivering with frozen fear.

"No! No, don't leave Julie here. Take her with you."

"Nobody's leaving anybody! We're going to leave here together! Now come on, don't be such a damn wimp! I can't do everything," Lela mocked, draping Jessi's arm over her shoulder as Julie did the same on Jessi's other side.

As they exited the ice room into the warm air of the hallway, they were immediately faced with stairs going up, and others leading down. Had Jessi been alert, she would have directed them up the stairs and through the CO2 room, but she was barely able to keep her feet moving, let alone give them directions. The down staircase was dark and clammy and dumped them into a hallway where they were faced with yet another heavy freezer door. Lela grabbed the heavy metal handle and pulled it open.

Julie's expression dropped and she faltered. Lela read the fear in the girl's eyes.

"We don't have a choice, honey," Lela replied as the three of them stepped into the frigid compartment where rows of butchered, frozen sides of beef hung from hooks, bathed in the dim, yellow glow of a bulb that was mounted over the door. As they half carried, half dragged Jessi through the icy room, Lela tried to bolster Julie's sinking spirits. "I've been in this room before, honey; we're almost out. Think how good you're going to feel when we walk out into the sunshine."

"I need to call my mom and dad," Julie replied, thinking of her mom's happy voice answering the phone at home.

"I'm going to take a nice, long, hot bath," Lela said as she stopped and adjusted her hold on Jessi's injured side.

They were within three feet of the exit door when it crashed open and a large figure burst toward them, wildly swinging a fire axe with a horrific scream!

"Ahhhhhhhhhhh!"

The glistening blade arched downward, barely missing Jessi and slicing through a side of beef less than an inch from Lela's head.

The three of them tried to retreat as the figure advanced. Kitty's bloody face came into clear view, her wild, unblinking eyes fixed and locked on Jessi as she raised the axe for a second swing, "She is mine! She belongs to me!" Kitty bellowed.

Jessi instinctively raised her 9mm, jerking off two wild shots that tore harmlessly into the thick wooden ceiling. As she tried to steady her arm for another shot, Kitty darted forward, hitting the gun with the axe handle, sending it clattering across the floor. Jessi pushed Lela and Julie away from the onslaught. She was totally spent and watched, almost dispassionately, as the crazed Kitty raised the axe for the final blow.

A *deafening blast* lifted the enraged Kitty off the floor and slammed her back across the room.

Cutler lowered the smoking shotgun and hurried to where Julie and Lela were kneeling on the floor, cradling Jessi's head. "What the hell happened?" Cutler shouted as he dropped to his knees and laid the shotgun on the floor.

"She saved our lives , that's what happened," Lela blurted.

"Her side is hurt bad!" Julie sobbed, wiping tears from her face as Cutler leaned over Jessi and took her hand.

"Do you feel you can be moved?"

Jessi nodded. "Get me out of here," she said in a throaty half whisper.

Cutler gently placed his hands under Jessi and picked her up.

Red and Kiko burst into the room, their side arms raised and ready. As Red advanced on the Kitty's bloody body, he froze momentarily. "For chris- sakes, it's Kathryn Weed," he gasped, reaching out and searching the woman's thick wrist for a pulse. "She ain't dead, but she soon will be."

As Cutler carried Jessi out the door of the freezer, he turned to Lela. "Where's the other one?"

"Back through there," Lela replied, pointing toward the far door. Her arm circled Julie's shoulder in a protective cocoon.

"We'll check it out. You get these folks outta here," Red said, moving with Kiko toward the rear door of the large freezer.

27.

❧

Lela, her worn carryall in hand and wearing hospital pajamas as if they were the latest fashion statement, paced nervously along the hospital hallway. Her bottom lip was puffy and looked sore from the six stitches it took to close the jagged tear. The numerous deep bruises and cuts on her arms, legs and fingers marked her ordeal.

Cutler watched her nervous pacing from the other end of the hallway as he talked on his cell phone. "Janie, all I know is she's out of surgery. Doc Carollo's in with her now. I'll let you know the minute we hear anything... Right. I will. Good bye." He hung up the phone and slumped down in a nearby chair. As he waited he picked up an old edition of *People Magazine* but found that the cast of "Friends" couldn't inspire him to get past the cover. He tossed the magazine down and returned his gaze to Lela, estimating that she had probably paced five miles in the last two hours. He had to admit that he was wrong about her involvement. He wasn't willing to go so far as to believe in her psychic powers, but she wasn't a murderer, and he was relieved without really knowing why. She was definitely more than a little eccentric.

Lela caught Cutler studying her and, moving quickly toward him, pounced aggressively.

"Why in the hell do they have to keep us out? What's the big secret? Probably afraid we'll see them screw up! They'd better account for every goddamn sponge in that operating room!"

Cutler didn't even try to stop her tirade. She'd been through hell, and she deserved a little slack.

"Well, I'm waiting."

"Waiting for what?" Cutler asked.

"For your apology.

Cutler gave her a look. "Would it make you feel better if I apologized?"

"Not really, because I'm thinking of suing your whole fucking department for defamation of my fucking character! You gave me a fucking lie detector test! How could you think I was involved with those...*people?* How could you even think I would hurt those little girls?"

Cutler saw the tears welling in her eyes and her angry attempt to wipe them away. He had just a glimpse of her exposed underside, and then she turned on him again, but before their exchange could reheat, Red, Murray, and Kiko entering from the side door entrance interrupted them. Lela glared at all of them before continuing to pace.

"How's Jessi?" Murray asked.

"She's out of surgery. That's all we know," Cutler responded.

Kiko crossed himself unconsciously. "Well, I'll tell you this. After looking at that place out there, I honestly don't know how they got out of there alive, boss. Swear to God, it looked like a scene out of a horror movie or something. We found poor old Charley Weed hanging from the rafters, gutted out like a slaughtered animal."

"Charley?" Cutler shook his head in disbelief.

Cutler and Red nodded, each appreciating the horror of Kiko's statement.

"We're ninety-nine percent sure that's Samantha Deavers' body in the block of ice.

"The others, we're not sure of," Kiko added.

"Others? What others?" Cutler asked, his tone reflecting his stunned surprise.

"We found five other bodies frozen in separate blocks," Kiko said.

"All young females," Red added. "And hold onto your hat, boss, 'cause I think one of them might be Kathryn's little sister, Molly."

"Oh my God," Cutler said, stunned as he recalled the countless hours his father had spent looking for that girl from one end of Grace County to the other.

"The FBI and State boys are thicker than fleas on a dog out there. They're taking the living quarters apart piece by piece," Red volunteered.

"What are they doing with the bodies?" Cutler asked.

"They're going to knock out the second story wall and lift the blocks out with a crane," Kiko answered. "That ought to be quite a sight, huh?"

The men stood for a moment, surrounded by an uneasy silence, each lost in their own visions of the horror they had witnessed. Red finally spoke.

"How do you explain Kathryn Weed? Hell, I figured her for just regular folk," Red asked, genuinely perplexed. "It never dawned on me she'd do something like this."

"Why should it have dawned on you? " Cutler flared. "Hell sakes, just because we're cops don't mean we can't have trust and faith in our friends and neighbors. Jesus Christ, where would that leave us?"

Cutler's statement hung unanswered in the air for a moment before the recovery room door opened and Dr. Carollo stepped out. The tall doctor wore the same tired half smile that he had worn the day he had slapped Cutler on the rear and welcomed him to Deep Texas thirty-five years previously.

"How's she doing, Doc?" Cutler asked as Lela shouldered him aside to push herself closer.

"She's okay, right?" Lela blurted. "She's going to make it?"

"The knife sliced right between her ribs. Missed her aorta by about this much." Carollo held up his fingers indicating about a quarter inch. "The muscles in her side were just shredded. Her lung was punctured, and it collapsed and filled up with blood and other fluid, but we took care of that. She has a couple of broken ribs, a dislocated shoulder, and plenty of cuts and bruises, but I'd say she's a pretty lucky young woman."

"Are you out of your mind? She was nearly killed by two maniacs, and you say she's lucky? She isn't lucky at all; she's just one tough cookie! What world do you people live in out here?" Lela asked, rhetorically.

"Hey, Doc, can we see her?" Cutler asked.

"Yes, but keep it short. She's still pretty groggy. She's going to be in a lot of pain for a few days." Carollo turned to Lela. "And don't bring up *anything* that's going to upset her."

"Ah, shucks. And I was going to talk about our old friend, Pinky, and seeing Sammy Deavers face staring at us out of a frozen chunk of ice–reminisce about the fun times we've had running from those maniacs." Lela turned away quickly, tears threatening again, and opened Jessi's door.

"Is that woman always like that?" Carollo asked.

"Pretty much," Cutler said, following Lela into Jessi's room.

When Cutler and the others entered the room, Lela was already standing over Jessi's bed inspecting the IV drip and tracing the lines of the beeping monitors that were hooked to her. Jessi was wearing an oxygen mask and raised her hand weakly to Cutler and the others, forcing a tired smile.

"Don't try to talk or anything," Lela said softly. "You're so high you'd probably say something stupid."

Murray stepped forward and took Jessi's hand. "You're really something. If I had a medal, I'd pin it on you, but it looks like you already have enough needles in you."

Jessi tried to take off her mask, but Lela stopped her.

"Leave that on. I'm not saying that it works as well as my crystals, but I haven't got them set up yet, " Lela said, setting down her carryall on the foot of Jessi's bed. She quickly brought out her precious crystals and began placing them on Jessi's nightstand. "I'm arranging these for maximum healing effect. Make sure the nurses keep their damn hands off them."

Cutler moved to the bed and lightly touched Jessi's hand. "I'm glad you're okay. Everybody at the office sends their regards."

Jessi nodded as Cutler's concerned eyes took in all the medical paraphernalia. " I just talked to your boss in Houston. They send their very best wishes for a speedy recovery. He said to tell you to make it quick. He wants you to get your butt back to work."

Jessi smiled through the mask as the door opened behind her and a man stuck his head in. "She up for a little more company?"

"Hey, look who's here!" Cutler said, moving to hold the door open as Gary Abbott pushed Julie into the room in a wheelchair. Julie's red-eyed mother, Terri, not willing to release her rescued daughter's hand for even the second it took to move through he doorway, followed closely.

Julie wore a loose fitting green hospital gown that did little to hide the bruises on her thin arms and legs. The girl's eyes lit up when she saw Lela and Jessi, and she struggled out of the wheelchair to give Lela a tight hug. "When they had me, I prayed that someone would come for me and you did. I know in my heart that God sent you to me. You're my guardian angels." Julie moved to the bed and, burying her head on Jessi's chest, started sobbing softly.

Jessi removed her oxygen mask and stroked Julie's long dark hair. "It's okay, honey. We're all okay now," Jessi half whispered.

"Thanks to *you* we're okay. Lucky for Julie and me that you just don't know when to quit," Lela said as she removed the quartz crystal necklace from around her neck and placed it over Julie's head. "I'm giving you this so we can keep our eye on you. Right Jessi?"

Julie laughed and fingered the necklace as Jessi reached out and took Lela's slender hand. "If you hadn't got that woman off me when you did, we wouldn't be having this conversation, Lela. Have I thanked you yet? You're *my* hero."

"Let's not get all sentimental here," Lela said, faking irritability.

There was an awkward moment of silence before Terri Abbott nudged her imposing husband toward Jessi's bed.

The sizable Gary took a deep breath to fortify himself, shook Cutler's hand, and cleared his throat. "I'm, ah, not real good at expressing myself sometimes, most of the time actually, but I, we, Terri and I, we just want you people to know that you have given us back something that we, ahh, pretty much figured we'd lost," Gary said, biting his lip as he rested his rough, calloused hand on his daughter's slender shoulder. "We're not wealthy. We don't have much to offer you folks except our gratitude and friendship. I want you to know that if you ever need anything, a place to stay, a new roof on your house, a room sheet rocked, hell, anything at all. I don't know what else, anything, I..." Gary's voice broke and his wide shoulders shook as the enormous relief finally caught up with him, and he turned away to hide his sobs.

Terri and Julie went to Gary, and the three of them embraced.

As Jessi watched the Abbott family console each other, Dr. Carollo entered and replaced her oxygen mask. "I'm going to give you something to help you rest. All your friends are going to have to leave now."

Cutler was the last out. He paused in the doorway and then returned to kiss Jessi lightly on the forehead. "I'll be back later."

She watched as the tall doctor injected something into her IV tube. "I'll be looking in on you every hour or so. Get some rest now."

Jessi was finally alone. Now she, too, could cry.

Jessi spent the ensuing forty-eight hours flat on her back in a morphine induced stupor that kept her balanced in the nowhere land between deep sleep and semi-consciousness.

She was aware of nurses poking and prodding, their whispered voices faraway, heard Dr. Carollo murmuring and Cutler's quiet questioning voice in the background.

She felt the touch of a smooth coolness being massaged on her temples and realized that Lela was plying her own crystal healing power. Even the sweet smell of burning incense was comforting.

Nothing really penetrated the thick fog that enveloped her. One moment she was crawling over a sawdust floor, fleeing from the monstrous vision of Pinky, the next moment she felt Cutler close, holding her hand. His face hovered above her for a few moments before being replaced by her Houston patrol partner's. Tom Odom's large hand touched her cheek gently as he smiled down at her.

"Hey partner, 'bout time you reported for duty."

Jessi smiled and raised her hand in a weak greeting. "You look nice," she said in a raspy voice that was barely audible.

"Why, thank you," Odom replied, standing and giving Jessi a 360 degree look at his dress uniform.

"Have you got a ceremony or something?" Jessi asked.

"Highway Patrolman Marty Burris' funeral is today. Since I was already up here they made me the official Houston P.D. rep."

Jessi fought to make sense of the information. "What day is it?"

"Wednesday."

"How can that be? What time is it?"

The burly Odom checked his watch. "0930 hours on the button. Lose a day or so, did you?"

Jessi shook her head and yawned deeply. "I lost something."

Odom sat back down. "The doctor was just in. He said you were doing great. Said you'd be going home in no time."

"Good. I'm ready."

"Everybody on patrol sends their best. We're all walking around with our chests out. We're real proud of what you did, Jessi."

"You should be." Lela's voice drifted up from the darkened corner.

"Is that Lela?" Jessi asked.

Odom nodded. "Yeah. She's been on duty since I got here. She's more protective than Mark Mooring and Friday," Odom joked, referring to a particularly aggressive canine officer and his German Shepard."

"I'll take that as a compliment," Lela said as she moved to the bed and assisted Jessi in taking a long drink of water. As she held the straw to Jessi's cracked lips she smiled at Odom. "Don't let him fool you, Jessi. You're partner's a much better watch dog than he lets on. And while he's on duty I'm going to go outside and stretch my legs a bit," Lela said as she handed the water to Odom and headed for the door. "No, no, don't see me out. I know the way."

With Lela gone, Odom's tone turned serious. "Jessi, I have to take off, but before I leave, I want you to be aware that there's blood in the water and the sharks are circling."

Jessi's lips were painfully dry. "I've got numb brain, Tom. What are you talking about?"

"You have a good friend upstairs. He wants you to know that certain members of the murder squad are under investigation for their lack of professionalism in the way they responded to this case from the get go."

"Let me guess," Jessi replied. "The suits are looking to cut their losses."

"Exactly. So don't be surprised if you're paid a courtesy call by the dynamic duo. Be very careful of what you say. In fact, if you can get away with it, say nothing. Tell them to fuck themselves and if they have a problem with that to look me up. I'm serious, Jessi, I wouldn't put it past the bastards to wear a wire in here."

"I don't care if they wear a wire. I have nothing to hide from anybody," Jessi said, exhaustion enveloping her like a heavy blanket.

"I know you don't. Just be careful," Odom said. "Go back to sleep, I'll see you after the funeral."

Odom stood, replaced the water on the nightstand and started out. Jessi was asleep before her partner had even cleared the door.

She slept fitfully before the overwhelming smell of flowers filled her nostrils. She forced her eyes open and looked around the small room which was overflowing with flower arrangements. Her brain registered chrysanthemums, gladiolus, irises, lavender and roses all in a riot of colors and fragrances, before settling on Lela sitting in a corner, framed by two especially colorful bouquets. She was aware that Lela was busy sketching and tried to get her attention before she saw her dad beckoning her from the Bloodworm and she joined him, falling back into a deep, and this time uninterrupted sleep.

On the third day, Jessi was able to sit up and eat solid food for the first time. She was famished and developed an intense craving for a strawberry malt that Lela supplied from the Artic Circle down the block.

Murray, Jessi and Lela watched the local television news coverage of Marty Burris's memorial ceremony. They watched in silence as Marty's polished brass urn was carried out of St. Michael's Church, through a sea of uniforms, lead by honorary pallbearers, John Cutler, Red Cordell, Kiko Avila, Frank Cortez, Louie Adams, and Jimmy Park.

The hearse drove slowly to the rural cemetery leading a procession of over two hundred law enforcement vehicles from over fifty jurisdictions followed by hundreds of cars and pickups of friends and neighbors who simply wanted to pay their respects.

A nurse's aide brought Jessi's lunch tray and stayed to watch as the solemn services played out under brilliantly blue skies. A Catholic priest presided over the grave site and Janie Cortez offered a final tribute. A rifle salute by the local VFW marked the end of the services. The flag that draped Marty's coffin was folded in a neat, tight triangle that John Cutler presented to Ellie Burris. When Ellie, flanked by her two sons, stood and embraced John, Jessi and the others wept openly.

Jessi was dozing when the two FBI agents who had worked the Julie Abbott kidnapping entered the hospital room.

"Ms. Cole, are you up to a little company?"

Lela stood, protectively, from her perch in the corner. "Can't you see she needs her rest?"

"That's okay, Lela, I'm awake," Jessi said forcing her eyes open.

Both men were wearing dark suits and sunglasses which they removed as they approached her bed. Jessi noticed that the taller of the agents was carrying a long, brown envelope. He was an older man in his mid fifties with pale skin, graying hair and a thin face which contrasted to his younger partner's dark hair, round face and florid complexion.

"Who the hell are you two, the Blue's Brothers?" Lela asked.

"We're from the FBI field office in Waco," the older man explained. "I'm agent David Stackhouse and this is agent Terry Barber."

Jessi nodded. "I remember you from the office. What can I do for you?"

Agent Barber stepped forward. "Actually, we were hoping we could do something for you." His eyes moved to Lela "What *both* of you did was truly incredible."

"Tell me about it," Lela nodded.

Agent Stackhouse held up the envelope for emphasis. "We wanted to bring you up to speed on what's come down so far." He opened the envelope and handed Jessi six Polaroid photos each showing a terrified young girl staring blankly into the lens. "We've identified all of the frozen bodies. The families have been notified and the remains are being shipped out today. The M.E. said all of them were strangled."

Jessi looked at each of the photos and shook her head. "What a waste."

"Having their children's remains returned to them for burial has brought a needed closure to a lot of folks," Barber explained.

Stackhouse took over. "Apparently, Wesley Covine, aka Pinky, was pretty active himself. We found a bunch of stuff in his suitcase: rings, necklaces, and a couple of ID cards. We've got an entire task force working overtime trying to track his movements over the last few years. We ran his DNA profile through our system and came up with five hits on unsolved female homicides, and this just a preliminary number. I have a feeling it's going to go higher."

Jessi noticed the troubled look that washed over Lela's face.

"After you get out of here and have time to write your report, we'd appreciate you sending us a copy," Stackhouse said.

Jessi nodded. "I'll get to it as soon as I can." Jessi held up the Polaroids. "Where did these pictures come from?"

"Kitty kept a scrapbook and journal. We found it under the floorboard in her closet. Besides the pictures, there were stacks of letters. Apparently Kathryn Weed traveled with church groups to prisons here in Texas and Oklahoma. She'd flirt with these hard-assed cons and get them to write her. Before long she'd offer them a job and a place to stay when they got out. The cons ended up helping her kidnap the victims. She let them rape the girls, but they weren't allowed to bruise them in anyway. And when the cons outlasted their usefulness..."

"Let me guess," Jessi interjected. "She froze them?"

"We can't be sure at this point, but based on some hints in her journal, we're betting she might made them into hamburger or sausage," Stackhouse replied matter of factly.

Jessi shuddered. "I knew there was a good reason for being a vegetarian."

"Apparently, one of her cons, Ralph Porter, went nuts and beat Michelle Sandoval so badly that Kitty aka Kathryn couldn't add her to her *collection*. After Ralph tosses the girl in the dumpster, Kitty does away with Ralph. This leaves her short of help, so she goes on a recruiting trip to Huntsville and she hooks up with Pinky."

Terry Barber took up the tale. "Including Marty Burris, we believe that Kathryn Weed is responsible for at least twelve murders. The FBI profiler called me this morning and gave me all this psychological mumbo jumbo. He thinks she's a textbook example of split personality disorder and about twenty other disorders all wrapped up in her low self-esteem and her jealously of her little sister. I guess each of the killings was somehow a reenactment of Molly's *last* birthday party. We found a birthday cake complete with thirteen candles and 'Happy Birthday, Molly,' written on it."

"To summarize, Kathryn, or Kitty was one sick lady."

Lela was silent and sullen in the wake of the agents visit. Jessi sensed she was troubled but she didn't want to press her. After a long fifteen minutes of silence, Jessi finally spoke. "Lela, are you alright?"

"He's the one," Lela replied flatly.

"What are you talking about? Who?"

"Pinky, Wesley, whoever the evil bastard was, he's been here," she tapped her temple. "Here in my nightmares. It seems like I've carried his stench forever."

"Not any more you don't," Jessi said soothingly. "That's over."

A rap on the door caused them to jump. Lela's expression fell when the door opened and Houston's murder squad detectives, Steve Tyley and Grant Eisom entered. The balding Tyley was smiling from ear to ear as he approached the side of Jessi's bed. "There's our hero."

Eisom was carrying a bouquet of flowers and a small box of chocolates which he handed to Jessi. "Glad to see you're doing better."

"What are you two doing here?" Jessi faked surprise.

"We bring regards and best wishes from you're fellow officers in Houston," Tyley explained.

"Hide your purse, Jessi," Lela interjected.

Tyley shot Lela a cold look. "This is a police matter. Could you please step out and give us a moment?"

Lela looked to Jessi for guidance. "If you want, I'll stay."

"No, that's okay. I'll be fine."

Lela glared at the men as she left the room.

Tyley sat down on the edge of the bed as Eisom checked out the abundance of flowers that seemed to diminish their own grocery store purchased contributions.

"Looks like a friggin' florist shop in here," Eisom said.

Jessi remained quiet, waiting them out.

"Actually," Tyley cleared his throat. "We're looking at this low life Wesley Covine for one of our cold cases."

"A Houston case?"

Tyley nodded. "Her name was Louise Brown, a 24 year old waitress with two kids who was brutally murdered and then tossed into the bay like so much garbage. The M.E. recovered semen from her corpse that has been sitting on the shelf in the evidence room freezer for close to eight years. When this thing popped up here, we ran the sample and *bang,* Covine's DNA matches.

Eisom walked to the window and looked out. "CNN, ABC, FOX, CBS, they're all out there."

Tyley nodded and patted Jessi on the hand. "This is a huge case. You play your cards right, you can build your entire career on it."

"Hey guys, I'm too tired to play games. Why don't you put *your* cards on the table so I can see what game we're playing."

Tyley and Eisom exchanged a look. "Fair enough," Tyley said. "This case is big enough for all of us to ride for a while."

"You've showed us that you deserve a spot on the Murder Squad," Eisom said eagerly.

Tyley continued, "All we expect is that when you write your final report you don't mention certain prior conversations that we might have had, and..."

Jessi held up her hand, effectively cutting Tyley off. "Doesn't it bother you guys to know that if you would have just listened to Lela, or even written a simple report, you might have prevented several deaths? Who knows, you might have solved this whole thing yourselves."

"That's water under the bridge. A good cop learns early on that you do what you can. No need to beat ourselves up over a small mistake here and there."

"That isn't what a good cop does. My dad was a good cop. Marty Burris was a good cop. John Cutler is a good cop. They do what they can and then they do just a little bit more."

The room was stone silent for thirty seconds before Tyley finally stood and followed Eisom toward the door. As he was leaving, Tyley paused, "You'll always be a social worker."

"Probably. But you know what? You'll never be a *good* cop."

28.

꧁꧂

Jessi checked under the motel bed before moving to the bathroom to look one last time for any stray items she might have missed. Her left eye still sported a deep blue bruise and her upper torso looked stiff from a bulky wrap-around bandage. She moved to the bed, zipped her bag awkwardly, and leaving the key on the nightstand with a twenty dollar bill, stepped out of room number seven just as Cutler's Blazer pulled to a stop. The sheriff hopped out to relieve her of the bag.

"You're moving much better. How you feeling?" he asked.

"I'm still stiff, but better than yesterday."

"You ready to hit the road?"

"Yeah, I just have to get Lela," Jessi replied as she turned and knocked on the door to number eight. "I thought I heard her moving around earlier. Lela!"

"Down here!" Lela's voice drifted up from where the maid's cart was parked outside room 18.

"What's she doing?" Cutler asked.

"Velma slipped and sprained her ankle yesterday. Lela's just helping out until the new maid takes over. She was supposed to be here this morning, " Jessi answered. " Lela, let's go!" Jessi yelled.

Lela exited the room and moved purposefully toward Jessi and Cutler. "You go ahead without me. I'm not going back to Houston just yet."

"What do you mean, 'not going back?'" Jessi asked.

"The substitute maid Velma was counting on turns out to be eight months pregnant, and there's no way Velma can run this place on crutches. She asked me to stay for a while, and I said okay."

Jessi gave the older woman a curious smile. "That's very considerate of you, Lela, but I thought you couldn't wait to get back to Houston, being a big city girl and all?"

Lela nodded. "That's true. I do miss Houston, and I was looking forward to getting back to my van, but Velma has been very good to me. It's the least I can do."

Jessi raised her eyebrows, and her eyes lit up. "Gee, Lela, does that mean you're going to be cleaning room seven?"

Lela looked sheepish. "Actually, Velma's agreed not to rent out a couple of the rooms…"

Jessi laughed and Lela glared back at her. "It's not Velma's busy season and, at least, *she* understands. I mean, she could hardly expect me to go into room 13, and 7 is definitely out," Lela explained, taking Jessi by the arm and leading her away from Cutler. "Come here, I want to show you something."

Lela used her passkey to open number eight and motioned for Jessi to follow her in. "This room might not look like much," Lela said as she leaned down and patted the tightly made bed affectionately. "But here I've got a comfortable bed; I can shower every day with hot water. Hell, I've even got a dresser to put my stuff in." She moved to the cheap, pine dresser and demonstrated by sliding the drawer open and closed as if she were showing Jessi a new invention. "Velma said I could use the washer and dryer. I can even use her kitchen. I've kind of grown attached to this room."

They sat in silence a moment, each remembering the events of the last few days and the incredible bond that would bind them forever.

Their eyes met, and they smiled, a resigned, almost sad smile, but a smile nonetheless. Lela broke the silence. "They say a true sign of friendship is when you can be comfortable around somebody and not talk."

"Yeah, I suppose so," Jessi agreed. "You take care of yourself, Lela."

"I will, and don't you forget to keep that crystal with you. That way we..."

"Can keep in touch," Jessi said, pulling the necklace from under her blouse and holding up the crystal.

They hugged, tears welling up in their eyes. "Don't let those other cops see you cry, or they'll eat you alive."

Jessi nodded, opening the door. "Oh, by the way, I talked to my boss about the matter of your twelve grand worth of parking warrants. They've been expunged."

"That's the least those assholes could do for me. What about my van? Is it still in the impound yard?"

"You'll have to ask the sheriff about that," Jessi said, stepping out of the room.

Cutler was still leaning against the driver's side of the Blazer when the two women exited the room and approached.

"What about my van?" Lela asked sharply.

"What do you mean?"

"Jessi said I had to ask you about my van."

"Oh, *that* van. Well, considering all you've done for me, Grace County that is, I figured we'd foot your impound fees. And seeing as you're staying with us, I guess we could pay to have it towed up here for you," Cutler said, taking off his Stetson and adjusting the brim.

"I'll be damned. Was that my apology?" Lela asked.

"No, it's just a free tow job," Cutler countered, handing her a business envelope.

"Money?" Lela asked, glancing at the contents.

"$378 to be exact. We found it in Pinky's rat's nest."

"I'll be damned."

Cutler smiled as he helped Jessi into the passenger side before sliding in behind the wheel of the Blazer.

Jessi looked back at Lela and waved as Cutler pulled the Blazer away from the motel.

"I have a couple of stops to make before we take off. Do you mind?" Cutler asked.

"Not at all."

A soft whimpering from the rear of the vehicle caught Jessi's attention. Turning, she noticed a cardboard box on the back seat and two well-fed puppies sleeping inside. She looked at Cutler curiously, but he simply smiled. Jessi reached into the back with her left arm and brought out the runt, nuzzling him to her cheek, then placing him on her lap where he immediately gave a huge yawn and went back to sleep.

They rode in silence for a moment.

"Funny, you sit next to someone in school, at the movies, at church, you see them at the grocery store–and you think you know them. Kathryn Weed was ..." Cutler's voice trailed off.

Jessi reached over and touched his arm. "There's no way you could have known."

"I know. It's just that, somehow... I should have." Cutler shook his head sadly.

The sheriff's Blazer turned onto the gravel road and headed west, throwing up a cloud of dust. After a mile it slowed and turned into the driveway of a small, neatly painted white farm house and pulled to a stop. Jessi stayed in the 4x4 holding the squirming runt as Cutler, carrying another of the puppies, got out and walked around to Jessi's side.

"Gimme one more kiss," Jessi whispered to the runt and smiled as the sweet-smelling puppy licked her chin. "You're a sweetie, you are." Jessi handed the little dog to Cutler through the open window.

"This'll just take a minute. Will you be okay?"

"I'm fine," Jessi answered, leaning back in the seat and watching as Cutler carried the puppies up the steps to the porch.

Before Cutler could knock, the door opened and a tall, grey-haired woman in a simple print dress stepped out.

"How you doing, Arden?" Cutler asked, his eyes moving past the woman to the open door where he saw the old, double-barreled shotgun, both hammers back, resting dangerously against the wall.

"I'm doing just fine, Johnny. Who said otherwise?"

"Nobody. I'm sorry it took so long to make it out here."

"From the sounds of things you've been awfully busy. I'm so sorry about Marty."

"Yeah, thank you. I'm sorry about your dogs. I know how much they meant to you."

Arden nodded.

"Actually, the reason I came by is that I need a favor. Somebody dropped these little fellas off out on the highway." Cutler held up the puppies for emphasis. "I'd hate to see them put down."

"For god's sake, why would you even consider putting them down?" Arden chided irritably, taking one of the puppies and cuddling it.

"They're going to be hard to place. They've been half starved and they've got a bad case of the skitters," Cutler added.

As Arden took both puppies and cuddled them to her wrinkled neck, Cutler continued. "I was hoping you might keep them out here for a few days. Get them healthy enough so that Marie Sisco can find homes for them."

"Come on in, Johnny."

Cutler glanced toward the Blazer and gave Jessi a smile and a discreet thumbs up before following Arden inside.

As she waited for Cutler, Jessi laid her head back on the seat, closed her eyes, and soaked up the morning sunshine that poured through the windshield. Since the experience in the icehouse, she had promised herself that she'd never complain about being hot again. She was asleep within thirty seconds, caught up in a wonderful dream where she was sitting lazily on a riverbank, high above the water line, watching her father drifting slowly downstream in the *Bloodworm*. She watched Big Deke cast out his line, making a long arch that seemed to float on the air forever before dropping lightly into the water where it sent out an explosion of circles that swept toward her. Big Deke turned and she could see him smile up at her. Jessi waved, and Deke waved back, holding up two fingers, and pointed at the plastic bucket to indicate how many fish he had caught. As her father continued drifting away, Jessi turned at the sound of an approaching car and saw Cutler's Blazer pull to a stop close-by. She smiled and walked toward the driver's side, but when the window hummed down, Pinky's gruesome face stared out at her! As his bloody hands reached out for her, she jerked herself backward, sending a shooting pain into her shoulder!

"You okay?"

Jessi opened her eyes as Cutler opened the door and climbed in. He was holding Arden's old, double-barreled twelve gauge.

"I'm fine. I...it was just a chill," Jessi replied as Cutler snapped the breech of the gun open and removed a plastic green shell from each chamber.

"That's not a bad trade off, two puppies for a shotgun," Jessi said.

"That's right. We call it the barter system," Cutler said, laying the shotgun on the back seat before starting the Blazer and pulling away from the house. Returning to the paved road, he glanced at Jessi. "Now, where did I leave off?"

"You were talking about a retirement package," Jessi responded.

"Right. Like I was saying, we'll pick up your entire package from Houston P.D., then we'll start you off at Detective First Class. You'll be the head of our detective bureau."

"The head? How many detectives are in your bureau?"

"Ahh, if you take the job...one."

Jessi laughed hard enough to jar her broken rib. "What makes you think I'd give up working in one of the most exciting police departments, in one of the most exciting cities in the world, to come out here to, to..."

"Deep Texas?" Cutler finished the question for her.

"To *really* Deep Texas."

"That's a good question, and I'm glad you asked it," Cutler said, bringing the Blazer to a sudden stop and turning to face her. "I think you'd like it here because I think you like working with real people. I think you like getting your hands dirty, and besides I think you belong here."

"Belong?"

"That's right, belong. But then again, that's not the most important reason I think you should stay."

"And that is?" Jessi asked.

"And that is because...because I don't want you to leave, ever."

They looked at each other for a full ten seconds before Cutler leaned over and kissed her lightly on the lips.

"I'm sorry, I -"

Jessi reached out and touched Cutler's lips. "Don't you dare apologize."

The second kiss lingered until the sound of a passing car broke them apart.

"I'll give it some thought," she said.

"Good," Cutler said. He slipped the Blazer into gear and pulled away.

Acknowledgements

☙❧

Our appreciation goes out to those in the law enforcement family: to our daughter, Jessica and our son-in-law, John, who have taken their oath "to serve and protect" to heart. Thank you to the numerous police officers who allowed us into their patrol cars and into their lives. To officers in Fort Lauderdale, Florida; Nashville, Tennessee; Petaluma, California; the Sonoma County Sheriff's Department in northern California and to our friend, Sonny Grosso, who gave me complete and full access to the New York City Police Department and Rao's Restaurant. Thank you to Jack Webb who introduced me to Officer Mark Mooring who in turn introduced me to the Los Angeles Police Department and in the process became a friend.

Thanks to family and friends whose names we have used for characters who have no resemblance to their namesakes. It is our way of saluting you.

Some people need to be given individual recognition: Jill Butler for her in depth reading and valuable suggestions; Haley Lela Kinghorn and Gina Mooring for their thoughtful reading and insightful comments; and to Janice Triplett, a fellow writer and friend.

A special thanks to our friend Robert Conrad who kept us regularly employed.

About The Authors

❦

David and Marilyn Kinghorn have been a writing team for some time.

David has written over a dozen MOWs and created two, one hour dramatic series for the major networks. His movie *Man Against the Mob* won the "Edgar Allan Poe" award for Best Television Mystery of 1989.

Marilyn has had work published in two anthologies and recently had her first juvenile novel *Allie Carson: Interpreter Extraordinaire* published.

The Kinghorns are publishing *Deep Texas* under the pseudonym of Cole Stallings as a tribute to their mothers.

CPSIA information can be obtained at www.ICGtesting.com
Printed in the USA
BVOW08s2316230215

389021BV00015B/147/P